DIVINER

DIVINER

Dawn G Harris

First published in England in 2018 by
Telos Publishing Ltd, 139 Whitstable Road,
Canterbury, Kent, CT2 8EQ

www.telos.co.uk

Telos Publishing Ltd values feedback. Please e-mail us with any
comments you may have about this book to:
feedback@telos.co.uk

ISBN: 978-1-84583-125-7

Diviner © 2018 Dawn G Harris
Cover Art © 2018 Iain Robertson

Contents

'Never give up, for what we feel today can teach us tomorrow.'

'Non deficere, nam hodie non doceat nos quid sentis eras.'

DEDICATION

I believe you don't always have to be related to be considered as family, so there are some further supportive people thought of in this dedication, under the umbrella of my wonderful family.

Also to our much missed, treasured friend,
the ingenious and quick-witted Jeff R Milchard,
who loved to read and truly made me laugh, always.
You sadly didn't get to read this one,
but I hope wherever you've drifted to, JRM,
you'll have echoes of music and our laughter,
and a book by your side.
We'll open a 1984 red for the Camembert now,
your own talisman;
it's time for me to tell *you* a story.

x

BEFORE

The Marbles

October 5, 1813

Lord Elgin sat completely still as he scanned the crowded salon, but it was the spring-loaded stillness of a predator with its eyes fixed on its prey.

He was holding a crystal brandy glass in his right hand and a pipe in his left, but he had not taken a sip of brandy for the past five minutes, and his pipe remained unlit. All of his attention was concentrated on the girl in the gauzy yellow dress who was talking flirtatiously to the youngest son of the Brimstone family, whose soirée this was.

Her name was Jessica Coldwell. She was plump-faced and plainish, with pouting strawberry lips and a mole on her left cheek, although Lord Elgin had to admit that she did have some attractive f̶ ̶e̶s̶. She had glossy dark-brown hair that was pinned up̶ ̶ ̶ ̶ ̶b̶le ringlets, a full bosom and a tiny waist, and she̶ ̶ ̶ ̶ ̶ ̶*i* with a natural poise, fluttering her eyelash̶ ̶ ̶ ̶ ̶ ̶and inclining her head as the Brimstone boy t̶o̶ ̶ ̶ ̶ ̶ ̶ ̶sing story.

It̶ ̶ ̶ ̶ ̶ks, however, that were keeping Lord Elgin's eye̶ ̶ ̶ ̶ ̶was her father's wealth.

̶ ̶ ̶ ̶ ̶ ̶ ̶young for Lord Elgin himself, of course, with h̶ ̶ ̶ ̶ ̶ ̶ ̶and his aquiline nose and the wattle under his ̶ ̶ ̶ ̶ ̶ ̶never respond to the advances of a man of his ̶ ̶ ̶ ̶ ̶, so set in his ways, who could never give her a ̶ ̶ ̶ ̶ ̶ ̶sn't to say that he *couldn't* have her: when a man ̶ ̶ ̶ ̶ ̶n he shall; but it would be far too obvious why he w̶ ̶ ̶ ̶ ̶rry her.

It was common knowledge that he was close to bankruptcy. He had spent £70,000 of his own money transporting the marble friezes from the Parthenon in Athens to Britain. After six years of haggling and procrastination, the British Museum had at last made him an offer for them, but it was only £35,000, and if he were to keep his family home and his social standing he needed far more than that.

The floorboards creaked as the crowd of guests moved from side to side, in conversation and curtseys. Sways of women and their chaperones moved through the candlelit salon, mingling with the herd of finely-dressed gentlemen. A lady harpist was seated in the far corner, and their shadows seemed to dance around the walls in time to the tinkling arabesque that she was playing.

The dance of life and death, thought Lord Elgin. *One day even their shadows will have vanished. But tonight it's the dance of seduction, and that's what interests me above everything.*

He sat back and swallowed his brandy and watched as Jessica's father came up to her. James Coldwell, portly and tall, with fluffy white hair and reddened cheeks. He was the owner of Coldwell Heath and over nine thousand acres of arable land surrounding it, as well as two villages. Lord Elgin had known James for more than twenty years. They had played cards together and gone out shooting pheasants together, but all Lord Elgin could think of now was his money.

James caught sight of him, waved, and weaved his way across the room. Lord Elgin put down his brandy glass, stood up and shook his hand.

'My dear Thomas, how are you?' James boomed. 'I don't think we've seen each other since that ghastly reception at Clarence House. How is Greece? I've been reading about your adventures in the *Morning Post*. You certainly *look* well, old fellow!'

'Well, but a little stretched,' said Lord Elgin.

'Pff! What's a little money, when you have done such a signal service for the nation, and for art? The bloody Turks would have smashed those marbles to pieces if you hadn't rescued them. Either the bloody Turks or the bloody Greeks, or some other bloody heathens.'

All very well for you to say, thought Lord Elgin. But he believed he already had the keys to James Coldwell's fortune, and those keys were Jessica, and his own son George. His plan was very simple. He would introduce George to Jessica, the two of them would marry, and his financial problems would be solved to the throwing of confetti and the celebratory ringing of wedding-bells.

'Your Jessica looks entrancing this evening, I must say,' he said.

'Yes,' said James, turning to frown at her. 'But she'll be twenty-one next birthday, and she's no nearer to finding herself a suitable husband.'

'You mustn't lose hope, James. The world is full of eligible young men.'

He deliberately didn't mention George. Of course George was devoted to his childhood sweetheart Cathella, Lord and Lady Huxtable's pretty young daughter, and it had always been assumed in society that the two of them would one day marry. But Lord Elgin had already discovered how George's ardour for Cathella could be cooled, and how he could be made to fall hopelessly in love with Jessica.

He knew that he couldn't do it by persuasion, or cajoling, or pleading. But during his time in Greece he had found out almost by accident that it was possible to call on a force so powerful that no man or woman had ever been able to resist it – a force which was said to be capable of destroying queens and bringing emperors to their knees. It was one of the most perverse and mischievous spirits that had ever infested the earth – a spirit without morals or conscience, which fed on human lust and faithlessness. As upright a man as he usually was, Lord Elgin had seen it as a Godsend in his hour of desperate financial need.

'Well, old fellow, let's toast your achievement in rescuing those marbles,' said James Coldwell, raising his glass.

Lord Elgin picked up his glass and raised it, too. 'Here's to love,' he said. 'Love and happiness. And to prosperity. And most of all, to Cupid.'

James Coldwell looked baffled. But 'to Cupid,' he said, and drank.

PART ONE

Shock Reminder

'Well, this is me!' said Paula, as they reached the corner by the courthouse. 'See you later at home, Clarry, thanks for the lift! Good luck in your new job – you'll do great!'

But Clarissa didn't answer. She was staring at the small crowd of people around the courthouse steps, and especially at the man in a grey suit who was trying to push his way down to the car waiting at the kerb.

'Clarissa?' said Paula as she took her hand off the car door handle. 'Hallooo? I said "good luck in your new job"! What's wrong with you? You're normally so calm but you look like you've seen a ghost!'

Clarissa hadn't seen a ghost. However, she was seeing something which she hadn't experienced since she had been at school. The man in the grey suit had turned his head in her direction before getting into the car, and as he did so, his face seemed to melt and boil until it looked only half-human, and became pale, wet-looking and swollen. His tiny eyes glimmered scarlet and his lips began to stretch back over a tangle of broken and rotting teeth.

Not only did he look grotesque, there was no doubt that he was staring directly at Clarissa. She felt as if he were challenging her to cross the road and try to explain what she could see in him to one of the court officials or to his lawyer, or to one of the newspaper reporters who were clustered around him. She felt light-headed and swimmy, and her hearing dulled. She reached across to Paula's arm and gripped it.

'Clarry? You're not going to *faint*, are you? I *told* you to have breakfast! Are you okay?'

The stocky man with the pale, swollen face turned away, and ducked his head down so that he could climb into a waiting car. As it drove off, he smiled out of the window at Clarissa; his face appeared to be normal, handsome in a self-assured way, with thick dark hair and a deeply cleft chin. Clarissa was almost sure that he winked at her.

Clarissa said, 'Who *was that*? Do you know?'

Paula looked at her with an exaggerated frown and said, 'Who? What – that guy who just drove off? Beats me! Looked pretty pleased with himself though, didn't he? Whatever he was up for he obviously got away with it! Looked like a douchebag to me. Never trust a guy who thinks he's smarter than his suit. That's what I always say.'

Clarissa stayed where she was in the car for a few moments, her hand pressed against her chest, breathing deeply and evenly to steady herself. *Not again,* she thought, *not again. I was sure that I'd grown out of it. Dear God, don't tell me that I'll always see faces like that.*

'Wait here a minute, P,' she said as she switched off the engine and climbed out of her red MINI Cooper, leaving Paula looking confused. She hurriedly crossed over the road to the courthouse steps where a young female reporter was jabbing at her iPhone.

'Excuse me,' she said. 'Can you tell me who that was? That man in the grey suit that just left?'

The reporter huffed at her phone and didn't raise her head, but said, 'You obviously haven't been reading your *Greywell Village Post* lately. That was Barry Kaile. *Damn you, phone,* what's wrong with you!' She huffed again and looked up at Clarissa. 'Why? Are you on the story?'

Clarissa thought on her feet and said, 'Yes. What happened in there?'

'He was up for burning his wife's lover to death on a bonfire. *A ritual sacrifice,* that's what they called it. Except that he didn't do it. Or the police couldn't prove it, anyway. His *wife* had said that he'd *threatened* to do it, but there was no other evidence, so they had to acquit him. I think it was his sister-in-law. An act of jealousy. But what do I know?'

Clarissa was tempted to say: 'But he *did* do it! I know he did! I saw his true face!' But she bit her lip. The last thing she wanted was attention here and now over something nobody would understand, or believe her about any more than they had when she was a little girl.

'Clarry!' called Paula from the car. 'I need to go, are you okay now?'

Clarissa smiled and said thank you to the reporter who was now taking a phone call and flapping her hand at her dismissively.

She walked back to the car and gave Paula a tight smile. 'Yes, I'll be fine. Have a good day.' She reminded herself: *Nobody's perfect but it doesn't necessarily make them evil.*

She waved at Paula as she drove off. She then parked near to the Milltower Gallery, where she was starting work.

She tried to tell herself that what really happened was nothing more than a fleeting relapse of her childhood awareness. Perhaps Kaile was so malevolent that he had stirred up some of the sensitivity in her which had been dormant for so long.

'I'm officially allergic to evil,' she told herself as she touched up her lipstick in the sun visor and checked that her dark blonde hair was neat and smoothly tied back in a low pony-tail.

She was calmer when she reached the gallery doors, and took in a deep breath and tried to focus on the new job ahead of her. *Gallery Assistant.* She was just about to go inside, however, when she glanced across the street toward Gretta's Bakery and felt a chilly, sliding sensation all down her spine, as if somebody had poured ice-cold water over the back of her shirt.

A boy was standing outside The Merrybank Model Shop next-door to the bakery, with his back to her, looking in the window. Mr Merrybank was outside, in his brown apron and smart white shirt, dusting down the windowsills. He noticed Clarissa, and waved. But he didn't appear to acknowledge the boy.

It can't be, she thought as she waved back. *Not that boy. Not again. But what if it is?*

Just then, the gallery's glass door opened, and a tall young man appeared. 'Clarissa! We've been looking forward to seeing you again! Come in. My name's Craig – Craig Arlington – I'm the senior gallery assistant.'

Clarissa turned. Craig smiled and offered her through the doors. 'Hi, Craig, yes, me too – thank you.'

As she went inside, though, she glanced back across the street, and saw that the boy was looking at her over his shoulder, staring directly at her in the same intense way as Barry Kaile. All the same, entering the gallery with Craig made her feel as though she was going to be safe. For now, at least.

The Return

'I hope that it's okay, Mrs Ball. To come to your house I mean.'

'Of course, Clarissa dear. You look as wonderful as I hoped, how long has it been? Five years? I was delighted when you phoned.'

'Yes,' smiled Clarissa as Mrs Ball gripped her arms and welcomed her.

'I'm sorry it's been so long, time flies and life gets so busy.'

'I understand dear, you're a young woman now! In fact, I've been expecting you to come now you are older. I have something very important to show you. Come in.'

Clarissa pulled off her blue wellingtons and stood them by a pot with a huge sunflower growing from it. 'Oh?' she said, unzipping her raincoat.

She followed Mrs Ball into the garden room. It was crowded with yellowing wicker furniture, Turkish cushions, candle lanterns and plants. A book called *The Shamanic Technique of Gazing* sat on the coffee table. A small lamp gave a wide yellowed glow from the corner of the room, and it felt extremely cosy. 'Smells lovely in here,' she said. 'Like homemade bread.'

'I've been trying to talk with my plants in here for good energy. They could be chattering away for all we know,' Mrs Ball smiled.

Clarissa always thought it was strange to enter a house through the back this way and not through the front door, which had a note pinned on it saying: *Come round the back!* But once she was in, she once more found herself stepping over piles of books and edging her way around half-finished ceramic statuettes and canvas paintings, and she realised that there was so much creative clutter that Mrs Ball probably still couldn't *get* to her front door. A little archway led them into the living room, and Clarissa began to feel more and more intrigued to see what had changed.

It was very warm inside the house, so she slid off her raincoat and jumper and laid them over the back of an armchair. The room was filled with a comforting baking aroma and a heavy, classic perfume, as it always had been. On the windowsill sat the most beautiful white cat she'd ever seen, looking almost ludicrously contented in the upstream of warmth from the radiator. Curling around her ankles was a handsome tabby, mewing as he greeted her. Clarissa looked down at him and thought he looked so happy, and if she could draw him now she'd draw him as a cartoon, with a cute squinting smile and bulging cheeks.

Clarissa loved Blue Persians the most, and sure enough, she was delighted to see one stretched out on the fireplace rug, eyes half-closed in the fire's warm, bright glow. Outside, the afternoon was a wet and dull one, yet inside it felt like a very comforting, and different world.

Following Mrs Ball toward the hallway, Clarissa reached out to lean on the wall noticing its lumpy texture as she stepped over two large books lying side by side, with tabs of paper poking out of them as bookmarks. One had written on the front in bold print: *Saddle Up, Ride Like A Psychic!* The other was called, quite simply, *Greek Mythology*.

'Cup of tea, Clarissa?' asked Mrs Ball, as she led her through to the kitchen.

'Oh, thanks, Mrs Ball. Yes, please.'

Clarissa's attention had been taken by a large, open wooden box, which stood on the front doormat. The front door itself was covered by a heavy orange curtain as if Mrs Ball were trying to prevent a draught. Clarissa peered into the box and it looked to be filled with little bottles, with a large curved animal tooth on top, reminding her of a tooth that she had seen on Mrs Ball's desk one day at school.

On the wall hung a hand-carved wooden sign: *Welcome to The Snug!* Clarissa had always thought The Snug was a perfect name for such a cosy little place.

She followed Mrs Ball into the kitchen.

The kitchen was small and untidy, yet smelled clean, with tea-towels hanging over the backs of the chairs and plates and mugs stacked up on the draining-board to dry. As the kettle boiled, Clarissa looked up and saw that there were even more books up on the kitchen shelf than she had remembered, and not all cookery books, either, although one was called *Cooking To Cure Your Love*, whatever that meant. Resting on top of that one was a slim book entitled *Neuro-Science & Forensic Psychopathy*. Clarissa was fascinated and realised why she had been so enchanted coming here as a girl.

'Now then,' said Mrs Ball. 'Would you like sugar in your tea now you're older?'

'One, please.'

They carried their cups of tea back into the main living-room, and over to the corner where there was a small oval dining table. As Clarissa placed her cup down, she could see herself in the mirror on top of the sideboard, and was surprised at how pale she looked.

'Do sit down, dear,' said Mrs Ball. She brought over three large books and laid them down on the table. 'Now then, you must tell me what it is that you've been feeling, and why you've come to see me today.'

'It's happening again.'

'What is, exactly?'

Clarissa spoke haltingly at first, because she hadn't had visions for years, not since she had last seen Mrs Ball, and she didn't understand why then, let alone why now.

'All of a sudden it's back. I keep having flashbacks, too. Visions of being at school, and the tormented faces I saw. Last week, on my way to my new job I saw a man at the courthouse – the real side of him – what he'd really done – his evil – only he was being set free. I *saw* his true face.'

'Were you alone?'

'No, I was giving my flatmate Paula a lift – she said I'd looked like I'd seen a ghost.'

'I see, did this man at the courthouse see Paula?'

'I'm not sure,' said Clarissa. Mrs Ball was worrying her now.

Mrs Ball nodded, and said, 'Go on, dear. Tell me the rest.'

Clarissa began by reminding Mrs Ball about the garden party that she had attended at Old Gorton Manor on her eighth birthday, and the room upstairs, and the strange book in a foreign language that she had found there. It was there, in that room, that she had first encountered the boy. The same boy who had stared at her across the street from The Merrybank Model Shop – or one who looked chillingly like him.

'I just don't know why I'm getting all of this sensitivity back *now*,' she said. 'I thought it was only children who can see what people are really like, and interact with spirits, or whatever they are. But it's happening again. I can tell what people are feeling, without them having to tell me.

'Sometimes I look at pictures and they're not *just* pictures. Sometimes they practically come alive and I can *feel* their emotion just from the expression on their face. When someone's sad – I know exactly what's wrong with them before they tell me. I've woken up with all of these heightened senses again – like I had when I was young, only more so. And I feel different, as though I'm not alone.'

Mrs Ball nodded. 'I see. You must be careful. Has anything happened to your knowledge that may have triggered this return?'

'Not that I can think of. I mean – I've started a new job – but I'm not particularly anxious about it. It's a job I've wanted for a while now in my local art gallery. I've seen a lot more of Ma and her best friend, Mrs Cawsley-May, recently – but I can't see why that should have affected me.'

Mrs Ball thought for a while, and then she said, 'I'd like you to take a look at these, dear.'

She picked up a large canvas-covered book and passed it over. 'Here – take your time and read page twenty carefully. Then I want to show you page one hundred and forty-seven, and the illustrations on that page. I'll just pop into the kitchen to take my flapjacks out of the oven while you start. I shan't be a mo.'

I shan't be a mo, thought Clarissa. *She sounds just like Nanna used to.*

Mrs Ball stood up, wrapping a bobbly green cardigan around her shoulders, and disappeared into the kitchen. Clarissa could see her through the serving hatch. She looked down at the book in front of her, and began to read page twenty, as Mrs Ball had told her. She didn't exactly understand why, but she began to feel a childlike excitement, as if she were just about to learn what all the strangeness in her life was all about.

There was a title on the page: *Leonardo da Vinci: The Grotesque Heads.*

The only pictures that she could remember of Leonardo's were all beautiful, like The Mona Lisa and his drawings of Mary and the baby Jesus. What were his *'Grotesque Heads'*? And what did they have to do with her?

But as she read on, she learned that Leonardo had been fascinated not only by beauty but by ugliness, and had drawn dozens of portraits of hideous men with hooked noses and jutting chins, as well as women with pig-like noses and warts.

When he was court artist in Milan in the 1490s, he had painted radiant pictures of John the Baptist and Narcissus and ladies of the court, but he had also walked the streets with his sketchbook, looking for depraved and demonic faces: 'stalking beauty's opposite,' as the writer had put it.

Mrs Ball returned with a plate full of flapjacks and gestured to Clarissa to turn the pages.

'Now you've read about Leonardo, turn to page one hundred and forty seven. *Diviners.'*

Clarissa did as she was told, and started to read more. She recognised many of the names, such as Salvador Dali, Pieter Bruegel; Diego Velasquez; Max Ernst and Francis Bacon, and according to the text, they had all shared one thing in common: they had all produced portraits of grotesque and hideous faces.

'You see?' said Mrs Ball. 'All of these famous artists were capable of painting exquisitely beautiful people, and mostly they did. But they also sought out ugly and deformed people. Or perhaps I should say: people who appeared in their eyes to be ugly and deformed.'

'Do you think they were ever loved, regardless of what they

looked like? They all look pretty sad or distressed to me.'

'Oh, now dear,' smiled Mrs Ball. 'Don't forget they are only paintings. Some people's love is unconditional. And love has many *different* faces, as you have learned I'm sure.'

Clarissa took a flapjack and started to nibble it around the edge. It was still warm from the oven. She finished reading. 'I still don't really understand,' she said.

'Turn the page,' Mrs Ball told her. 'Then you will.'

She turned over and was confronted at once by a teeming crowd of hideous, bizarre faces, with sagging skin and bulbous noses and elephantine jaws. Some had profiles like nutcrackers, or lobster-claws, with hooked noses and upturned chins. Others had beetling foreheads, with eyes that stared out at her like evil goblins hiding under a rock.

'Love and creation aren't always kind, are they, if this is what these artists saw?' Clarissa asked.

She turned over page after page, and on every page there was a mass of monstrosities, all drawn or painted by some of the finest artists who had ever lived. Some were in a lover's embrace, some of the faces were grinning and gurning, others had the wild lost expression of madness. Many of them were simply smears or scribbles, with no distinguishable features at all, as if the artists had painted them or drawn them properly but then deliberately defaced them, so that they wouldn't have to look at them anymore – or so that the face could no longer look out from the page or canvas and see *them*.

Clarissa sat back, fascinated. 'This is uncanny!' she exclaimed. 'These drawings – these faces – they're like the ones I used to draw when I was a child.'

'So you see, dear,' Mrs Ball responded, 'you're not alone, by any means. Why could you draw and paint so well, Clarissa, when other students could barely manage to produce a stick-person? Why can singers sing, and violinists play the violin, and why can some do it so much better than others? Many artists are capable of creating wonderful pictures, aren't they? You yourself are very talented, my dear, but some artists can do much more than create pictures – they also have the gift of seeing the world as it really is, not only its beauty, but its flaws, too. Well, I say it's a gift, but perhaps it's a curse, in some ways. Because if and when you see evil, you also have a responsibility to expose it – which is why you feel compelled to put down what you see on paper, or canvas, or even sculpture. Your talent can draw many people into your life, quite literally, including enemies, too.'

'Ah, okay.'

'All of these artists could see not only beauty, but the ugliness that often hides behind it. They had an insight which very few people possess, which is why they are known as Diviners.

'A Diviner is an artist who can see behind somebody's face and into their soul. They see people's true characters on their faces so most of these people didn't *really* look like this – not on the surface, anyway. But Leonardo and Bruegel and all of these other gifted artists, they could see how corrupt or evil or ill-intentioned they were, and that is how they represented them. They all felt, sensed, and experienced things in the way you do. It's an ancient gift, and at times extremely powerful.'

She reached out and took hold of Clarissa's hand. Her skin was thin and wrinkled like tissue-paper, but her hand was warm. 'It appears dear, doesn't it, that we have you to add to that list of rare talent. *You* – Clarissa. You're a Diviner.'

'Mrs Ball, do you remember what happened last time?'

'Yes, dear. And that's why you need to be very cautious. Things happen for a reason – and it's a Blood Moon next month. Things are due for a dramatic change and you have to be ready.'

Mrs Ball looked over her glasses at Clarissa. 'Remember, dear, some people always bring good fortune and happiness with them, wherever they go, but malevolent spirits are the opposite. They are the carriers of bad luck, and personal tragedy. Sometimes they bring nothing more than a sad feeling, unhappiness, or discontentment. But they can be very dangerous, and bring sickness and accidents.'

'But does that mean something's *meant* to happen to me? Is *he* back?'

'Only time will tell you that, Clarissa,' said Mrs Ball. 'Some Diviners never realise what they are, and never have to face any challenges. But one day you will understand why we all have a nemesis, and why opposites are created by nature. I do believe that what you are seeing are all warnings, of one kind or another. So – whatever you do – don't ignore them.'

'Now … I also have some chocolate brownies in the oven,' said Mrs Ball, 'and they should be ready by now. Would you like one? Or two, perhaps?'

Goodnight Kiss

'Well, well, the birthday girl,' said Craig, as Clarissa came up the gallery stairs to the mezzanine floor. 'I hope you're going to buy me a drink after work to celebrate.'

'Actually, my birthday's not until tomorrow,' Clarissa told him. 'And aren't you supposed to buy *me* a drink?'

'It depends if you're old enough,' Craig smiled at her. She almost hated herself for it, but she loved it when he smiled at her like that. His eyes crinkled slightly, as if he could see right inside of her mind, and what would tease her the most.

'Of course I am. I'll be twenty two.'

The lights of passing cars flickered through the glass panel walls of Milltower Gallery, so that long shadows danced a ballet across the immaculate white flooring below them. Craig stepped toward the champagne and canapé stand, where Clarissa was arranging a display of business cards, ready for the big event tomorrow – an exhibition by some modern artist.

'One day your name will be on a card like that,' said Craig. 'You're an amazing artist, you know. Just as good as half of these *arrivistes.*'

Clarissa looked over her shoulder and gave Craig a coy, coquettish smile. She liked the glint in his dark eyes. She found it difficult to define what it was that she found most attractive. He wasn't conventionally handsome. His black hair was thick and wavy and curled over his collar at the back in a loosely groomed style. His face was squareish with high cheekbones, a straight nose and a sharply defined jawline. Yet there was something feminine about him, with his clear skin, and the flamboyant way he dressed and the way he knew so much about art and opera.

'Are all the clients gone? I thought I heard someone at the back a few moments ago.'

'Yes – unless a statue has come to life. Probably just the

heating clicking off, or a ghost,' he said.

'Hmm, you're funny.'

Craig put his arm around her shoulders and half-turned her around, as if he were going to kiss her. 'Yes. I am,' he finished.

'Wait,' she said, placing her hand firmly on his chest.

'What is it?' Craig asked her, with one eyebrow raised. 'You do like me, don't you darling?'

'It's just that – well,' Clarissa felt clumsy and disorganised with her words. 'You're very enthusiastic. Too keen. *And* you're my colleague. Is it allowed?'

'Is that so bad? That I'm keen on you?'

'It's not what I want, Craig, not yet.' Clarissa liked the mischievous look in Craig's eyes but she didn't want to be rushed. She had been rushed by men before, and bitterly regretted it. Craig shrugged, and stepped back, raising both hands in surrender.

'I'm a hot-blooded male, Clarry, I can't wait forever. You're sexy, you're beautiful, I can't stop thinking about you. Give me a chance, darling?'

Clarissa blushed. 'I've finished here now. Can you take me home please on *your* way home? I didn't bring my car today.'

'Okay,' said Craig. 'Whatever you want. Let me just grab our coats. Two minutes.' Craig walked off, shaking his head.

Clarissa put the rest of the cards down and twisted the flower vase, which was bursting with large white roses, and stood back to admire her arrangement.

When Craig came back, she slid on her coat, and pulled her handbag onto her shoulder as they walked down to the gallery doors. Craig clicked off the last of the gallery lights and set the alarm. Before he left, he patted the glass case in which the reproduction bust of Mette Gauguin was silently trapped and on guard.

Mette had been the 29-year-old Danish wife of Paul Gauguin and mother of his children. Her broad forehead, sunken eyes and long nose captured her determined expression, which Clarissa found extremely lifelike and disturbing. She had learned that his sculpted family portraits were very few, and out of his only known works in alabaster, this bust had been one of his favourites.

'*À bientot, mon ami,*' Craig said, as he did every night to it. '*Until tomorrow, my friend.*' Clarissa wouldn't look at Mette Gauguin for long. She had such deathly-white marble skin and such a solemn, unwavering stare, Clarissa was both fearful and hopeful that one day her face would come to life and smile as they were leaving in the darkness.

As they drew up outside Clarissa's flat, she noticed that Paula's bike was already chained up by the front door.

'Your flatmate's home early,' said Craig, and she could sense the disappointment in his voice.

'Thanks for the lift, anyway,' smiled Clarissa, although she immediately despised herself for saying '*anyway*', as if she would have invited him inside if Paula hadn't been home. She was annoyed at herself for forgiving him so quickly for his attempted kiss in the gallery, and he had made no attempt to say sorry, as if he thought that her refusal had been only a temporary setback.

His arrogance overwhelmed her, but the way he crinkled his eyes when he smiled goodbye was still irritatingly gorgeous. Besides that, she'd had a soft spot for him since the first time she saw him, but refused to let herself get carried away. Not yet, anyway.

She opened the car door and stepped out into the empty street, wrapping her coat tightly around her because the wind was icy cold.

As Craig drove away, she felt the same pulling sensation inside her as she always did when he dropped her home and left, or when she had driven away from the gallery after saying goodbye. She wanted to call him back and kiss him, every time. But she didn't because she knew he wasn't the right man for her at the moment. She knew that he could hurt her, and badly. Her heart wanted him but her head told her it was wrong and inappropriate as colleagues. It was like the way she felt about the Mansuini paintings in the gallery – aching to touch them, and feel the texture of their brushstrokes, feel the passion from the artist's view, but knowing that she mustn't. Sometimes she felt as if a spell of tantalising torture had been cast upon her.

Clarissa walked up the steps and turned the key in the door, but as she did so, there was a whimpering noise, and she glanced behind her. 'Hello?' she said. 'Who's there?'

No-one answered. The trees rustled in the wind and she began to open the door she was certain she heard footsteps that weren't her own. She waited quietly for a moment to see if the footsteps continued, but they didn't. When she opened the door, she found Paula sitting in the hallway, on the floor, distracting her.

'Paula! What's the matter?' Clarissa closed the door and crouched down in front of her friend.

'I feel sick,' cried Paula. 'I'm so glad you're home. *I've finished with Max. It's over.*'

Clarissa took hold of her hand and moved a half-empty bottle of beer away to sit in front of her. 'Oh, sweetheart,' she whispered, soothing her as she tucked her long hair over her shoulder, out of the way, revealing a darkened cheek. 'What happened?'

'I just couldn't take it any longer.'

'Well, in that case it was the right thing to do. Take your time to tell me,' she said, aware that pressure about her bruised cheek wasn't what she needed.

'He's changed so much, although he doesn't seem to believe it!' Paula took a deep, shuddering breath. 'He doesn't seem to have any affection for me anymore, or make any effort to understand that I hate arguing. I promised I'd be with him forever, but I just *can't. Not like this.*' She shook her head as she wiped her eyes. 'I was talking to him about somewhere he went last year and then we had a massive row and he took my ring, *nearly pulled my finger off,* and I screamed at him to keep it, telling him we were finished. Oh Clarry, you should have seen the sad and angry look on his face, it was heartbreaking.'

'Take a long, deep breath.'

'*Then* – then he started *shouting,* and told me I was an *arsehole,* slapped me round the face, said that it was over for good – but I had just finished with him because of *his* actions – so how could he then finish with me? Or *call* me that, or *do* that, after everything I've endured from *him*? My God *something is wrong with him*. He says it's always my fault. If he's tired, it's my fault. If he's lost his keys, it's my fault. If he's drunk, guess what – it's my fault. He needs help. He's hard work. I tried so hard.'

'Take a breath,' said Clarissa.

'It makes me feel so tangled inside 'cause I can *see* the issues but they never get resolved, I thought he wanted us to work. I thought he loved me. It's been a one way street *all* the time. I'm such an idiot, why didn't I see? It's such a dragging feeling, like when you realise you're being used or dropped 'cause something better comes along, when you see the true colours of people you *thought* were friends, realising after a long time they've not been true to you, or that they gave up on you when you weren't at your best and useful to them.' She sniffed, and wiped her nose. 'It's the same, *gut-wrenching*. I *hate* that duplicity in people. Why are some *people* so *cruel*?

Clarissa smiled as she wiped tears from Paula's face. 'Go on, it's okay.'

'Look at me – us – it's *over*,' she sobbed, as she rubbed at her nose. 'He's gone mad, I don't believe he loves me anymore, if he ever *did*, and I've let him down by breaking my side of the bargain, *and* I don't even have the ring to remember him by.'

'Love isn't a *deal*, or *bargain*, P! Whether it's partners *or* friends! It's giving, on both sides, being patient and honest to one-another. You don't need a ring to give you nice memories, or false friends to make you see your own qualities far richer than theirs.'

'Really?' sniffed Paula.

'Think of all the happy moments you had – they'll never leave you. He's emotionally tormented you enough now. Don't beat yourself up: remember your most recent birthday? He asked you what you wanted to do. You said you'd always wanted to go to see that Skunk Anansie tribute band, at the stunning Gleeton Hall? And when he picked you up you were so excited, you looked amazing, too, but when he stopped the car, it was outside Pepper's Ranch Bar and Grill, because he wanted a fancy meal instead? What about the time he was due to pick you up but was *five hours* late because he was with another girl and thought it was okay? When you were sick with a throat infection and he shouted at you because *he* mis-heard you? Never mind the fact you could hardly speak – and he never apologised! He even stopped seeing you at Christmas, and told his friends to shut you out as some kind of psycho punishment for not spending equal money on him? Just remember all that, you deserved none of it. Just like you didn't deserve this.'

Paula nodded, and wiped fresh tears from her cheeks, sensitive to one side.

'People that behave that way, needing constant inflation of ego, have many issues – not always their fault – okay, but they try to make you out to be awful and wean you out, because they're unsettled by your independence, honesty and the fact people love you, for you alone. Even if you're of a gentle nature you become a threat because of it. And if you break down from being hurt or retaliate you become their excuse. But it's more honourable in *any* relationship to be brave, kind and honest rather than sneaky, shallow or selfish.' Clarissa squeezed Paula's hands and felt a lump in her throat at seeing her friend so distraught. 'It broke my heart to see your heart breaking; that was all so cruel. Remember when he accused you of embarrassing him because you didn't want to spend your only twenty pounds on a round of drinks for his friends that time, who were already drunk on cheap wine *before* you arrived? I *know* you love him and I know that he was really sweet to you *sometimes,* even romantic, but he was mainly very cruel and childish, his idol was *Crab Man* for goodness sakes. That'll tell you something.'

'But – I don't know. I felt so *pure* when I was with him, at the beginning, it must stand for something. I always hoped I could help him change. I thought I was the one for him. I can't believe all that happened. *I can't believe I let it.*'

'You shouldn't need to change someone if they're right for you. And that feeling *will* come again, only better! You were a winner's prize. And besides, he has his own journey, my darling, in a world that's dreary and no good for you. *You* haven't let *him* down. You've shown him more real love than he'd ever experienced. You did all you could to support him. With you he had more love and goodness than he'd ever experienced, but it takes a strong man in return to understand the strengths of a woman in love, and that is something that he simply couldn't see. You were treated poorly. But love is a game to his type: they don't change. It's his *major* loss. Just like those friends that hurt you. It's their loss, too, P. They'll not care that you had them in your heart every single day and did your best for them, if they can treat your emotions so cruelly. You've not been bad to anyone, you've just finally stood your ground.'

Clarissa kissed the back of Paula's hands as if to force some of her energy and affectionate strength into her.

'You're better off without the torment it brings, it's not healthy and you're above all that. Leave them to it. Put your energies into *you* now.'

Paula looked at her and sniffed.

'Come on, take a deep breath and try to smile,' said Clarissa. 'We'll get you fixed up, it's all going to be okay.'

Paula sobbed and looked at Clarissa with such sadness.

'Did you know, P, you're a wonderful person! Sweet, gorgeous, funny, imaginative just for starters! One day soon you'll find somebody who appreciates you for who you are and *believes* who you are. And that, won't come with all of this pain. You need a man, not a boy.'

Paula looked up again, Her sky-blue eyes were reddened and swollen from crying, and her skin flushed.

'What would I do without you, Clarry? You've always been there for me, unconditionally, you've never let me down. You always have my best interests at heart, thank you, babe,' she said, and then she started to whimper again, and the tears poured down her cheeks.

Clarissa hugged and rocked her but as she did so she thought: *Don't rely on me to heal your heart. I know almost as little about the way some people pretend to love as you do.*

Dreamcatcher

That night Clarissa dreamed of storm-set rolling waves, crashing and draining between the rocks on a rugged coastline. The sky was already grey but it gradually grew darker, and as she reached the crest of a cliff, a crowd of young children appeared, screaming and pointing at her. Their screams grew louder and shriller, until they suddenly died down. An old man came walking through them, and they parted to let him through, as if he was some kind of messiah. As he approached Clarissa, however, she could see that he was bleeding, and all of his clothes were soaked in blood.

'*Clarissa*,' somebody whispered, and Clarissa felt ice-cold breath against her cheek. She woke up, startled.

She opened her eyes but the room was totally black. She felt so disorientated that she wasn't even sure that she had woken up in her own bed.

'*Clarissa*,' whispered the voice again. In the darkness, she could hear the dreamcatcher chime that hung from her curtain rail tinkling softly in the draught that came through the open window.

She reached for the corner of the duvet and pulled it in tightly toward her chest, in the hope that any minute now she could snuggle her way back to sleep, the way she had done when she was a child, after a nightmare. *I must have been dreaming*, she thought. Was it the cheese and wine before bed, or the busy day at the gallery that had disturbed her, with all those haunting paintings and Mette on her departure? Whoever it was that had spoken to her – whatever it was – it gave her a horrible, cold, heavy feeling in her chest.

As she took a deep breath, she felt something prodding her shoulder.

'*Agh!*' she shrieked.

Outside it was raining hard and water was gushing from the blocked guttering above her window. Maybe the voice was really only the water noise that she had heard, chattering down the wall. But her shoulder was a different story.

She scrambled under the duvet as far as she could get and tightly closed her eyes. *I'm dreaming, I'm just dreaming,* she told herself.

Then she heard the voice again – '*Clarissa*' – and she couldn't work out if whoever was whispering was close beside her, or standing by her bed looking down at her. She felt panicky and vulnerable but she had no idea where it was safer to be: under the covers, hiding, or out in the open where she could face whoever it was. Or *what*ever it was. There was no point in screaming out for Paula because Paula was away visiting her parents following her break-up with Max.

Cautiously, she reached her hand out of the duvet cover into the cool air and clicked on her table lamp. Nothing.

Clarissa picked up her mobile phone from beside the lamp and pulled it back under the covers. She had plenty of signal, but who would she call if she needed help at this hour? The police would probably think she was just a hysterical, mad young woman.

The only person who might believe her would be Mrs Ball. *I can't disturb an elderly woman at four in the morning.*

She paused for a moment or two and heard nothing else. So she slowly slid herself back up and out from under the duvet and sat up. Out of the corner of her eye, however, Clarissa glimpsed a diminutive shadow flit across the room. It was like the shadow of a child, running from one side of her bedroom to the other to hide. She quickly turned around, but it had gone.

'*Hello?*' she said. Her voice sounded strangely flat and unconvincing.

How could anybody have managed to get in? She hadn't heard her door open and the round window was far too small for anyone of regular size to climb in anyway. Although her logical mind was trying to find a reason for it, she knew that it must be her imagination.

'Hello?' she said again, and listened, but there was no response. She knew that it was probably ridiculous, but in a tone that she had heard ghost-hunters use in the *Most Haunted* television show she called out, loudly, 'Do you need my help?'

What am I doing? she thought.

She heard a pattering sound against the window, so she climbed out of the bed and tugged back the curtains and opened the window. There was nothing outside to see but the empty street, and the pavements glazed with rain, being cheered on by rain–laden bushes. Her feet were cold on the laminate flooring and her skin was cold with fear. As she stood there and closed the window, however, she felt the presence of somebody behind her. Somebody very close behind her.

At first she didn't dare to turn around. She couldn't hear anybody breathing, or the soft rustle of clothing. Or smell anything. All she could hear was the rain pouring from the guttering.

She released her hand from the window handle and turned, as slowly as possible. On the opposite side of the room, beside the door, stood the boy. The same boy who had disturbed her when she was eight years old.

She froze.

There was no question in her mind. It was the very same boy, and still the very same age as he had been then – not fourteen years older, as Clarissa was now. The same boy with his scruffy curly brown hair and his pinched, underfed face. The same boy she had seen in the street.

He was standing with one arm held stiffly by his side as if he were on parade, and the other bent as though he was holding something in the darkness.

His head tilted.

'Who *are* you?' she asked, trying to sound forceful, but she could hear for herself how frightened she was. 'Why have you come back?'

Just then there was a deafening bang at her bedroom door, as if somebody had hurled themselves against it from the outside. At the same time, both taps in the bathroom washbasin suddenly started spouting water in explosive, intermittent bursts and the bulb in the lamp exploded, so that the bedroom was only dimly illuminated by the streetlight from outside.

The boy jumped toward her – although he didn't move his arms and his legs at all. His face remained expressionless and he didn't blink.

'Who are you?' Clarissa demanded. Then, in a much higher pitch, 'What do you want? Go away!'

The boy jumped even nearer – and then nearer still, until he was close enough to touch her if he had raised his arms out in front of him. If he had been as neglected and unwashed as he first appeared, she could have smelled him, he was so close. But he smelled of nothing.

'Go away,' she told him. 'Leave me alone.'

The boy stared at her, looking almost elated, as though he were quite confident that she couldn't escape him.

'Please!'

She reached behind her for the edge of her dressing table, trying to locate her mobile phone. She touched it with her fingertips, but in her panic it tumbled onto the floor, and she heard it bounce and skid against the skirting-board. Breathless with fright, she dropped to her knees, frantically patting the floor all around her. It was then she could see that the boy had no feet.

She found her phone, and sat up straight, holding up its shining screen in front of the boy as if to say, *you may think that I'm alone and defenceless, but I'm not. I can call on friends to come. I am not afraid of you.* Although she knew she was.

But as soon as she did that, the boy vanished. One second he was standing staring at her, and then he was gone. He simply wasn't there anymore. There was nobody in the bedroom but Clarissa herself.

Still trembling, she stood up. She walked over to the door and flicked on the ceiling light and looked around the other side of the bed, but the boy wasn't crouched down there. She took a deep breath, and then she opened her wardrobe. He wasn't in there, either.

Then she crossed over to the window to draw the curtains

back fully. As she was about to do so, however, she looked down into the street and saw two figures standing under the streetlamp. They were both holding umbrellas so their faces were in shadow but Clarissa recognised them immediately. The Olven twins. She had known them when she was younger.

They must have seen her at the window but they didn't wave. They turned around and crossed the street and disappeared around the corner by the newsagent's.

Clarissa stood by the window for a long time, holding it open. It was still raining, though not as heavily now, and she breathed in the cold refreshing smell of night rain to calm herself down. She didn't need to call Mrs Ball now. She knew what had happened. She could hear Mrs Ball's voice in her mind, as if she were standing next to her. *'You will instinctively be able to tell who is on your side, and who is not. Special and talented individuals like you will always have – how shall we put it – Watchers ... sort of guardians, if you like – people who are on your side and will look out for you and protect you.'*

A Hidden Man

The next morning the rain had stopped. Sunlight was streaming in between the curtains, lighting dust particles across the room. Clarissa woke up with a start and checked the time. *Nine fifteen. Better get up,* she thought. Clarissa was due to meet Ma at Gracie's Lodge just after 12 noon and she couldn't be late.

She scribbled a note for Paula on a pink post-it note and stuck it on the fridge. *See you tomorrow, sweetie when we're both back. Popping to see Ma and staying there, mwah! Got to talk to you when I get back. It's about something last night. Hope you had a nice time at your parents' and are feeling a lot happier. xxx*

The air seemed extraordinarily still today, with not a cloud in sight. Surprisingly there was not much traffic either. Clarissa shut the gate and began her short walk toward Mipsy's Lane, and along the footpath which was a shortcut toward the shops and tea room. She could smell the aroma of baking bread coming from Gretta's Bakery.

Halfway along the lane, under the trees, there was a wooden bench, and this morning she saw that a tall man in a dirty brown raincoat was sitting on it, with his back very straight, almost as if he were sitting in alert. Beside him on the ground was a can of Red Stripe beer, and a small brown dog that looked in need of a good wash. As she passed him, she glanced at the man's face. He appeared to be staring directly back at her, but he was wearing sunglasses with mirrored, rainbow-coloured lenses, which concealed his eyes. As she got closer, she could hear him gruffly singing *I saw three ships.* He was unshaven, with prickly white stubble, and his nose was a road-map of broken red veins. Clarissa felt a shiver go down her neck and her instinct told her to hurry past him.

As she walked off, however, he suddenly spoke, 'Hey! You wanna tell me what *you* know about love? It's poison, ya know, love.' His voice was gruff but he had spoken so softly that she wasn't sure exactly what he had said. But then, louder, he said, 'You wanna tell *me* something about love, Clarissa?'

Clarissa slowed, and turned. The man had placed his large hands on his knees, and was now leaning slightly forward, still staring at her behind his rainbow sunglasses. The dog jumped to its feet and shook itself, and stared at her, too, expectantly, the way dogs do when they want a biscuit, or a pat, or a walk.

'Well?' the man asked, but Clarissa walked away as fast as she could, trying not to look as if she were unsettled by him. She eventually reached the end of the lane and turned the corner so that the man and the dog were out of sight. She then crossed the grass mound that led to Gracie's Lodge tea rooms, where she could see Ma waiting for her on a patio table in the sun, talking to her friend, Mrs Cawsley-May.

But that afternoon, while Ma and Mrs Cawsley-May discussed all the details of the charity tea they were organising in aid of the Greywell Donkey Trust, Clarissa couldn't stop herself from picturing Barry Kaile's face, and the old man she had passed on her way here, and what he had said to her about love being poison.

Most of all, though, she couldn't stop thinking about the boy, and how he had first appeared in her life. She had truly believed that he had gone forever – that he was nothing more than a symptom of her childhood sensitivity, like an invisible enemy instead of an invisible friend. But now he had come back, as if she still had something that he desperately needed.

Maybe he was jealous of her happiness. Or maybe it was something much more than that.

Milltower Gallery

Craig held the door for Clarissa as they entered the gallery. He winked at her as if to say *after you, gorgeous*.

God, he's so irritating, she thought. And what was even more irritating was that she couldn't stop herself from smiling back at him in a flirtatious way.

Clarissa had been told that the French artist Archibald Argeils would be at the exhibition today. She had seen his work in several art magazines, and she was very much hoping to meet him, because his view of the world seemed to have striking similarities to hers. He painted beautiful, peaceful landscapes, but there was always a shadow in them, or an inexplicable shape, which gave a hint that something alarming was about to happen.

She lifted the hem of her suit skirt and began to clatter up the staircase. When she reached the mezzanine floor, she turned around. The gleaming marble grandeur of the Milltower Gallery still inspired her, even though she had worked here for months now, and today it was echoing with even more excitement.

The guests started to arrive, handing their tickets over to Marjorie Lennarch, the ever-smiling gallery administrator, with her smart grey suit and her steel-grey Princess Anne bun. She ticked their names on her clipboard, and announced them to the gallery's owner, Hugo Walker, so that he could give them a nod and a smile and welcome them to today's exhibition. Clarissa already knew him well enough to recognise that behind that nod and behind that smile he was thinking: *I hope they've brought their credit cards with them.*

'Nerve-wracking, isn't it?' Craig murmured, very close to Clarissa's ear. They were both standing at the top of the staircase in matching navy and white – Craig in his suit and his white silk tie, Clarissa in her smart little jacket and skirt, with their shiny name tags fastened into place.

As the guests climbed the stairs to the mezzanine, the noise level began to rise, especially since most of them were the kind of people who were used to commanding attention.

'Geoffrey – my dear boy – how are you? How's Biffy these days?'

'Annabelle! How good to see you! When was the last time? Antibes, I'm sure!'

Craig watched Mrs Cawsley-May throw her white fur over her shoulder before welcoming a champagne flute into her hand. 'It never ceases to amaze me – the money dripping off these women,' he whispered to Clarissa. 'What else are they going to do with their husband's money apart from buy great art and spoil their toy-boys?'

'*Shh*,' whispered Clarissa.

'Clarissa! Darling!' Mrs Cawsley-May called out.

'Look out, I'm in luck! My sugar Mumma is coming over!' teased Craig.

'Ssh, she's one of my mother's best friends!' said Clarissa. She gave a radiant smile and went over to greet Mrs Cawsley-May. 'Lovely to see you again, Mrs Cawsley-May! How are you?'

'Oh, pff!' said Mrs Cawsley-May. 'It's wonderful to see *you*, darling.'

Clarissa always thought that she must have been very beautiful when she was young. She still had extraordinary green eyes, but the years and the Caribbean cruises and the charity dinners had all taken their toll on her skin.

'My doctor says I should go on a gluten-free diet. I told him that the only diet which would work with me would be a *glutton-free* diet! How's your dear sister? I haven't seen her since that auction we held to raise money for the cause you wanted me to support – what was it – Cystic Fibrosis Trust! We raised so much money I remember. And who is *this* fine young man?'

'Maggie's well, thank you. I don't see her often but we spoke on the phone just last night. Yes I remember the auction, you raised a great deal of money. It was amazing.'

Mrs Cawsley-May flapped her hand as if to say *pleasure!*

'This is my colleague, Craig. Have you had a chance to look

around yet?' Clarissa asked.

'Oh darling, no, first of all I just had to come and see you, call me biased, but you look stunning, and pristine as always!'

Clarissa blushed.

'I heard that wiggly abstract one by T J Wells is here. What's it called?'

'*Illibrium,*' said Clarissa. 'Yes, it's just over there, in the main gallery.'

Mrs Cawsley-May leaned in closely to Clarissa and said: 'I wish somebody would paint *you,* Clarissa darling, truly I do! You're so pretty – your portraits would make a fortune!'

Clarissa felt slightly awkward at receiving such blatant flattery in front of Craig because he always seemed to have an answer for everything and she was beginning to like him a little more than she thought she would. But all Craig said was, 'I have to agree with you – Mrs Cawsley-May, is it? But the artist would need plenty of red paint – she's always blushing!'

'Come, darling. Let me show you what else will take my fancy. Come along dear, you too,' she said to Craig as she fluttered her false eyelashes at him, eyeing him up and down.

Mrs Cawsley-May took Craig by the arm and they made their way through the ever-increasing crowd of visitors toward the first wall where the paintings were hanging.

'This is *divine,*' she said, pointing with her champagne flute to a very simple seascape. 'I hear you have a new sculpture here too? A nude? I'm quite partial to nudes!'

Craig looked at Clarissa and winked.

Mrs Cawsley-May had taken them across to another two paintings, and then a watercolour by Mabel A Brookson – a riotous interpretation of flowering bougainvillea called *Hanging In Bloom.* She had obviously asked her a question about it, but Clarissa hadn't heard her, because she turned toward her with a frown and said, 'Are you quite all *right,* darling? You look a little pale.'

The chattering and laughter seemed to be growing louder and

louder and for some reason Clarissa had begun to feel strangely light-headed and the noise began to sound muffled, as if she were underwater, or being anaesthetised. Even Mrs Cawsley-May's voice had become an indistinct, high-pitched drone.

'Pardon?' Clarissa answered, quickly smiling back at her. 'Sorry, I feel faint. I think I need five minutes in the fresh air.'

'I was just wondering about the price. I do love it, don't you? So *expressive!* But seven thousand for the pair is a little on the steep side.'

'I'll have a word with Mr Walker,' said Clarissa, trying to focus. 'I'm sure he'll be willing to come to some arrangement.'

'You're a darling, darling.'

Clarissa took in a few steady breaths and both she and Mrs Cawsley-May walked back along the main level, leaving Craig talking with a client. There must have been well over fifty people there already, and the baying of wealthy bankers and stockbrokers and their wives reminded Clarissa of the painting *The Heythrop Hunt*. She recognised and smiled at some of the gallery's regular clients, like Mrs Prized and her very tall husband, who insisted their surname was pronounced *Preezèt*. Craig always called her Mrs Prize Pea.

'That's very odd,' said Mrs Cawsley-May, peering down the staircase. 'Look at that scruffy boy – is he *allowed* in here?'

'What?' said Clarissa. 'What boy?'

She looked down to the reception area below. She was so shocked by what she saw that she exclaimed '*No!*'

'What is it, darling?' asked Mrs Cawsley-May. 'Is everything all right?'

It was the boy. The same boy who had stared at her in the street and had appeared in her bedroom. The same boy who had stalked her and frightened her when she was young. She was sure of it, no matter how impossible it seemed that he had never grown up. He was standing in the middle of the reception area, amongst a crowd of visitors, staring up at her. Was *he* the reason she had suddenly felt unwell? Had she unconsciously sensed that he was here?

Without moving his arms or his legs the boy suddenly

jumped until he was standing at the bottom of the staircase. Then he jumped a second time, and now he was halfway up to the mezzanine. He raised one arm, as though he was reaching for something.

'Oh, God,' said Clarissa, desperately looking around to see where Craig was. She could see the boy, and Mrs Cawsley-May had obviously seen him, too, yet there were people walking up and down the staircase and they didn't appear to be aware of him at all.

He jumped again. And then again. And then he was standing only two steps away from the top, right behind Mrs Cawsley-May, his arms both down by his sides, with a sly expression on his face.

'Are you *sure* you're all right, Clarissa?' Mrs Cawsley-May asked her. It seemed she couldn't see the boy now, although he was standing right behind her. 'You are looking frightfully pale again. Perhaps you *should* go outside and get some fresh air. It's very crowded in here, isn't it? Craig can show me the art, darling. Oh, look – here he is now.' Mrs Cawsley-May caught Craig's eye and beckoned him over.

Clarissa nodded. *What am I going to do?*, she thought. She looked at Craig then back at Mrs Cawsley-May, with the boy still standing close behind her. How could nobody see him, with his soiled grey blazer, his shorts and his scruffy, curly hair? The atmosphere was filled with the smell of expensive perfumes so perhaps it masked any odour he might have.

'Here, darling,' continued Mrs Cawsley-May, 'I've just remembered.' She passed Craig her champagne flute and pulled a pink tissue-wrapped package from her handbag. 'Put this somewhere safely. Something out of the blue has just made me remember I had it on me for you. It's a special little old something and I thought it was high time that you had it. Sorry I missed giving it to you on your actual birthday, darling. Don't open it now, though. Open it later when you're feeling better. And – please – if only for your own sake – don't mention it to anybody else,' she winked.

'Th … thank you,' Clarissa stammered, taking the parcel,

although she found it hard to keep her eyes off the boy. 'I'll open it after work.' *Don't mention it to anybody else?* She thought.

'Good. It's *divine*, darling, in every sense of the word, and very, very special. Keep it safe. Now, who is the woman in that very striking portrait over there?'

'That's Elaine Grace, the actress,' said Craig. 'Did you ever see *The Reckoning*? She was in that. Well, and dozens of other plays too.'

Clarissa tucked the small parcel into her suit pocket.

The boy was now standing so close behind Mrs Cawsley-May that Clarissa could see only part of his shoulder. She didn't know whether to warn Mrs Cawsley-May or to stay silent and hope that he would simply vanish, as he had vanished in her bedroom.

Mrs Cawsley-May continued talking and laughing with Craig as they discussed the portrait of Elaine Grace. 'Was her nose *really* that large, or is that just artistic licence?'

Without warning, the boy took another jump, sideways and upwards this time, so that he was standing *next* to Mrs Cawsley-May. He stared first at Clarissa, as if challenging her to say anything, and then he turned his head to stare at Mrs Cawsley-May. He lifted both arms, each as stiff as a railway signal, and seized two handfuls of Mrs Cawsley-May's taupe silk dress, tugging at it hard.

'*Whoops!*' said Mrs Cawsley-May, as she teetered sideways, but the boy pulled at her even harder. She had seen him when he was downstairs, but for some reason she obviously couldn't see him now.

'*No!*' cried Clarissa, and tried to grab Mrs Cawsley-May's hand. Craig reached out to support her too, but the boy wrenched at her dress yet again, and this time she lost her footing. She snatched at the banister-rail, but her right ankle twisted underneath her, and she clattered awkwardly down the first few stairs as if she were trying to run down them as fast as possible.

Then, however, one of her heels broke and she lost her balance altogether, thumping and bumping down the rest of the stairs, as inelegantly as a bundle of washing.

'*Mrs Cawsley-May!*' shouted Craig and Clarissa, but it was too late. Mrs Cawsley-May rolled over and over, all arms and legs and silk dress and fur, and hit the marble floor at the bottom of the stairs with a sickening crack. Her pearl necklace had snapped, and dozens of pearls bounced and pinged down the stairs after her, and then rolled away in every direction across the gallery floor.

Clarissa looked down in horror. The gallery guests were huddled in groups and people were crying. Mrs Cawsley-May was lying sprawled on the floor with her arms and legs at awkward angles. Blood was seeping from her white bouffant hair. Was she actually *dead?*

Clarissa had never seen a dead body before, and she was so shocked that she could scarcely breathe. For a few long moments, the silence in the gallery was overwhelming. A bald man in a dark suit pushed his way through the crowd around the body and knelt down to lift up her wrist and take her pulse.

'Please – I'm a doctor. Please stay back. Give her some room. Can somebody please call for an ambulance.'

The crowd of visitors shuffled back. The whole gallery was quiet. The doctor held Mrs Cawsley-May's wrist for over a minute, and then he gently laid her hand back on the floor and shook his head. One of the women close by started sobbing, and then another.

Clarissa stood at the top of the staircase, in shock. She looked around for the boy, but she couldn't see him anywhere. He had been standing only a few feet away from her, but now he had disappeared entirely.

'*Clarissa!*' echoed a voice. She turned around, but nobody else seemed to have heard it except for a tall, blond man in a dark brown velvet jacket on the other side of the mezzanine floor, who gave Clarissa a quizzical look as if to say *what was that?*

'*Clarissa!*' screamed the voice again. Clarissa held onto the banister and took one stiff step downwards, but then Craig came up behind her and took hold of her arm.

'Don't,' he said. 'Don't go down there.'

Clarissa stepped back up to the mezzanine floor and Craig put his arm around her shoulders. 'There's nothing you can do,' he told her. 'It was an accident, that's all.'

She couldn't stop trembling. Mrs Cawsley-May's fall may have looked like an accident, but she was the only person in the gallery who knew that this wasn't the case. She looked around to see if the man in the dark brown velvet jacket was still there. He appeared to have heard the voice, too, so perhaps he had seen the boy also. But the crowd of visitors kept milling around and she couldn't see him anywhere.

She looked back down to the reception area, and saw that Mrs Cawsley-May's white fur stole was gradually soaking up her blood. Mr Walker came out of the side door from the storeroom, carrying a large sheet which was usually used to cover up paintings. He draped it over Mrs Cawsley-May's body and then stepped back, his face as grave as an undertaker's.

Craig said, 'Come on, Clarry. You don't want to see any more of this. Let's take you to the office.'

She turned away, but as she did so she heard a drawn-out screeching: an indistinct stream of words. It was coming from two young ladies standing near the body. Their arms were outstretched and pointing toward the back of the room. Clarissa gasped and had to cover her ears. The screeching made her feel as if her teeth were being pulled out.

In response, and without knowing why, she screamed out, '*Vges exo!*' over, and over, and over again.

She screamed so loudly that the people below stared up at her in bewilderment.

She felt Craig shaking her shoulder. 'Clarry!' he was saying, in a blurry voice. 'Clarry, Clarry look at me.'

Clarissa stopped screaming. Craig turned her around, and it was then she came out of her trance and threw her arms around him.

'Craig, why has this happened? What have I done? I invited her here – it's all my fault. *It's all my fault –*'

The crowd parted as the paramedics wheeled away Mrs

Cawsley-May's body through the front doors. Once she had gone, the shocked silence was replaced by a subdued murmur of conversation. The police had arrived and everybody had to stay in the gallery until they had taken statements.

'I'm sorry, Clarissa. I know that you and Mrs Cawsley-May were close.'

Clarissa raised her eyes and said thank you to Hugo Walker.

'Clarry, what were you screaming?' asked Craig, still holding her close. 'It sounded like a foreign language.'

'I don't speak any other languages, Craig. What are you talking about? Those two girls were screaming so loudly, I couldn't listen any more, I just had to cover my ears. They must have been mad at him,' she sobbed.

'Who? Mad at who? Only *you* were screaming sweetheart, just you – and it *wasn't* English.'

Peace

Clarissa pulled her sunglasses down from the crown of her head to shield her eyes. Alone, she walked along the path leading to East Greywell Cemetery. The air was still and not many other people were around.

As she walked, she thought about what had happened to Mrs Cawsley-May last month. She had tried to explain to Ma but she still wasn't sure that Ma had believed that she 'lost her balance' – or, if she had, that she had forgiven her, for without Clarissa she never would have been invited to the gallery on that fateful day. After all she was her longest standing friend. *Surely Ma wouldn't really blame me, would she?*

Maybe it was time that Clarissa explained everything to Ma.

She thought about Craig, too, and how mixed-up her feelings about him were. She wasn't even sure if she trusted his charming ways enough to become his girlfriend, and she didn't want to get serious about somebody who was never serious about anything. But the more time she spent with him at the gallery, the more she liked him. She couldn't help finding him attractive and extremely funny and his passion for opera and classical music really impressed her.

She waved to a little old man on a walking frame, and he grinned back at her with an irregular array of yellowed dentures. To her left she could see the old stone walls and lych gate of the cemetery. She could see over the mossy wall: a bench halfway along the cemetery path caught her attention, surrounded by dandelions and bathed in sun. There didn't appear to be anyone visiting the graves, so she spent a few quiet minutes looking around some of the smaller stones, reading the dates and messages before heading toward the rear of the cemetery to Mrs Cawsley-May's grave. It pleased her that it didn't upset her too much being in here, in fact she felt at peace.

She wandered over the grass, holding a bunch of hand-picked flowers, and the breeze gently blowing her hair. Being surrounded by singing birds and no human voices nearby, she felt a deep sense of self-acceptance and focus. As the breeze drifted around her, it brought with it a smell of freshly cut grass and a strong aroma of hyacinths.

As she got toward the back of the cemetery she reached out and felt the rough texture of a large headstone, and compared it with the smoothness and coldness of the granite one behind it. She wondered why smoother ones were placed amongst larger, lumpier ones – maybe it was a case of left-over space or family plots. She stood still and closed her eyes, and took in a deep breath, feeling the warmth of the sunshine sink into her, all over. To her left a bird chirruped as it landed on a branch of the yew tree.

Continuing to walk along the path and around to Mrs Cawsley-May's grave, she couldn't help but feel tearful at how fresh it all still looked, and wondered if after time it would look neglected just as many of them did. 'Mrs Cawsley-May we miss you, I promise I will do what I can to find an explanation,' she said, quietly, as she crouched down, as if in some way Mrs Cawsley-May would hear her and know she will always be loved. 'I know I'm here alone, but Ma is finding it still too raw, she misses you terribly.'

Clarissa felt as though everything paused for that moment and a lump rose in her throat. 'I know you can hear me, maybe you're with me, watching me. Maybe you're wondering why I'm here crying at a lump of stone when your spirit is laughing and sipping champagne somewhere luxurious.' She stood up and laughed as she sniffed and wiped her eyes.

'Aw, hi moggy,' she said, as what felt like the fur of a cat brushed the back of her leg. She tilted her head back and took in another slow calming breath and felt her heartbeat slow. She imagined herself sitting high on a clifftop, on a veranda, bathed in sun, while she painted the view with her troubles floating away, as wispy clouds floated around and the tide washed against the rocks and sand below.

Taking another deep breath, she slowly opened her eyes, and at first looked straight up to the sky. Then she lowered her gaze. Less than ten feet in front of her, near Mrs Cawsley-May's grave, stood the boy.

Eye Spy

Clarissa said nothing at first. The boy didn't speak, either, but stood motionless among the long grass between the unkempt graves, staring at her. Somewhere in the trees behind him, a pigeon kept monotonously warbling.

'What do you *want?*' Clarissa challenged. *'Can you talk?'* Her heart was now beating very fast, with a heavy thump, and her voice was angry. She walked away from Mrs Cawsley-May's grave so the boy didn't attempt to damage it somehow. 'Why do you keep following me? Why did you pull Mrs Cawsley-May down the stairs? *You killed her! She was our friend!'*

Still the boy said nothing, but plucked a stem of grass and began to twist it around his finger, around and around. His lower lip stuck out a little, as if he were sulking.

'Who *are* you?' Clarissa demanded. 'What do you want? You *killed* Mrs Cawsley-May! Do you know that? She *died*!' Her voice had risen now to a whispery scream, conscious that someone might hear her.

Abruptly, the boy jumped toward her, so that he was two graves nearer, standing on the gravel path. The pigeon continued to warble, over and over, but still the boy said nothing. Clarissa didn't know whether to back away or stand her ground. *He's scary, yes, but he's only a little boy.*

She was just about to ask him again what he wanted when she saw a flicker of yellow light off to her left. She glanced quickly toward the cemetery gates and saw two young women in lemon-yellow dresses. They were standing side by side behind one of the grey, ivy-covered tombs, staring in her direction. She couldn't believe her eyes. It was the Olven twins again, Sarah and Sally, she was sure of it. She was both bewildered and relieved. *What were they doing here? Was she in danger?*

Unlike the boy, they had grown up. Their bushy red hair was cut short now, but they still had pale, distinctive faces, and those bleached rainwater eyes.

When the boy saw that Clarissa was looking toward the cemetery gates, he turned, too, to see what had caught her attention. The second he saw the Olven twins, he jumped away, until he was standing three pathways away, half-hidden by the shadow of a weeping stone angel. As the twins began to walk slowly and serenely toward him, hand in hand, he jumped backward, and was gone.

Clarissa called out, 'Sarah! Sally!' But when she looked again, the Olven twins were nowhere to be seen.

The cemetery was still hot and sunny and deserted, just as it had been when she first walked into it. The trees stirred in the slightest of breezes, and the pigeon kept on warbling.

She briskly walked away from the headstones, looking over her shoulder intermittently, and kept going until she reached the cemetery gates. As she approached them, she saw that on the pillars on either side a life-size stone face had been carved, grotesque and grinning. She stopped in front of one of them and stared at it. It was a well-weathered stone, with blotches of yellow moss on it, but all the same it almost appeared to be alive.

It was then that she began to understand that her life was always going to be revealing faces, like a repetitive tapestry, and that the boy and the Olven twins were an integral part of that tapestry, like a grey thread and two red threads that constantly ran through it, and that she could never escape them – not without her whole destiny unravelling. This grinning stone face in front of her was reminding her that she was a Diviner, and that being a Diviner was woven inextricably into everything she would ever do and everywhere she would ever go and everybody she would ever meet, or be afraid of, or fall in love with.

Butterflies

Craig sat down on the wall of the fountain in the sunshine.

'Sit with me. Tell me your favourite things to do,' he said.

Clarissa looked around just in case the boy was watching them from somewhere, like behind a tree or under a bench, or in the water fountain ready to drown her. She was aware they had only an hour for lunch but a part of her didn't want the hour to ever be over. She looked behind her a final time and sat on the wall of the fountain next to Craig, placing her Greggs lunch bag and drink to her side.

People were wandering around the square, couples holding hands and a small boy running about holding the string to a bright red balloon.

'I like coming here, on my lunch break,' she said. 'There's a lot of people-watching to do, so it makes a nice contrast to the calmness and peace of the gallery.'

'Even the odd one–legged pigeon,' smiled Craig.

'Yes, that too,' Clarissa agreed.

'But what do you *really* like doing? What makes *you* happy? *Who* makes you happy?'

'Lots of things. Family, drawing, music, the coast, log cabins and champagne.'

Craig smiled. 'Go on.'

'And in a strange way, realising that life goes on. Of course we all have to die sometime, but when you lose someone you love in your family, your pain inspires you to be creative or build something for others – to honour what they were by creating something beautiful in their memory, to recognise that you are what you are because of *them*. That realisation of being free to be you, and that unconditional bond of loved ones makes me happy.'

Clarissa smiled, but her eyes were welling up with warm

tears. She lowered her head as a tear slid down her cheek. She wiped her face with the back of her hand hoping that Craig wouldn't see. But the beautiful thing about Craig, that she had seen and admired, was that he did notice everything. He knew when she was feeling creative; he knew when she had a hair out of place; he even knew if she'd changed mascara colours.

'Deep,' he smiled.

'And the sound of that water cascading behind us, it relaxes me,' she said as she looked up at him. Craig leaned across and wiped his thumb gently across her cheek.

'I love your passion, Clarissa.'

'What do *you* like doing?' she asked, trying to take the focus off her. As sympathetic as he was, she didn't like crying in front of him.

'Oh me? I like being with you,' he replied.

Clarissa blushed.

'But I love the sound of the fountain, too. And a wander through the Clatterbang market and large car boot sale on a Sunday. There's a great bistro up the road there that I like to go to afterwards. Even more, I like the way on a summer's day the clouds look lumpy against the bright blue sky. The sky amazes me, *how* it's so blue. It's like living inside a painting. Especially on days like this. Even if you close your eyes you can imagine what the day is going to be like by the noises and bird sounds.'

Clarissa looked up and smiled. 'It reminds me of being a child, when it's like this. I love it, too.'

It was then that she began to feel differently toward him. In spite of her newly-restored sensitivity, she hadn't seen any trace of evil or ugly secrets in his face and she really felt she had bonded with him. It's like living inside a painting – that was so close to the way that she sometimes felt about life.

She felt herself saying, quite unexpectedly, 'Craig, I – I'm sorry I pushed you away at the gallery, when you wanted me to kiss you. You see – I was embarrassed, and unsure. But if you ever wanted to again, I –'

Craig looked at Clarissa and smiled, reaching out his hand to place it on hers. 'We will, and I think it would be special.' He winked at her, and gently squeezed her hand. 'We will.'

Clatterbang

Clarissa had begun to see the Olven twins more and more frequently, although she had seen no sign of the boy for weeks. She wondered if it was the presence of the Olven twins, her Watchers, that was keeping him away, although she couldn't be sure. The twins never came close enough for her to be able to speak to them, and whenever she tried to approach them they walked away, and disappeared into a crowd, or round a corner, or simply vanished.

She had been on her annual leave for two weeks, including a week in Edinburgh, during which it had rained almost every day. Now she had only just arrived at the Clatterbang car boot sale on Curbine Street and already she had seen the twins. Their appearances were becoming so regular that Clarissa could almost predict the days that they would cross paths – last week, just crossing the street in front of the Milltower Gallery; yesterday at the fashion show that she had visited with Ma; and today, here at the boot sale. Their increasingly frequent appearances made her feel that something disturbing was going to happen, any day soon, but she also knew she'd be safe if they were near her. She knew that they were keeping a protective eye on her, but why so often?

It was another warm, sunny afternoon. Clarissa browsed through the dusty cardboard boxes full of books, watched by a market seller who was slowly biting his nails. She could smell his mug of chicken soup and the cooked sausage roll that were perched on the edge of his car boot.

"Right, love?' he smiled. She looked up at him and smiled back, but all the same there was something about him which reminded her of the man in the rainbow sunglasses – and there was a scruffy little brown dog sitting beside him, too.

She didn't really need any more books, but she adored them.

They fascinated her. She pulled out ones that had titles that seemed to relate to her life. *Daisy Did It* was the first that she smiled at. *The Little One* was the second, and *Don't Be Shocked, Be Strange!* was the third. She came across a big old canvas-covered book next, called *A Lover's History in Art*, a big book full of famous paintings, and although she loved it she felt she would be reminded of that fateful day that they lost Mrs Cawsley-May every time she saw it on her shelf so she decided to not buy it. One by one, she sorted through the next large box of books. She could almost hear the voices of the writers, with all of their different ideas, and babbling voices of the hundreds of characters within the books.

Tinny ballet music was coming from a record-player on another stall, *La Fille Mal Gardée*, and it made Clarissa feel amused and relaxed. The Clatterbang car boot sale was quite crowded, and people were jostling and bumping into each other as they made their way around the stalls. Clarissa could smell coffee, and cakes, and hear the clinking sound of bric-a-brac as people rustled their hands through the hundreds of items. She glanced over a bric-a-brac stall and was drawn to a tiny porcelain statue of Cupid. Looking up at the brassy lady behind the stall, she smiled, handing her a two pound coin. As she was putting it in her bag, she heard a loud familiar laugh behind her and turned around.

And there he was, in a jazzy red shirt with a zigzag pattern and beige slim-fit chinos. Craig. He was accompanied by a chubby, smiling middle-aged lady in a splashy green-and-orange dress and a floppy straw hat.

'Clarry!' said Craig. 'What the devil are you doing here? Excuse me, Mrs Ponting, It's my princess!' Clarissa smiled at Mrs Ponting.

'Craig! Hi!' She felt awkward for having interrupted their conversation but Mrs Ponting didn't seem to mind in the least. She made an odd wuffing noise, flapped her hand dismissively and scuttled off toward the cake stall. Clarissa and Craig laughed in unison.

'Oh, it's wonderful to see you! It feels like forever!' Clarissa beamed, as she tip-toed and reached for a big kiss on Craig's cheek. Craig's eyebrows raised and he smiled at her.

'You're right, darling, but it's only been two weeks,' he smiled. 'And your holiday leave is nearly over!'

'Oh – *sugar*,' she joked, fiddling with her bag to make it hang more comfortably on her shoulder. 'It feels like I've been off work for months, it's been lovely and relaxing, especially in this weather.'

'So, do you have time for a coffee or a glass of wine? Or are you too busy buying up every decent book in Lodsley?' He nodded at her bagful of second-hand novels. 'There won't be any left for anybody else at the rate you're going.'

He was talking about books but Clarissa could see in his eyes that his attention was entirely on her. Quite unexpectedly, she found that she couldn't look away from him, either. She thought: *this is ridiculous. This is like we've both been bewitched.*

'What?' she smiled, sensing Craig looking at her intently. She could feel herself blushing.

'It's *great* to see you,' he said.

Afternoon Delight

Afterwards, she couldn't remember if they had said anything, or moaned, or murmured, or whispered in each other's ears how much they excited each other.

The long curtains had remained open a foot or two, so that his bedroom had been flooded with sunlight, and when he had looked up at her, her hair had been shining like a halo, as if he had been making love to an angel.

Clarissa kissed his shoulder. It was tacky from cooled sweat, but his skin smelled sweet, and sexy, with a dulled scent of Gucci. She thought it one of the most sensual combinations of smells that she'd ever encountered. He was lean and muscular from swimming, and he had a tattoo on the left side of his chest that said *When words fail – music speaks*. When she had come close to her climax, she had gripped the pillow next to his head so tightly with both hands, as if she needed to stop herself from falling off the Earth, and kissed him hard before throwing her head back to flick her hair and scream in pleasure.

She had never given herself so completely to anybody. But he was so calm, and so assured, and so strong. His stare sunk through her and excited her at every gaze. He made love to her as if he were swimming. It was only when they approached the final few moments that he began to thrust harder and harder, relentlessly, and she had felt that the world was coming to pieces all around her.

They lay in each other's arms for a long while. Craig reached across and stroked her hair.

'You know what you are, Clarry?' he said.

She turned her head, and smiled.

'You, my darling – *you are divine.*'

My Girl

When they woke again, it was early evening and the bright afternoon sunlight had turned into the low, grainy, crimson glow of sunset. Reaching over to him, Clarissa stroked her hand across the width of Craig's naked stomach. He grumbled as it tickled and rolled over to face her, and opened one eye. He stared at her for a long time as if he didn't recognise her, or as if he couldn't believe that she was really here.

'Hi,' she said. 'Had a weird dream.'

'Was just a dream,' smiled Craig. 'You're with me now, safe.'

'It was like it was real.' She kissed him gently on the lips and said, 'Oh hey – I bought something from the boot sale for us.' She giggled, as she rolled and reached over the edge of the bed and into her bag, pulling out a figurine. 'Look! It's Cupid!'

'Cupid?'

'I'm going to put it here, by your bed, maybe it's worked some magic on us!'

'Clarry?' he mumbled with only a slight movement of his lips, and only opening one eye to look at her statue.

'Yes honey?' she softly replied, placing the figurine down and wriggling over toward him under the covers. 'You fancy some more champagne?'

'Mmmm, lovely,' he groaned.

'What shall we do this evening? I could dance, I feel so wonderful,' she said, as she stretched out in contentment.

'Sleep,' said Craig.

She couldn't believe that she'd spent hours making love to Craig. Her feelings about him at the gallery had been so mixed, but now her passion for him was vivid and clear, as if all her jumbled emotions had fitted together like a speeded-up jigsaw, and she could now see the sharpest, brightest picture of their affection for each other.

'On second thoughts, let's go out for dinner,' he said. 'Somewhere expensive.'

The white bed sheets barely covered the curves of her back, as she lay holding his hand. She rolled over and let the Egyptian cotton wrap around her body as she reached out for a champagne flute that stood on the bedside table. She took a sip, looking at Craig over the rim of the glass.

'You're so sexy, darling,' she smiled, seductively eating a strawberry from the pallet next to the champagne.

Craig opened his eyes to watch her as she teased her tongue around the tip of the strawberry. 'Come here,' he demanded.

A deep operatic voice filled the air as Craig turned up the stereo. 'Feel this through your soul,' he said. 'It's my favourite. *O Mio Babbino Caro.*'

He rolled back toward her and began to caress her soft skin.

They made love again and again, and lay listening to the music in between, holding hands, stroking each other and breathing in the emotion together, synchronised.

'This is what it must be like in Heaven,' she whispered into his ear, and gently kissed him on the cheek. 'Everything in Heaven must be flooded with sunshine, with wonderful music playing. And champagne. And strawberries, dipped in milk chocolate. I feel so happy and complete right now. I never want it to end.'

Craig smiled, more to himself than to her. *I've finally got Clarry. My girl.* He turned over, kissed her firmly on her forehead and said, 'I love you. Do you know that? I think I always have.'

Clarissa opened her eyes and smiled back at him. She was beginning to think that she might have felt the same about him.

Clarissa pulled the plug on the bath and thought about where Craig might be planning to take her for dinner, although it was getting quite late. She slipped into a grey satin gown that hung on the bathroom door and tucked her wet hair behind her ears. She had used so many sandalwood bath-balls that she could still smell the sweetness on her skin. *This man really pampers himself with lovely products*, she thought, as the cool satin slipped over her breasts and soft, glowing skin.

She walked back into the bedroom, tying the belt of the gown.

Craig was still on the bed.

'*Craig!*' she screamed. '*Craig!*'

She was so shocked at what she saw that she stumbled against the end of the bed, panicking. Craig was lying on his back with his arms raised helplessly in the air, dying. He was drenched in blood.

Both of his wrists were cut open, and blood was pouring down his arms and dripping from his elbows and soaking the white bedding all around him. There were loops and spatters of blood all across the pillows and across the headboard.

'*Craig! Oh God, Craig!*' cried Clarissa. '*Craig, what's happened?*'

Craig opened and closed his mouth, but Clarissa couldn't hear what he was saying because Pavarotti was loudly singing *Ave Maria*. She climbed onto the bed and tried to take Craig in her arms, but his blood was pumping everywhere.

'Clar – ry ...' he mumbled. 'There's some – bo – dy here ... somebody tried t – to kill me ...'

Clarissa stretched over and frantically slammed her hand onto the stereo off-button three or four times until it was silent. On the pillow, she noticed there was a broken champagne glass, with a bloodied edge and her statue of Cupid splattered with blood.

'*Craig, stay with me!*' She wrestled herself out of the satin gown and then wrapped it tightly around both of his wrists, pressing it firmly with her thumbs. But she couldn't stop him bleeding. The satin was slipping and sliming with deep red blood within seconds.

'Who was it, Craig? Craig – who was it? *Oh shit, Craig, stay awake!*'

She turned her head quickly to look behind her, terrified that whoever had done this to Craig might still be here, in his apartment.

'I – wa – sleep … I didn't s – see. I only f – felt … Clarry, I'm bl – bleeding to dea – I don't wa – want t – t – to *die!*'

Clarissa lost her grip on the blood-soaked nightgown. It was no good, she couldn't stop the bleeding. She kissed Craig quickly and then she clambered off the bed and grabbed the phone. She dialled 999, her eyes filling up with tears. When the emergency operator answered, it was all she could do to choke out the address.

She went back over to the bed, still holding the phone to her ear. 'It's okay, Craig. It's going to be okay! The ambulance is coming! Keep both your arms up as high as you can, that's what they said. Try to stay still. Try to stay calm. I'll be right back. Two seconds. I promise.'

She kissed him again, firmly and passionately and then stood up, her naked body streaked with impressionistic swipes of blood. She walked naked into the hallway, leaving bloodstained footprints across the cream bedroom rug.

The front door was shut, and the security chain was still fastened. She turned around slowly. The balcony doors were still locked. Nothing looked as though it had been disturbed, so it seemed that nobody else was in the apartment. She headed toward the kitchen. Her breathing was becoming heavier and she was increasingly nervous. But nobody was there either, and it was totally silent. She stopped still for a moment or two, and turned on the spot. Scared and cold, shivering, she began to start moving toward the door. She headed back along the corridor, past the kitchen door and toward the bedroom. As she did so, however, she had a feeling that somebody was following her, close behind her. She turned, quickly, but there was nobody there. The only sounds she could hear were her blood-stained feet sticking to the laminate flooring, and her anxious breathing. The door to the coat cupboard was ajar, which made her feel even more uneasy, because she thought he had closed it. She rushed into the bedroom and slammed the door shut.

'Oh Craig!' she cried, with both hands pressed against the

door leaving bloody hand prints. For a moment she wondered if she could see the image of an angel's face in the blood. She closed her eyes, leant her head onto the door and began to cry. *'Oh, Craig.'*

She almost felt as if she were going mad and heartbroken all in one go. She turned around, and gasped.

Craig was still lying in a widening pool of his own blood, but now his arms had dropped to his sides and his eyes were wide open and he was staring up at the ceiling.

She could see that he was dead.

She felt as if her heart were shrivelling, as if the whole room were closing in on her in time with the increased pace of her heartbeat.

She heard a strange whimpering sound, and looked around, slowly and nervously. Standing on the opposite side of the bed was the boy. With one hand he was twiddling his curly hair around his finger, the blood sticking his curls together. His other hand was pointing at Craig, and his sleeve was stained crimson. Only his fingers protruded from his sleeve and he was holding some sort of blade, but this too was smothered in blood. He suddenly stopped whimpering and looked across at Clarissa. Then he wiggled his fingers at her mockingly, and smiled.

Penitence

A female detective came into the room and stood patiently waiting while Paula gave Clarissa a tissue to wipe her eyes. Two paramedics carried Craig's covered body away.

The detective was a stocky young woman, with a badly-cut brown bob and an olive-green suit that looked as though it were a size too big.

'We've only just got together – now he's –' said Clarissa, but then she broke down in tears.

'Only hours ago we were smiling and –'

All she could think of was all that blood, and Craig staring at the ceiling. And the boy, who had wiggled his fingers at her and then jumped back and vanished, and how sticky the blood was.

'Take it easy, miss, just take it easy,' said the detective. 'You've seen something awful, you've had a nasty shock.' She had a strong Birmingham accent, keeping her teeth clenched together when she spoke. 'We don't have to talk now. We can call back in the morning, all right? Give you a chance to get over the shock. I'm sure your friend here will take good care of you. Try and get some rest. Go home.'

She buttoned up her flappy jacket, and then looked at Paula, who was squeezing Clarissa's hand to reassure her.

'All right, love?' she continued. 'See you tomorrow, around nine if that's all right.' Then she nodded to the forensic team dealing with the scene, then to her fellow officers and they all filed out of Craig's apartment. A younger uniformed officer took a look back at Paula as he shut the door behind them, although he didn't say anything to her.

Clarissa sobbed and gasped, crying uncontrollably.

'I'm so sorry, honey, come here.' Paula pulled Clarissa in tightly and cuddled her.

'It's my fault he was murdered. What am I going to do?'

Clarissa whispered through her tears. 'I mean, what am I going to tell the police tomorrow? That a ghost boy killed him? They'll never believe me. It sounds ridiculous! My prints are everywhere, and my DNA all over him and the bedding and – oh Paula they *will* think I've done it because there's no-body else's DNA, nobody else has been here, have they?'

Paula looked at Clarissa with a grimace as if to say: *honey, it was suicide. Why he should have wanted to kill himself I can't imagine, but he must have done.*

Just then, Clarissa's mobile phone jangled loudly, which gave Clarissa a sudden salty taste in her mouth.

'Caller ID says it's Hugo. From the gallery?'

'Oh, God. That's my boss,' said Clarissa. 'Why is he calling me?'

'I'll deal with it,' smiled Paula.

Clarissa could hear Paula on the phone to her boss in the other room as she splashed her face at the bathroom sink with icy cold water. She could hear words being used like *maybe soon, such a tragedy, they think suicide, it's going to take time,* and *bless her.* No matter what her destiny might be – Diviner or not – Clarissa didn't want to be a victim or to be treated like one. Without her, the boy would never have appeared, and Craig would still be alive. She raised her eyes and looked at the puffy, pale and angry version of herself staring back at her. Guilt was rising up inside her and swamping her heart, and she cried uncontrollably, feeling incredibly sick.

After a few minutes, she splashed her face with water again and dabbed it dry with Craig's hand towel. She sat on the toilet lid with her head in her hands and dropped the towel onto the floor.

She began to think. *First Mrs Cawsley-May, now him. Who is going to be next? It seems as if nobody I really care about is safe from this vindictive boy. People I love have died. What am I fighting against? Who is he, this child? Why is he stalking me like this, and trying to destroy everything I care about?* She needed answers. And soon –

before anyone else got hurt.

'Clarry are you getting ready?' Paula called from the doorway. 'There's an officer outside the door waiting to seal the room. We should get out of here like the detective woman said. Come on honey, let's go.'

I'll Be Seeing You

Clarissa made her way along the path and up toward the grave where Craig was going to be buried. With one hand she held her skirt to stop it from flapping in the wind, her other hand fastened tightly around her umbrella handle. The rain was as persistent as her sadness, but she didn't mind it pattering onto her skin as it became one with her tears, and refreshed her cheeks.

About thirty family and friends were gathered around the vicar, some staring at Craig's coffin, some huddled into the arms of loved ones to take shelter from the wind and the sorrow. She edged her way through to the front of the mourners and looked down. His coffin seemed far too small for the tall, well-built man who had made love to her on the day he had died. She bent down and took a notebook from her bag before placing it on top of the coffin. She had written on the cover: *Craig and Clarry's favourite things!*

'Keep our dreams of romance safe, my darling. I'll always miss you and love you,' she whispered. 'Thank you for your strength.'

She stood up but stayed close to his coffin. She turned to offer a smile of sympathy to Craig's mother, who was sniffling into her handkerchief and being comforted by a member of the family. In return, she nodded at Clarissa and shared a broken smile.

Clarissa sat bolt upright, holding her hand to her chest. She threw back the duvet and scanned the room. Her bedroom door was open and a half empty glass of brandy sat on her bedside cupboard. The room was hot, and her T-shirt was stuck to her skin from night sweats. She pressed her hand to her forehead for a few moments to soothe her headache and to focus her eyes. She thought of the first time that Mrs Ball had helped her to understand the gift that she had been born with – although now she began to feel that it was more of a curse. Would she ever be free from losing people she needed? From seeing the cruelty and deception in people's faces? Would the boy ever stop pursuing her, frightening her and hunting down her loved ones?

Maggie

'Come in!' smiled Maggie, as she welcomed Clarissa. 'I've got the room ready for you. Did you ever think your big sis would be a qualified masseuse? And working from home?'

'Ah, I always knew you'd be great at something,' Clarissa teased as she took off her coat and hung it up. 'It smells amazing in here, like lavender.'

'Lavender and chamomile. Silver birch too. I make my own massage oil.'

Maggie hugged her and held her close. 'I'm so pleased you decided to come and stay. You need somebody to turn to, after what's happened.'

'You're right. Paula's away now on business for two weeks and I thought I could manage on my own but I keep having nightmares. Last night I dreamed I saw Craig lying there with his arms held up, and all that blood, and looking so bewildered, like he didn't know what was happening to him.'

Clarissa didn't go so far as to mention the boy. Until she had found out who he was, or *what* he was, and why he seemed so determined to kill the people she loved, she would rather keep his appearances to herself. She still felt as if she were to blame for Mrs Cawsley-May falling down the gallery stairs, and for Craig's wrists being cut, although she didn't really understand why she should be. It wasn't her fault that she had been born a Diviner. Clarissa smiled at Maggie and gestured at her case, which she carried her into her bedroom along the hall. It was warm, and the lighting was subdued. She undressed and put on the chunky robe that was hanging on the back of the wardrobe door, and then she went back into the living-room where she had left Maggie.

'Right,' said Maggie. 'We're going to start by giving you a massage, to ease all of that stress out of you. Then we're going to sit down and have a good old sisterly natter. I'll make us some green tea. That'll help your detox. Get comfy and I'll be back in five minutes. Let the lavender fragrance and calming music soothe you. *This is where you start your fight back,*' she finished.

There was something in the way she said it that made Clarissa feel as if Maggie might be aware of exactly how she felt, and knew what had happened to Craig and Mrs Cawsley-May, and why. Did Maggie know that she was a Diviner, even if she didn't know about the boy? Clarissa didn't want to ask her outright, in case she *didn't* know, and she would have to explain it to her, and it would all sound too fantastic to be true.

'Clarry? Clarry?'

Clarissa could hear Maggie's voice in the distance, but when she opened her eyes she could see her sister next to her, smiling down at her.

'You were out for a while there, must have gone into a deep sleep. There's a glass of water for you here, and when you're ready pop your gown on and come through to the sofa and we'll chat.'

'Thanks, Mags.' Clarissa rolled over, holding the towel against her. 'Wow, yeah, I had a really weird dream, although I think it actually happened, when I was younger. The sky turned purple and I saw all these dead sparrows lying in the lane. I keep remembering all these things since Craig died. It's weird.'

'Maybe it was a memory, but maybe it was shock. Whatever it was, we'll work on calming your inner self. I promise you, you'll soon start to feel better, and stronger.'

Old Gorton Manor

As Clarissa approached the large iron gates of Old Gorton Manor, the sky was growing greyer and greyer, and the wind was making the trees dance as the first few spits of rain were beginning to fall. Shadows of low bushes looked like a dark crowd of children welcoming her in. A new sign at the gates said *Welcome to Old Gorton Manor, Hotel and Tea Rooms.*

It couldn't have been more of a low-lit autumn day, with clouds chasing each other over the slate rooftop. She admired her view, one that she'd always found interesting and inspiring. The grounds were littered with autumn leaves although a gardener in the distance attempted to sweep the leaves up.

This should be interesting, first visit back here in a while, she thought. She remembered how her family had visited often when she was growing up. As she approached the front entrance she noticed the round privet bushes behind which her friend Henry had hidden at her eighth birthday party. Now they seemed almost too small for *anybody* to hide behind.

Clarissa reached the door. Her heart was still thumping in anticipation of what she might learn today. She had a perfect excuse to come back here: her mother was having afternoon tea here with the Carragh-Hughs, and she hadn't seen her mother for months – partly because she had been so busy at the gallery, and partly because of Mrs Cawsley-May's tragic death. She could say hello, and chat for a while, and then sneak up to the room upstairs where she first saw the scruffy boy, to see if there was anything she could learn about the him coming into her life. Was he a ghost who resided here?

As she stepped into the porch, which now had raindrops dripping down from the ivy and rain-spattered cobwebs, she hesitated to open the door.

I'm here to get answers, she thought. *I mustn't get spooked.* All the same she wished that she had brought Paula or Maggie with her for moral support. She took in a deep breath and took hold of the large bronze knob, pushing the door open.

'Thank you for the delightful painting you gave me for my birthday, Clarissa darling, it's truly beautiful!'

Ma laughed and poured another cup of tea for Alice Carragh-Hughs and then for Clarissa. Clarissa could hear *Bach's Prelude No. 1* playing softly in the background, and she smiled. *I love this piece of music,* she thought.

'I remembered you saying you had a space in the study that needed colour, so I thought that Mary Loppers' *Days of Spring* would be perfect. All that yellow and green, it would tone with your curtains Ma. She's one of my favourite artists, we sell so many of her prints at the gallery. You should come and see it sometime.'

Ma pursed her lips.

Come to the gallery? Clarissa wished she hadn't said that. Seeing where her friend had lost her life was the very last place she'd want to go.

'Erm – thank you darling. Maybe one day,' Ma replied.

'Oh, Ma, I'm sorry, I didn't think –'

'Now, now, Clarissa darling,' Ma interrupted. 'We don't wish to bore our friends with past regrets.'

Clarissa finished her tea in awkward silence. She glanced at Alice Carragh-Hughs and Alice gave her a quick smile back. After a few minutes, Clarissa excused herself and left the room.

She walked along past the library, finding it hard to keep her tears back. She stopped at the large mirror and fixed her hair but she couldn't stop herself from letting out a sob of anguish. Her hands covered her face and she could feel her heart aching.

She wiped her eyes but as she did so she heard the floorboards creaking. *Oh dear God, please don't let it be the boy!* She turned around to see it was only an elderly couple who were walking along the corridor too.

'Good afternoon,' said the couple, with kind smiles.

'Hello,' she replied, trying to smile back.

'Are you all right, dear?'

'Oh yes, I'm okay, I mean I will be okay,' she smiled. 'Thank you, most kind of you to ask.'

'You know dear,' said the elderly lady, lowering her tone, 'a saint is not one who never falls, it is somebody who gets up and goes on every time he falls. You must believe you can stand strong, and then you will. Even at your darkest moment you will be able to find the strength and light you need. This is your time to fight back.' Smiling again, she reached out and touched Clarissa's hand, as if she were giving her a blessing.

'Thank you –' *Your time to fight back?* She thought. *She sounds like Maggie.*

'Joan,' smiled the little old lady. Clarissa took a deep juddery breath then smiled as she fiddled with a tissue that she'd used to dry her eyes. Clarissa noticed that a little girl was watching them. 'You're very kind. That was a lovely thing to say, Joan.'

The little old lady patted her husband's arm. He smiled at her, and off they went.

Clarissa dabbed at her eyes and composed herself, looking across the staircase for the little girl, but she had gone. She wondered why she had looked so much like her. She looked back toward the elderly couple but they too, had gone.

Although the billiard room at the back of the house had now been converted into tea rooms, most of the house seemed to look the same. The same stags' heads hung on the walls around her, and the same dark, dramatic paintings. The house smelled the same, too. *Old.*

As she walked up to the first-floor landing she could hear classical piano music, Beethoven's *Piano Concerto No. 5.* She saw a small room with its door open, and inside she saw a lit fireplace, where a man in a shawl-collared sweater sat in an armchair reading, quite a young man, with thinning hair. He looked up at her and smiled, and then he said calmly: 'Sorry! The answers aren't here, you know young lady.' He then returned to his book.

'Excuse me?' Clarissa asked him.

'People often look for answers here. But Old Gorton Manor is just part of the journey,' he replied, not looking away from his book. Then he continued reading in silence. On any different day Clarissa would have thought that his comment was intriguing and poetic, but today, nothing felt that simple.

Clarissa walked away from the room, although she stopped for a moment to write down what the man had said to her on her mobile phone's note page. She pushed her phone back in her pocket and continued walking until she reached the narrow staircase that led up to the room where she had first met the scruffy boy. It didn't look as steep as she remembered, and she placed her hand over the bulbous wooden newel post, noticing the carving around the wood.

Because it was still raining outside, and so gloomy, the autumnal light that shone through the red stained glass window looked blood-red and she couldn't help thinking of Craig, soaked in his own blood.

She looked around. She could see no-one, but could hear polite conversation echoing from the reception hall, and a distant clatter of china plates, accompanied by a faint aroma of baking scones. She decided to go up the stairs, which seemed narrower and she felt that her feet were almost too long for each step. *Intermezzo* began playing but it became quieter, the further up the staircase she reached. She couldn't help thinking that the room would now be used for something other than books but she had to find out if there was a connection, regardless.

She twisted the door handle and the door creaked harshly as she pushed it inward.

Inside, stood several coat and hat stands. In the opposite corner there was a desk, with a large manila folder on it and a metal spike with a thicket of paper tickets impaled on it. Clarissa walked in and half-closed the door behind her. Memories of that summer's day when she had first ventured up here flickered in her mind. *Was that really so long ago?* The room even smelled the same. She ran her fingers over the windowsill and glanced out to the stormy sky as raindrops dribbled stringy patterns down the window.

She heard footsteps on the stairs. The light clicked on and a tall grey-haired lady came into the room, humming to herself.

'Oh!' she said, in surprise, as she saw Clarissa by the window. 'Can I help you?'

'Oh, no, not really,' said Clarissa. 'I'm sorry if I startled you. I was just reminiscing. I used to play up here as a child.'

The woman lifted the glasses that were dangling around her neck and placed them on the end of her nose. She peered at Clarissa with her head slightly tilted back.

'Looking for something you once lost?' she smiled.

'Pardon?'

'Or your coat?'

'Oh – erm, no thanks, I left mine downstairs.'

The woman crossed over to a hat stand at the side of the room and began searching for a coat.

'Robert Stenson –' she muttered.

'I'm sorry?' asked Clarissa.

'Coat for Mr Stenson.'

Clarissa watched the woman as she sorted through the raincoats and heavy woollen coats and furs hanging together. Clarissa looked across the room, as though expecting to see the boy. But he was not there.

'Here we go,' said the lady. '*Robert Stenson.*' She took off her glasses, and tugged off a large ticket attached to the hanger and placed the coat onto the desk. 'Yes – it's surprising how many people are looking for something they once lost. But of course not everybody finds it. Not by a long chalk.'

Clarissa raised her eyebrows. Maybe it was her, but everybody she met today seemed to be talking in riddles about her life.

After a few moments, she asked: 'Excuse me, wasn't this once a library?'

'Oh, yes dear. Up until about ten years ago. But before that it was used as an office, for reporters researching local history and suchlike. All of the remaining books are downstairs, in the Taylor Suite – where the fire is lit. Just an old cloakroom *now* I'm afraid. Won't find anything exciting in *here*, dear.'

Maybe that's why the boy isn't in this room now, Clarissa thought. The woman walked over to the desk and stabbed the ticket onto the metal spike. 'Unless you have an interest in furs,' she smiled. 'Plenty of gorgeous coats and leather gloves reside in here too,' she smiled. 'Was there a book in particular you were after?'

'Erm – just a few old books I remember falling in love with and I was hoping to find some history on the house, too.'

'And without the books you love, you cannot *resolve* love?'

Clarissa said: 'Oh, no – urm, I suppose not, no.'

'Shall we?' gestured the lady.

'Erm – yes, of course.' Clarissa let the lady lead the way out of the room and onto the top of the stairs, and the lady closed the door tightly.

Clarissa wasn't entirely sure why she had encountered these few strange people in the house today, but she was pleased that she had because it seemed that each of them knew something, something that she didn't know herself, and that they were trying to give her guidance.

She walked back past the Taylor Suite but the man who had been reading by the fire had now gone and the fire had subsided into glowing ashes.

'Is it all right if I take a look at the books?' She asked the grey-haired woman.

'Of course, dear. Whatever roads lead to Rome. Or wherever you need to get to.'

Clarissa ventured into the room. It was very warm and smelled of book-leather. She slowly scanned the books on the shelves around the walls, but she didn't recognise many of the books that she had seen here as a child.

But right at the end of the shelf near the fireplace she saw a slim green book entitled *The Gift of Knowledge* and it looked very similar the little book that Mrs Cawsley-May had given her as a belated birthday present, at the gallery, just before the boy had dragged her down the stairs. Her heart thumped a little, and she checked to see if the boy was in the room with her. She took the book from the shelf and opened it up, but it was nothing more than a book on wild flowers. *That's strange*, she thought. She had looked at the book at home, time and time again, but it didn't make any sense, and had often wondered if there would be another one here to go with it, and this had looked the likeliest. Maybe it was nothing more than her own imagination, but she felt that her visit today to Old Gorton Manor was giving her several insights to what she should do next, and one of those clues was the title of the book *The Gift of Knowledge*. She needed to know more, why she had seen the boy, why he was with her that day and why she *could* see him at all. Who was he? Where was he from? Why was he so cruel? And if he resided here, where was he this very moment – was Paula safe? And what was the book all about?

Clarissa decided to walk the long way back down to the lounge, in the hope of seeing him, although he was frightening, she had her own questions and curiosity to answer to now.

She returned to the room where she had left Ma and Alice Carragh-Hughs, disappointed at having not seen the boy, but relieved at the same time. They saw her come in and Ma waved her over.

'Wherever did *you* get to?' she asked.

'I was looking for something that I saw here on my birthday, when I was eight.'

'And what was that?'

'It was a clue, more than a *thing*. I didn't really understand it when I was that age.'

'You are a funny girl. So have you found it, this *clue*?'

'Yes, I think I have.'

'And do you understand it?'

The way that Ma asked that question reminded her of the way in which Maggie had said '*This is where you start your fight back'* – as if she knew a lot more than she was saying.

There was a sudden boom of thunder right over the roof of Old Gorton Manor, like the dramatic emphasis in a play, and the rain began to hammer down even harder.

When she returned home, there was a voice message waiting for her on the phone.

'Ms Davenport? Detective Sergeant Mayberry. I just thought you'd like to know that the results of the DNA tests that were taken by our forensic team have just come in. Our initial tests on the broken glass that inflicted the fatal injuries on Mr Arlington showed us that there were none of your fingerprints on it. There are no traces of your DNA, either. I'll be sending you formal notification in due course, but we'll be reporting our conclusion to the coroner that Mr Arlington took his own life.'

Paula's Joy

Clarissa led her new colleague, Ben, to the front door of her flat.

'Can't wait for you to meet Paula,' she said to Ben, as she turned to close the door behind them. The hallway was cluttered with wellington boots of different colours.

'We love our wellies, as you can see!' said Clarissa, as she moved at least three pairs out of the way. 'Come in, Ben.'

Ben raised his eyebrows and said, 'Wow. I always like girls who can give it some welly!'

Clarissa had been thinking he would be perfect for Paula, ever since he had joined the gallery staff. Ben had a square face, neat blond hair and full lips. His eyes were hazel brown, good humoured and twinkly. His wristband and diver's watch suggested a love for a life at the coast.

'I thought I heard voices!' shrilled Paula, as she came dancing into the living room. She was wearing leopard print spandex leggings and a white Skunk Anansie tee shirt. Ben stared at her in disbelief.

'Oh, *hi!*' she said, when she saw Ben. 'I'm just having a wardrobe blitz, choosing my outfit for a fancy dress party on Saturday. You like it?' she laughed, one hand on her hip.

Ben raised his eyebrows and nodded.

'For sure,' he agreed.

Paula smiled.

'Paula, meet Ben. Ben, this is my flatmate – Paula. You wouldn't think she works for a sophisticated car showroom, would you?' Clarissa teased.

'I love cars,' winked Ben.

Paula blushed, and folded her arms in embarrassment as she remembered she had no bra on. But to Clarissa it was quite obvious that Ben thought she was hot, whatever she was wearing, *or not.* He nodded and kept on nodding and said, 'Great to meet you, Paula,' and he couldn't take his eyes off her.

'I'll get some drinks,' said Clarissa. 'What would you like, guys?'

'Wine, please,' said Paula, disappearing into her bedroom again to change.

'Beer, please Clarissa if ya' got one?' asked Ben. He sat on the edge of their sofa and looked around. 'Nice place you've got here. Love the boatwood furniture, great combination with the sage green and bleach white. Very artistic. Lived here long?'

'I think she likes you,' winked Clarissa as she walked back into the room handing Ben a bottle of Budweiser. 'Yes, years.'

When Paula returned, she picked up her glass of wine from the coffee table and smiled at Clarissa. 'Thanks.'

'Is that the top from COS I got you for your birthday? Looks great on you!'

Ben agreed, before taking off his coat and laying it over a chair at the entrance to the hallway.

'Thanks babes, yeah, it is. I love it. It's so different and feels great on, too. So then, what's *your* favourite car, Ben?'

'Favourite? Well, that'd have to be a Bugatti,' he smiled, facing the room again and smiling at Paula.

As they all relaxed, Paula gazed at Ben as he talked about the gallery, and how much he was enjoying it, after his move from a small gallery in Cornwall. Paula glanced at Clarissa as she took a sip of her wine and gave her an approving *he's hot!* wink.

'What's this song, Clarissa, printed on the cushions?' asked Ben. 'Can't read music. Maybe my dad's right, I need glasses. Or more education,' he laughed.

'An old favourite song,' she said, and softly smiled, with a fond, pensive look in her eyes. 'It's "Feels Like Home".'

By 9:30, Paula and Ben were still chatting and flirting, but Clarissa had an early start at the gallery in the morning, and so she had said goodnight to them and went to bed.

Once in her bedroom, before she turned out her bedside light, she picked up the book that Mrs Cawsley-May had given her and leafed through it for what must have been the twentieth time. It contained at least a hundred pages, every one of them densely covered in handwritten Greek characters, even into the margins. A little pouch that was tied to it had miniature pieces of bone in it. *What are these for?* she wondered.

She had tried three different online Greek-English translation sites, but even though the characters were definitely Greek, none of them had been able to make any sense out of it at all. Maybe she had never been meant to understand it, only to own it and keep it safe. She rubbed the soft, thick paper between finger and thumb, as if she could absorb its message by osmosis.

Opening the first few pages she had found a piece of paper, used as a bookmark. A motto had been written on it, in English, but even then she couldn't really understand its meaning. *Love is a face reflected in a pond, beautiful when the surface is still, but distorted when rippled by mischievous fingers.*

She read it twice. *A face, reflected in a pond.* It tugged at her memory. She felt almost as if this motto had been written especially for her, to warn her.

Meeting Mark

'Clarry! Hi!'

'Hi guys! Great to see you!'

Clarissa had headed straight from work to Kayz Wine Lodge to meet her old colleagues from the gallery, Marcel and Lisa. The gallery staff had bought them tickets for an exhibition in Paris for their first wedding anniversary, and Clarissa had been selected to hand them over, as well as buying them a celebratory bottle of champagne.

Clarissa gave them a wave as they walked in, and they came across and joined her.

Marcel and Lisa had worked closely with Craig so she was hoping they wouldn't want to talk too much about him. Months had gone by but she was still hurting badly and she wasn't sure how much they knew about her relationship with him, if anything at all. At the moment the slightest verbal reminder of Craig could still choke her up. Somehow paintings, or pictures of him didn't have the same effect. Maybe it was because she was looking at them in her own time, whereas someone talking about him was out of her control.

Kayz Wine Lodge was a warm and welcoming place, with large hand-carved wooden benches where Clarissa felt comfortable to sit alone reading with a coffee, or spending hours with Paula on Champagne Fridays. It was a chilly autumn evening and the log fire was lit, and candles were burning on top of the mantelpiece.

Sitting down beside her, Lisa said: 'We hope you don't mind, but one of our friends is joining us – Mark. He's new to the area and we wanted to show him around a bit. Hope you don't mind – I'm sure you'll like him!'

'Okay, fine,' smiled Clarissa. 'But I *am* quite happy being single for a while.' The waitress brought over the bottle of Moët that she had ordered, and opened it for them.

'Here's to your first anniversary,' said Clarissa, raising her glass.

'I'll drink to that,' said Lisa. 'I didn't think we'd make it past a month!'

'What are you talking about?' Marcel protested. 'I'm the most amenable man you could ever meet!'

'If "amenable" means that you're able to be mean, I'll drink to that,' laughed Lisa. 'You'd use your teabags twice if I let you.'

'Cheers!'

'Bloody awful news about Craig, wasn't it, Clarry,' said Marcel.

Marcel was a well-built man in his forties, with a dark, full beard and kind, truthful eyes which always made Clarissa feel comforted, somehow. 'Such a terrible thing to happen to him,' he said. 'Who would have known. He always seemed so – well, I guess you never can know someone's internal struggles.'

Clarissa began to cough on her drink and excused herself. 'Yes, very sad, sorry I just need to have a quick coughing fit, think it's gone down the wrong hole! I'll be back in a minute.' And with that she excused herself and headed for the toilets.

Marcel frowned at Lisa and they passed a mutual expression of *'did we put a foot in it?'* It was obvious they hadn't heard about her relationship with Craig after all.

Clarissa reached the toilets, looked at herself in the mirror and began to cry.

When Clarissa returned a short while later, Lisa said: 'Mark's called. He's just parking the car, Clarry, so let me brief you!'

Lisa held up her fingers and counted off everything that she knew about him.

'He's currently writing a novel called *Choosing You*. He's thirty-eight, and he has this great apartment at Luxbury Hill. He's got this – well – this male magnetism, Clarry.'

Marcel tutted and said, *'Women!'*

'You'll see what I mean when he comes in. He's really

attractive. He knows he's handsome and I know that might bug you, but give him a chance. He won't mess you around. Apart from that, he loves opera, and architecture, and art, and most of all he's recently single!'

Opera, thought Clarissa. *Craig loved opera, too. Opera was playing when he was murdered.*

Lisa glanced at Marcel, smiling and raising her eyebrows at this overload of information which she had piled on Clarissa. But then the door opened and she abruptly stopped talking and turned around. A tall, slim man with floppy fair hair walked in. He lifted his hand to show that he had seen them, and came over to join them.

He had a handsome, slightly squareish face, with high sharp cheekbones and a long slim nose. His eyebrows were blond to match his hair, but his eyes were very dark grey. He was smiling, but it was a very secretive smile, as if he already knew something about Clarissa that she didn't even know herself.

'Ah-ha, here he is! Mark, our dear friend – Clarry. Clarry works where we used to at the Milltower Gallery on Grosswell Street and she's actually a fantastic artist herself. Clarry, meet Mark, he's a fiction writer.'

Mark came forward, took hold of both of Clarissa's hands and gave her a kiss on each cheek. Then he stood back, still holding her hands, and stared directly into her eyes, as if he were searching for something. Clarissa looked back at him and found that as long as he kept staring at her she couldn't look away either.

After a long moment he released her hands and said, 'Very nice to meet you at last.'

At last? she thought. *What a strange thing to say.* Yet somehow she felt that she had always been destined to meet him, and that she might even have met him before.

All the same, when he sat down next to her on the oak bench and poured more Moët for everyone, he talked to her as if they had already known each other for most of their lives, although she couldn't think where, or when. And she didn't make any attempt to move away, enjoying his closeness.

Singer's Bookstore

On their first date, Mark took Clarissa to Singer's Bookstore, a small, quaint shop that was tucked away in a pedestrian precinct.

As they approached the shop, she felt as though they were being watched. 'Did you see that?' she asked him, but he just replied simply, 'No.' He took her hand and gripped it tightly. She didn't know if it was too soon to be holding hands, but she figured that she may as well let her guard down a bit, as she knew there would be a time to move on. Not only that, but Lisa was right. He did have a certain, strong magnetism about him, and to be holding hands with such a confident, handsome man made her feel safe again. She felt that people weren't looking at her anymore because she seemed so sad after losing Craig, but because she and Mark had the appearance of a perfect couple, and that gave her a comforting feeling which she hadn't enjoyed for far too long.

Mark led her to the fiction section. 'Search for me, my *nom-de-plume* is Mark Ross.'

Clarissa smiled but for some reason she felt uncomfortable at his sudden demand. *I can read people like books themselves, but Mark seems to have some form of shield, or way to block my ability to read him. Maybe he is just a very strong character.*

'*Go on!*' he insisted.

Feeling forced to play along, she scanned for the name amongst the line of books.

'Here. I've found you,' she said. 'Mark Ross.' She read some of the titles to herself: *Dead Above The Rest, Call Me,* and *As Guilty As You.* As she did so, she began to find that in spite of her natural defensiveness, her interest was aroused.

'So what's your inspiration? Is it your life experience?' She looked at him and smiled. He was already staring at her, with his grey, intense eyes, which Clarissa found strangely unsettling. 'Well?' she asked.

'Clarry, if I had ten pence for every time I was asked that question, I'd be a *billionaire.'*

Clarissa thought: *Oh dear, I have an exaggerator on my hands here – so I need to be wary. Exaggerations often go hand in hand with lies.*

'Okay,' she said, remembering what Lisa had advised her: *Give it time.*

'It's just inside your mind, that's all, Clarry. It's inexplicable really. You write, and see where the story takes you. For instance, this one –'

Clarissa didn't approve of the way he so effortlessly called her *Clarry,* it was exactly how Craig used to say her name.

Mark pulled out a brightly-coloured book and tapped the cover. *'Call Me* was inspired by a news story I read about a hooker who was desperate to be loved. Turns out, she killed *eighteen men* and never found love. She even killed her *dog.* And *that* was intended to be a love story of sorts. You can't predict how a story is going to turn out. You can't predict how life is going to turn out. Or love.'

Well, that's true, she thought. Her own experiences had taught her that. But there was something oddly rehearsed about the way he described his novel and showed her his work. Was he really Mark Ross?

'Fascinating,' she said, cautiously. 'So – coffee next?' Mark nodded and put *Call Me* back on the shelf.

Clarissa followed Mark away from the fiction section and toward the door of the bookstore, looking behind her. She couldn't think why, but she couldn't shake the disturbing feeling that the boy was close by, watching them.

Mark turned and said; 'So, a macchiato? Or maybe I can tempt you to lunch at The Well? They have a new winter menu.'

Clarissa smiled. 'A coffee sounds fine.' She buttoned up her jacket and headed out. *Most women would jump at the chance of being spoilt with lunch,* she thought. *But I don't want him to think he owns me. Not yet, anyway.*

Mark pulled a face as though her comment had displeased him, shrugged and said 'Okay, okay – if you insist, a coffee it is.'

Clarissa returned home by 5pm and dropped her keys in her pocket and slid her coat off, slumping it over the chair in the hallway. She wandered into the living room, where Paula was watching her favourite show, *Come Dine With Me*, and eating a pot of noodles.

'Hi sweetie, I'm home. What a strange day. Going to have a nice soak in the bath and drink a glass of fizz. Would you like some?' Clarissa went through to the kitchen, and opened up the letters that were waiting for her on the work surface.

'No thanks babes. Been anywhere nice?'

'Just to the bookstore with Mark, then for coffee,' Clarissa called out. 'I have to admit that he's gorgeous, although he's a bit full of himself. I'm not sure where it's going at the moment. There's something about him that I can't quite put my finger on, and he's fascinating to look at, like you're looking at a skin with someone else's behind it. Are you seeing Ben again soon?'

Clarissa wandered into the living room with her post and sat on the edge of the sofa.

Paula nodded, with her mouth full of noodles. She swallowed, and then she said, 'Tonight.'

'Oh fab!' Clarissa said, as she untied her hair. 'Pleased you like him, I thought you would. He's a nice guy, isn't he? Harmless and funny. What you need.' She stood up and wandered into the kitchen toward the fridge. 'Pretty good on his cars, too.'

'You seeing Mark again, babes?' called Paula.

'He's told me we're meeting on Thursday evening, without even asking me if I'm free or not, but I think I'll give him a chance. Maybe he's nervous, and he's just trying to impress me. Time will tell. I have to say that it's really nice to be given so much attention, albeit a bit different. Maybe we could make dinner for the four of us if you're interested?'

'Sure.'

'Great,' replied Clarissa. She reached out and took a bottle from the fridge and said to it: 'Come here Prosecco, tonight – you're *mine.*'

Frosted

'Now you can see into *my* world,' said Mark.

Clarissa was beginning to wonder if it was too soon for her to have agreed to come with him alone to his apartment. Thursday had seemed to come around too fast. She stepped into the hallway and he quietly clicked the door shut behind her. She wasn't sure what to expect from his home, or from him now they were truly alone. Although he was smiling, she sensed he was tense all the time. It was only the reference from her colleagues that reassured her that he'd loosen up, and with that she had to offer a level of trust. She turned round and smiled at him; but for some reason she didn't like how she felt – restless and uncomfortable, as if her 'alarm bells' were ringing inside her and warning her to be on guard. On the other hand, this was only the second time they had been out together, and maybe she was feeling cautious because it was all so new. Maybe it was her?

They were expected to meet Paula and Ben for an early dinner at Bucking Roger's Steak House in the High Street, but they had an hour to spare and Mark had insisted that they stop at his home on the way, as he wanted to show her his artworks, and in particular a painting by Henry Ludd entitled *Mainstream*, which blended old-fashioned streets with modern city life, like an up-to-date Lowry.

'I won't even *tell* you what it's worth,' he had told her, archly, but she had been working at the gallery long enough to be able to guess. Five figures, at least.

Clarissa texted Paula to let her know they were at his flat: *Here sweetie, at his. Let me know as soon as you are there, so we can leave!* XX She slid her mobile into her bag and placed it on an armchair while she wandered around in interest.

'Lovely apartment, Mark.'

The hallway had a polished oak floor and a cast-iron spiral

staircase that led upstairs, although Clarissa was surprised how bare it was for a man who Lisa had told her was an art and music lover, with no CDs or instruments, and only minimal pictures on the walls which had next to no colour. She carried on into the living room – and the first thing that caught her attention was the strong aroma. It was as though he'd sprayed everywhere with a scent of fresh roses. Clarissa had never known any man have such a fragrant home.

She turned to smile at him again, thinking that he was behind her, but was disconcerted to find that he wasn't in sight. Then she heard his voice from another room.

'Fancy a quick glass of fizz before we head out?'

'Erm – yes please,' she called out. 'Where's the bathroom? I'd like to use it.'

There was no reply.

'Mark?' she repeated, but he still didn't answer. She decided to take a seat and wait for him. At the opposite end of the room there was a large marble fireplace, reddish-grey, with a cold and empty grate. Above it hung a dark oil painting of a sad-looking girl in a grey dress, and in front of it lay a grey hand-woven rug. When she looked at it more intently she saw it had a pattern in the centre which resembled a sad woman's face, although maybe it was just an optical illusion.

In the light of a large copper lamp, she saw a book lying open over the arm of her chair, face down. She was curious to see what Mark had been reading, but hesitant to pick it up in case he returned into the room. *The Lost Love* it said on the spine. She was about to lift it up when she heard Mark's footsteps right behind her chair, making her jump. When she turned around he was smiling at her and holding out a glass of champagne.

'Sorry,' he said. 'Didn't mean to startle you.'

'No, that's all right, you didn't,' she told him. She didn't quite know why, but she didn't want him to think that he had managed to catch her off guard.

All the same, she wasn't expecting what he did next.

As she stood up, he took hold of her arm and drew her toward him, kissing her on the lips. The kiss lasted only a few seconds, but it was passionate. Then he stood back, grinning at her with teeth that were almost unrealistically white. He stared at her, as though he was waiting for her to say something flattering, but she was so taken aback that she didn't know what to say to him. She could actually taste his cologne, which was lemony and woody like Issey Miyake. She wiped her mouth as discreetly as she could with the back of her fingers and took an effervescent sip of champagne, trying to get rid of it.

'The Ludd's upstairs,' he said. 'In my bedroom.'

She felt awkward and surprisingly cross, because the last person to assume that he could kiss her like that was Craig. It was then that she realised no matter who kissed her from now on, she would never open her eyes afterwards and find that it was him. Sometimes, she actually felt that she would rather never be kissed or touched again, by anyone.

She put down her champagne flute down on a nearby table.

'Could I use your bathroom please, Mark? Where is it?'

'Of course. Upstairs, at the end of the corridor. You may want to admire my abstract *en route*, I was the lucky purchaser. It only cost eight thousand – a bargain if you ask me.'

Clarissa climbed the spiral staircase and walked down the long corridor leading to the bathroom. She felt irritated by his reference to his wealth. She had her own money and wasn't interested in his.

As she had reached the top of the stairs she saw the large black-and-white abstract painting on the wall in front of her. *'Eight grand,'* she whispered to herself. *'You were robbed.'* She reached the bathroom door and found that it had an oval metal plaque on it, saying *Le Loo*.

Le Loo Clarissa thought to herself, *how precious is that?* She started to push the door open but before she did so she took a long sideways look at the black-and-white abstract. It *appeared* to be abstract, nothing but circles and squares and jagged, overcrowded shapes in-between, and yet she thought she could see something else in it, like a figure with its back turned.

Stop being a Diviner all the time, she told herself. *It's just an abstract. You're starting to see faces and figures in everything now.* Yet she felt agitated in Mark's company today and she knew there must be a reason. He was attractive, yes, but he had some strong negative energy that he was trying to hide from her. She almost hated herself for allowing him to affect her like this, and for fancying him so strongly, so soon after Craig. *Why can't relationships just be easy?*, she thought.

Even the bathroom was minimalist, with no warmth or colour, not even a frame with something interesting to read in it. As she washed her hands, she looked at herself in the mirror over the basin and she thought that she was looking pale, too, as if Mark's home had drained all of the colour out of her. Even her mint green mohair cardigan looked frosted.

As she left *Le Loo*, she decided to pause and take a longer look at the black-and-white picture, just to make sure that there was no strange figure in it. As she stood staring at it, however, she became aware that somebody was standing at the top of the spiral staircase, although she hadn't heard any footsteps. She turned and saw that it was Mark. He was staring at her unblinkingly, completely rigid, his arms by his sides as stiff as wood. Clarissa shivered. *What's the matter with him? Why is he standing there staring at me like that, not speaking, not moving?*

'Mark?' she said.

He began to walk toward her. It was Mark, obviously, but not the responsive, good-looking Mark that he had been downstairs. His face looked older, with sallow and unhealthy skin, and his lips were cracked. His eyes looked black, rather than dark grey, and soulless. Even his teeth appeared small and yellowish-brown as he opened his mouth. She blinked furiously in the hope that his face would again appear normal. But it didn't.

What could she do? She covered her face with both hands so that she wouldn't have to look at him, and backed away until she bumped into the door of *Le Loo*. She wanted to run away as fast as she could, past him and down the spiral staircase and out of the house, but she was breathless and her heart was beating like a hammer and she simply couldn't move.

It's just my imagination, she told herself, over and over. *Lisa introduced him to me, and Lisa would never do anything to hurt me, so he must be nice.* There was silence, just like the moment of silence in the gallery, after Mrs Cawsley-May had fallen. But this time Clarissa was becoming terrified and could feel her heart thumping against her ribcage.

It's just anxiety. It's just me thinking the worst.

'Clarissa?'

Clarissa's eyes were tightly shut. She felt two hands wrap around her wrists and pull her arms slowly down.

A sick feeling rose in her stomach.

'Clarry, sweetheart, it's me – what's wrong?' She cautiously looked at the hands that were holding her. They were clean, and they felt warm, and firm, and they were framed by a sea-blue cashmere sweater.

'Darling, what is it? God knows how you've been treated before I came along to rescue you! I've just come up to find you. What are you doing?'

Clarissa looked up at his face, with hesitation, and he looked just like the Mark that she had first met. All the same, his eyes were expressionless. She said nothing.

'Paula just called your mobile,' he said. 'She and Ben are on their way to the restaurant and they want to know how long we're going to be. We really need to think about leaving. It seems like our time is up sooner than we thought.'

She couldn't believe his audacity – how dare he go into her bag and answer her mobile phone? She lifted her gaze again to see Mark smiling down at her. *Our time is up?* She thought. *What a formal way of saying we have to go. And he hasn't even shown me his wonderful Henry Ludd painting yet. What the hell just happened?*

'I'm fine,' she said, twisting her hands away. 'I – I'm sorry. I'm ready.'

Rescue me? she thought. *I don't need or want to be rescued.*

'I felt a little faint,' she said. 'That's all. I think I need something to eat. Let's go.' she smiled the best she could at him and regained her composure, deciding to think about it on the way for dinner just to get out, and fast.

'Come on, whatever it is Clarry, you're okay. I don't think you're mad or anything, don't worry! I actually think you're unique and that I'm a very lucky guy to have you as mine. Let's get going.'

She nodded, tucking her hair behind her ears. Taking a deep breath, she began to walk back toward the spiral staircase.

What had she just seen? It had appeared to be the most horrifying of faces but – it was Mark.

Clarissa gripped the rail of the staircase and hesitated. She didn't want to go down first. Her trust in Mark had been shaken and until she was sure who or what she was dealing with, she felt that she had to be wary of him. Her instincts had been right. Mark was smiling but Clarissa thought that his eyes still looked soulless and drained of colour.

As if he could read her thoughts, Mark said softly, 'Clarry – I'm really sorry if I scared you by creeping up on you like that. I didn't mean to. It's the soles on these new expensive soft Italian leather shoes – I'm as quiet as a mouse in them on this flooring, you know when they –'

Clarissa stopped listening and didn't say anything. Mark's voice faded. All she wanted to do was get out of his apartment, get the meal over with so she could go home. As she began to walk down the stairs, it occurred to her that he might not have realised that she had seen him looking so grotesque. Or *had* he known why she had been so frightened, and was attempting to convince her that she had simply been hallucinating?

She was not only embarrassed but irritated at herself for becoming so anxious in front of him. She didn't understand why he had this effect on her. Maybe it was the Diviner in her, being over-sensitive after losing Craig. Then again, she had read recently about men who purposely make their partner fearful and unsure of themselves in order to exert control over them, and if that was what Mark was doing to her, she needed to give herself a good talking-to. She found him so attractive, so why did he unsettle her so much? Was it something truly sinister? Until she understood why, she would have to appear as unaffected and normal as possible. However inexplicable his behaviour, she still didn't want to lose him without good reason.

As they reached the bottom of the stairs, a beam of sunlight was shining through the circular window in the door that led into the hallway, and it suddenly grew stronger, as if it were guiding her out of there. She scooped up her bag from the chair, knocking the book off of the arm by accident. Mark walked behind her and picked it up. He followed her out, much closer than she would have liked. When she stepped out of the front door she let out a quiet sigh of relief at the open space and put on her sunglasses against the low sun.

As they walked, her mobile phone rang again.

'It's Paula calling. They must already be at the steak house. Hello?'

Clarissa walked along the driveway with her mobile phone to her ear, and across to Mark's Mercedes. Mark followed her, with a wide grin on his face, as if something had amused him.

He opened the passenger door for her, and as he did so, he said, 'Pity we didn't have time for you to see my Henry Ludd. We'll have to make it another day, won't we?'

Pillow Talk

As they talked on the phone at midnight, Mark flattered her and charmed her and thanked her for being the most beautiful girl in the restaurant tonight. Maybe it was just the wine's influence softening her instincts, but she knew that she was allowing her heart to rule her head, because his good looks, the fine wine and his tactile compliments were making her feel adored, and special again, and were beginning to outweigh any of her doubts about him. It was as though he cast a spell on her over dinner, because he had been so frightening beforehand, which had put her off.

This evening, however unsettled she'd felt at his apartment, he had made her feel so wanted, and attractive, and she had warmed to the comfort that gave her, and the feeling that she didn't have to be alone anymore. The more she relaxed, the more she thought it had felt really good to be kissed on the mouth again, too. Maybe she should accept that no-one would ever compare to Craig. Maybe her love for Craig had left such a void in her life that she was being far too critical of Mark. Maybe he was just what she really needed. *After all,* she told herself, *no relationship is perfect, is it?*

Maybe tomorrow my Diviner instincts will be clearer, she thought. *Maybe he's always this persistent when he sees something he wants.* She snuggled her head into the pillow as their conversation was coming to an end, and put the phone to her other ear, thinking: *We must have crossed paths for a reason, and I'm going to see it out.*

'Where are we going on Sunday evening anyway?'

'It's called The North Chapel,' said Mark. 'You'll love it.'

A Mother's Roast

Maggie and Clarissa began to stack the dinner plates into the dishwasher.

'Amazing roast for lunch, Ma,' Maggie called out to her mother, who was tidying the dining-room table.

'So, Clarry,' said Maggie, as she poured some more champagne, watching the scores of bubbles cling to the glass as it almost overflowed with foam, 'I was thinking, would you fancy a night out soon, at Crystal Cluster? Their cocktails are amazing and there's a really handsome new manager that works in there, so –'

Clarissa smiled. Now that she and Maggie were spending more time together, they were becoming closer than they had ever been, even when they were little. 'Sure, sounds fun. Things didn't work out with Adam then I take it?'

'No, he was too immature. I really hoped it might work because he seemed so into me, and meeting at the gym I thought he'd really take care of himself and be a good influence and have similar goals. The trouble was, it turned out he not only collected dead beetles, but I began to find it all a bit depressing – not going anywhere new together, watching re-runs of *Who Wants To Be A Millionaire* every day, watching him drink milkshakes like they're going out of fashion all got really boring after a while. And fattening! Totally different to salon life.'

'He wasn't ready for a relationship I guess. Not with someone career-minded and boisterous like you,' grinned Clarissa. 'You're driven and you *were* older than him, too.'

'All that *talk* about us getting married – by week three! He didn't mean it. Just like he didn't mean it when he said he goes to the gym every day or enjoys mini trips abroad. He kept telling me that I was his princess, but who expects princesses to put up with sleeping in rarely-washed bedding? And who needs that lack of personal hygiene to look forward to for the rest of married life – on top a dead beetle collection? *Pfft!*'

'I know what you mean. They're never as they make out. Mine's obsessive the opposite way and a total minimalist in his home!' said Clarissa, thinking about Mark. There was something romantic and adventurous about him, she had to admit, but maybe that was because he seemed secretive, and unpredictable, and even dangerous, too.

The girls laughed together as they talked about some of the men they had dated. Ma leaned on the doorframe of the kitchen, clasping her coffee, admiring her two beautiful and loving daughters.

The North Chapel

Mark and Clarissa walked toward the tall, granite-grey chapel hand in hand.

'Remind me why you wanted to come here?' asked Clarissa. She felt slightly uneasy but she was really determined to find out more. Maybe this would give her some insight.

The chapel was built of limestone, weathered and pockmarked, with thick green moss clinging to the west-facing wall. Above the main doors there were two circular windows so that the chapel looked to Clarissa as if it had a startled face. The afternoon was silent except for the distant cawing of crows.

'Well,' said Mark, 'they call this The North Chapel. It has some very interesting history attached to it.' He looked at Clarissa to see if she was listening. 'There was a fire in a local orphanage in the 1950s which killed at least ten children and left several others seriously ill from smoke inhalation. While they rebuilt it the remaining orphans came to live here. There used to be a South Chapel but it was demolished during the Reformation. It was said to be built as a replica of an ancient Greek temple. The locals and churchgoers have meetings here every month to talk about their voluntary work for children. They also come to share any supernatural experiences they might have had – you know, like hearing from somebody on the other side, or seeing a sign from a long-dead relative.'

'So it's a spiritualist church?'

'Yes it is now. Its formal name is The Church of Infinite Wisdom. That's how some spiritualists refer to God.'

As they entered the chapel Clarissa shivered. She felt that they were walking into a building charged with static electricity, filled with voices whispering ancient secrets to anyone wanting be told. Inside, it was stark and bare and chilly, with a high vaulted ceiling and rows of dark oak pews. A little plastic fan heater hummed away near their ankles as they entered the room, making the air smell dusty, but it made little difference in heating such a large area. Several groups of middle-aged women stood whispering to each other and some of them turned to look at the newcomers. All the same, she wasn't sure that she felt over-welcome and she gripped Mark's hand a little tighter.

'Was this a good idea?' she whispered to him. 'It doesn't feel very friendly.'

The women continued to whisper for a moment, but then, as if they had been given a pre-arranged signal, they all gathered in the left hand corner of the chapel, around an old upright piano. Only one tall, balding man remained where he was, on the opposite side of the room.

'What's happening?' asked Clarissa,

'They're starting their discussion. Maybe we should go over and join in.'

'You're not serious, are you?' hissed Clarissa. 'I haven't had any supernatural experiences I want to share.' But then she thought – *if I do I may get answers about the boy. Maybe it was real. Maybe the way I saw Mark at the top of the stairs with that ravaged face and those snaggly little teeth – maybe that counts as a supernatural experience, too. And maybe that's why he's brought me here.*

'Oh, come on,' he said. 'There's nothing like a good ghost story.'

He tugged at her hand but Clarissa resisted him. She had heard disturbing stories about people who attended spiritualist churches. She was already wary of spirits, and knew from her own tragic experiences exactly what kind of harm they could do. If the boy who had murdered Craig hadn't been a spirit, then what else was he?

If there were any spirits here, she certainly didn't wish to disturb them. Not only that, she had an unsettling sensation that she was being watched.

Once the group had all gathered together, two or three of them began handing out leaflets. They whispered away, nodding enthusiastically as they pointed to different parts of the building and the piano.

'Come on,' said Mark. 'Let's go and join in. There's no point in us coming here if we don't.' He tugged her hand and reluctantly she allowed him to lead her down the nave.

They joined the crowd and smiled, and everybody smiled back at them, and nodded.

The piano was made of dark brown mahogany, although it looked tired and battered, with scratches of what looked like children's doodling along the top of the lid and down the sides. Next to Clarissa stood a short chubby woman, wearing a pink rain mac and clutching a rolled-up copy of Soul & Spirit magazine.

'We're obsessed with ghost stories!' the woman declared in a high-pitched voice, although her eyes were unfocused and Clarissa wasn't entirely sure that she was speaking to her. 'I don't think there's any such thing as ghosts! I believe that angels walk the earth! We do good works, we die, and we come back as angels!'

'Well, yes, it's a nice thought,' Clarissa replied.

She turned to smile at Mark but to her surprise he was no longer next to her. She scanned the chapel but she couldn't see him anywhere. As she did so, however, her attention was caught by two girls in grey raincoats standing in the shadows of the right-hand aisle. 'The Olven twins?' she whispered.

'What? What'd you say, love?' said the short chubby woman in the pink mac.

'Sorry, nothing, thinking aloud –'

The woman shrugged her shoulders. 'Angels.' she said. 'No doubt about it.'

They were here in the chapel, the Olven twins. Clarissa began to feel breathless and panicky but she stayed where she was, by the piano. Where was Mark?

'Mark?' she called out. Then, 'Mark?' a little louder. One or two of the women turned around to look at her, but none of them responded. The Olven twins, however, were staring at her intently, as if they were trying to communicate something to her telepathically.

They didn't smile. They didn't move. They stood rigid, hand in hand. They didn't look as if they had aged at all since Clarissa had last seen them. *Am I in danger?* she thought. Were they here to protect her from the boy, just as they had one day after school, and that night when he had appeared in her bedroom? She couldn't see the boy anywhere though. She tried to peer over people's heads to her right, but it was no good, everybody was constantly moving around and she couldn't see past them, even when she stood on her tip-toes.

She looked back toward the aisle where the Olven twins had been standing, but now they had vanished, too.

'Oh Mark where *are* you?' she said, under her breath. Unexpectedly, Mark appeared next to her and took hold of her arm. Clarissa squealed.

'Where have you *been*? I couldn't see you – I swear I just saw something – someone I –'

'Ssshh, Clarissa, I'm here, it's okay.' Mark turned to her, and lowered his head to kiss her. 'Let's look around.' he said.

Clarissa gave him a quick peck in return. She wasn't fond of public displays of affection, especially when she felt so unnerved.

Just then, the tall balding man stepped forward and began to speak loudly.

'And – a very good evening to you all! If you look behind you, you will see this is not just any piano. This is where Angela Turrows will continue, Angela – over to you.' The crowd shuffled around to face the piano.

A lady, presumably Angela Turrows, walked toward them and smiled and nodded, her thick curly hair bouncing as she did so. She looked delighted.

'Orphans used to assemble around this piano, to join in prayer and song, to help their little lost souls,' she announced, in a hoity-toity tone of voice. 'As some of you may know, the orphanage was burned to the ground back in 1954. One of the orphans set fire to the curtains and sadly many children lost their lives in the blaze that followed – twenty-three of them altogether. The surviving children were brought here for safety and housing. The piano was not in the orphanage at the time but was away being restored, and so was not damaged. It became something of a symbol for those orphans who had escaped the conflagration. Its music brought back memories of all those who had so tragically been lost.

'In fact, when it was played, and the orphans sang hymns, they said that they could hear the voices of those who had died, joining in with them. Some recordings were made and analysed at Dentworth Sound Laboratory, and it was proved beyond a doubt that when only eighteen children were actually singing, they could identify the voices of more than thirty. This has never been scientifically explained, but I think we all know that when it comes to spiritual manifestations, science does not necessarily have all the answers!'

Clarissa was listening intently, but Mark suddenly took hold of her hand and said, 'Come on!'

'What is it?' she said.

'Come with me.' He led her away from the piano and along the right-hand aisle. Several of the crowd frowned at them as he pushed his way past them.

'Want to show you something better,' he whispered.

'Mark, she's *talking,* and it's interesting. It's rude to just walk off.'

Mark shook his head. 'What *I* have to show you is much more interesting.'

As they started to make their way between the pews the balding male tour guide stepped out in front of them. Turrows glanced over at them, clearly irritated at being interrupted.

The tour guide beckoned them over to the opposite aisle. 'Roger, Roger Harding,' he announced and held out his hand.

He was smiling, but Clarissa thought that he was looking at Mark very warily.

'Er, hi. *Mark,'* said Mark, shaking Harding's hand.

'I assume Angela's talk isn't really why you came here?' Harding asked them.

'Not really, no,' said Mark 'The thing is, we heard that you had recently discovered some interesting relics here.'

We? thought Clarissa. *This is the first I've heard of any relics.*

'Well, we have indeed,' said Harding. 'Let me take you through to the back section of the building. It was bricked up for years – possibly for nearly two centuries. Earlier this year, though, we were given a grant by the National Trust to restore the chapel to its original glory, and about two months ago we came across some plans that dated back to 1813. These showed us that behind what we thought was a solid wall were several small storerooms. You can see for yourself what we found in them. Quite frankly, though, it's a bit of a mystery why they were sealed up so securely – without those plans I doubt if we ever would have realised that they were there.'

'Let's just take a look, shall we, Roger?' said Mark, impatiently. He had a firm grip on Clarissa's hand and even though she tried to twist herself free he wouldn't let her go. She was embarrassed by his rudeness and she could see that Harding wasn't very happy about being spoken to so abruptly.

'We'd love to see them,' she said, smiling at him.

'Very well, then, follow me. But watch your step. Some of the flooring is quite uneven. And I'm glad to see you're wearing something warm. It's unusually cold in here.'

As he turned to lead the way along the corridor, Clarissa looked at Mark and scowled. *'What's wrong with you!'* she hissed. Immediately he let go of her hand.

They passed an open door on the left-hand side of the corridor. Clarissa could see that its walls were lined with bookshelves, and that even more books were stacked on the floor. Clarissa noticed some pictures hanging on the wall but they passed too quickly for her to see what they were of.

'That's our library,' said Harding. 'Bit of a mess in there at the moment, because we've taken a lot of the older books out of storage, but we're gradually getting it in order.'

Mark stopped and stared. 'The older books,' he said. 'Where did they come from?'

'The orphanage, mostly, after the fire. Luckily the library wasn't burnt down, too. Very interesting, some of them. We have records of all the children who were taken in, and what their daily regime was, and what they ate, and who eventually chose to adopt them – those who were lucky enough to be adopted, anyway. Very few of them were. I'll show you the photograph we have to go with it. Strange, though, one of the boy's faces has been scratched away. We thought it was decay but apparently it wouldn't happen that way. Through here. Come.'

A few metres further on, they reached the place where the corridor had been bricked up. Clarissa could see the marks on the walls and ceiling where the bricks had been hacked away. Beyond here, there were no windows, and the only light came from a makeshift string of light bulbs that were hung from the ceiling. From here, too, the corridor was so narrow that they had to walk in single file, with Harding in front and Clarissa following close behind him, and then Mark. Harding had been right: it was unusually cold, even for an old building like this, and it was a dry cold, too.

It was then that Clarissa realised that she could no longer hear Mark's footsteps behind her. She turned around, but he had disappeared. She felt that he had disintegrated and there was nothing left of him but the echo of his ego in the atmosphere.

'Mr Harding!' she said. 'Before we go any further, Mark's just left us. Shall we wait for him?'

Harding turned around and smiled. 'Clarissa, it's *you* who needs to see this.'

Two of the lightbulbs had blown, so that Harding was standing in shadow, and that made his face look as if it had been shaded in by graphite pencil, almost like a Leonardo drawing. But his was a gentle face, understanding, not like one of Leonardo's grotesques. Clarissa realised that she was seeing Harding as he really was. She hesitated. She hadn't told him what her name was, so how did he know?

'Don't be concerned,' he said, holding out his hand. 'Here – it's just in here.'

The corridor widened into what looked like a gloomy prison

cell, except that it had no window and no bars. In the far corner there was a crowd of twenty or thirty earthenware pots, some of them glazed, some of them cracked, some of them broken. They were all large, but one terracotta pot was almost a metre and a half high, and teardrop-shaped, so that it came to a point at the bottom, and was standing upright in a metal frame. Harding walked her over to the wall, where a picture frame with the photograph of the orphans was fixed. 'This is the picture I told you about.'

Clarissa kept looking anxiously over her shoulder to see if Mark was catching up with them, but there was still no sign of him. She started to shiver, and it was all she could do to stop her teeth from chattering.

'Wow, what a picture. They always seem so *creepy* in the sepia colouring I think, as though people's eyes still show a part of the soul when everything else has faded. There's so many children, too, and is that the piano, that's here?'

Harding agreed.

'Who *is* the boy with his face scrubbed out? And why did they brick up all of these pots?' she asked Harding.

'That's the mystery,' he replied. 'Perhaps that's what brought *you* here.'

'Mark brought me here. I didn't really want to come.'

'I understand that. But sometimes evil is its own worst enemy.'

Clarissa frowned, and turned around again. Still no Mark. 'Look,' she whispered to Harding. 'What *is* it about Mark? I know you saw something. Are you a –'

Harding interrupted her, without hesitation. 'Come and take a closer look at these pots. Especially this very large one. It has something inscribed on it. Do you read Greek?'

Clarissa shook her head, but she remembered the words Mrs Ball once said to her in art class over her shoulder. *Deíte mesa apó tin kardiá sas, óchi ta mátia sas,* Somehow she had known what that meant, even if it was just instinctively. *See through your heart, not your eyes.*

'You may surprise yourself one day,' said Harding. 'But look at this.'

Who is this man to say these things to me, she thought, *and where on Earth is Mark?*

Harding beckoned her closer to the large pot standing in its frame. There were Greek characters engraved in the terracotta, in a triangular shape, the way that 'abracadabra' was usually written in spells. Harding took out a small torch and shone it on the letters so that Clarissa could see them more clearly, but she still couldn't understand what they meant.

Το βιβλίο που ισχυρίζεται ότι για να πει την ιστορία μου είναι ένα βιβλίο των ψεμάτων.

'One of our church members is an amateur archaeologist and a bit of a scholar, so he translated it for us,' said Harding. 'He said that it's an amphora, which the Greeks used to fill with oil or wine or other liquids, but he did say that it's exceptionally large. He had never seen one as big as this before. He said it reminded him of the jars that the forty thieves hid in, in the Ali-Baba story.'

'So what do the words say?' asked Clarissa.

'Freely translated, "*The book that claims to tell my story is a book of lies*".'

'Did he understand what that meant?'

'Not entirely. At first we assumed it was nothing but an aphorism, or a saying, or a quote from some Greek scholar. You know, like "the child is father to the man." But the more we thought about it, the more we began to believe that there was more to it than that. It says "*the* book" rather than "*any* book", as if it refers to a specific volume. And why does it say "*my* story"? Does that mean the story of the pot itself, or the story of what might have been stored inside it? And what was stored inside it? If it was oil, or wine, there would have been nearly a hundred litres of it. But who would write a book that told lies about oil, or wine?'

Clarissa nodded. 'This must have been engraved into the pot when it was first made, mustn't it? So how did the potter know that there would ever be a book about it, and whether that book would be true or not?'

Even as she was speaking, Clarissa began to think about the little book that she had seen at Old Gorton Manor, and the one that Mrs Cawsley-May had passed on to her in the gallery as a 'special' gift. Could that be the 'book of lies'? What an extraordinary coincidence that would be. But then again, perhaps it wasn't a coincidence at all. Clarissa was increasingly beginning to feel that her life was already worked out for her, that there are no such things as coincidences and that the people she met seemed to know more about her destiny than she did.

Roger Harding switched off his torch. 'We believe that there was a book – that there *is* a book – and that it tells the story of this amphora. It may have been recovered from the remains of the orphanage, along with all the other books, but it remains to be found.'

'You mean somebody might have taken it?'

'Yes. Perhaps it was one of the volunteers who helped to move the orphanage books out of storage.'

Harding had said 'perhaps' but Clarissa felt that he was much more sure of what had happened than he was telling her. First, he seemed convinced that the book had existed at all. Second, that somebody had taken it.

'Have you ever heard of a Mary Stebbings?' he asked her. 'Or Mary May?'

'Erm, sorry, who?' Clarissa didn't know what to say. The only May she knew was Mrs Cawsley-May, but could this have been her name before she married?

She didn't want to lie, but on the other hand she didn't want to tell Harding anything that might lead to thinking badly of Mrs Cawsley-May's good name. There must have been a reason why Mrs Cawsley-May had given her the book, if it was *the* book. Not only that, there must have been a reason why the boy had killed her. She felt a chill and tingle run through her left side.

'Mrs May,' Harding repeated. 'Mrs Mary May.'

Clarissa felt a lump rise in her throat and the tingling became stronger. 'Oh, erm, yes, yes I do – well, a Mrs Cawsley-May I did. She's – actually, she's dead now. She knew my mother. But what has she got to do with any of this? If it's her at all?'

'She's passed away?' said Harding, 'Oh dear, I'm very sorry to hear that. I didn't know. Well, Clarissa, we suspect that Mrs May may have had this book in her possession. We think that she probably kept hold of it with the best of intentions, but we'd very much like it back.'

Just then, Clarissa heard footsteps coming along the corridor and Harding glanced over Clarissa's shoulder. 'Mark!' he said. 'We wondered where you'd got to! We're just coming!'

Before she turned around, Harding gave Clarissa a quick, stern look, as if to say *don't tell him, whatever you do*. It was almost as if she'd *heard* him say it, too, without him moving his lips.

Mark stepped into the storeroom. He was frowning as he came in, as if something had annoyed him, but then he stopped, and his expression changed completely. Clarissa went toward him, but he didn't look at her or try to take hold of her hand. He was staring at the large amphora with look on his face that she found impossible to read. It was partly shock, and partly anger, but it was partly elation, too, as if he had been searching for this amphora all his life, and could hardly believe that he had found it.

'Mark?' asked Clarissa.

'What?' he said, still not looking at her.

'Mark, what is it? Tell me. Is something wrong?'

He suddenly turned and grinned at her. It was difficult to tell in the gloom of the storeroom, but she was sure that his teeth looked smaller and more crowded together, as they had when she had seen him at the top of the stairs. A child's teeth, rather than a man's.

'No, no. There's nothing wrong, darling. Nothing wrong at all. In fact, I'd say that everything's turning out to be some sort of wonderful.'

Harding said, 'I think I'd better be getting back. Once Angela has finished, I have to give my little speech about the orphanage. Sorry to rush you, but at least you've had a chance to see what we've found here. I need to lock up, now. Let's go back.'

Now Mark took hold of Clarissa's hand and squeezed it almost painfully hard. 'Yes, Roger, we have! And it's very much appreciated! I can't tell you how much! I'll be back!'

As they walked back, single file, to the chapel, Clarissa glanced behind her and looked at the door. She didn't know why, but she felt as if she had found another missing piece to the puzzle of her life, and what its purpose was. She had been meant to come here tonight. *The book that claims to tell my story is a book of lies,* she thought. *I wonder.*

The Gardener

Clarissa walked over to the window and drew the curtain aside, her eyes narrowing in the morning sunlight. She had woken early for two reasons. The previous evening's visit to The North Chapel had set her mind racing and she couldn't wait to get home to look at the book that Mrs Cawsley-May had given her, but Mark had insisted that she should stay with him that night. He had questioned her all the way home about Roger Harding and what they had talked about.

'The way you two were whispering together – you don't fancy him, do you? You didn't kiss him?'

'Don't be ridiculous! Of course I don't fancy him!'

'Well, the way he was looking at you –'

'Mark – you don't have anything to be jealous about! Stop being paranoid!'

Apart from that, she had slept badly, partly angry at herself for letting him control her that way. Mark had clambered out of bed at an early hour, and she hadn't felt rested for the rest of the night, because she was lying awake wondering what he was doing. What did he have to do that was so important to do at night? And now, at a normal time to wake up, he had come back to bed and was now fast asleep, snoring. His snoring hadn't even faltered when she had thrown back the covers in exasperation.

As Clarissa fully drew back the curtains the sun dazzled her. She turned to look at Mark to see if the sudden flood of light into the bedroom had woken him, but all he did was stir slightly and mutter the words '– *have to find … no.*' For some reason though, she felt he was aware of her watching him. She turned back to the window, shielding her eyes. The trees were dancing and dipping in the wind, and when she looked down at the garden she saw a black cat trotting across the lawn. She opened the catch and pushed the window wide open. The breeze blew in, running over her naked body like a stream of cool water. She closed her eyes and enjoyed the way it caressed her, and listened to all the reassuring noises of daybreak: leaves rustling; birds chattering; and the distant rattling of an early train. It was a refreshing contrast to the clinical sterility of Mark's house, with its white walls and its plain grey carpets.

The deep rumbling of a lawnmower suddenly echoed around the garden and Clarissa caught a sniff of petrol on the breeze. She opened her eyes and looked down to see a tall, elderly man, walking very slowly up and down the garden, mowing the lawn. He was bent over the mower as if he barely had the strength to push it, and could collapse there and then. But as she watched him he turned, and looked up toward the open window. He stopped, and set the lawnmower engine to idle, and stared at her. His eyes were small and close-together and his grey, tangled hair looked in need of a wash, as did his filthy, old gardening clothes.

Very slowly, he smiled at her – a thin, creepy smile that made his lips buckle – as if he had known that she was watching him and that he, all the time, had been watching her. She flinched in embarrassment, because she was still naked and she hadn't expected anyone to be out in the garden so early in the morning. She hurriedly stepped away from the window and pulled the curtains back. She could still see the gardener's face in her mind's eye as she walked over to the bathroom and reached around the door for Mark's thick towelling robe, and she couldn't help cringing with regret. Outside, the lawnmower revved up again as the old man carried on with his mowing.

Clarissa went over to the bed and sat on its edge. Looking over at Mark, she wondered if he would have been angry that she had even approached the window naked. She was beginning to learn how possessive he was. She had learned that love can become controlling in someone insecure, and some of her boyfriends had almost seemed to think that they owned her, but she had hoped that Mark would be more relaxed.

She watched him breathing slowly and deeply, his lips puffing out slightly as he exhaled. Her feelings about him were so complicated. She smiled, thinking how lucky she first felt to have met him, and how delighted she was that he was a creative type too, a writer and lover of music, and that he would understand the way she looked at life – as a watchful observer, more than a participant. But now she felt different, as though he wasn't all of those things, not *really*. He was becoming so supercilious, and so evasive. He never seemed to answer a question directly, or he would simply answer it with another question. Sometimes she felt as if she had no idea at all of what was going through his mind, or who he really was. As soon as she thought that she worked out the real him, he would change, dramatically.

Maggie had already openly quizzed Clarissa, wondering how she could put up with his complicated, arrogant personality that seemed to prevail more than his sweetness. His peculiar sleeping habits didn't help, either. In the small hours of the morning, desperate for sleep, but kept awake by his relentless snoring and sweating, she could have happily picked up her pillow and smothered him with it.

It was then that she made the decision to sleep in her own flat from now on, and much less frequently with Mark.

The Curse

Clarissa was deeply absorbed in drawing a dreamy woman's face when Paula hammered on her bedroom door and called out, '*Clarissa!*'

Clarissa had heard her call out a few minutes ago but had presumed she was telling her that the re-run of *Arrow* had started on television. She checked the time on her mobile phone, 22:12. She laid down her pencil and walked to her door to see what she wanted. As she opened it, Paula had her fist raised to bang on it again.

'What on Earth is the matter?' asked Clarissa. 'Are you all right?'

Paula looked behind Clarissa, as though expecting or hoping to see someone else in the room.

Paula's face was completely drained of colour. 'Somebody tapped me on the shoulder! *They did it twice.* But when I turned round, there was nobody there!' Her eyes filled with tears and she was so breathless with terror that she could barely speak. 'There – was – nobody – *there* Clarry, I swear it.'

'Come on, let's go and have a look,' said Clarissa. 'I'm sure it's all right.'

She tried to sound calm and reassuring but in fact she felt deeply uneasy. She had reconciled herself to the appearance of strange people and strange faces in her own life because she knew that she was a Diviner. But Paula was so bubbly as a person she didn't know why anything would want to frighten a girl like her.

It was dark in the hallway and Clarissa flicked on the light. *What if the boy was here? What if Paula was going to be attacked, like Craig? What if none of her friends, relatives or boyfriends would be safe – because of her?*

It almost seemed as if the boy was on a jealous rampage to

destroy everyone she liked and loved.

She took a deep breath and nervously cleared her throat. She couldn't let her thoughts run wild.

'P, stay close,' she whispered.

At that moment there was a deep rumble of thunder, and rain started to fall, suddenly and heavily, tapping onto the skylight directly above their heads. Paula looked up, clinging onto the back of Clarissa's jumper.

'I'm freaked out, babes,' she whispered, as she followed Clarissa into the living room. Clarissa wished Paula wouldn't pull on her jumper so hard: her nervousness was beginning to affect her, too.

'Stay here, and I'll look around.'

'No – I'll – I'm staying with *you*!'

They walked through the living room, around the sofa and into the kitchen. Clarissa noticed that the kitchen window was wide open and splatters of rain were hitting the work surface.

'I thought I closed this earlier,' whispered Clarissa as she pulled the sash window down. They walked back into the living-room, around the coffee table, and Paula sat down, perching on the arm of the sofa.

'There's no-one here darling,' Clarissa said, standing in front of Paula.

'But then what was –?'

Paula's bedroom door creaked open, and Clarissa felt a strong draught.

'Clarry – look, my door. It was *shut* –'

Clarissa shivered. Although Paula was with her, the last thing she wanted to do was to enter a bedroom and see another horrific sight like Craig, smothered in blood.

She took her hands off Paula's shoulders and turned toward the bedroom door, but Paula obviously sensed how frightened she was feeling, and why, because she took hold of her sleeve and said, 'Wait, Clarry, I'll go. *But come with me, just in case* –'

Clarissa nodded, and noticed a decorative whiskey glass that sat on the coffee table. She looked at it and frowned, indicating it to Paula with a gesture. On the bottom of the glass, in big red print, were the words *The Curse*.

Paula shrugged and whispered, 'Weird, isn't it? Ben gave it to me. It was some kind of a promotion in the pub. You don't think – it's –?'

'A little too uncanny?'

The girls walked gingerly toward Paula's bedroom door. As they did so, however, there was a deafening clatter in the kitchen as though all of the saucepans on the overhead rack had crashed into each other, like a mad peal of church bells. Paula screamed and grabbed Clarissa's arm.

'*What the hell was that?*' Paula was so terrified that she whimpered. 'Clarry – I think we should get out of here. *I'm scared –*'

Clarissa was trembling, too. But then she thought: *no, I'm not going to let this chase us out of our own flat. This is my home. This is my sanctuary. If we're too frightened to stay in our own home, then what have we got?*

She stalked across to the kitchen door. It was already a few inches ajar, but she pushed it wide open. The saucepans were still swinging, but there was nobody there.

'There!' she said, trying to sound dismissive, more for her own sake than for Paula.

'But what do you think did it?' Paula asked her. 'Saucepans don't just crash together on their own.'

'Maybe it was a draught, or the kids upstairs in Mrs Law's flat, thumping around. Now let's take a look in your bedroom.' Paula stared at Clarissa as if to say: *no, we both know it wasn't either of those things.*

'Clarry – I really am scared, I mean it.'

Clarissa went across and reached for the bedroom door handle. Paula was panting and she could feel her own heart fluttering.

'What are we going to do if it's a burglar? What if it's a ghost? What if –'

'It could be anything, even next door's cat. Let's go in. Okay, you ready?'

Paula nodded.

The girls walked in, as quietly as possible. It was gloomy inside the bedroom because Paula had only half-drawn the curtains, and the rain was dribbling down the window. Thunder rumbled again, although it was much farther away this time.

Clarissa was just about to say, 'There's nobody here, either,' when she heard a faint, husky voice.

'*Amorino!*'

Clarissa paused, holding her breath, and listened intently. She couldn't tell where the voice was coming from: in front of her; above her; or behind her. She felt as if a thousand red ants were crawling down her back, inside her jumper. Sure enough, the voice repeated itself. *I hate this feeling,* she thought.

The voice grew louder, and clearer, and gradually it rose from a husky whisper, to a shrill, unbearable screech.

'*Ammm – orrrrr – inooooo!*'

A breeze began to rise, too, until it was almost like a wind. Paula's bedroom door slammed shut behind them and the scented candle beside her bed flickered and dipped and was abruptly blown out. The bedroom was plunged into darkness.

Paula was hanging tightly onto Clarissa's arm, but Clarissa managed to scrabble for the light switch on the wall beside the door, and slammed her hand onto the switch to turn the lights on.

The wind dropped, instantly, and the voice fell silent. Paula's bedroom became ghostly quiet, except for the trickling of the rain down the window, and the ticking of the red alarm-clock beside her bed.

In fact, the room looked so normal that Clarissa found it even more frightening than if the bed had been soaked in blood, or if all of Paula's stuffed animals had been torn open, or her china ornaments smashed. The only indication that anything unusual had happened was the curl of the smoke from the candle.

She gave Paula a squeeze, and said: 'It's gone, P. Whatever was with us, it's gone.'

Paula looked at her, biting her lower lip and looking

extremely shaken up, her cheeks wet from tears. *'But what if it comes back? What then?'* she cried.

Clarissa looked at her for a moment. 'Then we'll have to be ready,' she said.

Memory's Window

Clarissa was walking along the hallway carrying a mug of coffee, and talking to Maggie on the phone. The front door was flung open, and Paula burst in, tugging Ben behind her. They were playfully pushing and shoving each other in fits of laughter.

'Clarry! Hi! Guess what?'

'Mags – sorry, I'll have to go. I'll see you later – yep – looking forward to it. 'Bye.'

Clarissa smiled, delighted at the sudden energy that Paula and Ben had brought into the flat, because she had been forced to stay in all day, waiting for the boiler engineer who had arranged to visit 'between eight am and six pm' and it was now half-past four.

'Hi darling!' Clarissa replied. 'Erm – I don't know, what? Don't tell me you bought those Jimmy Choo shoes you couldn't really afford?'

Paula giggled. 'No! Much more exciting than that! *We're engaged*!' she yelled, holding out her left hand. A modest ring sparkled on her third finger.

Clarissa nearly spilled her coffee. 'Oh that's wonderful! Oh my God! Really, *congratulations*!' She set her mug down and flung her arms around them both at the same time. She kissed Paula on the cheek first, then Ben.

'Ahh this is great news. Let's celebrate! Tonight?'

'Ah well actually we're just going to see my mum, then Ben's dad to tell him, then Ben's mates. But we wanted you to know first! Are you around Wednesday? We could go for dinner at Kayz and then cocktails at that amazing bar, Crystal Cluster? What'ya say?'

'Sounds great! On one condition, the bill is on me though guys, okay!'

'Aw thanks, Clarry,' smiled Paula, as she reached out and

hugged her. Paula turned to Ben. 'Come on, let's go.' She kissed Ben on the cheek and giggled.

Clarissa couldn't take her eyes off them, wishing she could still kiss Craig's cheek the way Paula had kissed Ben's.

'See you Wednesday, gorgeous!' said Paula, and left the flat, pulling Ben after her. Ben looked at Clarissa and grinned and shook his head, as if to say *crazy girl!*

Clarissa felt thrilled for them, and couldn't help smiling in self-satisfaction at her match-making skills.

All the same, she couldn't help feeling a twinge of envy, too. It was as though her world had just started turning again, like a fairground carousel, but then the carousel had slowed down as the horses' faces had changed expression, and the music slurred. She was in a relationship with Mark but she didn't experience that sense of comfort and flirtation with him, or the spilling, helpless laughter that she had once had with Craig. Was it because she missed Craig so much? Or was it because she wasn't in love with Mark at all? Or maybe she just knew that Mark was holding something back, and even when he did laugh it sounded forced, as if he could never let himself go or he had no happiness inside him.

Clarissa watched as Paula and Ben made their way along the pavement, still laughing and pushing each other playfully, as they disappeared around the corner.

She shut the door and went back to pick up her mug.She then realised she would always see life with the eyes of a Diviner, no matter how normal they might appear to everybody else, and that she must respect her ability, even when it unsettled her and made her suspicious of people who might mean her no harm at all.

Her phone beeped and abruptly she remembered that she had promised to help Ma prepare for her birthday dinner. She took her mug and walked through to the living-room and picked up the phone to text her back, and explain why she was running late.

Bubbles of Time

That evening, after Ma's dinner party, Clarissa stayed at Ma's house in her old bedroom, rather than travel back home to an empty flat. She sat on the single bed where she had slept as a child and looked around. There was the pale pink shelf where her Sylvanian rabbits used to sit still in their little chairs; and the shelf by her bed where many years ago she used to put her teddies; and there was the large wooden toy chest filled with drawings, pencils and expressionless dollies and their blankets, now used as a seat with three plump cushions on it. But this room contained more than souvenirs and reminders of her younger self mixed in with its new 'guest room' image. It reminded her of how she used to draw people from her window here – sometimes how they really were, and sometimes as she *really* saw them: distorted and strange, and now, at last, she had learned why.

On the wall by her desk Ma had framed several large sketches that Clarissa had drawn when she was about ten years old. Clarissa leaned forward to look at them more closely. One was a drawing of the house, from a distance, with an old man leaning on the gate. Beside the hedge stood a little boy with his back turned, and around the house there was a small veranda and upon it an old lady, in a rocking chair. She had named the picture *Old Love And Bones*, written in her childish handwriting under the image.

Next to it was the picture she had drawn when she was six, of the trees in a park and a Ferris wheel. But unusually there were no animals or characters in it, just autumnal shaded leaves on the trees and an empty Ferris wheel with no-one on it.

After she had undressed for bed, she sat at her dressing table brushing her hair in the oval mirror, with the frame made of sea-shells that she had collected from the beach a lifetime ago. It was strange to think that this same mirror had reflected her face when she was a child, and now it was reflecting her face again. Her skin seemed less plump, but her eyes held a certain unique sparkle. Her lips still looked youthful, but her hair had lost its natural golden glint. She stared at herself for a while, just to see how much she had changed, and wondering if it would explain the mysteries of her life as a Diviner. Although it was an unusual feeling to be sleeping here again all grown up, it felt strangely reassuring and grounding all the same.

Reflected in the mirror, she saw the drawer at the bottom of her wardrobe. In a flash of memory, she saw herself putting her precious diaries in there, to keep them safe from prying eyes.

I wonder ... I wonder if Ma has kept them all safe in there all these years? Clarissa got up and went over to the wardrobe. She remembered that the drawer was stiff, and so when she pulled at it, it jammed. With a little tugging and jiggling, she got it open enough to see inside.

They're still here! She pulled out a few diaries tied together with string, and a couple of A4-sized books, which must have been the latest ones there.

She felt pleased that Ma had preserved her childhood with such care and understanding: she recalled Paula telling her that when she had moved away from home, her room had been redecorated within a month and turned into a study.

Clarissa took the diaries to the bed and made herself comfy amongst the familiar fabrics and smells of her old bedroom.

She pulled the bow of the rough brown string open, and the past rapidly drifted through all of her senses; smells of the past awakening a thousand feelings. She selected the first diary, and opened it, the pages stiff and slightly bent with being cramped together for what seemed like an age.

In the safety of her room, she began to leaf through and read the story of her childhood, the words taking her back as though turning on an old film, remembering how she felt whilst writing each and every word that was written …

PART TWO

The 7th Warning

Seven years old

Clarissa sat bolt upright, in total darkness. She stayed completely still, listening, clenching the duvet cover to her chin. There was nothing she could see. Not even the usual glow under her bedroom door. She could hear her father's old long-case clock downstairs, ticking its way wearily through the night. But she knew she was not alone in her room.

She could hear more than the heavy pattering of night rain, more than the pendulum of an old clock. More than she wanted to. *Voices.*

Clarissa, come to us. She gasped and scrambled to the edge of her bed, frantically patting it for her torch that she had used to read with. The whispering was relentless whether she covered her ears or not, as if her bedroom were crowded. She wondered if she ought to call out, 'Who are you?' and 'What are you doing in my room?' But suppose somebody answered?

Clarissa, come to us! Clarissa! Each of the voices was whispering at her, coaxing her. Her skin was cold and she tried to keep her panting quiet, but mewled as she felt something touch her face. She rubbed at it, and cried out: 'You're scaring me! Leave me alone! Go away!'

But the whispering grew louder, and increasingly sibilant, and the number of voices seemed to grow, too. *Clarissa! Clarissssssaaaa!* as if they were relishing her terror.

At last she found her torch. She pressed the rubber button to switch it on, but nothing happened. '*Come on, please,*' she whispered, and shook it in an attempt to bump the batteries together. Getting to the edge of the bed, she sat and placed her feet on the floor, slowly. She stood up and tried the rubber button on the torch again. It worked and she took in a deep breath, before pointing the beam in front of her.

Standing there was a figure. A pale-faced girl, dressed in white.

In fright, Clarissa flicked the torch off, and jumped back onto the bed, terrified she would be grabbed, or see the faces of her nightmares: the desperate faces of the people that were talking to her. She clambered backward over the bed and crouched down on the other side. *'It's okay,'* she told herself, breathing heavily. *'It's okay.'*

She took a deep breath and repeatedly pressed the torch button again until it came on again, but its light was dim and orange because its batteries were dying. When she looked back across the bed, though, she realised that the pale-faced girl had been nothing more than her own reflection in her wardrobe mirror. She let out a sigh of relief, and as she shone the torch around her bedroom she could see that there was nobody there. But if there was nobody there, how could she still hear crowds of people?

Clarissa! We are here!

She listened intently, holding her breath. Maybe all of those whisperers were crowded on the landing outside her bedroom door. She stood up and crossed the bedroom and pressed her ear to the door, but as she did so the whispering stopped, and she could hear nothing, not even the slow, solemn ticking of the clock downstairs. She lifted the torch very slowly upward, until she could see the shelf where all her teddy bears and dolls were sitting, like an expectant audience. In the beam of light, amongst the dust particles, she smiled at them and one by one they all stared back at her. But surely it couldn't have been *they* who had been whispering to her? A large, worn-out looking brown bear with a glass eye and threadbare nose had fallen on his side, but he still looked as if he had a benevolent smile on his face. As she scanned the beam very slowly from left to right the bears looked as though each had his own story to tell: one had a missing ear and needed stitching on his face; others looked worn and tired; and some were still brand-new in their boxes. One doll had one of her arms in a sling that Clarissa had made out of a handkerchief. At the very end of the shelf sat a purple teddy bear, with *Sister* embroidered on its chest and a birthday badge pinned to its arm. For a moment she wondered if she would grow up to feel as much sympathy for other people, as she did for her collection of injured teddies.

Next to the shelf hung a large framed picture. Clarissa had painted it herself when she was six. She walked over to it, and looked at all the characters she had created. There was a crowd of people, both children and adults, as well as dogs and trees and a little house, and behind that a Ferris wheel. But something wasn't right. One of the figures looked as though it was pressed up against the inside of the glass, staring at her, pleading with her. Another two figures were leaning over and whispering to each other. She was sure that she hadn't painted them like that.

Clarissa went right up to it. The picture and all the people within had changed position since the last time she had looked at it. She leaned in closer again, and noticed there was a shining window in the cottage. *'But I didn't paint the windows yellow!'* she whispered to herself. Just then, the figure that appeared to be pressed up against the glass began sobbing into its hands.

Clarissa, there is danger, Clarissa beware! cried the voices, over and over, growing louder and sounding ever more panicky. The figures in the painting crowded towards the glass, jostling each other as they all desperately tried to shout at her.

'It's you! It's always been you! *You* are the ones who talk to me!' she said, in disbelief and excitement. 'But how – why? I created you, but I *painted* you!'

Another figure put its finger to its mouth to hush her. *Someone is coming,* it said.

At that moment, she heard a creak outside her bedroom door, and the landing light was switched on. She gasped, and turned to face the door. The handle slowly turned, and as the door began to open, she could see the silhouette of a tall figure standing outside.

'Who is it?' Clarissa backed into the corner. *'Who is it?'* she asked again.

The door opened wide.

'Clarissa! Why aren't you in bed?'

It was only Ma.

'Mama you scared me.'

'Clarissa darling what is going on in here? I heard you talking, and why are you out of bed, don't you know it's three o'clock in the morning. Did you have a bad dream darling?'

Clarissa shook her head and turned off her torch.

'Come on, sweetie. Pop to the toilet and get back in bed. Do you want some water?'

'No, thank you,' she replied, desperate to keep talking to her painting.

Ma took the torch out of Clarissa's hands and put it down on her bedside table. Patting the bed, she said: 'Come on, back to bed then.'

Reluctantly, Clarissa walked over to her bed and clambered in. 'Okay.'

Ma tucked her in, and then walked away, reaching up to the shelf to pull down the brown teddy bear. 'Here,' she said, as she tucked it in next to Clarissa. 'To keep you company while you sleep. Maybe you couldn't reach the teddies, maybe you were sleepwalking.'

Clarissa stared up at Ma, looking at her kind blue eyes. 'Goodnight Mama.'

Ma smiled, and stroked Clarissa's hair away from her forehead, then kissed her head. 'Goodnight, darling.'

The Visitor

When Clarissa woke, the people in her picture were all sitting down as she had originally painted them and the figure against the glass had gone. She stared at the picture for a long time, but nothing moved.

After breakfast, she took her notebook and pencil from her bag and sat on the bottom stair, pulling on her boots.

'Mama, I want to go for a walk to see the bluebells, can I?' she called out, as she stood up, tightening her hair bunches in the mirror's reflection. 'I want to draw them.'

'Okay darling,' Ma replied, 'But stay near the house, and where you can see the path. And be back indoors in an hour as we are going shopping to get things for your birthday cake, then we are coming home to make it.'

'Yes, Mama.'

Outside, Clarissa unlatched the garden gate and looked ahead at the bluebells dotted around the trees and in the woodland, and lining the stony path. It was a lovely warm day with only a few clouds in the sky. She looked up and smiled as a crow flew overhead, squawking loudly.

Skipping along the path, Clarissa stumbled to a halt. She stopped singing to herself and turned, and stared back at the man who was leaning on a garden gate at the side of the path. As she had skipped past him, she had stopped and looked around, her heart beating quickly, because she had caught a glimpse of his face out of the corner of her eye, and for a split second it appeared to be a blurred mixture of flesh tones, like an oil painting that an artist had wiped while it was still wet, with his eyes becoming a dark vacuum. She stared at him.

The man continued looking at her, his eyes returning to normal as the skin around them creased, and he winked. He was an old woodland vagrant. He had stubbled, drawn features, with deep-set eyes and yellowed teeth.

He looked back at her with a faintly mocking smile, as if he knew what she had seen but was challenging her to prove it. Yet the smeary face that she had seen as she had skipped past could have been half-human and half-pig, or the face of a sightless man who had once been involved in a terrible accident.

She was convinced that he had really looked like that, if only for a moment. It wasn't the first time that she had seen people's faces appear to be distorted, or a different colour, but never quite as scary as this. If only she had been carrying her pastels with her, she could have captured his face exactly – a chaotic scribble of pink and red smudges, with dark hollows for eyes and a gaping mouth.

'All right, love? Looking pretty!' he called out. 'What were you singing?' His voice was mocking, as well as his smile, but she didn't answer.

Something stirred amongst the hydrangeas next to her, and when she looked down she saw a thick-furred Persian cat staring up at her.

'All right, love?' the man repeated, and the cat looked round at him contemptuously. Clarissa thought: *If this cat isn't scared of him, then neither am I.*

All the same, she turned and ran back down the bluebell-lined woodland path and didn't stop until she reached her garden gate.

She ran in through the open back door, tugging her wellington boots off in a hurry. She ran up the stairs and into her bedroom, slamming the door shut behind her. She went up to the picture but to her bewilderment there were no people in it. The crowd that she had painted had disappeared, even the dogs.

'Where have you gone?' she cried. 'Was it him? Was it that man you were warning me about?'

There was no response. 'Where *are* you all?'

The painting was deserted, but it was moving. The Ferris wheel was spinning even though there was nobody on it. The grass was ruffled as if a breeze were blowing, and the trees were swaying, too. Clarissa stood watching it, uncertain of her feelings. She was unsettled that all of the characters she had painted had disappeared, but she was sad for them, more than frightened.

'Where have you *gone*?' she repeated.

'Clarissa? Was that you talking?'

Oh no, it's Mama, she thought. She unzipped her jacket and threw it onto the bed. She looked again at the painting, and now the Ferris wheel had stopped turning, and the trees and the grass were motionless. Baffled, and slightly breathless, she replied: 'Yes, Mama, just coming.'

Daisy Chain

After the previous day's encounter with the creepy man Clarissa decided to play in the garden. She went into the kitchen for a glass of lemon barley water that Ma had made her and then she went down the steps into the sloping back garden and started picking daisies. There were hundreds of them, thousands. It was a hot silent afternoon and huge white clouds were billowing high above her like a fleet of airborne galleons.

She loved daisies because of their cheerfulness, and their straightforwardness. She liked simplicity. Anything dark and complicated made her feel confused and unsettled, like the man at the gate watching her. She knew that she would be compelled to draw his face later, the way she had seen it when she went skipping past, but she also knew that when she had drawn it, she would crumple it up and throw it away. That was the way she dealt with dark and complicated things. She drew them, and then she crumpled them up and threw them away.

When she had gathered enough daisies in her dress, she tipped them out on the mottled concrete doorstep. She sorted out the longest ones first and formed a figure of eight out of them, because today was her eighth birthday. She began to pierce the stalks with her thumbnail and interlock the stems of the daisies. Her knees were dented by the edge of the step but the texture of her dented knees was interesting to touch, like the patterns in Ma's brocade sofa.

She sang 'That's Amore' to herself, in a thin, reedy voice. She had heard it again this morning on Ma's greenhouse radio, and it was her favourite song. It always reminded her of father, who used to whistle it around the house. Ma used to tell him that whistling indoors was bad luck, and perhaps it had been.

Ma opened the kitchen door. 'Clarissa! Time to ice your birthday cake, darling!'

Birthday Surprise

Clarissa put on her white *broderie anglaise* dress with the bows at the back. She stood in front of the mirror and admired herself, her hair shining in fine gold filaments in the sunlight. This was the prettiest dress she had and she loved it, but she was only allowed to wear it on special occasions.

Because it was her birthday, Ma was taking her to a garden party at Old Gorton Manor, where there would be lots of friends of the family, and they would all be dressed up, too – the men wearing summer blazers and straw hats and the women in bright, pretty colours. Clarissa liked to see how the colours that people wore matched their characters. Vivacious women in reds and yellows and splashy greens – shy, plain women in beige and brown. And the louder the men, the louder their blazers.

Clarissa had a strange feeling that her father might be there, among the crowds, although she had no real reason to believe that he would be. If he were, though – if he had surreptitiously come to see how his precious daughter was growing up – she was sure that she would recognise him, if only by the colours he was wearing, and the way he stood so straight.

Ma had always told Clarissa: 'You can tell a good man because he stands tall, like your father. Good men never cast a crooked shadow.'

Granny, when she was still alive, had always said, '*Pah!*' when Ma had told her how good a man her father was, and flapped her hand dismissively. But there were pictures of Father around the house with Clarissa on his shoulders, and he was always standing straight. She could remember how high up it had seemed, when he carried her around like that, as if she could lift up her hand and touch the clouds.

By comparison, the man with the smeary face had cast a crooked shadow. In fact his shadow had been even more crooked than it should have been, as if Clarissa had already drawn it and crumpled it up.

The Book and The Boy

By mid-afternoon the garden party was in full swing, with a local jazz band playing 'Didn't He Ramble' and all of the grown-ups talking and laughing louder and louder. The refreshment tent was becoming overcrowded, so Mrs Cawsley-May roped Ma in to top up the jugs of Pimms and scoop ice cream onto the knickerbocker glories.

Ma said to Clarissa, 'Why don't you go and play with Henry?'

She wandered around the gardens for a while. Several of the ladies leaned over her in their enormous hats and gave her lipsticky kisses and wished her a happy birthday, but apart from her cousin Henry there was nobody she knew of her own age, and she certainly wasn't going to play with him. He was podgy and perspiring with so much curly hair that he always looked as if he were wearing a clown wig. Apart from that, he thought that Clarissa was weird because she had once told him that his face was pale green. But it had been, if only for a moment. He had been pale, sickly green, like a boy who had drowned and had been floating undiscovered in a pond for two days.

Clarissa saw Henry next to the refreshment tent, queuing up for an ice-cream cornet. He was wearing a stripy red T-shirt that made him look podgier than ever. Before he could turn around and catch sight of her, she ran up the stone steps in front of the house and in through the open door.

It was cool inside, with dark oak panelling. Clarissa thought that it smelled of *old*. There was an oil-painting hanging beside the staircase of a pale, beautiful woman standing next to a window. She was wearing an ivory-coloured dress and for some reason Clarissa knew that she was very sad. Perhaps she had lost someone she loved, like Clarissa had lost her father.

She heard voices and sudden laughter and when she peeked through the crack in the living-room door she could see grown-ups lounging in armchairs. A woman in a salmon-pink dress came toward the door saying, 'I'll bring you some, Charles!' so Clarissa quickly tiptoed up the stairs. Breathless, she reached the landing just as the woman came out into the hall.

Halfway along the landing Clarissa saw another staircase, much narrower and much steeper, with a threadbare green carpet. She went to the bottom of it and looked up, and right at the top was a door with a crimson stained-glass window above it. The sun was shining through it, which not only turned Clarissa's white dress bright pink, and her face even pinker, but it made it look as if something magical was happening up there.

Clarissa glanced around. The grown-ups were still laughing loudly but nobody was coming up to the landing, so she climbed the narrow stairs until she reached the door. The door handle was heavy and unexpectedly cold. Cautiously, she eased it down and pushed the door open. Inside, of course, the room wasn't really shining red, but to Clarissa it was still magical and interesting. The sun was streaming in through the window and illuminating a dusty study with floor-to-ceiling bookshelves.

On a warm summer's day like today, there was a strong musky odour of old paper and books. It smelled as if nobody had been in here for a very long time. The windowsill was littered with dead spiders and skeletal moths and desiccated wasps. Scores of them, as if something had attracted them into the room, in the same way that Clarissa had been attracted into it, but once they were in here they had been unable to find their way out.

She went up to the bookshelves and tilted her head sideways to read some of the titles. They were strange, like books that had been invented by her favourite author, Lewis Carroll: *Treasure from Nature*; *Hunting For Lovers*; *Coffee Bean Carving*; and *Fly-Fishing for the Visually Impaired*.

She knew they were books for grown-ups but she couldn't understand why grown-ups would want to own such peculiarly named books, and why so many!

She ran her fingertips across the spines of the books, one after the other. The shelf was so dusty that it made her sneeze. She particularly liked the lumpy, leather-bound books; but she found one very thin one, smoothly bound in silk, and she couldn't resist sliding it out and flicking through the pages. It was written in some foreign language and shapes, like Russian or Greek, so she couldn't understand it; but she loved the feel of the paper and its perfumed aroma, like pressed rose petals.

The shelf below looked as though the books upon it belonged to someone: a student, or teacher, perhaps. She pulled out one that was covered in what looked like wallpaper, which said in capital letters on the front *BABY DEVELOPMENT – a study by Persephone May and Sandy Strowger, September 1966*. She slid it back, and wondered why anyone would keep a notebook from all that time ago. The books next to it were dictionaries and thin paper files.

Toward the end of the shelf her finger moved inwards, where a small, chunky red book seemed to be hidden, next to what appeared to be a photograph album. The book was covered in faded red fabric-like canvas, with strange gold letters embossed on its spine. Clarissa had learned to read up to Level Two English at school and could read English quite well, but this writing was unrecognisable to her. She tugged the chunky book out of its hiding-place, and was about to open it when she heard a creaking noise on the stairs. Hurriedly, she pushed the book back into place, and stepped away from the bookcase.

As she did so, a boy appeared at the top of the stairs and came into the room. He looked about nine or ten years old, with scruffy, curly brown hair. He stared at Clarissa as if he had caught her trespassing, but he didn't say a word, and he didn't look as if he belonged here himself. He had a thin, triangular face, with deep-set eyes, as if he had been ill, or never had enough to eat. He certainly wasn't dressed for a garden party. He was holding his cap, wearing a dirty grey blazer over a dull green jumper with a frayed neckline, and tired, grey flannel shorts. His brown leather shoes were worn down, with mismatched laces.

Clarissa noticed a large brown mole on his left cheek, and for some reason that reminded her of somebody she knew, or a doll she had. He stared at her, she felt frightened, and walked backward until she bumped into the desk.

The boy crossed the room and went directly to the small, chunky red book that Clarissa had been trying to examine. He pushed it back deep into its original hiding-place and then turned back to her. Although he hadn't spoken, there was no question what his eyes were telling her: you're a trespasser here, touching things that don't belong to you. Go away and don't ever come back.

Clarissa bit her lip for a moment, wondering if she ought to say sorry for intruding, but she felt that there was something very wrong about this boy. She ran to the door and hoped he wouldn't chase her, and made her way back down the narrow staircase, one hand holding up the hem of her *broderie anglaise* dress, the other clinging onto the banister rail to stop herself from losing her footing.

When she reached the landing, she looked back up to the top of the stairs. The boy was standing in the doorway, still staring at her with undisguised hostility, still saying nothing. Without him even touching it, as if it had been caught by an unfelt draft, the door swung shut.

Mrs Cawsley-May suddenly appeared at the end of the landing, and said: 'Are you okay, my little darling? Are you lost?'

Clarissa nodded her head hurriedly and went back downstairs.

In the living-room, the grown-ups were still talking and laughing and clinking glasses. It all sounded so normal, but Clarissa felt that something very strange had happened, something that would haunt her for the rest of her life.

An Undetected Gift

'Clarissa! Have you taken my hairpins again, you little pest?'

Maggie flung her coat onto the newel post at the bottom of the stairs. Then she turned around and glared at herself in the gilt-framed mirror that hung in the hallway, and started to pin up her hair.

With a Kirby grip clamped in between her teeth, her reflection kept glancing venomously at Clarissa, who was kneeling on the carpet on the living-room floor. The expression on Maggie's face said: *You're not even listening to me, are you? My stupid annoying perfect little sister.*

Clarissa was opening up Granny's button-tin. She didn't want to answer, because she had seen something very strange and unsettling when she looked at Maggie this morning. For the briefest of moments, when she had walked into the kitchen, Maggie's face had looked like a blank sheet of paper, as though someone had rubbed out all of her features. If Clarissa answered her, she would have to turn around and look at her again, and that was exactly what she didn't want to do, in case she saw that facelessness again. She couldn't imagine what it meant, but it had seriously disturbed her.

Maggie was always fussy and bad-tempered when she was on her way out with Deely, her boyfriend. Clarissa thought Deely was a silly nickname for a boy and it was even sillier that Maggie would spend time with someone if it made her feel so moody. Clarissa liked to be around people that made her happy, not miserable. The lid of the tin was lined with sheet music, and a peeling label – cut out of the title *Singin' in The Rain*. She touched the buttons in the button-tin, and they felt cool and smooth, like pebbles.

Maggie puffed out her cheeks in frustration that Clarissa

hadn't responded to her. She grabbed her leather jacket by the collar and dragged it off the banister.

"Bye, mute!' she snarled. Pulling open the heavy wooden front door, Maggie stepped out into the sunlight. Clarissa looked round and saw that Deely was waiting in the road outside. He was leaning on his motorbike with his arms folded, as if he were posing for a photograph. He was thin-faced, almost foxy, with spiky black hair. Clarissa always thought that he had no personality at all – as if he really was a photograph, two-dimensional, and that if he turned sideways he would disappear.

As Maggie slammed the door shut, she narrowly missed Craivers the cat, who had trotted to her heel in adoration. Craivers jumped back, lifting his paw and flicking his tail, and looked at Clarissa as if to say: *I love your sister too, you know, even if you don't understand each other so much.*

The back door creaked in the through draft and Ma peered through the kitchen window over her flower box. Her perfume drifted in with the breeze and reminded Clarissa of fresh flowers. Ma came to the back door and tried to coax Craivers outside with sharp kissing sounds.

'Was that your sister going out, darling?'

'Yes, Mama,' Clarissa called out.

Craivers finally gave in and trotted outside. Ma came into the house, peeling off her gardening gloves. Clarissa looked up at her. *Mama always looks very beautiful*, she thought.

'I wish Maggie would tell me where she goes,' said Ma.

Clarissa knew exactly where her sister was headed, and who with, but she didn't say anything. She understood loyalty and silence were as important as telling the truth if asked. But Ma hadn't directly asked her, so she hadn't given away Maggie's secret. Ma came into the living-room and showed her the few red dahlias she had picked. 'I'll put these in water for you and you can have them in your bedroom.' She paused, giving Clarissa the fondest of smiles. 'Sorting through Granny's old buttons again? You're a funny girl.'

Clarissa picked all of the pink and yellow buttons out of the tin first. Granny's tin was home to so many various buttons, of so many bright colours, and Clarissa thought they were colourful because Granny was always such a cheerful person. She loved buttons, for their smoothness and the varying sizes. She began to lay them out delicately and precisely, to form the number seven. 'Seven,' she whispered. She felt that number seven was today's special number, but she wasn't sure why. Before breakfast this morning she had already counted out seven pencils in her room, arranged seven teddy bears on her bed, and discarded anything left over into her large wooden toy chest.

Picking up a large button, Clarissa leaned on the sofa by her elbows, and cupped it. It was a so large that she could surround the rim with both hands touching at finger tips. It felt cold, as though it was made of bone. Clarissa imagined what clever things Granny would have made with buttons like this, perhaps old rag doll eyes, or teddy bear noses. She turned it over to look at the reverse side. It was engraved with a stream of letters around the top curve of the button. Around the bottom curve were those funny shaped letters again, like the ones she had seen on the book at the manor house. She couldn't pronounce it, but she knew what each of the letters was. The letters put together, spelled *PRAESIDIO*. As she stared at it, she felt her vision blur, as though she was looking at the pattern of a mottled egg.

Blinking in bewilderment, she lifted her head and looked around. Everything else was still normal. She could see everything clearly. She squeezed her eyes tight shut and then opened them again, and slowed her breathing.

She looked down at the button again. Somehow it was no longer a button: it was a brown, curved animal tooth. She gasped, and flung it away from her, and it skimmed off underneath the sofa.

But it was a button, I know it was a button! she thought. Taking a few short sharp breaths, she lowered herself and scrambled her hand under the sofa, until she could feel something other than the wispy ends of the rug. She withdrew her arm and sat back on her heels. She opened her hands. Inside, was just one large, cold button, not an animal tooth at all.

Unsure what to do, she thought it would have to be kept a secret, as who would believe her? Ma would say it was her imagination, but she knew that it was not. She couldn't just leave this button in the tin, she had to keep it somewhere hidden. *Maybe it has a magic spell cast on it*, she thought. The embroidered pocket on her T-shirt was the perfect place to hide such a button, so she dropped it in. She stood up, gathered her hair to one side, and ran to the kitchen at Ma's call for lunch.

As she sat up to the kitchen table, Clarissa looked out onto the garden and she could see Craivers sitting on the brick wall, basking in the sunlight.

'Maybe you could come out into the garden and get some fresh air after lunch, darling. You can help me pick the runner beans,' said Ma. 'In a few years you will be at big school and these little pleasures will be less, you will be learning your own things.' Ma smiled at Clarissa, and even though Clarissa didn't really understand what she meant, she smiled back, as if they were sharing a secret.

School Manifestations

Fourteen years old

Clarissa was staring out of the classroom window, wishing that secondary school wasn't compulsory, as she was more than happy being at home drawing and helping Ma with errands and her church fayres. She was still daydreaming when she gradually began to feel that somebody had their eyes fixed on her. Not just casually, either. *Intently.*

It was the strangest sensation. Her wrists prickled, and she felt instantly breathless, as if she had been running upstairs.

She turned away from the window and looked around. It was nearly the end of the practical science lesson and most of the class had got up from their seats and were milling around the laboratory, the boys laughing in adolescent honks and the girls chattering and giggling like a flock of starlings.

Clarissa hated all this bustle and noise, but she knew she wouldn't have to suffer it for long. The class were waiting only for Mr Wallace to collect up their work books and the bell to ring, and then they could go.

Most of the popular boys were crowded around the front desk, laughing at the rude drawings in Jason Arden's science book, and arguing over who was going out during break to buy the next packet of cigarettes. One or two of them glanced at her, but that was all. They all thought she was a weirdo, and they had told her so.

Apart from Olivia, the class boffin who blushed every time Mr Wallace approached her, the girls were gathered around the chalk board, with their elaborately over-styled hair and their glossy bubble-gum pink lips and their friendship bands around their wrists. Not one of them was staring at her or Olivia. Almost all of them had their eyes on Lewis Clastine-Rees, who was sitting on the edge of Mr Wallace's desk. Lewis had a wave of naturally blond hair, intensely blue eyes, full, sensual lips, and a languid self-confidence that went with his looks. Almost all of the girls adored him, but Clarissa had seen what was behind his eyes and it was nothing but arrogance, and the capacity to love nobody but himself. She had seen something darker, too, which she didn't really understand, and didn't want to.

Mr Wallace was walking up the aisle, collecting the workbooks, and it was only when Clarissa picked up her book and offered it to him that she lifted her eyes and realised who had been staring at her. It was him. But at the same time it wasn't him at all. He had the same short-sleeved white shirt and hairy forearms and the same unpressed chinos, but Clarissa gave a little mewl of fright and surprise when she saw that he had the face of a woman.

The face was grainy and unfocused, as if Mr Wallace's own features were being masked by a picture of a woman's face from a slide projector. She had drooping eyes and a mouth that was sloping downward in what looked like unbearable distress. She was staring at Clarissa without blinking, as if she were pleading for help. *Save me, Clarissa. Only you know how.*

Clarissa jerked her chair backward, trying to stand up, but Mr Wallace tugged her book from her hands and as he did so the woman's face dimmed and disappeared, and he was simply Mr Wallace, with his bulbous nose and his little ginger moustache.

'Didn't you want me to take your work book, Clarissa? Don't think you've got anything to worry about.'

One of the other girls, Cora, gave Clarissa a contemptuous glance and curled up her glossy pink lip, as if to say *freak*. But Clarissa was too shaken by the woman's face she had seen, and in any case she never cared what the other girls thought of her. If they wanted to be bitchy to her because she was quiet in class and good at her subjects, she didn't mind. She didn't want to belong to their group anyway, with their thick hairspray, matching bags and their empty heads and their stupid, thoughtless gossip. With every passing day, she believed more and more that she was somebody different, and special, with a very unusual gift. She didn't understand exactly what it was, but she was sure that it was precious, and that it was worth a thousand times more than being asked out by Lewis Clastine-Rees or trying to be the most noticed all of the time.

Granddad used to tell her: *'The reason dogs have so many friends is because they wag their tails, instead of their tongues'*. And if that made Clarissa the dog amongst her classmates, then so be it.

She glanced across to Eric, a boy that she was sure knew how it felt to be an outcast. He sat twiddling his pencil, trying not to make eye contact with anyone, and waited patiently for Mr Wallace to collect his book. *You're never alone in this world,* she thought, *there is always someone else just like you.*

The bell rang, and there was an immediate scraping of chairs, and the laughter and chatter grew louder still. Clarissa gathered up her books, slung her red tapestry bag over her shoulder and weaved her way out of the classroom as quickly as she could, past the girls, the scruffy, tubby boys who would stare at her chest, and the School Prefect, so that she wouldn't get caught up in the huge crush.

'Hey, what's the hurry, freako?' called out one of the chubby boys, Nigel Bell. 'Don't you love us anymore? Come on, I've never had a freak-job!'

She ignored him. She hated Nigel, with his incipient hair and his flaming-red spots, but she would never give him the satisfaction of telling him that she hated him. Inside herself, she knew that his own life would punish him for what he was, as with the silly gossiping girls.

She pulled back the sleeve of her grey school jumper as she climbed the wide staircase and saw by her watch that she was ten minutes early for her art class. Seeing the face of that distressed woman on top of Mr Wallace's face had not only frightened her, but made her feel totally disorientated and very alone, because nobody else in the class had seen it, had they, apart from her?

She turned to see who was behind her, as she could hear someone humming All You Need Is Love. But there was no-one near her. In fact, the closest person was Dave Earns, a pupil in her music class, and she knew for a fact he couldn't sing, or hum in tune. She carried on walking, decided to go to art class anyway.

At least the art room was reassuring, and full of the smells of paper and paint, and she had always felt more secure there than anywhere else in the school. In the art room, she knew that she could express what she felt. The art room was the only place in the whole school where there was any colour, apart from grey.

Clarissa's jumper was grey. Her pleated skirt was grey. The polished vinyl flooring underneath her feet was grey, and the walls were grey. Sometimes she felt as if she were spending all day inside a black-and-white photograph. Most of the teachers had grey hair, and all of them seemed to wear a shade of grey like the children, except for Mrs Ball the art teacher, who usually wore a dull shade of raspberry linen, or pond green, or blue.

Clarissa stopped for a moment where she always stopped, outside Art Class One, where there was a large photograph on the wall of a summer sky. For some reason she couldn't fully understand, this photograph always calmed her down, and made her feel peaceful, as if she were really standing outside on a warm July day, looking up at a long stream of mottled clouds, like white paint being rinsed out of an artist's brush into sapphire blue water.

That wide-open summer sky represented freedom, and escape from the drab grey surroundings of school, but each time she looked at it, little by little, Clarissa had begun to find in it a much deeper significance. She was growing to understand that a picture could be so much more than a picture: it could come alive. It could for her, anyway. If she looked hard enough and relaxed she could practically feel the warmth of the sun, and she could hear the birds chirruping and the wind sighing in the trees. To Clarissa, this wasn't just a photograph, it was a real day, in which all kinds of things were happening, even if they were out of sight.

When she looked at it, she always thought that after a while she could hear her father calling her, his voice very distant and almost swallowed by the sound of the wind. That was when she would turn around to look at the picture on the wall behind her, a delayed-exposure photograph of space, with a satellite crossing in a bright diagonal line from one side to the other.

Her father used to take her out into the garden on clear summer nights, in her dressing-gown and slippers, and point out the satellites sailing between the stars. He would tell her that we can only see them because they reflect the light of the sun. Back up in her bedroom, Clarissa would kneel at her window and pretend that the satellites were animals and people who had died and become angels, and that they were looking down on their loved ones, watching them.

Clarissa continued past Art Room Two, where the door was wide open and just inside the doorway were two teachers, laughing with each other. The next door was Art Room Three, but for some reason it was never used, and the door was chained with a heavy padlock. She always imagined that something terrible must have happened in Art Room Three, and that was why it always stayed locked. Perhaps a pupil had fallen from the window, or there was a ghost in there, or perhaps somebody had painted a picture of a monster, and it had come to life and killed the boy who was painting it. Or perhaps she was allowing her imagination to run away with her, as it did so often.

She reached Art Room Four, which was the only art room with a blue-painted door. She peered through the wired glass to see if there was anybody in there. No other pupils had arrived yet, and it was just her and a younger boy in the corridor, but she could see Mrs Ball the art teacher sitting at her large desk, her shoulders hunched, her bony hands cupped around a coffee mug. In front of her, stood the headmistress.

She was about to reach for the door handle when Mrs Ball looked up, as if she had sensed that there was somebody outside in the corridor. Clarissa felt a horrible crawling sensation inside when she saw the headmistress turn to face her. Her face looked grey, with skin that was bobbled like a toad's. She had eyes like a toad's, too: bulbous and shiny black; and suspicious.

For several long seconds, Clarissa didn't know what to do. She felt as breathless as she had when she had seen Mr Wallace's face look so different. Should she simply smile? Or should she go? Or just wait for some more of her classmates to appear? Maybe the boy behind her saw it, too. She turned to look at him but he was gone. She let go of the door handle and stepped back, feeling a rising sense of panic.

But then Mrs Ball made up her mind for her. Through the wired-glass window, Clarissa saw her leave her desk and walk up to the door, and the next thing she knew she had opened it.

'Clarissa! I thought I saw you outside!'

Clarissa's heart was still palpitating. She looked at the headmistress but her face had turned back to normal. As the headmistress walked over, she passed Clarissa the same as she usually did, with a tight, insincere smile.

'I'm glad you came early,' said Mrs Ball. 'You can help me to put out the pencils and the charcoal.'

Clarissa stepped cautiously into the art room, giving Mrs Ball several quick, uncertain smiles. Mrs Ball turned and walked back to her desk as if nothing had happened, but Clarissa knew that she knew.

Mrs Ball was fiftyish, with thick streaky grey hair that she had fastened into a large, untidy bun, with a lopsided ribbon at the back. She had one of those kind, motherly faces, with a slender nose which had ivory glasses perched on the end of it. Unusually for her, she was wearing an indigo-blue smock, and dangly blue crystal earrings.

Perhaps today was a different kind of a day, thought Clarissa. Perhaps today was a 'Mr Blue Sky' day, like the song that father used to play to her and her sister, as they'd sit down for breakfast and crack their boiled eggs.

She took the sketches of sailing ships that she had drawn for her homework out of her bag and set them down on Mrs Ball's desk, next to the usual clutter of dried-out paintbrushes and unsharpened pencils and torn-off bits of kitchen towel tissue and a half-eaten apple that was turning brown.

Beside Mrs Ball's coffee mug, she noticed a large curved animal tooth. It had a hole drilled through it and it had been attached to a long piece of string. She was about to ask Mrs Ball what it was and tell her that she had seen one very similar when the art teacher covered the tooth with her hand, quite emphatically, and looked at Clarissa over the top of her glasses as if to say: *Don't, dear. It's none of your business.*

In spite of this, she didn't see any hostility in Mrs Ball's look. In fact, she strongly sensed that the art teacher was trying to be protective. *It's better that you don't know what this is, Clarissa, or why I have it here.* And when she spoke, she was still motherly and sweet. 'You should do well today, dear. Today I'm going to ask you all to paint or draw your emotions. No restrictions whatsoever. Completely free expression. I want to see what you feel, all of you, and how you can put it down on paper! Now, what did you choose to draw for your homework?'

Mrs Ball picked up Clarissa's papers. 'How lovely, an old sailing ship, I do like those. You've drawn this one in particular, very well.'

Clarissa smiled and picked up the pencils and charcoal from the box and weaved her way between the desks, arranging two pencils and three sticks of charcoal at every place. When she had finished, Mrs Ball called out, 'Thank you, dear!' and Clarissa went to find a seat for herself.

Most of the desks in the front of the classroom had orange plastic chairs, but Clarissa didn't care for orange much, or the texture of the plastic chairs. At the very back row there were some smaller wooden chairs that she preferred. They seemed more natural, and over the years they had been scratched and stained and painted on, so she felt as if each of them had a story to tell.

Not only that, when she sat at the back of the class she could see everything that was going on, and there was more space to spread out her work, and there was nobody behind her, peering over her shoulder and making faces to the rest of the class.

It was comfortably warm in here, with musty smells of wet paper and poster paint. The windowsills were cluttered with clear glass jam jars crowded with paintbrushes and big lumps of tinted sponge sitting on paper towels. The windows were all smeary, where they had been repeatedly wiped over with damp paint-stained cloths, so that the playground and the school buildings outside looked like an Impressionist painting, rather than the real grey school which it actually was.

Clarissa rolled up her shirt sleeves so she didn't get any paint or charcoal on her new shirt, and laid out her own pencils. Only three or four girls had drifted in while she was doing this, which was good, as Clarissa liked to have her own peaceful space in which to prepare.

After a few minutes, however, the door burst open and the rest of Clarissa's classmates came jostling in. The calm was replaced by giggling and gossiping and scraping chairs.

'Settle down, now, girls and boys!' said Mrs Ball. 'I said, settle down! You can't create and chatter at the same time! Do you think that Leonardo was chattering to his friends while he painted the *Mona Lisa*?'

Once everybody had quietened down, she walked up and down the aisles handing out large sheets of white cartridge paper, which she did with an exaggerated flourish.

'Class – I have told Clarissa this already.'

Clarissa wished she hadn't said that. She didn't want to sound like the teacher's pet.

'Today you are free to express any feeling that you have inside you. It doesn't matter what it is. It could be happiness, it could be anger. It could even be boredom.'

Annika Nyman put up her hand and said, 'What about hunger, miss? Can I draw some sausage rolls?'

Jessie Williams said, 'What about love? I could draw my favourite singer!'

Mrs Ball raised both hands for silence. 'I've just told you. You can express any emotion you like. I want you all to free your minds. If you want to draw sausage rolls, draw sausage rolls. After that, if you're still hungry, you can draw yourself some cakes. If you want to draw your favourite celebrities, then go ahead, but make sure they're decent. It's the way you do it that will tell me what kind of an artist you are. And also, although you may not believe this … what kind of a person you are.'

Everybody in the class started to sketch and scribble. A few of the boys teased Jessie Williams by drawing hearts and breasts and making kissing sounds. Clarissa could tell that a lot of them weren't at all interested, even though Mrs Ball always tried to make her art lessons fun and interesting. But then she thought: *I don't like maths, so everybody's different*, and she surprised herself with her own feeling of tolerance.

She picked up one of the thicker sticks of charcoal. She had no clear ideas in her mind about what she was feeling, or how she was going to express it in a picture, but she started to draw curves – deep, swooping curves, pressing harder on the paper with every upward swoop. She pressed down harder and harder, and the drawing grew blacker and blacker. She wouldn't normally draw anything as ugly and lumpy as this, but she felt as if somebody was forcing her hand down. As she drew, a face began to appear – a dark, distressed face – a face that almost looked as if it were appealing to her not to draw it.

She paused for a moment, and looked up. The Olven twins were sitting at their usual desk by the door, and both of them had turned around in their seats and were staring at her. Not scornfully, like some of her classmates did, but calmly, as if they understood what she was doing. It was very strange. She had caught them looking at her in the same way before, but today she felt unusually self-conscious, especially since her sheet of paper was already a mess of black charcoal, covered with her own fingerprints.

Both Sarah and Sally Olven had bushy red hair that was always clipped off their faces by little ivory-coloured hair grips, and pale freckly faces, and eyes that were rainwater blue. They both wore the same home-knitted cardigans, and they always finished off each other's sentences, but nobody ever teased them or bullied them. They had each other, and they had a serenity about them which kept their classmates at a distance.

Clarissa went back to her drawing again. In large letters, along the bottom, she whispered the words as she wrote them: *enai ora*, although she had no idea what it meant. Then she wrote it again, even larger, and again.

Mrs Ball was patrolling up and down the aisles, looking down at everybody's progress. When she came to Clarissa, she stopped and watched. She stood beside her for a moment, and then she said, 'Why don't you stop, Clarissa, and start again?'

Clarissa said, 'I didn't – I don't –' But then Mrs Ball bent so close to her ear that Clarissa could smell the coffee on her breath, and her Estée Lauder perfume. '*Afiste mas,*' Mrs Ball said, very quietly. '*Afiste mas.*'

'What?' said Clarissa.

But without another word, Mrs Ball pushed her messy charcoal drawing to one side, and touched her finger to her lips. Then she went to her desk at the front of the class and came back with a clean sheet of paper.

'Now,' she said. There was such kindness, even in that single word.

Clarissa picked up her charcoal again and this time, with gentle strokes and subtle shading, she drew her garden back at home, and the grass clustered with daisies, and the kitchen steps. She didn't draw her mother, but she drew the kitchen door half-open, and she knew that her Ma was inside.

She did, however, draw the garden fence, and beyond the garden fence stood the man with the smeary face. She drew his face properly, with eyes and a nose and a mouth, but then she smudged it with her thumb.

Mrs Ball watched her as she did this. 'Tell me, who would that be?' she asked, gently.

'I don't really know, miss. He lives in the house up the road. He sometimes says weird things to me. He watches me.'

'So why have you rubbed out his face?'

'Because that's the way he looks. Not always. But sometimes.'

'I see,' said Mrs Ball. She paused for a moment, as if she were thinking, and then she said, loudly, 'Time's nearly up, girls and boys! I'm going to collect up your pictures and next time we'll talk about them. Make sure you write your names on them, won't you? We don't want our sausage rolls mixed up with our celebrities, do we?'

As the class came to an end, Clarissa packed up her things, feeling confused about what had happened.

'Clarissa, would you stay behind, please?'

Clarissa knew that some of her classmates would stare at her, or laugh at her, calling her the teacher's pet, but she knew that what had just happened was something serious, and not only had Mrs Ball noticed, but she knew why. Sarah and Sally Olven smiled at Clarissa as they left the room, but again their smiles were friendly rather than mocking.

After the classroom was cleared, Mrs Ball shut the door. 'Clarissa, what you were drawing was something very different. Do you understand?'

She walked toward her desk and leaned on it, and smiled. 'It's nothing to worry about, dear, but I'd like you to come and talk to me if anything like that happens again. I'll be speaking to your mother on parents' evening at the end of the week, and I'll give her my phone number, should you or she need to get in touch with me, okay? For now I want you to know the name of my house is The Snug, at the end of Greywell Lane. That's just in case you're ever out somewhere and something frightens you, or something strange happens, so you will know where to find me.'

Clarissa nodded. 'Okay. What was it that was making me do that scribbling with my drawing?'

Mrs Ball picked up a piece of paper and wrote 'The Snug' on it.

'Something you will learn about as you get older. You are very talented, and hold a special gift. But be wise about who you share your talents with, dear. You will instinctively be able to tell who is on your side, and who is not. Special and talented individuals like you will always have – how shall we put it – *Watchers* ... sort of guardians, if you like – people who are on your side and will look out for you and protect you. Do you have any other questions?'

Mrs Ball handed Clarissa the small piece of paper and walked toward the window.

'Not really, miss. Well, sometimes things happen to me that I don't always understand, and sometimes I see people looking strange, but –' Clarissa was interrupted by a crash outside in the corridor. There was laughing, and a pupil pressed his face up against the glass and puffed out his cheeks.

'It seems we are going to be distracted,' said Mrs Ball. 'We mustn't ignore signs. You go, we will speak another time. And well done again for your classwork, dear.'

The Boy at the Pond

Clarissa pushed open the school library doors and stepped out into the fresh air. At last her school day was over. It had been raining on and off most of the day, but now the clouds had cleared and the sun was shining.

As she walked through the school's iron gates, she decided to take a left along the street instead of turning right. She knew this road was leading away from the bus stop, but she didn't feel ready to go home yet. There used to be a large pond in the woodlands at the end of this road, which was overcrowded with reeds and bulrushes, where Granny and Granddad frequently used to sit with her when she was little. She hadn't been back there for months, but she wanted somewhere to sit and think, away from the interruptions of school life and noise of the bitchy girls, and she needed some quality time alone to think about the disturbing things she had seen today at school. She remembered the tranquillity of the pond and woodlands in the summer, and how she and Granny used to sit there without saying a word, while Granddad walked around looking at the wild flowers, listening to the ducks and the breeze blowing through the reeds and trees.

The pond was the perfect place for her to spend some time. A small bench made of a tree stump used to be perched on the bank and she decided to look for it and sit for a while.

Clarissa crossed the lane and there it was, at the entrance of the woodland – the pond, with the same small tree-stump bench, nearly overgrown with large clusters of grass and wild flowers. She approached the woodland and trod carefully toward it so that she wouldn't crush the little purple phlox flowers that were growing all around it. She sat down, and immediately felt as if she were close to Granny and Granddad, because this was where they used to have their own special time together and Sunday walks to see the bluebells. She looked across the pond and remembered the story that Granddad used to tell her, about the warty frog that turned into a handsome young man as it hopped out of the murky green pond. Every now and then Granny would announce with a twinkle in her eyes that she had baked them a sponge cake, to share when they reached home to have with a glass of cream soda.

Thinking about death was like thinking about a cold, empty room – but a room which Nana, Father, Granny and Grandad didn't belong in and had all stepped out of, saying as Nana always did, 'I shan't be a mo!' Except that now they would never really come back.

Clarissa searched through her school bag and pulled out her diary. She had promised herself to keep a journal of her memories about these very unsettling things that keep happening to her, in the hope that eventually she would be able to make sense out of them all. She opened the diary and the first entry was written in thick black felt tip. She read it twice, and it still made her neck feel prickly. It was what she had written about her encounter with the boy upstairs at her eighth birthday party. She still didn't understand what had happened that afternoon, but for some reason she felt that if she could, all of the other strange incidents might make sense.

Flicking through the pages to find a blank one, she took a pencil from her shirt pocket and began to scribble down all the things that had happened today, starting with her science lesson.

Why do I keep having these visions? What triggers them off? I need to understand what they mean and learn how to control them. Is Mrs Ball really here to protect me from something? Am I being followed by something evil? Does Mrs Ball know what it is? She seems to understand something that I don't.

She thought about all of the inexplicable things that she had seen, and now seemed to be catching her attention almost every day, almost like somebody tugging at her sleeve and saying: *look at these people's faces, Clarissa, and this old ivory button you thought you'd lost. Look at the headmistress's face, in the art room, and the animal tooth on Mrs Ball's desk that she tried so hard to hide. And what about the man with the smeary face, and the way that the Olven twins stare at you?*

What's it all about, Clarissa? Think, Clarissa! What does it mean and why is it happening to you?

She wondered what Granny, Granddad and Nana would say about all of the strange things going on. *Maybe they know, maybe they are up there in satellites,* she thought. *Maybe they're right here with me, at the pond or sat next to me, but I just can't see them.*

Even when a day passed without seeing something upsetting or scary, she was thinking about faces or drawing small sketches of the faces she'd seen, from her memory. Was it her own subconscious, trying to show her how special she was, because of what she could see? Or was it some influence that was trying to corrupt her and confuse her, and twist her talent to benefit itself? Something evil?

A butterfly flapped and flopped around the bush beside her, dancing in the pleasure of the afternoon sun. Clarissa shut her diary and put it away in her school bag. She pulled out a rolled sheet of paper: another thing she had been working on.

She unfurled it and laid it on her bag. It was a picture. Sketched out in pencil was the pond, with the trees behind. It was a scene she loved, of a place that felt secretive, and sometimes eerie, but mainly beautiful and calm. In her own way, she was trying to capture it all in one drawing.

She pulled out a dark green pencil from her bag and started to add some colour to the trees.

Something suddenly caught her attention. She saw something moving among the reeds, on the opposite side of the pond. She squinted as she saw the reeds swaying, trying to see what was causing it. Sometimes she and Granny had seen herons here, especially in the spring. She shaded her eyes against the sunlight, and as she did so a boy appeared from behind the reeds, and then stood absolutely still at the bank on the other side of the pond, his arms by his sides, staring back at her.

The boy was wearing a dirty grey blazer, and his face was very pale. His reflection was wavering upside-down in the pond as if another pale-faced boy had drowned in it, and was floating just below the surface staring up at him. But then a large cloud began to hide the sun, and the whole afternoon darkened, and the image of the drowned boy disappeared.

Clarissa felt fear sink into her, all the way down to her toes. She half-rose from the bench, ready to run away. Before she could do so, however, two young girls in grey school dresses appeared between the trees, holding hands, and they stopped only a few yards behind the boy, standing just as still as he was. To Clarissa's surprise and bewilderment, she saw that they were the Olven twins.

If the twins said anything to the boy, Clarissa was too far away to hear. He turned around, not hurriedly, but as he turned around he vanished. One second he was there, the next second he had gone.

The twins stood still for a few moments, staring at Clarissa. They both gave her a calm, self-satisfied smile and walked back along the path into the woods.

Clarissa stood there, by the bench, watching until the twins had disappeared from view.

She realised she had been holding her breath, and let it out with a relieved sigh. At the same time all the sounds of the countryside came flooding back to her. Pigeons frantically flapping their wings in between branches, bumble bees dipping toward flowers. The water gently lapped at the edges of the pond as a heron landed, while a car horn sounded in the distance.

She looked down at the picture of the pond, and thought she saw a movement in it. She looked closer. Some of the pencil marks looked disconcertingly like the small figure of the boy on the river bank. She moved her pencil's eraser to where she had seen the movement and rubbed gently, blurring the marks into a grey haze.

Clarissa carefully rolled up the picture and put it back in her bag. She made sure she had her pencils and other things, and then made her way back home. She was certain her life was unlike any other's. And she wasn't sure she liked or even understood it sometimes.

PART THREE

Revived

Clarissa woke up with a start. It was still dark, and at first she couldn't think where she was.

Her mind was still at the pond, as a child, and she could hear the sounds of rain hitting the water.

She sat upright and switched on the bedside lamp. It felt strange to wake up in her old bedroom after so many years, with familiar smells surrounding her, but it was very comforting. She soon realised she had fallen asleep for quite some time and rubbed at her eyes.

As her eyes adjusted to the light, she leaned over and took a sip of water that had now gathered small bubbles at the sides of the glass. She took a few moments to collect her thoughts. Around her on the bed, open, were all her old diaries, the writing executed in her precise childish hand.

Writing. I wonder.

Her pen and notebook lay on the table under the lamp, so she moved the diaries and decided to try something that Mrs Ball had once suggested to her, for times when she felt as though she needed explanations – automatic writing.

On the first empty page of the notebook, she wrote: *Spirit guide, please answer my question. Will I see Mrs Ball again? Am I focusing too much on my Diviner talent – am I missing out on other things and friends by focusing so much on this?* She closed her eyes, tented the duvet and blanket higher over her and remained still for a few minutes, with the pen in her hand.

Then, without consciously thinking about what she was writing, she began to write.

Within a short while her hand had stopped moving, and she was no longer writing. She felt a sinking sensation and knew that was very quickly the end of her automatic writing.

She looked down at the page and read what was written

there.

If you can see a turning it is yours to take. Speech, vision she will be with you again. Always. Others are there but you are here and a purpose is your direction. Not wrong to follow gift as choices made by higher realms.

'It *worked*,' she whispered.

Never Forget Me

'Hi!' shouted Paula as she walked into the hallway and shut Clarissa's front door behind her. 'We had a problem with the smoke alarm at the new flat I'm getting with Ben so the landlord wanted to get it fixed before we moved in. Health and safety, he said. Clarry! Are you all right? Where are you?'

Paula headed into the kitchen. Clarissa was standing high up on a stepladder.

'Hmm? I'm fine, just trying to get this light bulb changed it's – so awkward trying to get my hands in between all the fancy metal bits of this shade. I want to make sure all the bulbs work, so if it goes dark on me I know it's the boy playing tricks. So I'm putting new bulbs in everywhere.'

'Don't you think that's a little over the top?'

'He's not the kind of thing you want to be alone in the dark with! Believe me!'

'It's so *creepy*, what does he want?'

'Trying to find out. There, last one done.'

'Fancy going for a bite to eat?'

Clarissa pulled a face. 'Yeah, sounds great. I'm going to miss you P, when you move out.'

'Oh, come on, you could use my room for a mini art studio – got a lovely view, once you see past Mr Wigmore's garden and his mad trellis addiction,' she said as she poured herself a glass of apple juice from the fridge. 'Want one?'

Clarissa shook her head. 'I wish I could, but I'll have to find a lodger to cover the mortgage.'

She climbed down from the stepladder and wiped her hands on a cloth.

Paula gave her a hug. 'Going to miss you too, Clarry,' she smiled. 'You've been like the big sister I never had. And an amazing friend, I couldn't ask for better.'

Clarissa hugged her in return and then made a performance of folding up the stepladder to distract herself, because she felt a lump in her throat at the thought of soon saying goodbye. After all, their wedding and honeymoon were fast approaching and then Paula would be gone.

'If you've got a minute, Ms Electrician, I've made something for you. Before we grab some food.'

They sat down together on the sofa. Clarissa plumped up the cushions and made herself comfy, while Paula got up and went to the hallway to get her bag. She carried it back in as though it was heavy, sat down and pulled out a thick red leather-bound photo album. She thudded it down onto the coffee table and said, 'Ta-da!'

'What's this?' Clarissa asked her.

'I've been making this for you. Kind of a Never Forget Me! present. I was going to give it to you next week, but I don't know – I think today would be perfect.'

'So what is it?'

'It's a Memory Album,' said Paula. 'And *this* one –' she said, tugging a thinner green album out of her bag and banging it down on top,' – this one is only half full, so it's a Future Memory Album. There's still plenty of space for more pictures. Maybe we'll even get Mark and Ben together if they're lucky! So – I thought we could look through them together, with a hot chocolate or a nice bottle of wine, and have an evening of laughs and reminiscing. Maybe even take some more pictures. It'll be fun. What'dya think?'

'Oh P, I think it's a *lovely* idea! Thank you, this is so special.'

Paula nudged Clarissa with her knee. 'I can always see Ben tomorrow instead of tonight. That's if you don't have plans already this Valentine's evening?' And with that, she took out her mobile phone and started to tap out a text for Ben.

'No I don't. Absolutely nothing planned actually. Mark is away,' she scowled playfully. 'Tell you what, just remembered there are some new films out on Netflix. We could watch one of those, too.'

'Okay, sure! So long as it's not a ghost story!' laughed Paula.

'Got our own one of those – who needs fiction,' grinned Clarissa.

Clarissa drew the curtains to shut out the evening light and switched on a lamp while Paula poured them both large glasses of merlot. Paula handed Clarissa the thick red album. 'Take a look at this big one first.'

Clarissa took a sip of her wine and opened the book. Paula watched her bright-eyed, eager to see the expression on her face. In the front of the album, she had written a message:

> *Dear Clarry. This is a little forget-me-not gift! You are so special to me and I wanted you to see how special you always have been, year after year. You're so loyal and always love me unconditionally. Other people could learn a lot from you. (And how stunning your hair always seems to look, regardless of when you feel miserable!) Your friend, Paula. XXX*

Clarissa said nothing, but reached out and took hold of Paula's hand and squeezed it.

The album started with photographs of Clarissa when she was a baby in her cot, and in the garden amongst the daisies. She saw another one of herself standing knee-deep in snow, pouting because she wanted to go home where it was warm and cosy, and another lying on the beach in summer with a crab in a bucket.

She had forgotten how different photographs used to look and feel and even *smell* before everybody took pictures with their smartphones. Some were thin and glossy, while others were thick and matt-textured, with crimp-cut edges. And the colours were strangely muted, as if they had become distant memories and silenced the moment they were taken.

'Where on Earth did you get these from?' Clarissa smiled, shaking her head in disbelief. She was so touched that Paula had gone to such trouble.

'Your mum let me have most of them after she'd made herself copies. I told her I wanted to make something special for you, like *This Is Your Life* in pictures. Here – turn back – look at that one of you as a baby! That has got to be one of my favourites! What a sulky face!'

'Oh, I think that's Maggie, not me.'

'No, it's definitely *you*, look –' said Paula 'There's Craivers, your cat. He was a kitten when you were born, wasn't he? So it must be you because he's tiny and so are you. It's such a cute picture, pity about those white spots all on it there.'

Clarissa looked at the photo more closely. She had seen it before, years ago, and she had noticed the white spots, but she had always assumed that they had been specks of dust on the negative. Now she could see that they were tiny white spheres, perfectly round, and they were dancing around her head like a crown.

'They're not just white spots. Mrs Ball showed me a photograph just like this, of her mother. They're called elemental orbs. Oh my goodness.'

'What?' said Paula. 'What are elementary orbs when they're at home?'

'Ele-*mental*, not elementary! They're like the spiritual forces that surround you, in your aura. Not many people have them, and usually you can't see them, but under certain conditions they can sometimes appear in photographs. You know – like ghosts sometimes do.'

'So what does that mean, if you've got them? Is that good or bad? I've gone all cold.'

'I suppose it's a bit of both. It just means that you're closely connected to the spirit world. Let's see if they show up in any more pictures.'

'I was looking through my own album a couple of weeks ago. I didn't have any orbs around me.'

'Then you're lucky,' said Clarissa. 'You can live a perfectly normal life and marry Ben and have loads of children and not have to worry about spirits, ever.'

Paula frowned and laid her hand on Clarissa's arm. 'The other night – in the kitchen, when all the saucepans started banging – that wasn't spirits, was it?'

'I don't know what it was, not for sure. But I have seen that ghost – well I think it's a ghost – of a boy here. And in other places. Look – here's another picture, taken at Rhystone Peak on the Isle of Wight, when I was about four. Can you see all of those orbs just above my head?'

Paula nodded, rubbing her arms.

'You could easily mistake them for dust, or small flowers on the bush behind me, but see – they're perfectly round.'

Paula stared at Clarissa intently, and then waved her hand around the top of Clarissa's head. 'Do you think you've still got them now? I mean, I can't *feel* anything.'

Clarissa shrugged, still looking at the four-year-old self in her little pink dress with the elemental orbs dancing over her head. 'I don't think they ever leave you, P. They're something you're born with around you.'

'But are they good or are they – you know – like, *evil*?'

'I'm not sure. Maybe they're both. Maybe they protect, guide – or harm. That's just something I'll have to find out.'

Anonymous

When Clarissa returned home from work she picked up her mail from the mat then kicked off her heels and unzipped her suit dress, dropping it onto the floor and stepping out of it. She walked to the sofa and flicked on the television for some reassuring background noise before she went through to the kitchen. She clicked the kettle on and then crossed over to look at the calendar. Standing just in her underwear she tapped at the page of the calendar and let out a long sigh. It seemed ages since Paula had moved out and into her own place with Ben. She missed Paula even more than she had expected. Her laughter and companionship, even her messiness, but her friendship more than anything else. The place was very quiet without her. Her new flatmate Laura, who now rented the room, was company at weekends, but nobody could replace Paula.

Just then, the letter-box squeaked open and something fell onto the mat. Clarissa frowned and went back out into the hallway. A small brown padded envelope was lying on the floor. She picked it up and then she opened the front door, peeking out around the door toward the railing where Paula always used to chain up her bike. There was no-one close by except for an old man coming out of Gretta's Bakery on the far corner and stopping to take out his handkerchief. A chilly breeze was blowing so she stepped back inside the flat, shutting the door behind her. *That's weird*, she thought.

She placed the envelope on the sofa and sat down next to it. For a moment or two she just stared at it. *Who was it from?* There was no name or address written on it, and no stamps, so it must have been hand-delivered. She tucked her hair to one side. She knew that for some reason she was reluctant to find out what was in it. *Too many weird things going on already*, she thought.

She tugged and tore open the envelope. Inside, she found a small package of stiff brown parchment paper. When she unfolded it, she found a large ivory button, and a handwritten note.

Dearest Clarissa,
You forgot this a long time ago. You will need it now.
Come and see me at The Snug. It's important and we will be waiting for you.
Much love, dear.
Persephone Ball.

Clarissa took in a short, sharp breath. *Mrs Ball!*
Who had delivered it? And how did she get it? And who was 'we'?
Clarissa wrapped the note and the button back up together.
I've got to go and see her, now.
Just then, her mobile phone rang from the hallway.
She hurried into the hallway, pulled the phone out of her handbag, and saw that it was Mark calling. She hesitated to answer, but if she didn't, she knew that he would make a paranoid assumption that she was out with one of her male colleagues from the gallery. He was becoming more controlling and possessive every day.
'Mark! Hi. I'm just about to go out.'
'Where are you going?'
'To see a friend, that's all.'
'Well, come around my place first.'
'I don't think I have time. I want to get a cake on the way back, before the bakery shuts, and then I promised to –'
'The cake and your friend can wait. I really need to see you.'
'Why, is something wrong?'
'I really need to see you, that's all.'

Clarissa drove the short route past Mipsy's Lane, and past the tea-rooms. Behind the steamy windows she could see Mrs Babda and Mrs Wells at their book group, chattering and laughing. As Clarissa drove slowly by, she tooted so they noticed her and waved. Clarissa waved and smiled in return, but secretly hoped they wouldn't beckon her to join them, because she was desperate to get to Mark's and then straight to Mrs Ball's. Her head was becoming a jumble of confusion. 'None of this feels right,' she muttered. *'None of this.'*

When Mark opened the door for her he seemed perfectly calm.

'So what was so urgent?' she asked him. He said nothing, but headed into the living room, and she followed him. Had he lied to get her here? Mark's LCD flat-screen fireplace was flickering on the wall to make it appear cosy and warm, but it gave off no heat at all, and the house was chilly. Clarissa shivered. Mark sat down on the sofa next to her.

'The way you were talking to me on the phone I thought something was wrong. So you're okay now?'

Mark didn't reply. What was the phone call about? Maybe he was just having a bad day.

'How about some coffee?' he said flatly. Without waiting for her to answer, he got up, and Clarissa looked around to see if anything was different to give her a clue to his behaviour. There was a large, old book on the floor entitled *Searching*, and over the arm of the chair was another book, called *Fury & Trace*. There was also a neat pile of first editions of his own books, but there was nothing unusual about that.

'Mark, I have to go shortly, I have to be somewhere and I want to go before it gets dark. What was it that you wanted to see me about?' She was becoming extremely unsettled and annoyed. She stood up from the sofa and went to the kitchen door.

'But I've made coffee,' he said. His face and his tone of voice were both expressionless.

'Mark what's *wrong* with you? Talk to me, what was wrong when you called me?'

Mark blinked rapidly as he placed his coffee mug onto the table and passed Clarissa hers.

'There's nothing wrong with me, why do you keep on about it?' he smiled. A false, perfect-toothed smile.

'Well, you worried me!' she said. 'It sounded urgent!'

'I'm okay, sweetness,' he said. 'Now, tell me who you were going to see? I can give you a lift there if you like.'

For a moment, Clarissa didn't want to accept his offer. Or to stay with him here any longer either if he was going to act so strangely. She was beginning to feel angry.

'It's okay, I'm driving. It's getting late, I should go.' Clarissa took a sip of her coffee but it was too hot and in any case, she didn't really want it.

'You're not going to drink that, are you?' he smirked. 'In that case, let's go. I'll follow you, just to make sure that you get there safely.'

'No. No need,' she told him. *What a wasted journey. What was the matter with him? And what's the matter with me for putting up with him? From now on I am going to be stronger with him, I am not going to be in a controlling relationship. They never end well.*

Memory Lane

Mark stopped behind Clarissa outside The Snug, although he didn't get out of his car. She turned and waved a thank you as she opened the garden gate. He waved back to her and smiled. When she turned around a second time, however, to close the rusty latch of the gate behind her, she saw that he had stopped smiling and that his engine had been turned off. In fact she thought he looked almost angry. It seemed obvious that he hadn't really needed to see her – he had just wanted to know exactly where she was going and who she was visiting, and to remind her that he was in charge.

Clarissa approached The Snug. The pathway was overgrown and unkempt. She followed it around the back of the house, feeling tingly with apprehension, because of all the memories that were suddenly coming back to her. She was eager to see what Mrs Ball looked like now, and if there were any changes in her creatively cluttered home. She had no idea why Mrs Ball had asked her here and what she wanted to tell her that was so important.

As she came closer to the garden room she paused. A flash of movement by the apple tree made her look, but there was nothing to be seen but the natural movement of the grass and branches in the breeze. Her mind started to create shapes of a child from the foliage and tree trunk, but Clarissa blinked, and the growing image in her mind, vanished. By the back of the house, the same large flowerpot was standing by the door, but with no sunflower in it this time, just dry soil. There were overgrown shrubs and in the runner, a spiky spread of lavender awaiting the summer. Two pairs of brown leather boots stood next to the door. She knocked three times against the glass.

Stepping back, she unbuttoned her jacket and ruffled her hair. She didn't know what to expect. A few moments passed and to her surprise it wasn't Mrs Ball that came to greet her. It was Sally Olven, and right behind her, Sarah Olven. They had transformed into beautiful young women, but still held their angel-like looks with their bleached rainwater eyes and, now, cascading red hair. Just then, she heard a car engine start up and assumed it was Mark, finally leaving.

Clarissa felt her heart thumping. A cold shiver ran through her and she wasn't sure if it was the boy watching her from behind the apple tree, or apprehension that something might be wrong, or simply a chill from the stiff breeze. She didn't turn around and check again for the boy, but instead smiled at Sally, who said, in her soft, sing-song voice, 'Halloo again, Clarissa.'

'Sally! Sarah! I didn't expect to see you two, how are you?'

Clarissa followed them into the garden room. As she entered the house, she looked back and hoped that Mark had gone. She was greeted by warmth and a familiar smell of classic perfume and baking. She stepped over some books and saw that the fire was lit, and Mrs Ball's white cat was basking on the rug in front of it. She looked to the right and her throat tightened with emotion, because there she was, Mrs Ball, sitting in a large high-backed armchair with a loosely-woven blanket wrapped around her.

She was holding an open book in her hands and without looking up, she said: 'Clarissa, dear, welcome! Do have a seat.'

Clarissa walked over to the table, pulled out a chair and sat down.

'Hi Mrs Ball. It's so good to see you! I was only thinking about you the other day. How are you?'

'Starting to feel older, my dear, but quite all right apart from the troubles that come with it, thank you. But how about you? Are you alone?'

'Thank you. I'm a bit unsettled to tell the truth. I'm alone but my boyfriend, Mark, is so possessive, I think he's only just driven off. He followed me here. I'm not entirely sure why.' She looked up at the Olven twins, who were standing side by side, both smiling. She couldn't believe how little they had changed.

'Unsettled?' said Mrs Ball. 'That doesn't surprise me. A great deal has been happening to you and still is.'

Sarah and Sally Olven walked across to the window and glanced through the curtains to look out. 'He's gone.'

Clarissa smiled at Mrs Ball. 'Good.'

'Do you remember what we last talked about? It was that day of terrible rain. We talked about *protection*, didn't we?'

'Yes. I remember.' Clarissa was bursting with questions and happiness at seeing Mrs Ball again, but she had learned that if she wanted to understand her life even more, she had to curb her natural impatience, and so she let Mrs Ball finish.

'The girls are here with me today because we all suspect that you may be in some kind of trouble. If not now, then very soon. Have you had any unsettling experiences recently? Anything that you can't quite understand, apart from this Mark following you?'

Should I tell her the terrible way in which Craig died first? Or Mark?

'Well, the main thing that's not right at the moment is Mark. I'm not altogether sure why I'm attracted to him sometimes, as he can be awfully strange and quite frightening. Why does he insist on knowing where I am and who I'm with, also? It's a bit *Jekyll and Hyde*. I feel as if he has some kind of *power* over me. It's difficult to describe. I feel drawn to him, but he sometimes he makes me feel really uneasy.'

'Tell me more, dear.' Mrs Ball took off her glasses and placed them on her lap.

Clarissa looked up at Sarah and Sally Olven, who were standing together again.

'Late this afternoon, once I was home from work, Mark phoned me, panicking, *demanding* I go to see him. This was almost immediately after I got your package, which I thought was a bit weird. But when I arrived it was like nothing had happened and his mood was, well, *dark*. And just the other day he was staring at me when I was talking to him, but his eyes gave me the shivers, they looked so – *cold*. It's disturbing sometimes. But like I say, I feel drawn to him and I'm starting to wonder why, because an aloof or creepy guy isn't usually my type! I might catch his reflection in a mirror if I'm tying my hair, or putting my earrings in, when he's actually not there. But then, I sometimes think it must be purely my Divining on overload, which is why I keep giving him the benefit of the doubt. He acts as though I'm the problem, and sometimes, I actually wonder if I am.'

Clarissa looked down at her hands. 'Perhaps I should try to forget that I'm a Diviner now and again, and just pretend to be like everyone else. But it's so hard to try and be the same when I know I'm not. Or have a relationship when you can't help keep seeing their soul in people's faces, and being constantly on guard because of it.'

'Listen, my dear,' said Mrs Ball. '*Trust* your feelings. Your *instincts*. As Diviners grow more experienced and more mature, most are able to read other people almost at a glance, as you already can a total stranger most of the time, and make a balanced judgment about them. What you see in, or *feel* from someone, is real. Diviners can see everything good in people, and yes the evil – the ways in which they sometimes appear grotesque. Because of that, we are able to act on what we see.'

We? thought Clarissa. *Is she a Diviner too?*

'You need to ask yourself why you are remaining attached to this Mark, if he's so difficult for you to read. He could be linked to the boy and have placed a certain spell on you of confusion and self-doubt.'

'At first I think it was because I was lonely and he made me feel wanted. It *is* like there's a spell on me, and I don't mean love. I mean like a *real spell*.'

'A Diviner will also know true love, when they see it. You will know the difference, in your heart, and in your own time but *don't*, whatever you do, *don't actually* fall in love with the real him, or the nice version of him if you will. If he's susceptible now, he always will be.'

'Okay,' Clarissa said. 'So what do I do about him? It would make sense just to end our relationship.'

Mrs Ball placed her glasses back on her nose. 'Yes, dear. As I say, listen to your instincts. Good looks must not sway good intuition. In fact, I had a feeling that a man like this Mark would enter your life, although I didn't expect him to meet you this soon. Interesting, attractive, but secretive, too. Is that the way you feel about him?'

'Well, yes, that's exactly how I feel about him. He's very good-looking, and he has so much charisma when he's not being stand-offish. I guess the nice side is the *real* him, as you mentioned.'

'Where did you meet him?' asked Mrs Ball.

Clarissa pushed up her sleeves and sat back on the chair. She began to feel embarrassed because she realised that these were questions she should have asked of herself. Mark had never told her his real surname, and although they had become so intimate, she knew practically nothing about him. *How could I have been so casual?*

'I met him a while ago, through my work colleagues,' Clarissa said. 'The funny thing was, when he met me, he acted as if he already knew me. I was seeing someone at work, Craig, but he … he died … but my friends were insistent that Mark was really nice, and so I found myself letting my guard down a little. I trusted them.'

Clarissa realised just how strange and silly that must have sounded, especially since she should know better, and how odd and unlike her it actually was, because she was normally so inquisitive and self-protective.

Mrs Ball smiled sadly.

'I don't know his surname, or his mother's maiden name – or even met her – come to think of it, I've never seen any post with his name on. I've never asked, and he's never told me. He just told me his *nom de plume* – Mark Ross – he's a writer.' 'I see.'

'He lives in one of those new apartments in Luxbury Hill.' Clarissa paused, then said with remorse in her voice: 'I'm beginning to think I've been too trusting – I feel silly. It's normally a man's character that attracts me, not just his looks.'

'So even though your friends introduced him to you, you'd never heard about him before then?'

'No,' Clarissa replied. 'No, I've known them for – well – a few years from the Milltower Gallery and I'd never heard them mention him before that day,' she said.

Just then, Sally left the room and shortly after returned with a tray of warm chocolate brownies. 'Straight from the oven,' she whispered.

Mrs Ball said, 'It seems to me that this Mark has shaped himself into something that will draw you to him. In the same way that the most delicious-looking berry can be poisonous, and a Venus fly trap lures its prey in order to trap and dissolve them. Do you follow me, dear?'

'Yes. Yes, I do.'

'Remember, the boy himself cannot easily kill a Diviner: you have an ancient gift, but, he will possibly possess other bodies to get close to you, with evil intent and terrible consequences. Does he read? What are the books he reads himself? Have you noticed any religious memorabilia or Greek mythology?'

'Erm, yes he has very serious books, and one of them that I saw today was called *Fury & Trace*. There were others, but I can't remember them. I do know I have seen books with Greek titles there.'

'Whatever you do – be very careful from now on. We need to find out who, or indeed *what* Mark is. I have a very disturbing feeling.'

Clarissa didn't know what to say. But she knew she could trust Mrs Ball entirely.

'Oh my – you don't think – think that he's actually –?'

Sarah and Sally sat down.

'The boy spirit? Quite possibly,' said Mrs Ball. 'Mark himself might be just as good as your friends believe him to be, but the boy may have temporarily taken control of him. It is often the best people who are most susceptible to possession, because they don't recognise evil intent when it enters their souls.'

'I feel sick. That would make sense. And explain the complications of his character.'

'We must bide our time a little longer, dear. Just to be sure. Maybe the boy was there that evening, watching you all, and seized the opportunity. Be strong. Malevolent sprits tend to find a way to take advantage of insecurity and offer false comfort.'

'Yes, okay. I can do that. So I'm not mad, after all?'

'Mad? Oh, no, dear, quite the opposite! In fact I think you're a little too sane for your own good.'

Clarissa sat and looked at the fire. The jumping flames and popping, crackling sounds were relaxing, as was the smell. She watched them and let everything she was being told sink into her.

Phylactery

Clarissa took a bite of the last brownie. 'Thanks,' she smiled. 'Extra amazing when they're freshly-baked like this.'

Mrs Ball beckoned Sally Olven toward her. Sarah stood up and walked toward the fireplace, turning to face them at the table. 'Get me the holy water for Clarissa please, Sally dear. And a tooth vial, and also a black tourmaline, one of the larger ones. They're in the red box over there.'

'Holy water?' said Clarissa. 'I'm not a Catholic, Mrs Ball.'

'Now, now, dear. Holy water doesn't have to be Catholic – it depends who blessed it. It's the most powerful protection against evil, and it will help keep you and your loved ones safe. Pour a little into the tooth vial, for an antidote if anyone should be hurt in any way. Think of it as an extra layer alongside your own talisman – the button. I don't think we can be too cautious when it comes to your protection considering the circumstances. The black tourmaline will act as a psychic shield – it has been used by magicians for centuries as a way of warding off evil. Just keep it in your pocket. It seems the boy is getting to you in any way that he can, and it doesn't look as if he's slowing down. Remember. He *could* be Mark. Now, did you bring the button with you? Or the Praesidio as other Diviners would call it.'

Praesidio? thought Clarissa. She reached into her pocket to take out the button. 'That word is engraved on my ivory button.'

Sally approached Clarissa and handed her a small leather pouch.

'Here you go, Clarissa,' she said softly. 'Holy water. And antidote. Put the tourmaline in your pocket, keep it close to you always, within your aura. Also, keep this smokey quartz pendant on you. It used to be mine. It's cleansed. Ready.'

'Thank you.' Clarissa wasn't sure if she understood crystals properly but she took them anyway, in good faith and gratitude.

'This pendant is beautiful.'

Sally nodded, and smiled at Clarissa, as the white cat next to her flicked its tail and sat upright.

'Why would the boy hunt for me?'

'It's my belief that he needs a Diviner to free him and give him what he needs.'

'But killing and scaring and causing sickness is no way to go about getting help,' she said.

'Ah, true, for mortals, your everyday humans. But this boy is pursuing you so relentlessly for a reason. He wants something from you – something only a Diviner can give him. I don't exactly know what it is, but it's very clear that he wants it so badly that he will destroy everything and everybody that you hold dear in order to get it from you. Let me tell you this, though – whatever it is, you must never give it to him, under any circumstances. Once he has it, he will be able to hurt not only those around you, but you yourself.'

Clarissa looked across to Sarah Olven, who was still standing by the fireplace. She was also smiling reassuringly, although she hadn't said a word.

Mrs Ball nodded, raising her eyebrows as Clarissa handed her the button. 'That word on my button. *Praesidio*,' said Clarissa. 'What does it mean?'

'Yes. *Praesidio* means "protection". It's Latin. Although everything is appearing to be Greek, Latin is used for Diviners as it is our oldest language and cannot be destroyed, or changed, by a spirit that is hunting you. The spirit will have great intent to cause harm to those a Diviner holds in their heart. You must help protect them.'

Clarissa felt alarmed.

'For instance, if "protection" was written in Greek on here, the spirit could change it to draw you to him. But as it is in Latin, it's a warning and, a form of protection that should give you reassurance. It's your talisman. You must keep it with you always, for added protection from very strong entities. At what age did it first come to you?'

'Okay. I remember it well. I was eight. Just after my birthday party. I found it in my granny's button tin. It seemed magical, or bewitched, because just for a moment it looked like a tooth. You remember that tooth you had on your desk at school? Just like that. I've loved it ever since.'

Mrs Ball nodded and pushed her glasses further along her nose. 'It was making itself known to you, in a favourite thing of yours – such as a button – so that you would see it, and take notice of it. If you love something purely, a higher power will know. Mine, when I was your age, was a little ornament of a cat.'

'A cat?'

'Yes. It sat on my mother's mantelpiece for years. I told my mother, but she insisted I had an overactive imagination.'

'Sounds like my Ma.'

'Since then, I've loved cats. You see, all Diviners see the tooth within their talisman when their gift is ready to be used. It's the ancient symbol of Divination, originating from the tooth of a hyena. Some try to suggest that its history is linked to witchery, but any Diviner knows that it's not, nor is it anything sinister – and you're the proof.'

Clarissa nodded. She was already feeling less alone in the world. 'Ma used to say that I was a "funny little thing" when I used to enjoy sorting through Granny's buttons. Now I'm glad I did, because it seemed I needed to find this.'

'Everything happens for a reason, dear. There is no coincidence.'

Sarah and Sally Olven smiled at each other.

'I always knew I was different,' said Clarissa. 'When I was at school they used to tease me. But I knew I couldn't help being how I was, knowing when someone was lying, or knowing how someone was feeling before they told me. I sensed things about them. I knew their insecurities. I knew their fears. I was kind, always, and I didn't think it was a bad quality to be different, not like those girls who couldn't seem to survive or be happy unless they were in their bitchy groups, jealous of anyone stronger or prettier than them. I always found that behaviour all so sad and a waste of time. I was always strong enough to stand alone and rise above it, regardless of sometimes feeling isolated.'

'It's wonderful to be different,' said Mrs Ball. 'And strong. Nothing at all wrong in those things. In fact, you're not only different from those silly girls years ago, or those ignorant people who are jealous, judgmental or threatened by anyone gracious or talented – you are wise to it. Even a man that leers at you in a bar, or indeed anyone in your future who will be slanderous or malicious, you must be strong enough to grow from it, and there *will* be some. You are very special, well-loved and above anything, *genuine*. You're also grounded and becoming a very capable woman.'

Clarissa sniffed into her tissue. 'Sorry, I don't know why I've got upset,' she smiled. 'Thank you.'

'My dear, strengths like these knock spots off all of those others that wish you harm. Sadly, because of your gift, and the way you can interpret a situation so quickly, others can find you threatening. You may not think they notice, but to them you give off an air of Divine grace, a feeling of peace and positivity that they don't like. They may even try to perceive you as someone other than worthy of being liked and be slanderous about you to make themselves feel better, to protect or inflate their image; especially the insincere. It will make your journey in life very challenging. But being kind and strong, accepting and correcting your mistakes is vital. Not using someone for your own gain, is one of your qualities and their weakness, dear. And may I add, there are others like you. Not many, but your paths will cross when it's required.'

Clarissa felt tears well up in her eyes again and she looked down. She'd never had anyone say such powerful things to her before that touched a nerve, and she'd never spoken so much about herself, either. *Don't cry, don't cry!* she told herself. She was trying so hard not to sob that she could hear the blood rushing in her ears.

'Clarissa,' said Mrs Ball, 'you're an extremely shrewd and perceptive young woman. *A true Diviner.*'

When she said that, Clarissa couldn't hold herself together any longer. She pressed her hands on her forehead but she couldn't hide the fact she was crying, or stop.

Sally passed her a fresh tissue.

'No-one's ever understood before, or known what I was going through, not really.' She looked gratefully at Mrs Ball. She felt a deep sense of relief and release sweep through her.

Finally someone understands me and my life she thought. *After all these years.*

Sally passed Clarissa some more tissues and sat beside her. Mrs Ball glanced up and across at Sarah, and asked softly: 'Make a sugary cup of tea for Clarissa please, Sarah.' Then she nodded, knowingly, giving Clarissa a comforting smile, and closed the book that was on her lap.

'Let's have tea', she said in a soft, grandmotherly tone. 'Why don't we move to the comfy chairs nearer the fire. Oh, Clarissa, did I tell you, that Sheridan – the grey Persian – is having kittens in a few weeks' time?'

Clarissa lifted her head, and tucked her hair behind her ears. She looked at Sally, whose eyes seemed to glow, as though Clarissa was looking into a tunnel of peace, or an angelic light. She looked at Mrs Ball and offered a doleful smile.

'I thought that might cheer you up a little,' said Mrs Ball, offering the warmest of smiles, as she reached out and held Clarissa's hand.

The Library

The next morning Clarissa felt that a whole new world was opening up ahead of her, as if a dead weight had been lifted from her shoulders.

She was now focused on finding out who or what Mark was, as well as about the book. *Was Mark an orphan who had once been given shelter in The North Chapel? Was he possessed by the boy's spirit? Perhaps he had never made a point of telling her his name because he had never known his original name? Or does he know exactly who he is?*

Clarissa closed her umbrella and shook the rain from it as she approached the foyer to the Wood Bay Library. She had come here because it had extensive historical and local newspaper archives. If there was anywhere she could find out more about The North Chapel, it was here.

She took her mobile phone out of her bag to check the time and then she switched it off. She didn't want to be disturbed by anybody right now, especially Mark and his strange sixth sense.

As she reached the library doors underneath the foyer she paused to let a young lad wearing Marshall earphones go first, seemingly absorbed in his music. As she waited, her attention was caught by a notice-board covered with local advertisements and so she glanced at them. On it, were adverts for a local babysitter wanted, psychic night at the local village hall and the odd business card for plumbing and roofing specialists. But as she stood and listened to the rain falling, what really caught her attention was an inscription in the framework, and on a closer look she saw that it was a rhyme by R L Cooke called 'Time Will Tell'. She leaned in and whispered it to herself as she read it:

> *Soft speech and silver phrases do not prove*
> *the soul is sweet,*

And perfect manner do not tell how true a
heart can beat.
For God has often tied the tongue, yet
opened wide the hand,
Has closed the lips and yet has made the
heart to understand.
Judge not upon acquaintance when its first
brief meeting ends,
For time alone can prove who are the
worthiest of friends.

Just then, she was tapped on her arm by an elderly lady, who was pulling a little shopping trolley behind her.

'Excuse me dear, are you going in?'

'Oh sorry,' said Clarissa, pulling her out of her gaze. 'I'm blocking the way. Yes, after you,' she smiled.

It was cool inside the library, and musty smelling – a smell that fondly reminded her of visits to libraries with Ma as a child, the used paper and plastic covers of a thousand books warmed in people's hands, as they absorbed the information and fictional stories, then the dull bleep at the desk as an assistant scanned and piled up selected books, knowing they'd return home to a warm house and have a quiet afternoon by the fire.

She approached the reception desk, where a tall, angular lady was standing, frowning at a clipboard.

'Can I help you?' she asked, looking up.

'Hi, yes, I'd like to find out about The North Chapel,' said Clarissa. 'I don't know whether you can help at all.'

'The North Chapel? Oh, I think so, yes,' said the library assistant, as she tapped the clipboard with her pen and placed it onto the counter. 'We have quite a lot on file about it. I'll show you.'

Clarissa looked at her name badge, hanging from her blouse. *Allison Dragby. Historian Assistant.*

'Just follow me,' she said.

As she led the way between the bookshelves, Allison's long skirt flapped from side to side. Every now and then she turned to Clarissa and smiled. Clarissa wondered how old she was. Her hair was fine and silky, mousy brown and elegantly styled into a loose pony tail. The second time she turned around, though, her thin face seemed almost rat-like, and there was something unnerving in the way she smiled, almost as though she was baring her teeth, but Clarissa tried not to let it distract her. Stop *Divining*, she told herself.

She followed Allison along a corridor, down a few shallow steps and through another corridor which opened up into a high, chilly room, with narrow windows.

'So here we go, this aisle has all the records on The North Chapel. I presume you'd like to know about the relics that were recently discovered there, too? There was a feature about it in the local paper. Greek pottery, some of it quite old, apparently, and very rare.'

Allison took a pair of white cotton gloves out of her blouse pocket and elegantly pulled them onto her hands. Clarissa followed her along the aisle, past row after row of metal shelves, each of them crammed with books and files: filled with so much history; so many stories; so many secrets. She felt that every book and every file was crowded with ghosts, crying for discovery or release.

She could hear nothing but Allison's shoes clip-clopping along the old parquet flooring. Eventually Allison stopped and reached up to one of the upper shelves, pulling out a huge black leather file.

'Here we go,' she said. 'I think this will help you.' She laid the file down on a nearby large desk. 'Let's look in here. The North Chapel was built in 1797 by an offshoot of the Methodists, the so-called Redemption Methodists, but when they returned to the main Methodist Church, the building had been taken over by the Church of Infinite Wisdom, who are spiritualists, as you may know.

'One of the many good works done by the spiritualists was to open the Berkwood Home for Children, to take in orphans and mistreated children, to educate and protect them, and in their own words to – *keep them safe from malevolent spirits in the hands of God.'*

Clarissa was reassured by Allison's confident tone, as if she really knew her subject well. She zipped up her jacket to keep warm and leaned in to take a look, pulling a notebook and pencil from her bag as she did so, and scribbled on the top page: *The Library.* Allison pointed to a yellowed newspaper cutting headline and tapped it. She read on: '"Following last month's devastating fire at Berkwood Home For Children, sufficient donations have been made by neighbours and other benefactors to provide for the orphans who lived there. For the foreseeable future they are being housed in The North Chapel, and the funds will provide them with clothing, bed, books and educational materials and other essentials. The children and staff would like to express their profound gratitude to all those involved."'

'Is there anything more about the fire?' asked Clarissa. 'Does it say how it started?'

Allison nodded. She pulled out another binder from the shelf below. 'There's a whole section in here, purely about the fire.'

She placed the binder on top of the larger file, and opened it.

'There are several theories about the fire. Most accounts suggest that it was started by accident, because in the '50s the rooms were kept warm by paraffin heaters. However one report from a member of staff seems to suggest that it might have been deliberately started by an orphan called Thomas. Apparently he was always so badly-behaved that he had to be kept apart from the other children. But there's something about the fire which I personally think is very strange indeed, although all my colleagues think that I have an over-active imagination, and that it can only be a coincidence. But I don't believe in coincidence,' she grinned.

'Go on,' said Clarissa, really warming to her. Allison's eyes were almost lighting up with passion. It was obvious she knew a lot about the Chapel and its history.

'*Well,'* said Allison, very emphatically, 'in 1815, in the original orphanage, a boy who was *also* named Thomas was admitted to the orphanage, and he too was almost uncontrollable. Just look at this.'

Allison leafed through the binder and picked out a photocopy of a page from a notebook. At the top it was dated 14 February 1815. It was written in steeply-sloping italics, so faint that they were almost indecipherable, but Allison read it out loud almost as if she knew it off by heart. Clarissa shivered, partly because the room was so chilly, and partly because of what Allison was reading.

'"The boy we have named Thomas after the man who passed him to us, is continuing to act aggressively and to blaspheme without let. With regret we have had to keep him in isolation under lock and key, as Mr Bruce suggested we might have to when he first brought him to us. Mr Bruce explained that the boy was found hiding in a ship, and he is certainly as foul-mouthed as any sailor, although every effort to determine who his parents may be has been fruitless. He has attacked our staff on numerous occasions, hitting and kicking and biting, threatening them with sticks, and we are afraid that he would bully the rest of our children relentlessly, apart from exposing them to an endless stream of ungodly oaths. We tried to baptise him, but we had to abandon the attempt because of his shrill, loud screaming and we could not force him into the water.

'"Most alarming of all, he set alight on Thursday evening last to a curtain in his chamber with his bedside candle. Although Mr Borage was alerted by the smell of smoke, and managed to extinguish the flames, this incident has meant that we have been obliged to deprive Thomas of any lights at all during the hours of darkness."'

Clarissa said, 'That is so weird. That was – what – almost 140 years earlier than the fire in the '50s?' Allison nodded. 'Almost too much of a coincidence to be a coincidence, wouldn't you say?'

A sharp screech from the far side of the room distracted her, making her turn her head and frown like a nervous animal.

'Those horrid filing drawers in row thirteen, they still put my nerves on edge,' said Allison. 'You always think you're alone down here. But you're not.'

Clarissa looked up, and around the room. It was dull and chilly with a sweet smell in the air and she wasn't surprised that Allison felt that way. A door creaked and then clicked as it closed as the person from row 13 left the room. Allison turned back to look at Clarissa and gave her a strange, slightly rat-like grin. 'In truth, I really don't like it down here.'

'Allison, has anyone else looked at these files?' Clarissa asked her. Allison raised an eyebrow.

'Yes. A man did two days ago.'

'What was he like?'

'Oh. Erm. Quite good-looking, mid- to late-thirties. He was very polite – I mean polite to the point of being formal – but there was something about him that made me feel a bit uneasy around him. He seemed very *distant*. It's always spooky enough down here regardless, without being alone with someone like him. But I try not to let it worry me. I get used to it. You get all sorts. At least he didn't smell of stale body odour like some. Actually he didn't smell of anything at all, which was strange, in a way. I would have expected somebody like him to wear a fancy aftershave.'

'What was he most interested in?'

'The relics. The Greek pottery that they've just discovered in the back of the chapel. It's funny. There were no pictures of the pots in the paper, and that made him quite angry it seemed. He kept saying, "There's nothing about the book. Not a word. Why haven't they mentioned the book?" I didn't know what book he was talking about.'

Clarissa and Allison continued to look through the files related to The North Chapel for over half an hour, with Clarissa taking notes as they did so. There seemed to be so much about it, much more than she had expected. Allison began to read out snippets of information that she thought may be relevant, as if Clarissa's interest in The North Chapel and the man's visit had rekindled her curiosity about it, too.

'This is rather interesting,' she said. 'It's an article from the *Berkwood Weekly Advertiser*, about the chapel library. A local schoolteacher called Clement Trott was going through all of the old books that had been rescued from the orphanage, because he was writing a history of the village. It says here that, since the fire, nobody had catalogued these books or put them in any kind of order, so he was doing it himself. He found them fascinating because they recorded the day-to-day progress of every orphan who had ever been cared for at Berkwood.'

'*Every* orphan?' said Clarissa.

'Apparently so.'

'Then at least one of the books must have mentioned these two badly-behaved Thomas boys.'

'Presumably,' said Allison. 'It has several interesting snippets from the records that were kept about the lives of other orphans – especially children who grew up to be noted or famous, like George French, who was an early aviator, and Dorothy Quinn, the artist. But the odd thing is that the article doesn't mention either Thomas at all. You would think it would, especially since the second Thomas was suspected of starting the fire that burned the orphanage down.'

Clarissa took the binder from Allison to read the article for herself. The headline was *Rediscovered: The Heart-Rending Records of Berkwood's Orphans*. But it was the byline that made Clarissa catch her breath. *By Mary May*.

Roger Harding had been convinced that a book about an amphora still existed. Perhaps the same book contained a record of Thomas's life at the orphanage. Harding had suggested that one of the volunteers who had helped to clear up after the fire may have kept it as a souvenir, but he had also hinted that Mary May could have taken it from the chapel library – perhaps when she was interviewing Clement Trott.

Clarissa was sure now that it was the same book that Mrs Cawsley-May had given her, and that it was the same book that Mark was looking for, and had become so angry when he couldn't find. The implications of that gave her a sudden prickly chill, and she saw tiny sparks of light floating in front of her eyes. She swayed, and had to hold onto the table to steady herself.

'Miss? Are you okay?' asked Allison, with a worried frown.

'You look as if you're just about to faint!'

'It's – it's all true. She must have stolen the book from The North Chapel library – they must have all known each other – and her dying – it's – I need to talk to Ma –'

Allison took hold of Clarissa's hands and rubbed them vigorously. 'My goodness, you're cold! You need to sit down. You look very unwell. What do you mean, '"It's all true"?'

Clarissa stared at the floor, feeling increasingly dizzy. 'I'm sorry, Allison. I have to go.' As she turned around her vision clouded.

'Miss?'

Allison's voice faded.

'Miss!' she cried as Clarissa slumped to the floor, her eyes rolling upward. 'Help me! Somebody!' she screamed. *Somebody help!'*

I Don't Know You

Clarissa folded back the covers of her hospital bed and stepped into her slippers. *Today's the day*, she thought, as she glanced up at the clock. *Eight fifteen – Mark will be here in a couple of hours.*

She listened to the window blind *rat-tat-tat* in the breeze, which during the night had made her wonder if the boy was stood there, his grubby fingers knocking at the window pane. She picked up her notepad from the bedside table and looked at her list of pros and cons of remaining in a relationship with Mark. *How can I let this continue after Mrs Ball's warning? It has to end. But how can I end it without ever knowing for sure who he is? Or – more importantly, perhaps, what he is? Is it worth the risk?*

The trouble was – in spite of her suspicions about him – he still had such magnetism. What if she found that she couldn't end it? What if she had fallen in love with him so deeply that she was prepared to forgive him anything? She had to tell him that they were finished – as lovers, anyway.

'*Knock knock!*' sang a cheerful voice, as the door clicked open to her room.

'Morning,' replied Clarissa.

'Would you like a tea or coffee this morning?'

An attractive lady in her mid forties with loosely-curled blonde hair walked in smiling, pushing a drinks trolley. 'They say it's going to be a nice day out there today, you may like a walk in the rose garden.'

'Tea, please,' Clarissa said as the woman walked toward her. *When Mark gets here, maybe we can walk through the rose garden together. Maybe that's where I should tell him it's over*, she thought.

'Thank you,' she smiled.

'The rose garden is nice and private, although part of the

hospital looks over it,' said the lady, and it was as if she'd known what Clarissa was thinking about, or as if she was providing some guidance.

'You know, dearie,' said the lady as she fussed with the tea, 'you are a very beautiful young woman. You remind me of my niece.'

'Thank you, although I'm not sure this hospital nightgown is very flattering,' she joked.

'I wish you well, it's been lovely coming in here most days and seeing a friendly, pretty face. There you are,' she said as she passed Clarissa a packet of shortbread biscuits. 'Just for you. See you tomorrow.'

'Ahh, thanks.'

She smiled as she watched the lady wheel her trolley out of her room and along the corridor, leaving a soft aroma of perfume and tea in her wake. Before she closed the door she leaned out to look around. At the far end, a staff nurse was sitting at a desk, talking on the phone, while a young girl was shuffling her way slowly toward her along the corridor using her intravenous drip stand to support herself.

There was a dull smell in the air, like mushroom soup, and it made Clarissa feel sad and sick, because it was the smell of illness and confinement. She shut the door and took a sip of her tea, hoping she'd be allowed home soon.

She took her notepad and tea to the windowsill and began to think about what to say to Mark when he arrived. It was obvious that he was urgently and angrily searching for the book, and that he had been highly disturbed by the sight of the amphora. But couldn't he tell her why he needed the book so badly, and what it was that upset him so much about a piece of antique Greek pottery? They were supposed to be lovers, after all, and in spite of his secrecy and his controlling ways she still found him deeply attractive, and she knew that it would cause her terrible heartache to tell him that they were finished.

The most painful question was, did he find *her* equally attractive, or was he continuing their relationship only because he sensed that she could help him get whatever it was he so desperately wanted?

'Thanks,' said Clarissa as the nurse helped her on with her jumper.

'That's okay, enjoy your afternoon. Handsome man you've got there. The roses should smell lovely.' The nurse picked up her empty cup and nightgown, saying: 'I'll get you a fresh one on your return,' and then she left the room.

Clarissa sat on the bed and waited for Mark to come out of the toilet. Her heart was beating quickly, but it wasn't because she was unsure if she was doing the right thing, it was because she was unsure how he would react. *I shouldn't have to feel like this*, she thought. She pulled her cosmetic bag from the cupboard. Opening her compact mirror, she groomed her hair and started to apply some blusher. She noticed how rested she looked, and how her complexion had already begun to improve.

She ran through what she wanted to say to him in her mind as she applied some mascara. *Mark, I don't feel comfortable in our relationship anymore, you're becoming too domineering. I know there are things that you're not being honest about, and you have been acting very strangely. I personally can't build a relationship that harbours deception. How do you feel? I think we should remain friends.*

'Here goes,' she said to herself, putting her cosmetic bag away.

'Don't these roses smell fantastic?' she asked Mark, desperately trying to break the ice and remembering that his apartment had smelled strongly of roses the first day when she had gone round there. *Strange that his home should always smell so fragrant but he never smelled of anything.*

He didn't answer her. They walked along the little cobbled path until they reached a bench. The garden was much larger than she had expected and immaculately kept. Three gardeners were weeding it and clipping the privet hedges. The sun was out but there was a light breeze blowing, and when she sat down Clarissa closed her eyes and took in a refreshing breath of fresh air. A few moments later, she felt Mark sit down next to her, in silence. She opened her eyes and looked to him.

'Mark, I wanted to talk to you –'

'It's not an option, Clarry.'

'What isn't?'

'Remaining friends. I can't handle that.'

Clarissa hadn't begun to tell him, but somehow he must have sensed it, which explained the silence and tension between them.

'Oh Mark, I'm sorry, but it's just that recently you've changed so much. There's so many things that you won't tell me or talk about –'

'It's not an option,' he repeated, leaning towards her. 'List the options.'

'Sorry?' Clarissa didn't like the change in his voice or body language. 'Mark don't get cross, we need to talk and explain why it –'

'I said, *list the options*,' he interrupted.

Mark was frightening her now. She had expected him to be upset but she hadn't thought that he would become so hostile – and so quickly, too.

'I don't really know what you mean by "options",' she said.

'Options, choices, whatever you want to call them,' he snapped.

'Well, all right, the choices are that we keep our happy memories and remain friends, or we part and lose contact, or there's total honesty and no weird behaviour and we make it work. But, I feel Mark that I've waited long enough and been very patient, so really the only way forward is we have to stay fr–'

Mark stood up.

'Do you think I'm stupid?'

'Mark,'

'I see the way you look at Ben. And every other man. You're a flirt. You're seeing someone, others. You act like a whore.'

'Mark, how dare you say that? I don't behave like that *ever*!

Who do you think you are, talking to me that way? They're my friends and I'm a friendly person – and it's not about that, it's about the way your character is always changing. You always have an excuse for everything, and I never feel that you're telling me the truth. In fact, it's quite –'

She was about to say 'disrespectful and creepy' but she saw something dark in Mark's eyes, and she stopped. Her heart was thumping with anxiety.

Mark placed his hands on his hips and stood still. His eyes were intense and angry.

'Please, darling, tell me how you feel,' she asked him, speaking in a softer tone to calm him down. 'Do you *really* think that everything is okay between us? To carry on?'

'I love you, Clarry,' he said, although his tone was oddly flat. 'I realise that strongly when I see you with your friends. Laughing and joking. Fluttering your eyelashes. But you have to understand that you're *mine*. Not theirs. You belong to me. Everything about you belongs to me. It has to.'

Clarissa frowned, completely focused on what he was saying. Some of her previous boyfriends had been jealous when she talked to other men, but not obsessive, like this. He was making her feel very agitated and hemmed-in, almost claustrophobic. Even in this breezy rose-garden she felt as if she couldn't breathe.

'*This* Mark isn't the Mark I have feelings for. You accuse me of being unfaithful, you call me a whore. Then you say how much you love me. This isn't love, Mark. I don't know what this is. I think we need to be friends only, because frankly, I don't know who you are. You're creepy, arrogant – I don't know *this* Mark at all.'

'Friends isn't an option. I need you.'

'Can you answer me properly? You're not behaving normally and I can't put up with it anymore, not unless you tell me why. You talk in riddles all the time!'

Mark walked away from Clarissa and didn't turn back.

'You say that you need me?' Clarissa called after him. 'Yet all you can do is you walk away from me, leaving me feeling upset, and not even say why? How can you do that?'

She was tempted to shout, 'What about the book? Why is the book so important?' but she remembered what Mrs Cawsley-May had said when she gave it to her. *'If only for your own sake – don't mention it to anybody else.'*

She thought about getting up and going after him to get the answers she wanted, but she was too tired. He had exhausted her over the past few months, both physically and emotionally, and she was sure that her instincts about him were right. Her exhaustion and stress probably accounted for why she had fainted and ended up in hospital for a couple of days.

She stayed on the bench, feeling upset and embarrassed in case one of the gardeners had overheard. Tears welled up in her eyes but she promised herself that this would be the last time she'd ever cry over someone that didn't deserve her tears.

A juddery breath filled her and she wiped her eyes. She had never felt so hurt or let down. One of the gardeners was planting a small bush at the edge of the garden, and he looked up from his digging and smiled at her. As if to say, *I understand, my lovely. Don't you worry. He was no good. You know what a wonderful gift you have. You can see what others can't. You're not alone in this world, even if you feel alone.*

Death Is Nothing At All

It was one in the morning but Clarissa was still awake. The hospital was noisy, and heavy rain was hammering against the window. She leaned over and switched on the light beside the bed. She was grateful to be in her own private room, now more than ever. Not only that, it also gave her privacy to figure things out when she couldn't sleep, without disturbing anyone else. Somewhere in the hospital corridors was a woman screaming, and she found it distressing.

She decided to stay awake to read through her notes, put on some handcream and brush her hair to feel fresher, rather than lie awake in the dark listening to somebody else's pain and sadness in the distance. She took a sip of orange juice while thinking about all the things that she had discussed with Allison.

She wrote: 'Why does Mark seem to want the book so badly? I can't make any sense of it, so how can he? Could it be that he was once an orphan at The North Chapel, and the book had some kind of special meaning to him? But if so, what on Earth could it be? And where does the boy fit into all this, the boy who murdered Craig and Mrs Cawsley-May? He seemed to want the book, too. Is it – somehow linked?'

She took another sip of orange juice. *I'm sure it all fits together somehow*, she thought. *I wish I could just understand how.*

'Am I in danger?' she scribbled.

Just then, there was a shuffle and loud squeak outside her door, and the sound of low, urgent voices. She climbed out of bed and walked over to the door to see what was happening. Through the circular window she could see three nurses crowding around a trolley. One ran off calling for a doctor. The corridor was well lit and she could see that there was an elderly lady on the trolley and that the nurses were trying to resuscitate her. Clarissa swallowed hard. She felt an urge to help, although she didn't know how she could, however great her gifts were. Still, she opened her door, and stood watching.

The elderly lady's face was wrinkled and pale yellow and her hair was white and frayed. Inside her mind Clarissa said a short prayer for her. *Dear God. Please help these nurses to save this old lady. But, if she's too tired, please take her in peace to join her loved ones.*

As she thought these words, she saw the wrinkles on the elderly lady's face fading, and her cheeks flushing pink. Her hair, too, started to darken, and take on a sheen. For a moment, she looked like the young and pretty girl that once she must have been. Only for a moment, though; the wrinkles returned almost immediately, and her hair whitened again. Clarissa realised that none of the nurses had seen this. Only she had seen it, because she could see what and who people really were.

One of the nurses checked the elderly lady's pulse, holding fingertips against her throat for a few seconds. Eventually she shook her head.

It was then that Clarissa saw a man standing at the foot of the trolley. A tall, elderly man, wearing a navy-blue jumper. Clarissa couldn't think why she hadn't noticed him at first, but all the same she had to strain her eyes hard to focus on him, as if he were a figure in a fog. She knew there were no visitors allowed at night. Then he became clear.

Clarissa moved back slightly, into her room. The man was staring at the elderly lady, with one arm outstretched toward her. He looked sad, as if he couldn't reach her, no matter how far he stretched out.

'Come home, Betty,' he said, although his mouth didn't appear to move. His voice was so clear that it sounded to Clarissa as if he were standing right beside her. Clarissa gasped, and a tear rolled down her cheek, and the man turned his head and stared at her directly.

'All I want is my wife back with me,' he said. 'I've come to take her home. I miss her.' Then he turned back to look at the elderly lady. 'Ada, come home.'

He turned the palm of his hand upward, and gestured as though he were about to receive a gift, or a blessing.

There was an eerie silence, and Clarissa even felt herself holding her breath.

'I'm sorry, we've lost her. There's nothing more we can do,' said the nurse who had taken her pulse.

'One sixteen am,' said another nurse, looking at her pocket watch.

Clarissa swallowed again, and felt an aching lump rise in her throat. Her lower lip puckered as her eyes welled up, and another tear slid down her cheek.

Just then, the tall old man turned to Clarissa and smiled as a short, elderly lady appeared beside him and took hold of his hand. 'I've been waiting for you,' he said softly to her, then they embraced each other and turned to walk away.

The silence turned into soft chattering and a bustling sound as the nurses moved and squeaked the trolley away slowly along the corridor.

Clarissa's sadness warmed into a feeling of peace as she watched the ghosts of the elderly couple. They turned one last time, smiled at her, and then they faded.

Visiting Hours in Bell Ward II

Toward sunrise, Clarissa had a dream about the elderly couple, walking along Mipsy's Lane in the sunshine, past the flowerbeds and the laurel bushes. She was on her way to see Ma and they were strolling towards her, arm-in-arm. They smiled her at her as they passed her by, and the elderly lady, very quietly, said, '*Thank you, Clarissa.*'

She woke up, and lay there for a while looking at the patterns of sunshine dancing across the ceiling. She realised now that yesterday night she had been shown how strong her gift was. If she could see that dying lady for what she really was, then she must be able to see Mark, too, for what *he* was, if only she could summon up the courage to confront him. She had seen him only once with a different face, when he had come to the top of the stairs at his apartment, and she had never seen him look like that since. She wondered if he suspected that she could see that side of his personality, and had made sure that he concealed it from her. Maybe that was the reason he had changed so much.

She was still lying there thinking when a plump African ward nurse came into her room and announced with a grin: 'Miss Davenport, you have a visitor.'

Right behind her came Paula, laden down as usual with shopping-bags and a large canvas satchel.

'Aww, Clarry!' said Paula. She put her bags down on a blue plastic chair beside the bed as Clarissa shuffled herself up to a seated position. Paula reached out to cuddle her.

'I came as soon as I heard. How are you feeling, babes?'

'Better, thanks. You smell *heavenly*,' she replied.

'Oh thanks! It's called Moi, by Grenatchie. Heaven in a

bottle, isn't it? Here, have some – it's in my bag. Hold out your wrists, sugar.' Paula scrambled about in her bag and pulled out a square perfume bottle.

'So are you feeling a *lot* better?'

'A little,' Clarissa replied, smiling. 'Thanks so much for coming.'

'Aw *shushh*, nonsense, you're part of my heart. In fact, Ben wanted to come too, but I said you may not be up to it. I know how you'd rather have a touch of make up on and be smelling of Chanel before you see a handsome man!'

Clarissa laughed.

'Oooh, talking of Chanel, I have a gift for you. From us. Here.'

Paula handed Clarissa a small bundle of wrapped boxes. 'I know, I know, Ben wrapped them – he wanted to be *involved*,' she smiled. She blushed slightly and encouraged Clarissa to open them.

'Ah darling, thank you – you shouldn't have. These must have cost you a *fortune!*'

'Just a little pick-me-up-slash-get-well present. It's their new mist and cream. I remembered number five was your favourite. Wanted to bring flowers, but they wouldn't let me in with them. Something about germs and insects. So I gave them to the tramp that I'd noticed at the end of the road. Made her day,' she smiled.

Tears welled up in Clarissa's eyes and she cuddled Paula again. 'Thank you, you're very sweet. And thank Ben too for me, will you?'

Paula nodded and made herself comfortable. 'You seem a little – flat. Talking of handsome men, how's Mark? I half expected to see him floating around in the corridors here, between coffee machines. And how is work going?'

'Oh, don't.' Clarissa used the edge of the sheet to wipe her eyes. 'Work's good, Hugo, my boss, is being very understanding. But it's over between Mark and me. He came to visit yesterday and I made the decision. It was horrible, but I know I've done the right thing. We went for a walk and talked in the rose garden. It's very pretty down there.'

'And what did he say? Did he try to change your mind?'

'He called me a whore. And he wouldn't discuss our relationship at all – just kept saying that us being friends wasn't an option.' Clarissa fiddled with the bed throw. 'I dunno, he's so strange. I'm so disappointed.'

'That *bastard*! How *dare* he call you a whore? You're loyal, and caring, and God knows you've been *patient* with him beyond belief! Jesus the arrogance of him! Who does he think he is? He's nothing so special. I'm so *mad*!'

'Hey, it's fine, I'm done with him.'

'You're too bloody nice.' Paula got up and paced around the room. 'What a tosser. Ben was right.'

'What?'

'Sorry sweetie, but I didn't really want to tell you – but Ben said that Mark was always staring at other women when you and I had gone to get drinks from the bar, and he even swapped numbers with this girl. He didn't think you should trust him an inch.'

Clarissa patted the bed. 'Come, darling, sit down. He's not worth you getting all worked up. You want a coffee?'

Paula walked over and sat down. 'Sorry, I just love you, you know, we both do. You're such an amazing and supportive person, all you need is a man to be the same with you. Especially after losing Craig.' She leaned over and gave Clarissa a hug. 'What an idiot Mark is.'

'Mark was wearing me down. I didn't want to admit it because I thought maybe it was me being over-cautious. I found him so attractive. In a weird way – can you believe it? – I think I still do. But I guess he just wasn't the right man for me after all. The doctor says that I'm suffering from exhaustion and emotional stress.'

'Ah, listen, I'm not bloody surprised.'

'My blood-pressure and my heart-rate are now fine. I had blood tests done yesterday and I should get the results tomorrow. I was just tired out, my confidence has been majorly knocked though by him, and I haven't been eating properly because of it all. Mark's been causing me much more strain than I realised. Then I had a shock that caused me to faint. I seriously need a break.'

'What was the shock?'

Clarissa frowned. 'I was doing some research in the local library about that chapel that Mark took me to – do you remember?'

Paula nodded. 'You said he was acting strange, even then.'

Clarissa told her all about the historian's suspicion that somebody had stolen the book from The North Chapel, and how she thought it was the same book that Mrs Cawsley-May had given her.

'That amazing lady, who died when she fell down the stairs at your gallery was involved in the orphanage?'

'She didn't *fall*, Paula. I never told you before. I haven't told anyone, because I knew that they wouldn't believe me. She was pushed.'

Paula stared at her in disbelief. 'She was *pushed*? Oh, my God! Who pushed her? And I mean – *why*?'

Apart from Mrs Ball, Clarissa had never spoken to anybody about the boy from Old Gorton Manor, or how much she dreaded his appearances. But she knew this was the time for her to gather all the strength and support that she could, not just from inside herself, but from everybody who loved her. She had a divine gift, like angels did, but she realised now that even angels need friends to give them fortitude.

'It was a *boy*,' she said, trying hard to keep her voice steady. 'A horrible little boy who's been following me all my life. The one that visits the flat. He killed Craig, too.'

'Clarry,' said Paula, frowning and taking hold of her hand. 'Are you sure you're all right? Do you want me to call for the nurse? You've gone pale.'

'No, I'm fine, Paula, honestly. In fact I feel better now than I have for ages. I'm not having a nervous breakdown and I haven't been hallucinating. I don't know who he is, this boy, or where he comes from, but he first appeared when I was eight years old, and after that he kept appearing, again and again. He looks very grey, and thin, as if he never gets enough to eat, and he always wears this scruffy grey blazer, and shorts, like an old-fashioned school uniform.

'My God, Clarry, that's so creepy. Why didn't you tell me everything about him before? I knew there were creepy things happening but this is massive.'

'Because I didn't see him for years and years. And then he appeared again, on the very first day I started at the gallery, and he's been stalking me ever since. The really creepy part is that he's never grown up. He still looks the same age as he did when I was eight. But he's real, P. I swear to you that it's the same boy, and he's absolutely real.'

Clarissa was so serious that she could see that Paula believed her – or at least believed that *she* believed it. 'Go on,' said Paula. 'I'm listening.'

'You need to be careful, keep in touch with me and if either of you notice anything weird in your new home will you let me know.'

'Yes, of course.'

After lunch, and Paula had gone to let her rest, Clarissa fell asleep.

She dreamed again, but this time she dreamed that she had reached the end of Mipsy's Lane and was walking through the bluebell woodland on her way to Ma's house. Through the trees she could see the smeary-faced man who had haunted her childhood staring at her, and raggedly-dressed children were skipping around a gnarled old oak tree. Then she heard Ma's voice, calling her in for tea. As Ma's voice echoed around the woodlands, all the children stopped dancing and all the squirrels stopped scampering between the trees. Every living being turned to stare at Clarissa as if they were blaming her for their life coming to a sudden stop. The colour drained from the vibrant bluebells and air turned foggy and chilled.

Then she woke up.

A cooled sweat had coated her skin, making her gown stick to her. She looked up and toward the door, as she heard the nurse coming.

'Well hello Miss Davenport, how are you feeling after your nap?' asked the ward nurse.

Clarissa looked at the nurse's name-badge. Grace Day.

'Hi, Grace. Okay thank you, I think. Is there any chance I could put my own pyjamas on? I had another nightmare, and I'm well – a bit –'

Just then a light knock sounded from the open door.

'Clarissa Davenport?' asked a smart, stocky doctor with a neat goatee beard. He walked directly to the edge of her bed, holding a red clipboard and a long blue pencil. Behind him, a young nurse shuffled in. She too was holding a clipboard, and she was frantically scribbling notes.

'Of course you can change, Clarissa, once the doctor has seen you,' the nurse told her, in a soothing tone.

'Nurse Day, do you have her recent notes?' asked the doctor. The nurse lifted a blue folder from the rack on the end of the bed, and handed it to him. 'Mm hmm. I'll be at my desk, doctor, should you need anything else.' As she did so she pouted and batted her eyelashes flirtatiously, but the doctor appeared not to notice; or, if he had, he had chosen to ignore her.

'I'm Doctor Reed,' he said, in a businesslike manner, as he scanned Clarissa's notes. 'Doctor Phoenix Reed, I'm a neurologist. I know Doctor Humphreys has been looking after you, but he asked me to come and see you because he was very interested in some of the answers you gave him when he first talked to you.'

'I'm not sure I understand,' said Clarissa.

'Oh, there's nothing at all to worry about. He's quite happy with your physical condition, although he says that you're underweight and could probably use a tonic. But when he told you that you were stressed, you said to him, "yes, in the same way that you are." And you made some comment about one of the nurses being very upset. He was interested to know how you could have known that she had just broken off her engagement.'

'I didn't know,' said Clarissa. 'I just thought that he did look rather stressed,' she said, trying not to make eye contact. 'And that nurse did seem very unhappy and tearful.'

Doctor Reed sat on the bed beside her and said, 'Take hold of my hand and squeeze it as tightly as you can.'

Clarissa did as he asked her. All the time Doctor Reed looked into her eyes and said, 'What year is it?'

She told him, and then he said, 'What's your address?'

She told him that, too.

'You can let go of my hand now,' he said, and then he handed her his clipboard, and his pencil. There was a blank circle on his clipboard and he said, 'Can you fill that in with numbers to make clock-face?'

After she had done that, he asked her to climb out of bed and walk towards the window and back. She felt embarrassed in her damp gown, but she did it.

'Any dizziness?' he asked her.

'None at all.'

'Very well, Clarissa,' said Doctor Reed, standing up. 'I know those seemed like very simple tests, but they showed me that you have no neurological problems. If Doctor Humphreys is happy, you should be fine to go home tomorrow. You need to take it very easy, that's all, because it's chronic stress that has landed you here. Relax as much as possible for a few days, and rest whenever your body tells you to.'

Clarissa said, 'Thank you,' and climbed back into bed, feeling relieved and reassured. Doctor Reed put on a pair of rimless spectacles and jotted some notes on his clipboard, but as he did so she saw that he had tears glistening on his cheeks.

'Doctor?' she said.

He glanced across at her, too off his spectacles and gave her a smile, and his tears were gone. *It must have been a trick of the light,* she thought. The sun shining through his spectacle lenses. Or maybe she had perceived that, like so many people, he was suffering some pain in his life that could only be seen by a

Diviner.

'It's okay, nothing.'

Doctor Reed smiled. He took his pager from his lab coat pocket and paused, frowning at it. Then he said: 'Take care young lady.' And with that, he walked away toward the door, with his assistant shuffling along after him.

Listed

The next morning, the sun was shining brightly again. Clarissa got out of bed and walked over to the window ledge, where she sat for a while and looked out across rooftops and suburban streets. She wished she could be out in a field somewhere, underneath a tree, reading. She wondered what the new collections of art at the gallery were like, how Maggie's holiday was going and how Ma was. Although she kept visiting her in her dreams, she hadn't seen her for over a month and it would be another week yet until she was back from her Mediterranean cruise with the Carragh-Hughs.

She sighed and fiddled with the plastic name tag on her wrist, feeling alone. *Miss Clarissa Davenport. DOB 2/2/80.* What would it have been like had she and Craig had more time together, would it say Mrs Clarissa Arlington? *Mind you if he was alive and we were married, I wouldn't be here in hospital at all,* she thought. *Not unless we were having a baby.*

A loud knocking came from behind her and disturbed her thoughts. She turned to see a tall, slim figure at the door.

'Come in,' she called out. To her surprise, it was Allison Dragby.

Allison smiled, gently closing the door behind her.

'I hope you don't mind,' she said. 'I wanted to see how you were, so I phoned the hospital and they said you were ready for visitors. The nurse just told me you are going home later today?'

She walked over to the blue plastic chair and took off her coat. 'Warmer than I expected out there today,' she said.

Clarissa smiled. 'Yes, it looks heavenly.' Clarissa tucked her hair behind her ears, remembering that the last time she felt that her life was heavenly was with Craig.

'Yes I get to go this afternoon. They'll be around with tea and coffee shortly – I'm sure they'll let you have one.'

'Tea would be nice.'

She walked over to the window ledge and sat on it next to Clarissa, and unzipped the brown satchel in her hand. 'Here. I brought this for you.

She handed Clarissa a large brown envelope. 'I thought you'd want an interesting read while you're in here, or take it home. It's yours. Maybe it will help you find some of the answers that you came looking for.'

'What is it?'

'A copy of all of the orphanage registers from the day it was first opened until the day of the fire. A complete list of all the children who were ever taken in and cared for. Well, I say complete – there's one book missing from World War Two, when the children were temporarily evacuated, but otherwise they're all there. Every single name.'

'Is it okay to keep this?'

Allison nodded. 'Of course. I made a copy for you.'

Clarissa took the envelope from her and pulled out a thick sheaf of printed pages. 'Thanks. I think I've read every copy of *Woman's Own* and *The Peoples' Friend* in the hospital – twice.'

'They're all photocopies but I think they're clear enough,' said Allison.

Clarissa leafed through the papers. 'Thank you so much, I'm sure this will really help.'

Allison blushed. 'It's one of the things I love about my job, putting puzzles together with other people. Sometimes it's for coursework or families, but sometimes, a real mystery – like yours.'

Clarissa looked at her and smiled. *It's a mystery all right*, she thought.

'How can I ever repay you?'

Allison waved her arm dismissively and smiled 'It's fine, really,' she said. 'So long as you find what you're looking for.'

That night when she was home again, Clarissa sat up poring over the papers that Allison had given her. Name after name of children who had come to the orphanage.

Clarissa pondered on why there were so many children. So many kids who ended up with no parents and nowhere else to go. So sad.

She turned another page and scanned down the names.

P Tempkins.

J Overton.

R Layard.

T Bruce.

A Stevens.

J Gold.

She stopped and looked back. *T Bruce.*

Clarissa had seen that name before. Thomas Bruce. It was the name of her firestarter.

She turned back several pages to the previous year. There it was again: *T Bruce.*

She shuffled the pages back ten years. There he was again.

She paused and gazed into space.

Strange.

She quickly looked at the latest set of sheets that she had. There, on the third page, was the name again. *T Bruce.*

T Bruce, Thomas Bruce, appears continually, in every register, every single year! How is that possible? Could there have been more than one? Or brothers?

Clarissa yawned. It was now two am. She put the papers back in the envelope and placed it beside her bed.

I must get some sleep now. It couldn't be a coincidence.

Could it?

The One

Clarissa looked around her bedroom. She was pleased to have been released from hospital and back at home. Her room felt cosy and comforting, as it always did. Sitting on her bed with a cup of tea, she looked at all the memories of Craig around her – paintings on her wall, books from the gallery, even one funny art book he'd bought her, called *Don't Fry Them Too Soon!* Maybe she would never get over Craig.

She looked up at the reproduction of Dante's painting of Beata Beatrix that hung by the wardrobe, and she remembered the emotion she had felt the first time she saw it. Craig had bought it for her as her twenty-third birthday present from the gallery, and she had fallen in love with it, just as he had fallen in love with her.

She flicked the light switch on and took the *All Angels* CD from her collection that Craig had bought her. She selected their song, *Sancté Deus*, Elgar. Turning the volume up high, she crouched down to open the drawer under her divan bed. She sat on the faux fur rug on the floor and made herself comfortable. Pulling a soft throw onto her shoulders, she reached into the drawer, and pulled out a satin pouch, which had a label hanging from it. In Craig's hand-writing it said: *Be mine, be my girl.* She remembered the Valentine's Day when he had given it to her. Inside the pouch she had found a silver necklace with a pendant of a feather. *Fly with me, through life* was engraved on the feather. Clarissa felt her throat tighten as she placed her hand onto her neck, caressing the necklace. She hadn't taken it off since the day he'd given it to her.

She opened a small flowery-patterned envelope, and unfolded the note inside. She remembered the rainy day that he had left it for her, taped to Mette Gauguin, saying to her 'tonight, my angel, you must say goodbye to dear Mette. She has something for you'.

She smiled and read the note:

> *My darling Clarry, my new heartbeat.*
>
> *You brought me back to feeling, back to my heart and its true purpose!*
>
> *Into my heart you crept, and in my heart you will always remain.*
>
> *Sometimes I feel it will be forever until you notice me.*
>
> *As I sit here with the angels on the hill with the evening sun glowing upon me, and wind blowing the blades of grass,*
>
> *I think of your face, smiling, and a power within me is falling for you –*
>
> *I wonder if you know how I feel? I'll let your heart choose, as I want you to feel freedom and happiness, and your heart to choose for you.*
>
> *But my dear, I am yours, forever and a whisper away,*
> *Craig.*

'You were the one, Craig,' she whispered. 'You *always* will be the love of my life. I miss you so badly it *hurts*.' She held the note closely to her chest and fell silent for a moment or two.

She slowly folded the note back up, and kissed it before tucking it back into its envelope.

The next thing in the pouch was a yellow handkerchief, in which Craig's favourite bracelet was wrapped. As she unravelled it she felt an overwhelming sadness. She knew it would smell of Craig, and she wondered why she was torturing herself – but she needed to feel close to him again, even if just for a moment.

She visualised Craig wrapping it around his wrist and fastening it. So she placed it on her wrist, and admired it. She closed her eyes and smelled it. It was then that she felt him with her.

'Clarry, why are you so sad?'

A tear rolled from the corner of her eye, and it felt cold as ice as it trickled down her cheek.

'Why won't you let me hold you at night when you cry, why are you so sad? You are so pretty. Why are you afraid? I can protect you. Let me hold you Clarry, my love, my darling angel.'

'You left me, *you left me,*' she sobbed.

At first she wasn't sure if she'd said those words, or cried them in her mind.

Clarissa felt a firm touch on her shoulder.

'But baby why would I leave you? I love you!'

'You were taken from me, by evil! Evil took my heart, it took *you!*' she cried. 'I never got to say goodbye, it was too soon, we had so much time to give, *oh Craig –*'

There was a moment of silence, although the music was caressing her ears, and her wrists cuddled into her chest as she whimpered.

Just then she felt a ripple of energy beside her. It then surrounded her and she felt internally lifted and comforted within seconds. She held his bracelet tightly and looked up.

'I'm so sorry, come back to me Clarry, please don't cry. I'm here, my darling, always and a whisper away.'

'I can't see you Craig, you're *dead,*' Clarissa's throat was aching so much and felt so tight that she was struggling to breathe normally as she once again sobbed into her hands.

'Open your eyes and see me.'

A chill swept across her back and Clarissa took in a long, strained breath.

She opened her eyes again slowly. As she lifted her head, Craig smiled.

'I'm never leaving you. I'm here my darling, I'm here,' he said.

There he was. Craig. She could see him just as clearly as she had seen the elderly man in the hospital corridor.

'Craig?' she cried.

She could not only see him, she could *smell* him – she was sure.

'But – but Craig –'

'Shh, darling, everything will be okay. Be at peace with yourself, forgive yourself. I am *always* only a whisper away. Just hold my bracelet whenever you need me. You must find happiness now my darling. I will see you smiling one day at the altar, I want you to find happiness now.'

Bartholomew

The following afternoon, Clarissa showered and dressed to Elgar's *Salut d'amour*. She felt lifted, and the music danced in her heart. It was though there was now confirmation of, and comfort from, an angel within her soul.

She wanted to visit Mrs Ball again, because there was so much that she needed to ask her.

Her emotional strength had been renewed more than she could have hoped by the support that she had received from Paula and Allison, and also from seeing Craig again. Now she was determined to discover why the boy had been plaguing her again, and how she could be free of him – or at least, how she could prevent him ever again from harming any more people she loved and fight back.

Clarissa took off her wellingtons as she entered The Snug and shut the garden room door behind her. She shivered, and rubbed her hands together, but she was greeted with warmth from within the house.

'Ahh, it's lovely and warm! It's very nippy out there today. Winter's arrived!'

She smiled at Mrs Ball and made a tutting sound at the cats as they sat by the fire. A fat tabby looked up at her and squinted.

'Hello, dear. Yes. The cats know the right place to be in life, look at them all by the fire. Where does the time get to? The seasons seem to come and go so soon! I hope you are feeling better, dear.'

Clarissa took off her coat and smiled. 'Much better, thank you.'

'Help yourself to a cup of tea, this is a fresh pot here,' she said, patting the multi-coloured bobbles of the tea cosy.

'Thanks, very much needed.' Clarissa went into the kitchen and returned with a china tea cup and saucer.

'I asked you here today, dear, as I have something very special for you.'

Clarissa took a sip of tea. 'Oh?' she said. She put her cup down and pushed up her sleeves to make herself comfortable.

Mrs Ball reached out and handed Clarissa a small bundle of blueish-grey fur. It was so soft that Clarissa's fingers sank right in until she felt a bony little body.

'Your very own Persian kitten,' smiled Mrs Ball. 'He's a gift from me. A bundle of magic, you might say.'

Clarissa gasped in delight. 'Aaah! He's beautiful! Thank you!'

She felt such excitement that she thought if she were a balloon she might burst. Clarissa sat down next to Mrs Ball's rocking chair and cradled the kitten, looking in his big stormy blue eyes.

'I'll call him Bartholomew!' Bartholomew blinked, and expressed a weak mewing sound. 'He likes it!' she giggled.

'Bartholomew it is dear. Bartholomew is the patron saint of bookbinders and leather-workers and also those with unusual mental powers.'

'Really? I didn't know that. Aw I can't thank you enough! I've always wanted a Persian Blue!'

'I know, dear.'

Mrs Ball smiled with pursed lips. Clarissa made some soft kissing sounds while looking at Bartholomew, stroking his head and the back of his tiny ears.

'Mrs Ball, I have something I need to talk about with you.'

Mrs Ball took her glasses off and smiled at Clarissa in a knowing way. Clarissa felt as though she could tell her anything. After all these years and at her age, she still needed and appreciated her friendship and guidance. She looked her in the eye, and knew that her affection was returned. Looking back down at Bartholomew, she felt strangely as if she had gained an energy from him.

'Have you ever heard of – or witnessed, someone coming back to life? Even for a brief moment? Someone you thought was – *dead?*' Clarissa didn't look at Mrs Ball, because although she knew she wasn't mad, she was, however, slightly embarrassed.

'Tell me more dear. If you're asking me if I've seen a ghost, then yes, I do believe I have.'

'Not a ghost. Well, I don't think so. I actually spoke to him. And saw him. He looked – real. Solid.'

Mrs Ball patted her lap, encouraging her white cat onto it, and stroked it into a comfortable position. 'Can I ask who we are talking about?'

Clarissa stopped stroking Bartholomew. 'My – someone very close to me. *Was* close to me. Craig, my boyfriend that I mentioned.'

She shook her head in sympathy but Clarissa had the feeling that she already knew about it all– in fact, that she already knew everything that she had come here to tell her.

'I'm so sorry,' said Clarissa. 'At the time, I didn't think that even you would believe me. The police thought that he committed suicide, but he was murdered by the boy. I saw him, just after he'd done it, and then he vanished. I didn't tell anybody apart from Paula – who would have believed me? It was the same boy who killed Mrs Cawsley-May. Craig was the love of my life. And it was Craig who I saw yesterday. He came to me.'

Mrs Ball raised her eyebrows. She didn't say anything.

'He came to me last night in spirit. He was wonderful. I still love him. Thing is, he was really there. In my room. With me. But I wasn't scared, it was very different to any experience that I've ever had before.'

Clarissa stood up and with Bartholomew in one hand, she took her tea cup into the kitchen and placed it on the draining board.

'The thing is, I can't understand why this boy is killing people I love. I can't believe how powerful he must be to have changed Mark like that, and for me to doubt the power that I've been given. You were right – it must be because of the boy. But what does it all mean? I ended my relationship with Mark because he was making me feel so frustrated and frightened. He became so complicated that I couldn't take it anymore. But now, all these weeks later, I'm certain I can still feel Mark near me at times, or the boy, or whoever he is. Sometimes I think he's following me when I leave work alone, or when I walk into the kitchen late at night I'm sure he's there, standing in the hallway. Sometimes I think he's standing in the corner of the bathroom watching me when I'm taking a shower. It's really creepy, it's like he won't leave me alone.' She sat back down at the table. 'It must sound so crazy, I know. And now that I've seen Craig ... well ...' Clarissa stood up again, cradling Bartholomew in her arms and began to walk around the room.

'Craig told me to forgive myself. That he wants me to find happiness. But he also wants me to be careful.' She stopped by the archway and looked at a print of a large oil painting that hung in the hallway, opposite the handmade sign saying *Welcome to The Snug!* The painting was called *A Girl with a Kitten*, dated 1745. It was one of her favourite pieces. The black Bombay kitten was perched on the girl's lap, but as Clarissa she looked at it, it turned its head away from her and nestled into the girl's arm.

She stared back at it, but it didn't move again.

'I know that this boy wants something from you,' said Mrs Ball. 'As I said to you before, though, you must never let him have it, no matter how much he frightens you.'

Clarissa took another quick look at the kitten in the painting, but it hadn't moved again. She walked slowly back towards Mrs Ball, still cradling Bartholomew in her arms, 'I don't really understand what I have that the boy could possibly want. Whatever it is, he wants it so badly that he was ready to kill the one person I've ever truly loved. I'm terrified that he's going to kill me next.'

'Don't be afraid for yourself,' said Mrs Ball. 'Your talismans and your holy water will protect you from malevolent spirits. Apart from which, very few spirits have the power to harm you. Diviners are descended from very much higher powers than most demons.'

Clarissa sat down beside the fire. 'I'm so confused,' she said.

'You don't sound overly confused to me. You are thinking clearly and wisely.'

Mrs Ball watched as she settled into her armchair, stroking

Bartholomew, and tucking her hair behind her ear as she always did when she was thinking. She could see how worried and confused Clarissa was, and how deeply she was breathing but she didn't say anything. She just smiled.

Just then, Clarissa felt a chill run down her back, although her cheeks were flushed from the warmth of the fire. Mrs Ball sat up straight, as if she too had felt some disturbance in the room.

Bartholomew mewed and the white cat leapt off Mrs Ball's lap and cowered by the door, its back arched and its hair on end. It bared its teeth and hissed, staring at Mrs Ball with wild eyes.

'He's not – he's not *here*, is he?' asked Clarissa. 'He's not listening to us?'

'The cats certainly seem to think that there's something here, dear. And I can feel it, too.'

Clarissa didn't know what to say. Had their conversation about Mark and her worry attracted his presence into the room, in the same way that she had felt his presence close behind her when she was vulnerable on her way home from the gallery, or in her flat? Was he actually here somehow? Now?

A moment later, though, the chilly feeling passed, as if the front door had been closed, and the room was warm again. Mrs Ball seemed to relax, and made kissing noises at her white cat. She shook her head and said:

'What's wrong with you, you silly thing?' But the white cat turned sharply, and ran off toward the kitchen. 'Silly kitty. You had me worried there for a moment.'

'Are you okay Mrs Ball? I mean – I really thought I felt – and you said that *you* felt it too.'

'It's all right, dear. Whatever it was, it's gone as quickly as it came in. Now, where were we again?'

Clarissa let out a sigh of relief. 'Phew, for a moment there, I thought –' She looked down at Bartholomew and began stroking him again. 'Never mind.'

Mrs Ball looked down and across at Clarissa and stared at her, curiously, and smiled.

'Clarissa, dear, I will explain something to you. Diviners are not mediums but they can feel the presence of people that have passed over. If a person is possessed they can sense that, too, and sometimes actually see it in their face as you did with Mark. But some malevolent spirits can hide themselves deep inside the person they possess and are very difficult even for Diviners to detect. This is why it can be hard to sense good from bad, or figure out if they just have a bad side. Sometimes they will make themselves attractive to Diviners in order to deceive them and allay their suspicions. Be very choosy who you befriend, my dear.'

Ghosts of the Gallery

Following the 'all clear' from the doctor, Clarissa felt ready to get back into her daily routine, although remembering his advice: 'Take it easy Miss Davenport. Work minimal hours and rest when your body tells you to. You allowed yourself to become exhausted.' He had told her.

It was raining as she walked today, but she didn't mind with an umbrella because she loved the way everything smelled earthy during the rainfall and she felt refreshed and inspired by it.

As she reached the gallery doors, she pulled a large bunch of keys from her jacket pocket and took hold of a flat silver key.

She unlocked the doors and turned off the alarm before placing her umbrella in the tub. *Eight twenty.*

The gallery was cold inside, and although she'd missed being there, it felt extremely eerie even in the morning. Every step she took echoed. She'd never been in here alone before, and in the past Craig had always unlocked and opened up ready for work, and was always there to greet her with a wide, delighted grin, and sometimes even a glass of champagne, although it was often only nine o'clock in the morning.

'Breakfast!' he used to tell her, and then kiss her.

She wondered if Craig ever felt afraid or strange coming in here when he was the first to arrive, in this cold empty space, with all the figures and artistic interpretations of stories hanging on the walls.

As she closed the door and locked it, in the half-light she saw the replica bust of Mette Gauguin to her right. A sad, reminiscent shudder went through her as she looked at it. Then Craig's voice ran through her mind: *'A bientot, mon ami'*. She raised a half-smile. *Pull yourself together Clarissa,* she told herself. *He'd want you laughing at Mette Gauguin being trapped in a glass box on her own in here, not feeling sad at something he'd always said. Now come on.* She straightened herself and exhaled heavily.

'Craig,' she whispered, 'please be with me tonight and look after me, and make sure I get home safely. I am going to walk because my car's in the garage. They offered me a temporary car but I declined. I bought that black Alfa Romeo Spider that you always liked, it's so chunky and sporty, I love it. Anyway, let me know you're here with me. Please.'

She closed her eyes, trying to picture Craig's face. As she did so, she felt a cool breeze on the back of her neck, almost as if he were standing close behind her, and her heart tingled.

She walked over to the large panel of light switches on the wall. One by one, she flicked the switches on, watching the vast empty space of the gallery gradually light up. Each section and recess became illuminated by soft lighting. Once the main room downstairs had lights on, she clicked on the switches for the mezzanine floor.

She walked across to the staircase and looked up. A flashback of Mrs Cawsley-May ran through her mind, lying right here, dead. Blood. Pearls. Fur. Screams. She placed her hand onto the thick metal handrail at the bottom of the staircase and looked around the room to take her mind off the flashback images, before she began a solitary, slow walk up the stairs. She wished she'd put the music system on quietly, so that she felt less alone.

When she reached the top, she stopped and looked back, over the balcony. She remembered how Craig once stood here, assuming he could kiss her. She smiled to herself: *I never thought that would have been a fond memory,* she thought. *Now it's a very precious one.*

She let go of the handrail and walked to the far wall. The echo of her footsteps, and the rustle of her jacket sleeves as she walked, made it sound as though there was somebody else walking with her.

She felt drawn in one particular direction, and went with her feeling and walked until she found herself stopping in front of a modern and rather uninspiring painting of a crow. It was entitled *Le Caroslaid Crow.* She remembered how much Craig had disliked this painting. He thought it was a stupid and crudely executed picture, with no depth or reason, except that the crow had a cruel beady look in its eye. She could almost hear Craig's laughter as she studied it. For a moment, she thought she could smell him, too. It made her smile as she remembered what he would say about it. In a strange way, something about the crow reminded her of Mark's inane *Le Loo* sign on his bathroom door. *Maybe,* Le Caroslaid Crow *would be a perfect picture to hang in* Le Loo, *she thought.*

She carried along the central part of the mezzanine floor. She walked past *The Temptation of St Anthony,* and as she looked at it, it was though she could hear all of the beasts in the painting groaning and squawking.

She reached a small recess and smiled, as she instantly thought of Granny and Granddad. She was standing in front of a large painting of a dahlia. *I don't remember seeing this before,* she thought. *It must have arrived while I was in hospital. It's beautiful.*

Ma had once told a story of Granny and Granddad loving this flower and when they had died, Ma had planted their precious dahlias in her garden, and then grown even more in their memory, of all different colours. Next to the painting, was written: *Dahlia: Named after the 18th century botanist Anders Dahl. As a symbol, a dahlia flower can offer a great deal of meaning. In general, they are thought to symbolize dignity and elegance. But they are also thought to express an eternal bond between two people.*

Clarissa remembered when Ma had cut some dahlia heads and placed them in water, for her to keep in her bedroom. *They are thought to express an eternal bond* – she thought. *I wonder if Ma knew?*

At that moment Clarissa could hear a burst of muffled, male laughter and voices. She turned and walked to the edge of the mezzanine floor so she could see the entrance of the gallery. Through the rain-smothered glass she could see four men outside wearing high-visibility coats, with WATER emblazoned on the back. They were laughing loudly, even though that laughter was muffled by the glass doors. Strangely, Clarissa felt a sense of safety because she now knew she physically wasn't alone here anymore, and felt relieved.

She headed to the rear section, toward Burne-Jones' *The Mirror Of Venus*, an oil painting showing Venus and her maidens gazing at their reflections in a pool of water. The landscape around them was arid and rocky. She looked at the women in it, and the mixture of passion and distress on their faces. She wondered if she stared at it long enough, would the boy appear in the lake, as she had seen that day after school, at the pond? Or like these women, would she see a reflection that disturbed her?

As she stared at it, she thought she glimpsed a shadow flitting across the mezzanine floor, off to her left. When she turned to look at it directly, though, there was nothing there.

There were two paintings by John Everett Millais. She read the sign beside the first: *A Huguenot, on St Bartholomew's Day, Refusing to Shield Himself From Danger by Wearing The Roman Catholic Badge.*

'Bartholomew, what a coincidence,' she whispered. *But there's no such thing as a coincidence*, she thought.

Next to it was another of Millais': *The Woodman's Daughter*. She stepped closer. Something seemed very familiar about this painting. She felt very drawn to it, as though it knew she was looking at it. She felt a sensation of tingling across her face, and she felt the fine hairs on her face stand on end as she got closer. The painted woodman was in the background, behind two children. Clarissa felt that if this piece were alive, as though she was looking through a window into a woodland, and that the woodman would turn and grin at her as he stooped over a fallen tree. In front of the woodman, stood a little boy, holding out his arm toward a little girl. Clarissa leaned in even closer and squinted.

She felt her heart thump. She shuddered as though those horrible red ants were swarming over her body again, in that all-too-familiar warning. It was then, that she realised why it appeared so familiar.

The girl was her, as she had looked when she was a little girl. And the boy was *the* boy.

She gasped in shock and stepped back.

'Oh my God! This can't be happening,' she whispered. Panic was rising inside her. She could feel herself trembling. She leaned in again to get a closer look at the picture.

'It – really is – *it's me.'*

A banging sound echoed from downstairs. It banged again. And again.

Clarissa stepped backwards, away from the painting. She didn't like how she was feeling and how the woodman was looking at her, and she had no idea who was making the banging sound.

There it was again.

She pulled out her holy water and tooth from her jacket pocket. She stood still.

The banging stopped.

'This way,' whispered a gentle voice. She wasn't sure if she was right, but it sounded like Sarah or Sally Olven's voice. *'This way, Clarissa. hurry.'* it repeated.

Without hesitation, she let the voice guide her. She followed the voice along a narrow walkway and up another set of stairs and stopped outside the office.

'Safe, here,' whispered the voice. *'Be still.'*

Clarissa closed the door behind her. It was warm in this room. Warm but pitch dark: there was no window. She flicked the light on, and tugged her mobile phone out of her pocket and began to text Paula. *Never going to believe this. Call you asap. In gallery alone. Something scary is going on.* She leant in close to the door, and listened carefully.

She could hear it. It was here. Clarissa stepped away from the door and crouched down, covering her eyes. *What do I do? What do I do?*

There was a cracking sound and the air turned instantly, freezing cold.

'Afiste mas!' screamed the same voice that had led her into safety, into this dark office. *'Afiste mas!'*

Clarissa recognised the Greek from Mrs Ball as *leave us.*

There was an overwhelming roar, so loud and cracking in the

air that Clarissa had to cover her ears.

Then, gradually, it faded. She opened her eyes and the lights had gone out. The door was still shut. There was total silence and Clarissa was alone once again, in the darkness.

Panting, Clarissa scrambled for the door and pulled it open. She hurried down the gallery stairs, being careful not to lose her footing or slip on the marble flooring. She re-set the alarm, flung the door open and hastily locked it behind her as the alarm bleeped.

As she locked the door from the outside she felt hesitant, as though she wasn't meant to leave without telling her boss or being accompanied by Craig, or someone else to keep her safe. Regardless of Craig's flamboyant effeminate nature, she was beginning to realise just how safe he had made her feel. The workmen had gone and she stepped back and looked at the empty space behind the locked doors. Anything could be in there, watching her.

She crossed the road and walked through the fine rain towards Ma's house for some reassurance. Realising she'd forgotten her umbrella in her panic, she tapped out a message to Hugo Walker explaining that she wasn't feeling up to being at the gallery but that the initial checks for the day were complete ready for opening. The clouds were low and grey, and the silhouettes of the shop buildings looked increasingly menacing, as though they were closing in on her, and she was being watched from their dark upstairs windows.

As Clarissa made her way along the dimly-lit street, she glanced into Gretta's Bakery, where a three-tier wedding cake sat at the front of the large bow window. The two small figures on top of it made her think of herself and Craig, and what a life they could have had together. She thought she heard footsteps behind her, and when she looked over her shoulder she was sure she could see a shadow moving in the doorway of a shop on the opposite side of the street.

She walked faster, breathing hard, until at last she reached

Mipsy's Lane. Although she was only a fifteen minute walk from her home, now that she could smell wood-smoke, it reassured her that she wasn't alone, and that there were normal, comfortable people at home. As she turned the corner, however, she stopped dead.

Someone was standing under the streetlamp halfway along the lane – a tall man wearing a long black raincoat with a hood. He was motionless, with his hands in his pockets, and he was facing in her direction as if he had been waiting for her. She gasped, and felt a deep palpitation of sheer panic. She stood rigid, uncertain what to do next. She looked across to the cottage chimney where the smoke was coming from. *Perhaps I could run to their front door, and knock on it. Even if he caught up with me first, perhaps they would hear me scream.* She looked back at the man, who hadn't moved. This was the only way to Ma's cottage, and so she had no option but to walk past him. *Perhaps there will be a police car driving around, or a dog walker. Perhaps I should ring for a taxi. Why didn't I arrange for one to meet me from the gallery as soon as I took my car into the garage for its service? If I turn back now the man might follow me. And the boy might be at the gallery.*

Taking a deep steadying breath, she continued walking. As she walked, she gripped the handle of her bag, and put her other hand in her pocket where her keys to Ma's house were, and gripped them, as a defence weapon. The figure raised his head, as though looking at Clarissa, but his face was hidden by the hood. She tried to walk briskly and confidently, but she was silently praying that she would be kept safe from harm. She didn't know to whom she was praying but she hoped that if anyone was listening – Craig, or God, or any of his angels, or the spirits of past Diviners – that they would help her now.

Determined not to appear frightened, she looked at the figure as she passed the streetlamp. He lifted his head again, though not enough for her to see more than his lips. His chin looked pitted and unshaven with prickly white stubble that sparkled in the lamplight. He didn't say anything, and neither did she.

Her heart beating hard, she carried on walking as fast as she could and reached the end of the path without looking back.

The Secret

Clarissa sat on Ma's sofa, with a throw over her. She was exhausted, as if she had relived all the troubled events of her recent past, and all the emotions that had come with them. Looking at the clock, she saw it was probably time that she got up and went home. Although it was only just midday the fire was lit, and she could hear the floorboards creaking outside the room in the hallway, and Ma talking on the telephone. However, she sat there for a while, just to allow the tumultuous emotions that she experienced in her current nightmares to fade away.

When Ma came back into the room, Clarissa said, 'I can't keep it to myself any longer, Ma. It's all too much.'

Ma took hold of her hand as if – like Mrs Ball – she already knew what Clarissa was going to say.

With tears in her eyes, Clarissa told Ma how Craig had really died, and how the boy had tugged Mrs Cawsley-May down the stairs, too. She told her about Mark, and the man along the footpath, and how she could see people's true character in their faces, whether they were good or evil.

'Ma, *oh Ma,*' cried Clarissa as she cuddled into her shoulder.

'I'm so pleased that you've told me all this,' said Ma. 'I knew this day would come, I just didn't know when. I'm so sorry I couldn't be there for you, why do things always happen when I'm on one of my cruises?'

'So that I go to Mrs Ball instead, for guidance. It probably happens for a reason,' sniffed Clarissa.

'I need to tell you the truth about your father, darling, you were just too young before. At least now you will believe me, and understand for yourself.'

Ma pulled away and tucked Clarissa's hair behind her ears for her.

'It's the right time now. But before I tell you, darling, please believe me when I say that everything will be all right in the end. I promise you.'

Clarissa felt tired and confused and her head was aching from crying and talking with Ma for most of the day.

Very gently, Ma had explained to her that when she was only five years old her father had been found murdered. For weeks before he had been killed, he had told Ma that he had seen a boy hanging around outside their house, almost every day, and that he had seen him several times watching Clarissa in the garden as she played. Once he had caught him following her along the path to her friend's house, and he had confronted him and told him to stay away.

'He was a sulky-looking boy, very scruffy, dressed in grey, that's how your father described him. But he wasn't just sulky. Your father said that he could see wickedness in him, and that he was frightened for you. "I'm really scared that he wants to hurt Clarry," that's what he said.'

'He sounds exactly like the same boy who killed Craig, and Mrs Cawsley-May. But how could he be? Father died over seventeen years ago.'

'I don't know,' said Ma. 'But your father was like you – he could see things that other people couldn't see. He didn't like to talk about it much, but he told me once that he could see spirits. However unlikely it seems, I believe that it was the same boy.'

'I still can't believe Father was murdered too' said Clarissa. 'Why was nothing reported?'

'The truth didn't come out because it was simply unbelievable. A scruffy young boy murdering a fit, grown man, and without any apparent motive? A boy that nobody else had seen around the neighbourhood? I couldn't tell the police, and I couldn't tell you when you were young – I couldn't have my little girl scared of the dark, or what looked like ghosts – especially since you were a Diviner and your life was always going to be filled with phantoms, of one kind or another. I didn't tell you for the same reason that you didn't tell the police detective about the boy when Craig was killed. There are some things that officials don't understand – some things that society can't understand, or *accept*, more to the point.'

'How did father die?' asked Clarissa, although she wasn't sure that she really wanted to know. Her mind would create a picture of him lying dead, and she would never be able to erase it – instead of the way she remembered him now – smiling and laughing and carrying her on his shoulders.

Ma's eyes filled with tears. 'Your father was found in Gorham Woods, by the motorway. He'd been stabbed, several times. Once through the heart. He told me that morning that he had seen the boy hanging around again and that he was going to chase him away for good and all. You and I know the boy was responsible, darling, just as he was responsible for murdering Craig and Mrs Cawsley-May. But he police think that they were purely random attacks by deranged individuals or with poor Craig, a suicide, with no connection between them, so you won't be implicated. In any case, even if they *did* believe us, the police can't arrest and charge ghosts, can they?'

'But I *am* to blame! If Father hadn't tried to protect me, he wouldn't have been murdered! And if wasn't for me, Craig and Mrs Cawsley-May would still be alive, too!'

'Now, now, darling. That's not true. Do you *really* think you or I are to blame for your father's death, or Craig's murder? You can't blame yourself. *You* didn't do anything wrong. Please don't feel guilty, darling.'

'Does Maggie know about all of this – about me being a Diviner and Mrs Ball, and father?'

'Yes. That's why she gave you such a hard time growing up – because she knew you were special, too. It seemed cruel but she was jealous, although she really had nothing to be jealous about.'

'Special? You mean a Diviner – she knew *and* you knew? But – how –'

Ma patted the sofa seat next to her, encouraging Clarissa to sit down beside her. She gave her a warm, saddened smile.

'I'd watch you play with those little buttons, line your teddies up on your bed, knowing you were sensitive to numeric coincidences and people's energies. One day when you were counting buttons you stopped at seven – and I felt alarmed, and when you came back from the toilet you soon completed what you were doing – to fourteen.

'I'd often look through your sketch book while you were asleep, too. Those faces that you used to draw darling – I was concerned for your own safety that it would be true. That you *were* a Diviner. But once I knew, I also knew you would find your talisman and have your Watchers when the time was right, when you were ready to receive it.'

'You mean the button and the Olven twins?'

Ma nodded.

'All along you knew.'

Clarissa stood up and took a tissue from the box in the centre of the coffee table, and blew her nose.

'I don't mean to sound angry with you Ma, I'm sorry It's just such a shock. I do understand why you had to wait,' she smiled, and gave Ma a hug. 'It couldn't have been easy for you.'

Ma hugged her in return, then said: 'After seeing your school sketchbook I arranged to meet your art teacher, Mrs Ball. Because your father was exceptionally good at drawing faces too – it was the first sign. Actually, I'll show you his work later if you'd like?'

Clarissa nodded enthusiastically, still feeling shocked that her mother had been able to keep this secret from her for so long, trying not to let any frustration rise.

'Mrs Ball confirmed my beliefs about you. It was then that I realised how advanced a Diviner you were, even at that tender age.'

'So father really was a Diviner too. And so is Mrs Ball.'

Clarissa shook her head disbelief and exhaustion, and settled back onto the sofa next to Ma.

'Yes. And Maggie was always worried she'd lose you, too. The easiest way for her to deal with your father's death was detaching herself from you.'

Clarissa frowned. 'So how did she find out about me?'

'Maggie overheard a conversation I had with Mrs Ball. Let's

just say that Mrs Ball has been in the background of our lives for a very long time. It wasn't a coincidence that she was your relief art teacher at school, either. Maggie thought it was a curse of some sort when your father had died.'

Ma plumped a cushion and placed it behind her back.

'Life may seem cruel darling at times, but everything has its reasons and ways of working out. Who was I to interfere with what God had intended for you?'

Ma clicked on the standard lamp and placed a large folder down onto the table in front of Clarissa followed by a glass of whisky.

'Are you okay, darling?'

'Yes, Ma. Just getting my head around everything.'

She opened the large file. A small black and white photograph slipped out and landed on the floor. Clarissa tried to catch it and spilled her whisky on the table.

'Whoops!' said Ma, protecting the file. 'I'll get a cloth.'

Clarissa picked up the photograph with both hands. Suddenly, she had a sick feeling in the pit of her stomach and felt the blood drain from her face.

'Clarissa?' Ma walked back in the room and wiped the whisky slops. She looked at Clarissa. 'Whatever is the matter?'

'Who – Ma – *who is this* in this photograph?'

'That's the vicar who married your father and me, darling, when he was very young. Such wonderful memories. Oh, he was a character.' She smiled a fond, calm smile. Ma folded the cloth and put it aside.

'Why?'

'That,' Clarissa said, '*that is the boy.*'

'Oh don't be silly, darling. Look, look where he is. He's at church with his friends and his mother. He's not *evil*. Goodness, he grew up to be a vicar!'

'I see the boy in his face! What if – what if this boy had possessed him, and – and *he* killed father?'

'Nonsense. It's not the boy. Vicars are like God's messengers. They may not all be perfect but they are not demonic. They are protected.'

'Ma –'

'I'm sure it wasn't him. Here. Look at some of your father's drawings.' Ma said, as she sat down and picked up the file.

'But –'

'Come on. You're tired. Let's relax now and look through these pictures. I promise you it wasn't the vicar.'

Clarissa didn't want to contradict Ma, or upset her memories, so she decided to stay quiet. But *it is him*, she thought. He wasn't only following when I was little. He's been following me, even before I was born.

The file of her father's drawings was filled with toothless women and grimacing children, and grotesque struggling images of dogs killing angels, and dark, countryside landscapes.

'Your father became very depressed, he'd have nightmares about being stranded in evil woodlands, where every living being around him was watching him. Look at this one.'

Clarissa felt sad for her father, and wondered if he had anyone to support him, as she had with Mrs Ball.

'Did Mrs Ball help him, too? Who were his Watchers? Did he have anybody like the Olven twins?'

Ma hesitated. 'Oh, those are things we don't need to concern ourselves with, dear.'

'He didn't tell you, did he?'

Ma looked at Clarissa as if to say *No*.

Clarissa sat up for hours looking at all of the old photograph albums. Here she was, as a child, playing in Granny's garden, here she was at school, one eye closed against the sunlight and here were the pictures that Ma had shown her tonight.

How could she sleep alone tonight knowing that her father was buried in the very cemetery in which she had always found peace? Was that why she had always felt so calm there, so connected to the dead who were lying around her? She still had a dull headache and her mind was racing. She held the little photograph of her father in her fingers.

'What happened, Father? What *really* happened? And how do I stop myself or anyone else being killed by the boy? I can't, can I? Sometimes I feel as though there is nothing I can do.'

The Cemetery

Clarissa waved to a neighbour as she crossed the road with Ma towards the cemetery.

'What a lovely sunny winter's day it's turning into!' said Ma. 'Thank goodness we didn't bring our hats too!'

Clarissa smiled, but didn't really want to discuss the weather.

'Where's Father's grave?' Clarissa asked her.

'It's in the very last row, on the left-hand side.' Ma gave Clarissa an understanding look and said: 'I'm just going to have a wander around as the sun is out. I think I will visit Mary's grave, too. I'll come and find you, darling, when you've had some time alone.'

Ma squeezed her hand and walked off.

Clarissa stood still. The cemetery had never made her feel unsettled, she had always found it private, and quiet, and she had always felt happy here. It had been months since she had last been here and now the grass was yellow and straggly and wet from the recent rain and thick, and uncut, and some of the headstones were nearly hidden.

Clarissa heard footsteps crunch across the main gravel path, and looked to her right to see a dark-haired man, wearing a black suit and a long, heavy coat. Ma had walked out of sight. Clarissa watched the man. He walked past her without noticing her. In his hands he held an iPad, and rubbed his forehead as though following information or directions from it. She continued to watch him, intrigued. He walked to the far left of the graveyard and Clarissa felt tempted to follow him to see what he was searching for. Was he looking for something – as she was today? He finally stopped and crouched in the distance to look at a headstone, disappearing from Clarissa's sight behind the long grass.

She began walking in the direction Ma suggested. Across the

path was a nearby bench facing the wintry sun with a robin hopping around it. It felt wonderful to have the sun's glow on her face and Clarissa began to relax a bit.

Beside her was the chapel, and on its roof stood a noisy crow. Clarissa listened to its squawks before it flapped and flew off. She thought about why crows always appeared in cemeteries, and remembered a detective book she'd read called *The Crow's Eye* and on its front cover, there was a picture of a crow on a church steeple. She remembered *Le Caroslaid Crow*, too, with its one beady eye.

She began to feel deeply apprehensive that she was about to see where her father was laid to rest. There was a crunching sound on the gravel and she opened her eyes to see the man with the iPad walking towards her. This time he had noticed her.

'Hello,' he said with a wide, respectful smile.

'Hi there,' said Clarissa.

'It is what you make it, you know – *life*,' said the man. He stopped and looked around. Then he smiled again.

'Some people would find you morbid, you know. Standing here amongst all of these dead people. Gone, every one of them, never to return. Once loved, now gone.'

Clarissa looked curiously at him, expecting to see something frightening in his face at any second. *What an odd thing to say to a stranger*, she thought. *He doesn't know why I'm here.*

He looked at her, and she saw a softness in his grey eyes, and genuine, kind face.

'I'm here to visit someone,' she replied. 'I like the peace, it's strangely beautiful in here.'

The man nodded and looked down at his feet as if he expected them to start walking off before he was ready. Then he looked back at Clarissa.

'Beautiful? Yes, it certainly is, in its own way,' he said. 'Even when the crows are making all that racket. It reminds you that beauty can be found in the most deathly of places. But – vice versa, of course.'

Like Leonardo's grotesque paintings, she thought, and like the beauty of the gallery, in spite of the death that happened there.

The man put his iPad underneath his arm and began to walk off. "Bye now.'

"Bye, you too –' she said softly. She watched him go, her hand raised to shield her eyes from the low winter sun.

She then felt an extraordinary surge of urgency, as if she had been meant to cross paths with this man and that he hadn't finished what he had intended to say to her, and had an urge to call him back.

'Sir! Excuse me!' Clarissa shielded her eyes and waited for the man to turn around. As he did so, she walked towards him.

'I hope you don't find me rude, but can I ask, if you're researching a family member?'

The man smiled.

'Yes. It's quite fascinating. Would you like me to walk with you to the headstone you are looking for while I tell you? If I'm not interrupting your peace, of course.'

She didn't understand why, but she nodded and said, 'Yes please.'

Clarissa walked beside him. His tie was loosened and she couldn't help but notice his trousers that were slightly too short for him.

'I put this coat on at the office. That was a mistake, it's unusually so warm today, isn't it?'

'It's my father,' she said. 'It's been a very long time since I last saw him, and I've recently learned that he was laid to rest here. We were too young to understand death then, of course.'

The man smiled at her and after a while they stopped walking.

She wasn't sure why, but she felt comfortable telling a stranger something that had been very painful to talk to Ma about.

'Here,' said Clarissa.

'That's funny.'

'What is?' she quizzed.

'This is where I was looking, too.'

Clarissa looked down. They crouched down together and the man rubbed his hand across the stone.

'See this?'

'Yes,' nodded Clarissa.

'This is bush-hammered granite from the De Lank quarry in Cornwall. Good quality but very cheap. All these headstones were supplied by a local stonemasons, called Humber's. It was a family business – I believe they still are today.

Clarissa leant toward it and touched the stone.

'It's rough and really lumpy,' she said. 'It feels like the pebble – dash on the side of Granny's old house,' she smiled.

'Yes. Not your typical choice for a headstone because they can't be engraved very easily. They used these because they were cheaper than Devon granite and more unusual than normal stones. I suppose they hoped that people would notice these stones and be curious, and upon reading the plaque they'd see *Humber's Stone Mason* on it, eventually bringing them more business through word of mouth.'

'Uh – huh, self advertising even when it's inappropriate,' said Clarissa.

'That's business for you. After a tragic fire at a local orphanage, these were given by the Humber family to The North Chapel to commemorate the poor orphans who lost their lives. In fact the one next to it appears to be the same. Apparently there was a bit of a difficult battle with the parish about accepting them, as they weren't "official or traditional". But given the nature of the donation and Humber's solid and respected reputation, it was eventually allowed. Reverend Briggon was in charge back then I believe.'

A robin fluttered and chirped on a nearby headstone.

'Nice and easy for the birds to land on while they look out for dinner though, this stone!' smiled the man. 'Just mind the Yew trees – they're very poisonous.'

'Erm – sorry, these were orphans? But my father's stone is this one, right next to them. He wasn't an orphan.'

'Yes, all of these,' he said, gesturing to the line of headstones. 'Orphans, every one.'

Clarissa felt confused. Had Ma kept something else from her? Perhaps it was simply chance that he had been buried alongside the orphans.

Clarissa gently touched her father's headstone.

Is this true, Pa? she thought. *Were you an orphan?*

'My father's stone – it's different from all the rest. It's not made from the same kind of granite.'

'All the same,' said the man. 'This row is for orphans only.'

Clarissa had to wipe her hand across her father's headstone to read the inscription. *You Will Know When It Is Time,* it said.

What a strange epitaph, she thought. It was almost as if her father were speaking to her personally, trying to warn her to be cautious. *You Will Know When It Is Time.* Time to do what?

The man looked at his watch and stood up. 'Gosh, I'd better be going,' he said, giving Clarissa a grin. 'All the best, anyway.'

'Before you go,' said Clarissa, 'can you make out what this orphan's name is, next to my father's stone?'

She took out a tissue and rubbed the tarnished plaque at the base of the headstone he had shown her.

'It's not very clear,' she said. 'Dorothy *somebody*?'

The man frowned at it, too. 'No. I can't make it out, either.' He pressed the screen on his iPad and tilted it toward Clarissa.

'Here. Just before I go, this is the orphanage before the fire. And this next photograph is when they were housed temporarily at The North Chapel.'

Clarissa looked at the images sadly.

'If you have more questions,' said the man as he glanced at his watch, 'here's my card, get in touch and I can tell you more. What is your name?'

'Clarissa,' she said. 'It's Clarissa.'

The man typed her name into his screen and stood up. 'Okay, Clarissa. I'll be hearing from you, then. By the way, I very much like your wellies.' He smiled again, and walked off.

Clarissa looked at her wellington boots and smiled. *Wellies but no rain, winter coat but sunshine – we have something in common already,* she smiled.

'Father?' she whispered. 'Did you hear that? He likes my wellies.'

Contact

Clarissa walked into the kitchen and dropped a large bundle of washing onto the floor in front of the washing machine. She checked the pockets out of habit and from her jeans pocket, she pulled out a business card: *Gordon Norton, Family Investigator.* She sat back on her heels and read it again.

'Clarry, your sister called.'

Clarissa turned to see Laura in the doorway, chewing gum and scratching her arm.

'Oh, thanks, Laura,' she replied, and started to stuff the washing-machine with socks and tops.

Clarissa's new flatmate was only nineteen, younger than Paula. Paula's room had been occupied by Laura for months now and Clarissa had initially felt that having some company in the flat would take her mind off Mark and all of the other mysteries in her life. She hadn't seen Mrs Ball for months either, and felt that if Mrs Ball hadn't contacted her, then everything was settled for the time being. Recently, however, she had begun to feel slightly unnerved with Laura around, because sometimes she would come out of the bathroom and find her right outside, staring at her, or she would appear behind her in the hallway just as she was about to go out, as if she had been watching her closely for hours. Clarissa was beginning to think twice about letting Paula's room and perhaps she should use it for an art room and begin to paint again, as Paula had suggested.

'Oh, Laura!' she called out.

But Laura hadn't moved a step. Clarissa turned around to see her still leaning on the door frame, watching her doing her washing.

'Yeah?' she replied, as if to say: *You don't have to shout. I'm still here.*

'Oh, sorry! I thought you'd gone back to your room! Did

Maggie leave a message? Was it urgent?'

Why do you watch me all the time? she thought. *You give me the creeps, like the boy does. It's almost as if he's behind your eyes, using you to follow me everywhere I go.*

'Um – dunno. She only phoned a minute ago. I figured you were busy.'

Clarissa felt irritated that Laura hadn't even given her the choice of talking to Maggie, but she just smiled, turned back to her washing and said, 'OK, Laura, thank you.'

'What's that you got there?'

Clarissa shut her eyes and wished she'd go away. 'Just a business card.'

Clarissa stood up and turned on the washing-machine. As she put her mobile phone on the work top she noticed out of the corner of her eye that Laura was still watching her. *What does she want?* She thought.

'Oh. Can I see?'

Clarissa had second thoughts about leaving her mobile phone where it was and tucked it into her pocket. *Need to get a lock fixed onto my bedroom door.*

'Erm – yes, here.' Clarissa handed her the card, leaving her hand outstretched to await it back into her hand. She noticed a strange unfocused look in Laura's eyes.

'Family Investigator hey? What does a family investigator do, then?'

'Exactly what I'm going to find out,' smiled Clarissa as she took back the card.

In The Office

Gordon Norton lifted an untidy heap of papers from the green leather armchair facing his desk so Clarissa could sit down. His computer frame was plastered with post-it notes and photographs.

'Excuse the chaos,' he said. 'Genealogical research generates so much paper. I keep meaning to put it all on computer, but – you know.'

Clarissa thought that he looked like a man who lived on his own. His brown suit was mismatched, his shirt was crumpled and there was a certain air of loneliness about him.

'Thanks for seeing me this afternoon,' smiled Clarissa. 'I just wanted to talk over one or two things.

'Of course, no problem. Please, take a seat. After our little chat in the cemetery, it does seem as though we have some interesting things to talk about!'

Clarissa took off her coat and flopped it over the back of the chair, and then sat down.

'Coffee?' asked Gordon, as he slid a cardboard cup under the nozzle of a coffee machine half buried in papers on one side of the desk. There was a dull smell of body odour. His office was large, with huge windows that overlooked the trees of Luxbury Park. The sun came out from behind the clouds and lit up the dust particles in the air. They reminded Clarissa of the elemental orbs that she and Paula had noticed in the old photographs. And reminded her even more of why she had come here today.

'Now,' announced Gordon as he placed a black coffee in front of her. 'Let's get started. So, the orphanage – The North Chapel.' He tugged up his trouser legs and grunted as he made himself comfortable.

Clarissa glanced at the clock above the door. *Two forty-five. Nearly that time when our Guardian Angels are preparing for sunset and releasing a white feather or robin to those who are grieving.*

'Now this is what is most interesting,' said Gordon. 'Twenty-three children died in the fire in 1954, and were buried in the cemetery, all together. But one child was buried far away from the others on the opposite side, amongst the graves of people who had died unidentified – vagrants, for example – and elderly people who had no known relatives, and paupers.'

'Why was he buried there? I thought you said that all the orphans were buried in that one row.'

Gordon Norton peered at his computer screen. 'The orphanage manager didn't even want him interred in the same cemetery, according to this, because he had been almost uncontrollable and made the life of his staff a misery – attacking them whenever he could, kicking and biting and scratching and so forth, and using the most appalling language. However, the Reverend Briggon insisted that he had a right to a Christian burial, no matter how obnoxious she might have been. In the end they reached a compromise and buried him away from the others.'

'What was his name?'

'Doesn't say, I'm afraid. His is the only gravestone without a plaque on it.'

'The *boy*.' said Clarissa, under her breath.

'I beg your pardon?'

Clarissa waved her hand dismissively. 'Sorry. Just thinking aloud.'

'You said *the boy*. What boy were you referring to?'

Clarissa hesitated for a moment, but then she said, 'I don't know his name, not for certain. I have a strong suspicion who he might be, but considering I actually see him, it's very hard to believe that it really could be him.'

'I'm sorry,' said Gordon. 'I'm afraid you've lost me there. You *see* him? How can that be?'

'All right,' Clarissa told him. *Even if he doesn't believe me, at least I will have told somebody, and I can't keep this to myself much longer.*

'There's a boy who's been appearing in my life ever since I was young. He always behaves in a very threatening way and I think that he's responsible for the deaths of at least two people that I knew.'

'*Ye-e-es*?' said Gordon, raising one eyebrow.

Clarissa was aware that what she was saying must sound unbelievable, if not downright insane, but she carried on anyway. 'I have very good reason to believe that the boy you're talking about – the boy who's buried apart from the other children – well, he's the same boy.'

'The same boy?' Gordon repeated. 'You mean, a dead boy has somehow come back to life again?'

'I know it sounds ridiculous. But I think he may be the same boy who was originally put into the orphanage by somebody called Thomas Bruce, back in 1815.'

'Excuse me? How is that possible? That was nearly two hundred years ago.'

'I know. And, like I've said, I know it sounds ridiculous. But it's possible that he was possessed by some kind of malevolent spirit. That was why he was always so aggressive to the orphanage staff. It may even have been him who started the fire. I also think it's possible that he managed to escape from his coffin either before or after he was buried. Or maybe he didn't escape, but the spirit did, and found another boy to possess.'

'You'll forgive me for saying so, but this all sounds more than a little far-fetched,' said Gordon.

'Please believe me,' said Clarissa, 'I've seen the boy for myself. I'm not mad, and I'm not making it up. I saw him push – well, *tug* really – one of the benefactors of our gallery down the stairs – Mrs Cawsley-May. She died from her injuries. And I saw him again after he had stabbed my boyfriend to death.'

'Did you tell the police that you'd seen him?'

'What would have been the point? Nobody else saw him, so they would never have believed me. But I think he could have possessed other people that I know – my boyfriend – well, my *ex*-boyfriend Mark – and I sometimes wonder if he's possessed my flatmate, Laura, just so that he can keep an eye on me.'

'I'm not too sure that I *believe* in evil spirits,' said Gordon. 'However, I'm convinced that I did see saw a ghost once – my dead father, sitting at his desk – so I'll allow you that your boy might have been some kind of supernatural manifestation. But an evil spirit? From two hundred years ago? I'm not at all certain about that.'

'You do believe in *love*, though?'

Gordon fiddled with the knot in his narrow green tie to loosen it slightly. 'Well, yes, but in any event, what's that got to do with it, and why would this boy – if he truly *is* an evil spirit – why would he choose to pick on you?'

'Because of a book, I think,' said Clarissa. Choosing her words carefully, she told Gordon how Mrs Cawsley-May had given her the little book in the gallery, immediately prior to the boy tugging at her dress causing her to fall down the stairs to her death. She also told him about Mark's anger when he hadn't been able to find the book in The North Chapel library.

'Well, I don't know,' said Gordon, shaking his head. 'It might make a difference if you had the book studied by a professional, to find out what it was all about. Perhaps then you'd discover then *why* these various people seem to want to lay their hands on it so badly. I know from some of my previous research that many boys and girls keep their own private journals, so to speak, and that sometimes they're very reluctant to let anybody else read them.'

'I don't think this is a journal,' said Clarissa. 'It's all in some kind of Greek, too, although not Modern Greek, and not Classical Greek. I thought you might have had some idea what it was. Stupid of me, I should have brought it with me.'

'I'm afraid I never studied Greek, Modern or Classical In fact I was no good at languages at all. My French teacher called me a *nigaud* and my German teacher called me a *dummkopf*.'

There was silence between them for a moment. Then, Clarissa said, 'You don't believe me, do you? I can't say that I blame you.'

'But Clarissa, this was *so* many years ago, and surely the fire investigators would have discovered if the fire was set deliberately. As for this boy you keep seeing. Unless he's a ghost, he may be nothing more than a figment of your imagination, when you're under stress. It does happen, you know – if something traumatic happens to us and we have no other way of explaining it, we think we can see things and people who weren't really there.'

'No,' insisted Clarissa. 'This boy is real. He's not a ghost, and I haven't imagined him. He's real. So is the book, *and* the amphora.'

'Amphora?'

'That big Greek pot that they found at The North Chapel recently, when they were extending it. It has an inscription on it which mentions a book.'

'Amphora,' Gordon repeated. 'Amphora … let me see.' He skipped through the pages of his file until he found what he was looking for. 'Yes, here it is. And, yes, you're right. It does bear an inscription that refers to a book. I wonder if it's the same book that your mother's friend gave you, Mrs – what did you say her name was?'

'Cawsley-May.'

'Well, as I say, it might be worth having the book translated and studied. Perhaps the Greywell Museum could help.'

'Let's just say the fire was lit by an orphan, a very angry orphan. He might have done it in revenge or in order to escape.'

'Why escape? He would have had nothing to escape to,' said Gordon. 'Where could have gone?'

'But let's suppose that he started it, and that all of the allegations about him assaulting the staff are true. And that the amphora is more than just an antique pot. Did the boy attack the staff and set fire to the orphanage because they knew the truth about him? Or did he simply do it out of revenge?'

'There's no proof of murder. All of the orphans died of smoke inhalation, natural causes, or suicide. Just as humans do and will always continue to do. Mind you –' he said, shuffling through the papers on his desk, '– there *was* quite a nasty murder at the orphanage in nineteen twenty-seven. It made all the papers at the time.'

'Who was killed?' asked Clarissa.

'A temporary care assistant. Here we are. Her name was Turner – Clara Turner. She was found nailed to the wall in the laundry-room, upside-down, with her mouth stuffed full of chicken-feathers. The *News Chronicle* called it "The Fallen Angel Murder".'

'Oh, my God. Did they ever find out who killed her?'

Gordon shook his head. 'The only other occupants of the orphanage at the time of the murder were children, and the police concluded that no child could have been physically capable of nailing her up like that. The case remained unsolved.'

'I think it was the boy,' said Clarissa.

Gordon said nothing for almost ten seconds, his mouth half-open as if he couldn't think what to say to her.

'You mean the same boy who's been haunting you?' he said at last.

'You can think I'm delusional, Mr Norton. You can think what you like. But from what you told me in the cemetery, and what you've told me today – I'm almost one hundred percent convinced of it.'

'Well, you certainly have a very interesting view on life, Clarissa'

Gordon glanced up at his clock and from the way he was biting his lip, he either had something he was not telling her, or he was hungry for his lunch. Either way, she felt that he was anxious for the meeting to end.

'Well, I hope us discussing things has been of some use,' he said. 'Goodness! Would you believe we've been talking for nearly two hours?'

Clarissa looked up and smiled. 'Yes, thanks for your time and for seeing me at such short notice. But before I go, what do –'

'I think we've covered quite a lot, don't you?' Gordon interrupted her. He closed his file and stood up.

She collected up her notebook and her bag.

'Oh, okay.' *What is he not telling me?* she thought.

She put on her coat and looked at him for a moment, hoping that his face would suddenly allow her to divine his secret, but all she could sense was impatience and hunger. She imagined that he'd have something like a Cornish pasty for his lunch, and a black coffee with too much sugar that he was eager to begin.

'If you have any more questions, you know where I am, and you can always phone or email me. It's all been very interesting. Do let me know how you get on, won't you?'

'I'd just like to know what this boy wants from me, and what he might do next.'

'Better off visiting a medium then,' said Gordon. 'He's a spirit, after all.'

'Funny you should say that,' Clarissa said, 'I've got one in mind!'

They shook hands and Clarissa walked toward the door. As she did so, Gordon slid open his desk drawer to put away his file. He hesitated as he stared eagerly at a cellophane-wrapped sausage roll and Cornish pasty, accompanied by a can of diet Coke.

'Thank you Clarissa,' he said, closing the drawer. 'I'll see you out.'

She couldn't help smiling to herself as she waited for the lift outside his office. *I divined his honesty and his good intentions,* she thought. *I divined that he was single, and had never been married. I even divined his lunch.*

Clarissa's phone buzzed, and she pulled it from her pocket to see that it was Mrs Ball.

'Hi Mrs Ball, great to hear from you,' she said.

'Clarissa?' said a male voice in her ear.

'Yes … hello?'

'This is Lucas? Mrs Ball's son. She's asked that you come here to The Snug as soon as you can … she … she wants to see you …' Clarissa confirmed that she'd be there as soon as possible and terminated the call, her heart full of apprehension. A feeling of weight sunk into her, *what's happened?*

Bedtime Stories

The door to The Snug was opened by Lucas. Its paintwork was peeling from neglect and it was so old and weathered that he had to tug it hard, twice, before it would open.

Clarissa looked saddened, it was different to the last time she was here. She could sense something was terribly wrong.

'Oh, Clarissa,' he smiled. It had been years since she had last seen Lucas, and even then she had met him only briefly when he had come round to mend Mrs Ball's electric kettle. He had changed a lot, grown more mature and more handsome. He had wavy light brown hair and hazel eyes and very white teeth, and he was wearing a smart navy- coloured suit.

'Hi, Lucas,' said Clarissa. 'How is she?'

'Comfortable, but that's about the best we can expect. She's in good spirits but she's very weak. The cancer's taken over very quickly. It's spread to her liver and the doctor doesn't think she has very long.

Clarissa felt a knot in her stomach. *Cancer? She must not have wanted to worry me.*

'Oh Lucas, I'm – I'm so sorry.'

He paused, and then he said, 'I'm sorry we had to meet again under such sad circumstances. How are you? Still working at the gallery, so Mum tells me.'

Clarissa nodded, taking a deep breath and feeling a little sick with the shock. 'I love it.' Clarissa noticed that he was wearing a wedding ring.

'Can you stay for a while?' Lucas asked her. 'I've been here since early this morning and Mum keeps nagging me to go and get something to eat and have a bit of a break.'

'Oh, you should do that. I'll stay here with her until you get back. Really. I'll look after her. I can read to her, too I have my notebook in my bag. Goodness knows she's always been there for me – more often than I can remember. Will your wife be coming over, too?'

Lucas looked at Clarissa and smiled awkwardly. 'No, we aren't – well, we are going through a divorce. Seemed working in New York had one too many large plus points for her, if you know what I mean,' he said with an air of a grudge. He then took a black overcoat down from the peg behind the door and shrugged it on. 'I really appreciate this, Clarissa. You and me, we should have a bit of a catch-up when I get back, although I bet your life has been a darn sight more interesting than mine, from what Mum's told me. I'm in graphic design. Promotional brochures, mostly.'

Clarissa laid her hand on his arm. Although she found him attractive, she was well aware of how grief can draw souls together and now really wasn't the right time for any romance. 'I'll see you later, Lucas. And take your time. You don't have to hurry back. I'll be fine. Go.'

'Mum's birthday cake is on the dining table. Help yourself to a slice if you feel like it.'

Lucas hesitated for a moment before he stepped out of the door and looked at her as if he was seeing her for the very first time, and liked what he saw. There was something in those hazel eyes that said, *I know you've been round to see Mum so many times – why didn't I make sure that I was there, too?*

Once Lucas had gone, Clarissa closed the door and took a steadying breath. She pushed off her boots and went through to the living-room. It was gloomy in there, and for the first time it was cool, with no fire burning, and it didn't smell homely – only musty – the smell of fabrics that hadn't been washed in a while, and precious books that hadn't been opened in even longer. On the table she saw the white-iced birthday cake with blown out candles. A triangular slice with the word 'day' on it had been cut out.

She turned and walked through Mrs Ball's main room, stopping to stroke a marmalade cat that was sitting by the cold and empty fireplace.

'Hey, kitty,' she whispered. 'You okay? Everything will be okay.'

The cat mewed and dipped its head into the curve of her hand.

She climbed the stairs, each one of which was stacked with old books. As she approached the half – open door of Mrs Ball's bedroom, she prepared herself by taking another deep breath and beginning to force a smile. She knocked gently and opened the door wider. Mrs Ball opened her eyes and looked up at her. Clarissa instantly felt the room was too warm and stuffy, but somehow it was comforting to still have some warmth in a once such cosy home. She could tell that Mrs Ball hadn't been downstairs for a long time, and so she chose not to mention the chill and solemnity of the house. Instead she kissed her lips sharply to call the cat from the staircase. 'Come here kitty, be with us in here.' The cat trotted in between her ankles and looked up at her. 'Come on, it's okay.'

'Hi, Mrs Ball,' she smiled. 'Happy birthday, how are you feeling today, are you comfortable?'

Clarissa walked slowly toward the bed. The room was filled with flowers – lilies, roses and daisies, and birthday cards stood in a row on the dressing table. She leaned down to Mrs Ball to give her a kiss on her cheek. All the blue seemed have faded from Mrs Ball's eyes, but they still held a familiar comfort, and magic.

She took hold of Mrs Ball's hand, which was lying flat on top of her quilted bed throw.

'Beautiful Clarissa. Thank you. I didn't want to concern you with sadness before. It was your birthday week.'

'Hi,' smiled Clarissa.

'I'm very weak, now dear. But tell me, did you have a nice birthday yourself? I can't believe you are heading towards thirty. Where does time get to dear?'

'Ah, it flies,' she smiled, settling on the chair by the side of the bed. I got your lovely card and gift, thank you. I had a lovely time. I had a huge afternoon tea party at the traditional family place – Old Gorton Manor, and then a few of us went along to

Crystal Cluster for cocktails and dancing. I printed out the photographs to post to you, but they're still in my bag so I can show you today. I got you a birthday card, too, here, we can open it together.'

Mrs Ball smiled, and said, 'Crystal what?'

Clarissa smiled. 'Cluster.'

'That's nice, I'd like very much to see your birthday pictures.'

Clarissa looked around the room, at the dull, wintry sky outside the window, framed by flowery curtains. The flowers and birthday cards were trying desperately to make the room seem more cheerful, but Mrs Ball would never have another birthday and somehow that made the atmosphere unbearably sad.

'I will be with you for a while, if that's okay with you,' said Clarissa. 'I have some other bits in my bag I can read to you, that I'm working on.'

Clarissa pulled out a smart notebook and placed it gently onto the bed throw. 'I just saw Lucas. He's changed hasn't he? He's gone out for a while, to get some rest and dinner, like you told him to but he said he'll be back later.'

'Okay dear. Yes, Lucas is a good man. He posted your birthday card for me. He had to help me write the card as my hands don't seem to have any strength in them any more.'

Clarissa smiled the best she could. 'I understand.'

'I'm sorry I couldn't make it to your birthday party, dear, at Old Gorton Manor. The cancer is just too strong now. It commands my physical body now. People talk about battling cancer, but it's not really a battle, it's one long retreat.'

Clarissa became so emotionally choked that she had to look away. She kept biting the insides of her lips to stop herself from sobbing, and a heavy, dragging sensation of sorrow weighed down her heart and a salty taste filled her mouth.

Mrs Ball continued slowly: 'We Diviners often pass on our birthday. I was expecting it. It may feel sudden to you, but I have known a while how quickly things are turning inside my body. You must take something you love from here that gives you strength and warming memories. You know dear, Lucas is destined to meet a much nicer girl, like you, he's a very special soul and still young enough to start a family.' She smiled at Clarissa and gave her a reassuring pat on her hand. Wipe your tears, dear. It's so lovely to see you after all this time. We cannot change what is done.'

Clarissa smiled, cried, and squeezed Mrs Ball's hand.

After a few moments, Clarissa took out some photographs of her and Ma, her friends and her in their dresses, and the cake that Ma had had made for her birthday.

'You look lovely as ever, dear.'

After they had looked through them all, Clarissa said: 'I can read you the story I've been working on if you'd like to hear it?'

'A story, how wonderful.' Mrs Ball slowly turned her head to face Clarissa. 'There's coffee in that flask over there that Lucas made, would you like some, dear?'

'Thank you.' Clarissa leaned over and poured some coffee and the refreshing smell filled the room. 'Okay,' she said as she calmed: 'Let's open your card.'

Clarissa had drawn a detailed picture of Mrs Ball's cats in the garden of The Snug.

'Oh my dear it is lovely,' she said. 'Truly. Please put it over there where I can see it.'

Clarissa stood the card next to the one Lucas had given her. 'There.'

As she settled back down again, she smiled and took out the rest of her things she had bought with her. 'I actually found this story amongst my old artwork last month. It's a little silly, but I was only eight years old. So I'm working on adapting it, and hopefully I can sell it one day if it's good enough.'

Mrs Ball's smile widened, as though she remembered Clarissa when she was eight.

She opened the notebook to the first page and made herself comfortable.

'Chapter One. The Magic Path.'

Clarissa looked at Mrs Ball, who had closed her eyes to listen.

She had a slight smile on her face, waiting for Clarissa's words to take her to another world; perhaps to ease her from her pain for a short time. For a moment Clarissa paused, as she took in everything she felt about her; her kind ways, her reassuring support. *You're a wonderful, lovely lady*, she thought. She hoped she would tell her, too, in the right moment. A low wintry sun broke through the clouds and cast golden light over Mrs Ball. *You look like an angel*, she thought. She coughed and continued.

'I was in my room, staring out of the window when I noticed a falling snowflake. I was sure it was the first of the winter. I decided to take my coat and go into the garden, telling my mum that I was going outside.

'I walked along the old stony garden path, feeling snowflakes falling onto my face. As the path led me into the woods at the bottom of the garden, I noticed a small wooden house through the opening. I tiptoed across the crunchy leaves to have a closer look. Suddenly, a man wearing a long navy blue gown appeared in front of me. *Hello little one* he said. He looked very, very old and had a long white pointed beard. Hello, I replied. *Would you like to see some magic? Follow me and I'll show you something amazing!* And with that he tapped his wand on a tree, creating a big bang and flash of light.'

Clarissa looked at Mrs Ball. She looked so peaceful and still had a smile on her face.

'You always were a creative little girl, my dear,' she whispered.

Clarissa eyes welled up.

'I realise I have you to thank, for so much, you helped me so much, you were the only one who made me feel okay to be myself,' she replied. 'Ma told me you've always been in my life. She's told me so much. Thank you for everything. You've protected and strengthened me. I admire and respect you, you're lovely, and inspiring.' Mrs Ball didn't look at her but tapped her hand with affection.

Clarissa took a sip of her coffee to distract her emotions, and went back to the page.

'Chapter Two. The Crystal. *There's nothing to be frightened of young one*, said the wizard. *It's my great grandfather's crystal, from the magic mines*. It sounded scary to me, because I'd never met a wizard before. The wizard put the crystal next to a big book: *The Book of Spells. Did you know, young one, that anything you dream of can come true? Anything magical you hope for can happen if your belief is strong enough. More than that –'*

Clarissa felt a disturbing sense of emptiness float into her, and her voice turned flat. She sensed that Mrs Ball was no longer listening.

The rays of the sun faded, and the room suddenly felt cool. The cat by the heater mewed continuously and Clarissa put down her story. Clarissa looked at Mrs Ball's white cat that had sat up right on her legs, also mewing.

'Mrs Ball?' Clarissa whispered amidst the cats sorrowful mews. 'Is there anything I can do?'

Clarissa heard her voice, although her lips didn't move. *No, I'm okay now dear. I will never be far from your side, just ask for me. Thank you for reading to me, it was truly lovely. Such a clever girl. Please look after my kitty cats. Always be strong, our talented girl.*

Clarissa's heart thumped and her eyes welled up again. She put the story onto the bed and grabbed Mrs Ball's hand with both of hers.

'Oh Mrs Ball, I'm going to miss you so much,' said Clarissa as she stroked her hair. 'Please, please don't leave me I need you in my life! You mean so much to me!'

I'll always be with you to guide you, dear. You are strong. A true Diviner. Please tell Lucas I love him, and I said goodbye, dear.

Mist

Clarissa looked up to the sky as a fine mist of rain fell, as if to see something comforting above her as Mrs Ball's coffin arrived at the crematorium. Crowds of guests slowed their murmuring and some lowered their heads. Clarissa squeezed tightly onto her clutch bag and glanced at Lucas, who had his head bowed and hands interlocked, as a tear rolled down his cheek. Soft whimpers from Mrs Ball's family filled Clarissa with an overwhelming sadness but she had promised Mrs Ball she'd be strong, and so she had to be. She gritted her teeth and pouted in an attempt to prevent tears from falling and curtseyed slightly, looking to the coffin as Mrs Ball was removed from the hearse.

Inside, there was a song playing as they took their seats, and Lucas whispered to Clarissa: 'Ne Me Quitte Pas. Nina Simone. Mum loved this.'

After everyone had left the wake, Lucas handed Clarissa a bundle of envelopes, fastened with a wide red ribbon. 'Mum left these for you.' He was smiling, but she could see it was a slanted smile, as if he was doing his best to hide his grief.

'Your mum loved the spring,' said Clarissa. Look at all of her beautiful crocuses beginning to flower out there. I can hear all the birds singing their songs, too.

She placed the bundle of letters on the armchair and picked up a vase, which was crowded with half-opened daffodils. 'Look at these too, they'll be open in a couple of days if I sit them in the sunlight. I think I'll put them over onto the kitchen windowsill.' She placed them down admiring them, then turned and watched Lucas as he made the tea, and looked at his soft, dark wavy hair. She yearned to comfort him, she felt so sorry for him.

'Mum always said you liked a fire. Now everyone's gone I'll light it.'

She picked up the letters again and walked over toward the fireplace, noticing how lumpy the rug felt beneath her bare feet. She stepped over Mrs Ball's white cat, smiling at it. 'Hey girl,' she whispered. In return the cat squinted her eyes and mewed.

'Yes, I love a fire.'

She slid off her smart jacket and un-clipped her hair, letting out a sigh of relief. Actually Lucas, I have something for you, too. More like something to *tell* you. I'll help clear up the tea cups, first.'

The room had a different atmosphere now, with no statuettes or books or cushions lying around. It was strange not seeing Mrs Ball here, but it also felt as though her spirit wasn't far away either, as though she had herself too, watched her funeral and stood by their sides. She noticed that the picture frame on the mantelpiece had gone.

'Lucas?' she called out. 'Where is your mum's picture of a cat that always stood on the mantelpiece?'

'Oh that old thing?' he replied from the kitchen. 'She loved it. She said it was her special picture and wanted it upstairs next to her bed while she was ill. Did you like it?'

'Oh – I just noticed that it was missing that was all.'

'It's still upstairs. I've not felt like packing much away yet, it still smells like a hospital up there. Can't face it to be honest. It's all I can do to get through downstairs in an orderly fashion.'

Clarissa smiled with sympathy. She felt sorry for Lucas. He was an only child and although he was forty, she knew he had found it difficult to cope with all the winding up of his mother's estate. A strong sense of sadness filled her, her eyes welled up and she looked across to the dining room table, where she and Mrs Ball had spent so many hours together over the years.

'I was extremely fond of your mum, Lucas. If there's

anything I can do to help, please know I will, any time – or anything. Don't feel alone.'

Clarissa didn't get a response, but she heard a teaspoon tinkle against a teacup, followed by a loud sniffing sound.

She untied the red ribbon on her bundle and took the first envelope into both hands. *Clarissa, dear,* was written on it.

Lucas returned with a large silver teapot, cups and a selection of biscuits.

'Here we go,' he said. 'I'm afraid I didn't make the cookies or sandwiches for today, I bought them all from M&S I'm useless at hosting, not like mum.' Lucas sniffed again, smiled at Clarissa and poured the tea.

'Ah, that's okay,' smiled Clarissa.

Clarissa opened the envelope she was holding while Lucas settled next to her.

'Mum gave me that bundle one day before – well, before she left us.'

'Okay,' smiled Clarissa.

> *Dear Clarissa,*
>
> *My dear, I am sad to say I will be leaving you soon. I have left the books for you, please keep them safe, and refer to them as you need. Remember the Olven twins. They will always appear in times of need. Do not worry, they will never let you down as it is impossible for a Watcher not to not know where you are. You will find the books by my chair at the table.*
>
> *Don't be frightened to trust your instincts. Be wise. Be happy. Don't rush your decisions. Beware of love for it has many faces. Remember everything you are and the talents you have.*
>
> *As a Diviner you will reflect other's attitudes from within when face to face, so be patient with yourself and know this as a Diviner – you have the powers to dissolve any sadness, anger or deception you see, or reflect it straight back to them should you feel their bad energy. Trust your gift. You have been put on this Earth for a purpose. Remember this whenever you face*

the boy.

Live in a way that leaves you no regrets but maintain composure in all circumstances. And when you marry, dear, I wish you every happiness. Know that I shall be with you although you may not see me.

'"Know that I shall be with you, although you may not see me,"' Clarissa repeated.

'I always believed mum would be here forever.' Lucas sniffed, and smiled. 'I'd like to believe she's not really gone, that her spirit is here. I'm sure I can still hear her talking in the other room.'

'She'd be telling us not to cry,' smiled Clarissa, her face smothered with tears.

'Do you ever get that?' he asked. 'It's like you can hear her talking, or sometimes other people's voices, you know as though they are right next to you?'

'I get lots of different things.'

Together they laughed a broken laugh. 'Like what?'

'Wow, where can I start?' she sniffed. 'I can sense someone's emotions and describe to them their personality before I know them. I can feel when I'm in danger. There's lots of stuff. You will find it hard to find people that understand. But your mum always did.'

Lucas leant forwards and fell silent for a moment.

'She will always be with us, Lucas.'

He put his head in his hands. 'I just can't help it, she was everything to me,' he looked up at her with tears in his eyes.

'It's okay, it is. Time will help. And being here.'

Lucas sobbed.

Clarissa put the letter aside and found herself holding Lucas as he cried, and she kissed his forehead.

'It's okay, it's okay,' she whispered to him. He held on to her so tightly, as though she were slipping away, too. 'It's all right,' she reassured him. 'I'm here. Let it all go.'

They held each other for a few moments, and eventually Lucas raised his head and looked deeply into Clarissa's eyes. Within seconds, quite un-expectedly, they were kissing. Clarissa could smell Lucas' musky fragrance as she pushed her fingers through his hair. She felt a natural, spiritual connection, but also a rush of guilt drifted through her for Craig's memory.

Lucas broke the kiss and looked at her. 'Oh, Clarissa!'

She was sure, against her desire to be in a relationship for fear of loved ones dying, that they both just experienced something incredible. A strong, grieving desire to be held and secured, by a force within both of their hearts lifting them into their own safe world, leaving the pain they had felt behind them, if only for a moment or two.

Afterwards, Clarissa wondered how Mrs Ball would have felt about their kiss, and part of her realised that it was probably what she'd wanted for years. But for now, she had to think of his emotions running high as he grieved, and she didn't want to be hurt again.

'Here, have this to take home with you.' Lucas unhooked a picture in the hallway of Mrs Ball with her white cat. 'It's a lovely one of her.'

'Thanks, Lucas. It *is* lovely. I'll put it with my things. I should go before it gets too late, I'm sure you have lots you have to sort out or that you want to do alone here in your own thoughts.'

Lucas smiled and walked her toward the back door. Clarissa stopped by the table and ran her fingers across its textured wooden surface. 'Your mum always had a velvet dark pink cloth on here. It's silly how little things like this bring back nice memories and suddenly become sentimental.' She looked up at Lucas.

'Stay for a little longer? If you want to, I mean. I have a really good bottle of Châteauneuf-du-Pape in the kitchen that one of my clients gave me. It's crying out for somebody to drink it, and I don't feel like drinking it all on my own. Or *being* alone tonight, for that matter.'

Clarissa smiled. 'Thank you, but I must go. Save it for another time, okay?'

'You're right. Probably a good idea.' Lucas looked up and

sighed. 'I'm sorry if I came on a little strong – it wasn't the right time.'

'It's okay, we're both struggling a bit today, don't worry. It was nice, but too soon. Let's forget it. Friends?' she smiled as she offered a hug before fastening her coat, but knew something so passionate and spiritual would be on her mind for a while.

'And thanks, Clarissa. I feel a little better. You've been great today.'

Madame Cronsieur

'Come in, Clarissa.'

Clarissa lifted aside the heavy rose-coloured curtain with its fawn silk tassels.

'Hi,' she said, a little nervously.

'Make yourself comfortable, *ma cherie*.'

Madame Cronsieur smiled, and watched Clarissa as she settled, making little sucking noises with her lips as she watched, as if she approved of her new client, and understood why she had come.

Clarissa sat down on a wide antique armchair, upholstered in a patterned navy velvet. She unzipped her jacket feeling both nervous and pleased. Maggie had mentioned that she'd gone to see Psychic Sally on tour, and that had given Clarissa the idea to research and visit the best local medium. Now that Mrs Ball had gone, perhaps a medium could give her knowledge as well as comfort and guidance. Madame Cronsieur raised her eyebrows. 'You have *love* in your heart,' she said.

Clarissa couldn't help but smile.

'You have been blessed, Cupid has visited you.'

Clarissa blushed. She was alarmed that Madame Cronsieur had mentioned Cupid so early in the session, before she had told her anything about herself.

'And your card-reading – everything you were shown in your cards is becoming true? No?'

Clarissa nodded and made herself comfortable. 'Yes, how did you know I had my cards read?' she said.

'And this is the first time to a medium, too,' replied Madame Cronsieur, smiling. Her eyes were so dark, that they seemed big somehow, and filled with knowledge and strength.

'Yes,' nodded Clarissa. 'I'm fascinated.'

'*Captive*,' said Madame Cronsieur.

There were a few moments of silence.

Madame Cronsieur closed her eyes and puckered her lips. Clarissa took that opportunity to look at her. She had short wavy, dark hair, heavily-pencilled eyebrows, and she was wearing a dark blue jumper with a brooch in the shape of a frog, embellished with green crystals. From reading stories as a child, Clarissa had expected a medium to be a fairy-tale-like woman with long fingernails, thick long black hair, no eyelashes and a crystal ball. Instead, Madame Cronsieur appeared to look fairly normal, regardless of her eyes; the sort of woman you might find behind the counter in an old fashioned sweet shop or a flower stall. All the same, Clarissa felt that she had an unusual energy about her, and could tell she was in the presence of someone very powerful. It was as though the air around her was filled with static electricity and power. The room was warm, and the light glowing through thin, red curtains gave the room a cosy glow.

'Your troubles have passed but you have to fight them off as they will return. While you grieve they will come to get you but you must be strong. Something is going to change in your personal life, not an event, but a person.' She opened her eyes. 'You have a very light energy, your aura is light blue at its strongest today. You are connected.'

'Connected?' replied Clarissa.

'You are connected to everything psychic. Do you hear things?'

'Yes.'

'And when you don't hear, you see and feel the emotion of what you see?'

'Yes, yes I do.'

'You can learn more, *mon cherie* and you will indeed.'

Clarissa smiled.

'Who is Elsie?' asked Madame Cronsieur.

'I'm not sure. Elsie? No-one springs to mind.'

'Well she is with you. You are protected and very, very wise. *But!* Beware of deceit from a female friend. *Trahison – oui,* betrayal – someone is not being nice about you. They are being malicious and may try to harm your reputation. The more you share, the more you will be hurt. *Trahison.'*

'Oh. Okay.' Clarissa ran through her friends in her mind. *That's horrible. I've given no reason for a friend to turn on me. That's not what a true friend does. That's not okay.*

'Stay away from an argument and be very careful of a journey – an accident comes.'

Clarissa wondered why she was being given such alarming warnings.

'Okay,' she said. *Why isn't Madame Cronsieur saying anything about Mrs Ball's passing?*

Madame Cronsieur continued. 'Your losses have been necessary. Necessary for your survival. They have gone so you can be here. Beware of the clown's face, a malleable person in your life. A troubled young man always brings discord. *He who fits a purpose is fitting purely his self.* Love has many faces, Clarissa. *Soyez forts, ma petite.'*

Madame Cronsieur opened one eye and looked at her. 'Do not *overthink* a situation. Jealousy is not necessary. No. Take what you learn, move with it. Trust your instincts. But beware –'

Clarissa took out a little notebook from her bag and started to write things down.

'But wait –' halted Madame Cronsieur.

Clarissa wondered who she was talking to, because she had raised her left hand as if she were trying to listening to someone else.

'Mrs Ball wants me to tell you she is here. *Oui.'*

Clarissa felt her heart skip a beat. *She's here?* Her heart filled with excitement.

'There's so much I need to tell her, and ask her! I miss her so much!'

'She is *joyeux* you and Lucas connected. It is very much what she wanted, since you were young and heart free. *Cygnes sur l'amour.* She also spends time with Lucas, the cats, and now, now she is showing me a picture, a small wooden picture with *Snug* written on it. What is it, Snug? This Snug will be very important in your life. She wants you to remember a small room, in an old house. She spent many years there, working. She also shows me a box, with photographs, this will become very important to you.'

'Yes. Oh my goodness!' Clarissa felt that she could burst at Madame Cronsieur's accuracy. 'The Snug is where Lucas lives now, Mrs Ball's house down toward the valley.'

It was then that Clarissa recognised the beautiful piece of music, coming from the radio in the corner of the room. She softened in her chair and looked over at the little radio. She couldn't help but listen. It was Mendelssohn's 'Spring Song'. It was like the first songbird of the morning, or the hesitation in a first kiss.

Madame Cronsieur smiled, her eyes remaining shut. '*Oui*, Mendelssohn. The violin is playing, like stroking the strings of your heart, Clarissa. *La douleur, la passion et l'amour.* Mrs Ball's favourite. She wanted you to hear it. Sprits like to play with radio playlists. Which is why we listen, they message us with music. *Le sentir dans ton coer.*'

'I remember. She used to play it from a CD.' Clarissa stared at the radio. The music had indeed played with her heart strings. 'It's beautiful.'

They both sat silently for a while, listening. Then Madame Cronsieur continued softly: 'Things will happen around you that will be her. She says she knew about the saucepans. She is showing me a tall, dark haired man.' Madame Cronsieur's expression changed. 'Oh dear, he met a tragic end. *Il repose.* What does this mean "dangerous with Laura"? She shows me something – a door that is locked. She is worried for your safety, with Laura. Does this mean anything to you, Clarissa?'

Clarissa brought herself out of the trance of the violin. She pulled her sleeves over her knuckles and folded her arms tightly as she did when she was a child, to concentrate. Looking at Madame Cronsieur, she said: 'Yes, Laura was my lodger. She's not now, I have a new one. A man my age. He's called Dave.'

'Be sure Laura is gone from your life,' she warned.

'Okay.'

'Mrs Ball is showing me a blond-haired man, she is saying beware of old traps with him. *La souris ne peut s'echapper une fois –* The mouse can only escape once – There is a name … Mark …

yes *Mark* – And now she is showing me a boy, in a room? I'm looking at this boy then I'm looking at a white room and a handsome man next to me. He was brought here by a money man, greed. A master of greed.'

Clarissa knew. 'Oh my God.' She covered her mouth. It had been the boy again, coming into her life as Laura. Just as Mark had. The same person, over and over, but with different faces, like the multitude of faces from a pack of fortune-telling cards.

'You will be with Craig, do you understand? If Mark or Laura remains in your life, you will be unwell. You must also beware of a clown. No – no – I feel your clown is close to you, *beware* Clarissa! *Prenez garde!'*

Clarissa sat silently for a moment, feeling alarmed, remembering just how strong he had become by being close to her, through Mark, and how it had affected her.

'*Shh, ssh,*' said Madame Cronsieur very quietly.

'Okay.' Clarissa looked at her. She had the impression that she was reassuring Mrs Ball in some way.

'Mrs Ball is worried. So she has something for you. She says it is critical to your safety, and all of those you love. Also for your unborn child.'

'My unborn child?' said Clarissa. For a moment she was totally bemused. 'But I'm not even – *pregnant.'*

Madame Cronsieur raised her hand to interrupt her. 'This gift is unique and can only be passed on from beyond the grave. It is forbidden in waking life, because even the hearts of wicked people must be allowed to keep their secrets. *Clarissa, it is the gift of translation.* Never, never before this have I known it to come through. She wants you to use it as often as you can from now on.'

'Really? But how?' asked Clarissa. 'How will I get it?'

'Ah, you will, and you will know when. Be patient. Use it. Use it often, and use it wisely.'

The gift of translation, thought Clarissa.

As she drove home from Madame Cronsieur's, she stared

hard at the passing road signs in the hope that she could translate them into other languages. But the road names only blurred slightly, as if they were trying to tell her that this gift wasn't meant for anything so inconsequential as *Billers Lane* and *The Maltings*.

In her heart, she knew what Mrs Ball had been telling her through Madame Cronsieur. *The gift of translation is only intended for one very special purpose – and that purpose is to protect you, and Lucas too, from terrible harm. And any child you might have.*

She knew with complete clarity why Mrs Ball had given her the gift of translation. It was for the book. At last she would be able to discover what all its crowded pages of incomprehensible Greek actually meant. And at last she would be able to find out why the boy and Mark were so desperate to get their hands on it.

I Know You Are There

Once Clarissa reached home she kicked off her shoes and settled into the computer chair and wiggled the computer mouse to activate the screen.

'Come on, come on,' she whispered impatiently as it slowly resumed. It had been a while since she'd seen the boy appear in her life, but she realised such a thing wouldn't last for long, and he'd be back. She leaned across turning on the radio while she waited, and settled for AC/DC: *Highway to Hell*, turned it up and took a sip of her drink, tapping and flicking her head about to the music.

A few moments later, she turned down the radio to background noise as the computer became ready.

'Ahhh. Right Google, let's see what you've got. Give me something I can read in another language.' She typed into the search bar: *North Chapel Orphans amphora*.

She scrolled down the screen until she came to: *Orphanage Burns in Fire. Humber's Family Stonemasons donate headstones for orphans' graves*. She blinked and stared again. 'No good, still English,' she said. The heading was followed by a list of all those children who had lost their lives.

Clarissa murmured to herself. 'The book, I must go and get the book, maybe I can translate it now!'

Just then, her mobile phone vibrated. She pulled it out of her pocket to see that it was Laura calling. *Oh great. Good timing, as ever* thought Clarissa. She clicked the red button to cut the call off.

It rang again.

And then again.

'Oh for goodness sake, Laura. *Leave me alone.*'

Laura had called her six times and sent her four text messages since Clarissa had terminated her tenancy and this was becoming invasive.

'Dave!' Clarissa called out, hoping her new lodger was home. He appeared out of his room a few moments later with earphones around his neck, and a half-eaten slice of pizza in his hand.

'Did you call me?'

'Yeah, sorry, but has anyone been calling to the house for me?' she asked, leaning back in the computer chair.

'No,' he said. 'But then, nah I don't think so, anyway, I may not have heard the phone ring.' He paused again, and then he said, 'I don't mean to be personal or anything, but I thought I heard you shouting the other night. Everything okay?'

'Yes, I've just had some awful nightmares lately,' she smiled. 'Thanks, though.'

'Fair enough,' he said, as he looked at her slowly up and down taking in her appearance, and then wandered back into his room and shut the door.

Clarissa was really beginning to feel that she was being harassed by Laura after talking to Madame Cronsieur. She didn't want to be horrible to her, but she couldn't forget the warning that Mrs Ball's spirit had given her. She was much more sensitive than usual to anything that seemed to be threatening or even out of the ordinary, and Laura's persistent calls were certainly that. She turned up the radio as Lenny Kravitz' *It Ain't Over 'till It's Over* came on, and sang along.

The phone began to vibrate again.

Clarissa looked at Laura's name flashing up on her mobile phone screen again. She held up her phone and as it was vibrating in her hand, and said clearly to it: 'Laura, I know who you are. I ask you to stop calling me. I don't trust you – get out of my life. Enough now.' And with that, the phone stopped vibrating, and it didn't ring again.

She got up and went into her bedroom and took the book from its hiding place. 'This could be it, little boy. Maybe I can read this now and know all of your secrets.' She took it back to the desk, opened the book carefully, shut her eyes and counted to three, then opened them. The page was still unreadable – nothing but a mass of squiggly symbols.

'Hmph,' she said. She hoped she hadn't misunderstood what Madame Cronsieur had meant by 'the gift of translation'. But what else could she have meant?

She frowned intently at the page again, but all that happened was that she ended up with green after-images of Greek letters floating in front of her eyes.

Nature's Way

The wind whipped at Clarissa's legs as she turned the corner from the gallery to the cafe. It turned her umbrella inside-out and made her skirt lift, just as a delivery van drove past, making the driver smile.

As she approached Cafe 29 her phone rang. She pushed open the heavy door and shook off her umbrella, juggling her phone into her hand and to her ear.

'Hi!' she mimed to Kelly who was stood behind the coffee bar, waiting for her next customer. Kelly waved back and signalled at a cappuccino mug. Clarissa nodded, and smiled. 'Hello?' she said into her phone. She took off her coat and settled into a sofa by the bookshelf and open fire.

'Yes, yes that's right. Why, what's happened?' her expression sank as she just knew something was wrong.

'Okay Ma, don't worry, I'll phone Maggie now. Love you, bye.'

A few moments later, Kelly walked over with her coffee.

'Here we go,' she whispered. 'Got the fire lit today as it's raining, toasty huh!' Clarissa looked up at her plump, smooth face, like a woman in a Rubens painting, with perfectly applied make-up and thick chestnut hair. She could see that she was contented, and good-natured. It was always heart-warming when her gift showed her that somebody was happy, and that they enjoyed sharing their happiness.

'Just pay later, it's fine,' Kelly said. 'Enjoy.'

Clarissa stirred a sugar lump into her cappuccino and dialled Maggie's number. 'Maggie?' she asked, wondering how she was going to tell her. Then she thought that the kindest way was to be as blunt and calm as possible. 'Maggie,' she repeated down the phone. 'Ma's just phoned me. Maggie I've got some sad news, Craivers has been run over. He just couldn't get out of the way in time.'

Maggie said nothing, but then Clarissa heard her sob.

'Don't cry, Maggie, he was very old,' she said, 'nature always takes its course,' but then her eyes filled with tears in spite of herself. Somehow, although she was younger than Maggie, she felt a responsibility for her. Maybe their grief wasn't so much for their beloved cat as it was for grief in their childhood, for the father that they had lost, and all those days that had passed which they could never get back.

Cheers!

Clarissa stumbled across the hallway with morning light glaring in through the kitchen window, picking up clothing that was strewn on the floor as she made her way to the bathroom.

'We must have slept well!' she laughed, as she called out to her flatmate, wrapping her robe around her body and tying it, looking at the clock on the bathroom wall. 'Eleven-thirty! How many beers did we have Dave?'

'A case. That's what days off are about,' replied Dave from the sofa, as he watched *Star Wars: Rogue One*. How is your stomach today? You said you felt ill last night. Not surprised, you can drink me under the table!' he finished, chewing on some Galaxy chocolate.

'Eugh. Too many beers. Not what I should do on my days off!'

Clarissa picked up her mobile phone and dialled the number for The Snug, to talk with Lucas. Lucas listened as Clarissa continued: 'I've got so much on my mind at the moment. This book, I thought I was going to be able to translate it, but it still doesn't make any sense. And I've just remembered, I have a launch Wednesday evening, at the gallery.'

She walked into the bathroom and stared at her face in the bathroom mirror. She picked up her face cleanser, squirting some onto cotton wool.

'It's the new, young artist Eliza Cardnia. She's very talented, I think she'll do well. You can come if you'd like, I could get extra tickets, you could come along with Paula and Ben.'

She looked long and hard into the mirror, and then, for a split second thought she saw Craig standing behind her. She caught her breath and turned around.

There was no-one there.

She turned back to the mirror and felt guilt swamping her heart. She remembered Craig's voice, telling her he loved her, and how she was just as good as any of the famous artists at the gallery. She wished she could tell Craig she hadn't forgotten him, just because she had become friends with and had a subtle affection for Lucas. She looked down to ease the guilt, rather than look at her own reflection; her eyes that he had longingly looked into, and her lips that he had kissed.

She cleared her throat and said: 'I think I'll suggest putting Cardnia's work right at the front of the gallery. It's very bold and eye catching for passers-by along the pavement.'

'Just make sure you get your commission then,' Lucas replied.

'Lucas, I'll come over for a while. I'll be an hour. Something I want to look at, at The Snug if it's okay with you.'

Clarissa cleared down and looked back into the mirror. She looked pale. She splashed her face with icy cold water and stared back at her long, dark eyelashes, and the mousy brown eyebrows that desperately needed re-shaping. And what's more, she now felt as though she had somehow betrayed Craig. Why else would she have thought she saw him, standing staring at her while she was on the phone to Lucas?

Clarissa whispered: *'I'm so sorry, Craig, I kissed him but that's as far as it went. I miss you so much.* She hoped that somehow, somewhere, Craig could hear her. She picked up a hair band and walked away from the mirror, wiping the corners of her eyes. For a split second she thought she felt the boy near her, watching her, too. She untied the belt of her robe, took a deep breath and pushed the door closed to see if he was behind it. She couldn't see him there, but she knew he was here, somewhere. She could sense him. She opened the door again, to look out onto the landing. There was nothing there. She pushed her hair back and dropped her robe to the floor. Leaning into the shower cubicle she turned the huge dial, stepping underneath the hot spray.

'*Aaah,*' she whispered as the water splashed over her. She raised her face and held her breath as she stood directly under the falling water, keeping her eyes shut. *That's good. Heaven,* she thought.

The smell of breakfast drifted through the flat as Clarissa dressed and put on her boots. As she grabbed her keys off the worktop, Bartholomew sat eagerly awaiting at the kitchen chair, flicking his tail in hope for a scrap of bacon as Dave cooked a fried breakfast.

'I'm off out, Dave. See you later. By Barthy.' Bartholomew squinted in response but kept watching Dave's every move.

'Yeah, okay, see ya!'

When Clarissa arrived at The Snug she saw Lucas in the garden, under the apple tree. The way he smiled at her as he waved made her heart skip a beat.

Lucas walked across the uncut grass toward her and smiled. Leaning in, he pressed his lips softly onto her cheek to welcome her, and pulled her body in close to his to hug.

For Clarissa, time seemed as though it had frozen for those precious few moments. *Please don't let me fall for you,* she thought.

Clarissa opened the back door of The Snug and as she stepped in, found herself smiling back at a picture frame that was sat on the windowsill of Mrs Ball, and stared into her powder-blue eyes.

After a few moments of being alone, Lucas emerged from the garden, rubbing his hands on a towel.

'You okay?'

'I miss her, Lucas.'

Lucas smiled. 'Me too.'

Clarissa closed her eyes, wishing he could read her mind, and understand every moment of her heartbeat; every beat that beats for her losses, and her overwhelming fear that everyone she cares for will die at the hands of the boy. *Maybe he can*, she thought. *Maybe, just maybe he can.*

Clarissa took off her coat and placed it over the back of a chair, before pulling out a seat at the table.

'What a lovely crisp day!' she called to Lucas, who was now watering the bird table in the garden.

'I think a chicken coop would be perfect out here, you know,' said Lucas. 'Fresh eggs every morning!'

Clarissa gave him the thumbs up. 'Good at making omelettes, are you?' she teased. 'Funny,' he returned, laughing as he came back to the house.

'Thanks for letting me come over today. I wanted to be here, you know to I feel your mum is near me, because we used to sit here and talk for hours. Do you remember everything I told you on the phone the other day? About the book, and my visit to Madame Cronsieur? Well I'm going to have another go at translating this book. I thought that I'd be able to do it by now, but it's still just a whole lot of scribble.'

Lucas was leaning on the door frame and took off his wellingtons. 'Maybe you're right. Maybe Madame Croissant didn't literally mean "the gift of translation".'

'I still think she must have done. And it's "Cronsieur" not "Croissant"!'

'Oh, *excusez-moi*,' he said. 'And by the way, what were you muttering about on the phone last night?

'What?'

'Last night. Well, it must have been the early hours you left a voicemail because I could hear the blackbirds chattering away as well as you. My phone was on vibrate so I missed it ringing. I couldn't really hear what you were saying but you sounded well peeved about something.'

'But I didn't ring last night?'

'Really? Not at all? Oh. I must have dreamt it, then. Serves me right for eating all that Brie and red wine for supper. How about some coffee?'

Clarissa nodded and smiled. 'Strong coffee. Thanks.' But she couldn't help thinking: *if he did hear somebody's voice from my mobile but it wasn't me – who was it? The boy?*

'Today I'm really going to have a serious go at putting together all the different pieces of this boy thing,' she called out to Lucas. 'I mean, he really scares me. You know he does. But it's like a massive puzzle, like when you research your family tree. One person connects with another person, even if you didn't think they knew each other. One event makes sense of another event, even if they didn't seem to be related. If only I can find out exactly why the boy is here, and what he really wants so badly.

She paused for a moment, tapping her pencil thoughtfully against her teeth. 'The trouble is, what if I find out how to expose him, and get rid of him, but it turns out to be dangerous?'

She heard the clinking sound of a spoon against a mug, then a few moments later Lucas came shuffling across the floor in his moccasin slippers. 'Let's take it one step at a time, okay?' he told her. 'I know it's something you have to do, but we're not doing Tarot cards here. We're putting together whatever pieces of information we have in order to find answers and a way forward. Here we go. One strong coffee. Hangover, by chance?'

Clarissa grinned.

'It is a *little* like Tarot if you think about it – hints, and warnings, and secret messages.'

Lucas took his iPad off charge and turned it on, putting it onto the table ready for Google. First Clarissa laid out photographs of her eighth birthday party and one of her father's small drawings and a birthday card from Mrs Cawsley-May, which she hadn't opened because of grieving her death. Next to them, she placed Mrs Ball's huge canvas book, and arranged on top of it her large black tourmaline, her talisman button, holy water, a tooth vial, photographs of Ma's of her father, and a diagram of her family tree. Then, right in front of her, she placed the book.

'Wow, what's this?' asked Lucas as he studied her button

talisman.

'That's my talisman. They come to us when we're ready to accept our destiny, in the form of whatever you love at the time. Your mum's talisman was a cat ornament. The one she had by her bed. It'll be a good idea to keep it. '

Lucas looked at her and frowned. 'Okay. But that book. Remember, *it's only a book*. It can't hurt you. And besides, you know that I won't let any harm come to you.'

'*It never seems to be me that gets harmed,*' she murmured. 'I don't know what I'd do if I lost you, too, Lu. You've become such a good friend, I care a lot about you.

'I'll be all right, I'm my mother's son, remember? I'm not leaving you. *Ever. I care about you, too.*'

She took a sip of coffee and looked across to Lucas, who just smiled back, his eyes twinkling in the sunlight. She began to realise she cared more than she was letting on. And maybe sticking together was becoming the safest option.

'Okay. I'll read this birthday card. I haven't felt able to open it since she died, it seemed too personal somehow: I wasn't ready. Strangely I was keen to read your mum's letters when she passed, but not a simple card from Mrs Cawsley-May.'

'You know, this book. It's definitely the same book from Old Gorton Manor that I wanted to look at when I was a child. The book was the *start* of the problem for me. The boy didn't want me to know the truth about him. He must have known my power as a Diviner and my duty to expose evil.'

'Will it all make sense now?' asked Lucas.

'Oh God, I hope so.' Clarissa looked to the mantelpiece and nodded at Mrs Ball's photo. 'Wish you were here,' she said. *Please be with me now, Mrs Ball while I look through all this, and protect us.*

She picked up the book. 'That's strange,' she said. 'I can read the words on the spine easily now.'

Lucas looked at her, puzzled.

'They've never made any sense at all. They've always looked like funny shaped squiggles. But I can read them now. I can't believe it. *Éros: Proeidopoiíseis kai Entolés.*' She paused for a moment. *'Cupids: Warnings and Commandments.'* She looked up at Lucas with a horrified expression across her face.

'Here, let me see.' Lucas reached across the table and took the book.

'Careful,' she flinched. 'There's little bits of paper in between the pages, and something loosely sealed in the side pouch.'

'Eros – pro *what* did you say?' he raised an eyebrow. He picked up the iPad. 'I'll check Google translate. Just looks like Greek letters to me. No idea how to pronounce this. I didn't study Greek.'

Clarissa swallowed. 'Lucas – it's happened.' Mrs Ball's white cat appeared at the leg of her chair, mewing. He looked up at her and blinked, as though he knew how she was feeling and that she could now speak cat.

'Clarry, this is what it says on Google, and you're right. It's pronounced: *Éros: Proeidopoiíseis kai Entolés.* It roughly translates to *Cupids: Warnings and Commandments.'* He fell quiet for a moment.

Looking at Clarissa in disbelief, he said: 'Clarry –'

'I know. I've just said that – I've just *read* that straight away – in *Greek.'*

'But Cupids? What's all that about? Cupids have wings, don't they, and fly around shooting arrows at people so that they fall in love?'

'Yes, but if my experience of love is anything to go by –' Clarissa stopped speaking. She had started to think about the boy, and Mark, and Craig with his blood-smeared hands uplifted, begging her for help.

But if she could translate the book now, and find out exactly what the boy really was, and what he would kill for, maybe that would go some way to setting her heart at rest.

Clarissa opened the birthday card from Mrs Cawsley-May and held it in her hand for a few moments.

Much Love darling girl. Buy yourself something pretty! xx

A fifty pound note fell out, and another little envelope.

'There's a letter,' she said.

'Open it.'

Clarissa bent down and picked up the fifty pound note. She placed it on the table, showing Lucas.

'That's so sweet,' he said.

Clarissa nodded and opened the envelope and began reading the letter to herself:

Dear Clarissa.

I was the researcher of The North Chapel in the fifties. At that time I learned of some horrific stories involving the orphans. From my grandmother I also acquired a little book there. It was explained to me by someone I cannot name that I must pass it only to another Diviner should I feel at risk. It must remain a secret. I stored it amongst my books and work in Old Gorton Manor. I am passing it to you now.

In 1814 a ship called the Mentor *was sailing from Athens to London laden with Greek antiquities and also with an amphora containing a Cupid. Because she was a Diviner, my great-grandmother was hired by a Lord Elgin to guard this amphora, and he entrusted her with the book that told her everything about the Cupid and how to control it. The* Mentor *sank in a storm, but its cargo was recovered, including the amphora.*

I have convincing reasons to believe that the spirit which was contained in the amphora has now come looking for the book. I am too old and my powers as a Diviner are no longer strong enough to fend it off, but you are young and a very powerful Diviner.

'It confirms it's hereditary,' said Clarissa, 'and I think your mum knew Mrs Cawsley-May was going to be killed. But maybe not where, or when.'

'What's hereditary?'

'Being – well, a Diviner. It must be.'

'So let's say – we had kids – just saying, for argument's sake – we fell in love – then our kids may be like you?'

'Depends.'

'Depends on what?'

'I don't know. Fate. Genetics. Who knows?'

Clarissa carefully opened the book and read the first line on the first page. *'I am passing this book into your hands, my lord, with the greatest gratitude and respect, but also to advise you that you are now in possession of powers that rightly belong to the gods.'*

'I don't think we have much choice in it, Lucas. It's meant to be. That's why I need to translate this book, and keep it safe.'

That evening, Clarissa welcomed Paula into The Snug.

'Great to see you again, how are you?'

'I'm quite excited.'

Lucas walked out from the kitchen and asked: 'Do you want a glass of wine?'

'I'd love to Lucas, but I've got nine months to wait! Raspberry leaf tea for me please!'

Clarissa smiled. Paula was obviously bursting to tell him.

'Ah, congratulations!' he looked at Clarissa with a look of *why didn't you tell me?* across his face.

'A best friend's confidence,' she grinned.

'Aah. See. You can trust her with your diamonds *and* your secrets!' smiled Paula.

'If I had any,' winked Lucas.

Clarissa blushed.

'We've made it past the first few months of pregnancy. We can tell everyone now!'

Lucas hugged Paula and congratulated her again. Just then a knock sounded at the front door.

'Oh that'll be Ben, he was just parking the car. Got himself a new Audi, he's chuffed to bits, thanks to you helping his promotion to gallery assistant,' she said to Clarissa.

'I hear congratulations are in order, mate!' Lucas said to him as he walked in. 'Really happy for you, you stud!' He hugged Ben in a manly way, as if he had reunited with a long lost friend.

'Thanks, mate. I'm going to be a *dad!*'

Lucas looked at Ben and smiled. He knew he was going to be like a little brother he never had.

Clarissa and Paula walked into the living room and sat at the table.

'So how are you now?'

'I still miss Mrs Ball terribly. So does Lucas, of course, but it's getting loads easier. Mostly because she's out of pain and in another place, watching over us.'

'Good, that's good, babes. And how's everything going with you two? Any romance? And all this weird creepy stuff then?' Paula asked, settling into the armchair and taking a sip of her raspberry tea.

Clarissa thought Paula looked healthy and very happy, and although a long way off birth, she thought that being a mum was going to be just perfect for her.

'Well, strange you should ask. We are close', she blushed. 'And I may stay here a while for protection. It all seemed to go quiet after Mrs Ball died. I mean nothing strange has happened, and I haven't seen anything unusual. No people with horrible faces recently. I don't know whether being here loads has done that – this house must be very protected from anyone undesirable. Even the postman has a kind soul! The last one I knew was a real creep. We've been talking about moving in together for that reason of being ultra – safe, but keeping my flat rented to Dave until we want the money for a bigger move. I just hope it wouldn't be too risky.'

'*Risky*?' asked Paula. 'What do you mean?'

'I often wonder if our time is running out here, as though Mrs Ball's energy can protect us only for so long, now that she's gone. Now you've moved out too maybe Lucas and I could share here until we feel ready to buy a place elsewhere, perhaps the coast. I used to dream of living by the sea, so maybe it's happening for a reason. Maybe it was meant for me. When I think back to everything weird and sad that's happened over the years – all the signs that I've been given, all the omens – and how I've always managed to escape danger myself – each time there was somebody to take care of me. But I'm not sure that will last forever. And besides, I don't want to rely on that – I grew up strong by feeling alone. Everything has an expiration day.'

Paula looked at Clarissa with both empathy and respect. 'You think you and Lucas are in danger now you know *why* this has all been happening?'

'Yes. There has been a reason why this boy has appeared and killed people I was close to, and – Mrs Cawsley-May – I think she was the link to the book. I think he gets stronger with time and definitely more angry.'

'I'm a bit confused.' Paula picked up the pouch in front of them and tipped a few little tooth-shaped objects onto the table from inside it. 'What are these?'

'They are made from bone. Take one, keep it with you. They're like good luck charms.'

'O – kay –'

'So anyway, when I was eight, I found this book in an old house that we used to visit as kids. It was my birthday and I wanted to explore – and it was in an old attic room. Then this angry little boy, about my age, appeared in the doorway. Do you remember I mentioned it once?'

'Yep,' she said studying the bone.

'Well, I now know he appeared because I disturbed some old books – and one of them was *his* book or at least a book about him, and how to handle him. Just before she died, Mrs Cawsley-May gave it to me to look after, although she never had the chance to tell me what it was all about, and why I needed to look after it. The book's all written in some really obscure Greek dialect, and I was never able to translate it. Well, not until now.'

Paula blinked, but didn't say anything. She was used to Clarissa talking in what seemed at first to be riddles, and so she waited patiently to hear her out, all the time clasping the bone tightly in her hand, as if that would help her to understand.

'I'm sure the boy's haunting me, following me and hurting the people I care about because I have it. It explains about what and who he is, and it has instructions on how he can change his appearance and how he can return to his true self. Without it, he can't return to that. He can *possess* other people, yes – take over their appearance and their personality. I'm almost sure now that he did that with Mark, and maybe with Laura. But he can't do any more than that, not without this book, and not without his amphora.'

'His *what*? Can't we burn the book and hope he'll die with it if he's a ghost?'

'No. His amphora. It's like a huge jar. As far as I can work out, holy men in ancient Greece used to catch spirits and seal them in amphora, so that they could take them from place to place and let them out whenever they needed them – say, to help somebody whose crops had failed, or to make two people fall in love, especially if they didn't particularly fancy each other.'

'That sounds cool! Well, it *would* have been cool before I met Ben!'

Clarissa smiled. 'From what I've managed to translate so far, spirits always have to go back to their amphora if they want to regain their original form. The boy's a boy now – but if he could return to his amphora, he could become a man, a cherub, a demon.'

'Or whatever shape he desires?' finished Paula.

'We all need our truth and our guidance in life and this book is his. Everything has happened to me because this book contains the secrets of his existence – the secrets that even *he* doesn't know – and that's why he'll do anything to get his hands on it.'

'So – this amphora,' said Paula.

'It's in storage in The North Chapel. At least I'm pretty sure it's the same one. It's been there ever since the boy was first handed over to the orphanage. And that was in eighteen-fifteen. There was a photograph of all the orphans there too, but one of the kid's faces was all scrubbed out, as though on purpose.'

'Do you know something, Clarry?' said Paula. 'This all sounds totes insane. I mean, if he was put into that orphanage in eighteen-fifteen, he must be –' She tried to work out the figures on her fingers, but eventually gave up. 'Well, *old*, anyway.'

'Yes,' said Clarissa, simply. 'He is old. *Very* old, as far as I can work out.'

'And he can't be human, can he? If he's that old, and he used to live in a jar –'

'He's *not* human, Paula. He's a kind of a spirit. In fact the book says that he's a Cupid.'

'You're joking! You mean like those –' and Paula flapped her hands like little wings.

'I'm serious. They were always painted like that, Cupids, but I don't think they looked any different from ordinary children. Or adults, when they wanted to be.'

Listen Closely

Clarissa passed the book to Paula. Paula sniffed it and said, 'It certainly smells old. Smells like the inside of my granny's shoe-cupboard.'

'See if you can read it.'

Paula gently opened the cover and began to turn the pages.

'It's beautiful. Delicate pages. God – what sort of writing is this? No chance.'

'That, my sweet, is a very obscure Greek dialect.' Clarissa held out her hand. 'May I?'

Paula nodded and passed the book back to her. Clarissa turned a few pages into the book, where she had left a marker and began to read out loud.

'"Love between two people is not a feeling, it is a state of mind, and it is cupids, or erotes, who induce this state of mind. Their arrows are only symbolic, but like real arrows they can infect you with love or poison you with it. They can inspire bliss, or the blackest of jealous rages."'

'Does that mean that if you've fallen in love – if *anybody's* fallen in love – then Cupid did it?'

'Yes. But, of course there's more than one Cupid, which explains the world being *infected* by love and hate, if you like.'

Clarissa turned a page. 'It says here: "Shadows don't exist as living entities in themselves. They're just the absence of light. When the gods created the universe, they spread light around, created everything *good*. After they were completely satisfied, they stopped creating, but they left many dark crevices where light had yet to penetrate. That darkness gave an infinite number of breeding-grounds for evil. Cupids grew from the darkness within their own amphora. They need that special darkness – the darkness that the gods forgot to shine on."'

Paula put her tea mug down, remembering there was no

English in the book.

'What the *hell*?! You didn't – you haven't just read all that from the book – *oh, my, God.*'

'Stop saying God. I'm beginning to think we might need Him.'

Paula raised her eyebrows. 'Sorry,' she winced. 'I don't know what to be more shocked about! I'm so amazed you can read it! *It's Greek!* It's not even modern Greek, it's – it's gobbledy-Greek!'

'Tell me about it,' said Clarissa. 'That's why I know that we could be in genuine danger now. I don't think I would have been given the ability to translate it if it hadn't been urgent.'

She didn't tell Paula how she had been given the gift of translation. She was already stretching her belief to the limit, and besides, she didn't want to think about Mrs Ball, not at the moment. It was too emotional.

'It says in the front of this book that it was given to the seventh Earl of Elgin by a holy man called Father Cadmus on the Greek island of Kythira. It's almost like a manual for how to control a Cupid, and – *listen* – this is the important bit. "Release the spirit my lord when your son and his intended meet together, and she should be filled with uncontrollable desire for him."'

'Wow,' said Paula.

'It seems to me that Lord Elgin bought this Cupid in order to make some young woman fall for his son,' said Clarissa. 'I did some Googling and found out that Lord Elgin was practically bankrupt in 1815, because he had spent seventy-thousand pounds of his own money bringing the Elgin Marbles to Britain.'

'Is that why they're called the Elgin Marbles?' asked Paula. 'Because of him?'

'That's right. He offered to sell them to the British Museum but they would only give him thirty-five thousand pounds for them, so he was close to losing his family home and everything. He kept writing letters to his bankers saying that his son was about to marry the daughter of a rich landowner called Coldwell. He wrote several times that the marriage was "almost signed and sealed". I think that was when he brought Cupid back from Greece.'

'So this girl fell for his son, and Cupid did it? That's incredible.'

Clarissa shook her head. 'I'm reading between the lines, but it's a historical fact that they never got married because Lord Elgin's son developed an incurable skin rash that nearly killed him, and Coldwell's daughter became physically sick every time they met. That's what I think Cupid did. He was so angry that Lord Elgin had taken him away from his homeland that he ruined everything for him.'

'So is that when the boy got sent to the orphanage?'

'I'm sure it was. And there, in the orphanage, the boy was never allowed to return to his amphora, which he might have been able to use to grow up to adult size. This was kept under lock and key with written instructions that he was never to have access to it again. And the book was given to a Mary Stebbings – Mrs Cawsley-May's grandmother. Mrs Cawsley-May married a Mr Cawsley, hence her double-barrelled name.'

'Your mum's friend – at the gallery – who gave you the book – *wow*.'

Clarissa nodded. 'The boy himself was never permitted to leave the orphanage, and after he had assaulted members of staff several times, he was kept in solitary confinement. From 1815 to the present, he remained in the orphanage, never growing older.'

'Oh my God.'

'Then, one day, in 1954, there was a disastrous fire at the orphanage, killing some children, and the boy escaped – I think he started that fire, too.'

Clarissa looked across at Paula, who was totally focused on her.

'It was then that the surviving orphans were temporarily homed at The North Chapel, alongside pots and relics, the piano – and the amphora. All they had left of their own were old books and a few photographs. Lucky the library didn't burn down or else there would be next to no record of all this.'

Paula was astonished. 'And now he's after you – because of this book?'

'Seems so,' said Clarissa.

'I don't know … why don't you just give it to him? Maybe then he'll leave you alone.'

'I can't,' said Clarissa. 'Mrs Ball was quite clear about that. He's been able to hurt other people around me, but so long as I have the book, he can't hurt *me*. If he ever got hold of it, and got back to his amphora – well, I don't know what shape or form he would be in, but he would certainly tear me apart. I have no doubt of that at all.'

'So what are you going to do?'

Clarissa looked firmly at Paula. 'Expose him. When the time is right.'

'But how?' asked Paula.

'It will weaken him so that he won't have the strength to possess other people anymore, just think of Mark, and Laura, and that creepy man from my childhood. They were *all* him, I'm sure of it. The only thing is, I'll never know the moment of exposure until it happens. As long as I have my Watchers protecting me, he disappears, but one day they won't – and neither will he. Until I expose him … which means exposing his truth by reading this book to him.'

Clarissa realised just how strange and surreal all of this must sound, like something from Netflix but actually happening in their daily lives.

'Read me more from the book please – although I'm a little scared now,' said Paula, 'I'm fascinated too. And I didn't know you could read Greek!'

'I can't,' winked Clarissa. *'But something Divine inside me, can.'*

Unfinished Business

Clarissa frantically tapped at her mobile keypad to find *Lucas Mob*. After it had rung for a short while, Lucas picked up.

'Lucas – I'm not sure how much more of this I can take.'

She looked around. 'I've seen him again. The boy. When you left for work he was standing in the garden watching you. I'm so scared he's going to hurt you. I'm so sorry, maybe I shouldn't have stayed over, maybe it was the wrong decision. I've drawn him towards *you*. Maybe he'll attack *you* next thinking we're in love. Oh God.'

She walked into the front room and sat on the sofa, staring at the back door.

'When we talked about moving in together, moving to the sea, do you think there's any way at all that we could? Away from here? Away from him? Maybe it's just my imagination but I don't think it is. It's like the boy is always watching me, or at least I feel that he is. Lurking round the corner at the end of the street, or behind the trees in the park. I can even feel him standing behind the shower-curtain in the bathroom in the evening when I've returned from my run as though he's followed me through the park and along the streets. I'm so scared that one day he'll show up and hurt you, so if I can't control the moment to expose him and get rid of him, I at least want to be able to take us out of danger. If we move, he'll be left here, right? He can't follow us, can he, if he doesn't know where we've gone?'

Clarissa held the phone closely to her cheek while her other hand rubbed and soothed her face. 'I know, I know, I'm tired and emotional but really, I feel like I'm running out of hours for myself, I mean I feel I'm constantly thinking about him, looking out for him – I feel it's all I do. I can't concentrate at work. I want to think about nicer things, like falling in love again, and enjoying life more. I need a distraction and moving to somewhere different will do me so much good right now.'

She pushed off her chunky socks, settling herself on the sofa. 'I know it's a lot to ask, The Snug is so special, we wouldn't have to sell it of course not, but I'm so tired of being frightened and having so many reminders. I really am. Please just say we can look again at all our dates and options,' she sniffed, chewing her thumbnail. Nodding, she said: 'I care about you too. Okay, talk to you tonight when you get back. Bye.'

Clarissa put her phone on the sofa next to her and let out a long, deep sigh. She picked up the TV remote but when she looked up, she saw that the boy was standing in front of the television, staring at her with an extraordinary expression on his pale, grubby face. It was a chilling mixture of hatred and amusement – the smile of somebody who knows that they can do you harm, and fully intends to one day.

She screamed and clambered up onto the sofa.

'*Go away!*' she shouted. '*Go away! I hate you! I hate you!*'

The boy tilted his head and whined, as if he were telling her that he had heard everything that she said to Lucas on the phone and was proving he was getting stronger, and without Mrs Ball's powers protecting the house, he could finally enter what was once *her* sanctuary. Clarissa realised that she could see the television picture right through him, and then, gradually, he faded away. Cautiously, she climbed off the sofa and looked around the room but he was gone. She waited a moment, and listened, but all she could hear was the distant sound of traffic. She slumped back down onto the sofa and sobbed. 'Leave me alone, *please*! I can't help you. I *won't* help you. Leave me alone!'

Think Twice

'This is it,' said Clarissa, looking at Ben, Paula and Lucas in turn. 'The North Chapel. Time to end this.'

It was seamlessly dark with only one small torch, but the four of them groped their way along the path to the chapel door and pushed at it.

'It's locked,' said Clarissa. 'Let's see if there's another way in.'

'It's really creepy,' whispered Paula. 'And I can hear owls. Actual owls, like a ghost story! It's so spooky.'

As they crept around the side of the chapel Clarissa turned around, feeling as though they were being watched.

'Here,' said Ben. 'There's another door.'

Lucas clicked the button on the torch. 'There's a padlock, no good.'

Clarissa turned back to them and smiled. 'Old fashioned – I have a hairpin, let's try.'

She fiddled with the padlock for a few moments, and then it clicked open.

'You missed your vocation,' said Lucas. 'You should have been a burglar.'

As they walked into the chapel, a chilly breeze blew over them and tugged the door back in a draught, as if somebody were impatiently trying to pull it shut. The door creaked as Clarissa gently closed it.

'I hope God understands what we're doing in His house,' said Paula. 'I really hope He does.'

'He sees everything,' said Lucas, 'but He'll definitely understand we are trying to save lives by stopping evil. He'll protect us, too, and your miniature unborn baby, so don't be scared.'

Paula grabbed at Ben's arm. 'Ben, I haven't been to church in years. I hope God still loves *me*. We've got pregnant before marriage!' She was smiling but Clarissa could tell how frightened she was.

'I don't like the way our voices sound in here,' Paula whispered to Ben. 'All echo-ey.'

Clarissa led the way along the corridor through to the room where Roger Harding had shown her the pots and relics. 'This is it. It's open. Mind your footing.'

'What's in *there*?' asked Paula as they passed a closed door.

'Library,' said Clarissa.

'Can't you just put the book in there and leave it, so all of this will go away?' asked Ben.

'No, she can't,' said Paula with empathy, 'because it *won't*.'

'Smells damp, doesn't it, and it's really cold,' said Lucas.

Clarissa stopped, and as she did so she thought she heard a whispering sound. '*Sssh*! Did you hear that?'

'Oh God, don't freak me out,' said Paula. 'Keep going.'

Clarissa walked forward and they all followed her. Clarissa knew the whispering meant they weren't alone. It was as though she could hear the books the other side of the library door, all desperate to tell her the tragic stories of their lives in the orphanage.

As they reached the cold, cell–like storeroom, Clarissa stopped. 'Lu – can you give me the torch, please?'

Clarissa swept the room with the beam of the torch and Paula gasped. 'Whoa, look at all these *pots*! There's *loads* of them!'

'They're amphoras,' Clarissa confirmed. 'Jars that the Greeks used to use for wine, and oil. And Cupids, apparently.'

She took a step forward and leaned close to one of the amphoras. 'I wonder which one is his? It must be one of the larger ones, if he can get inside it.'

'Look!' said Paula. 'This big one here has a plaque!' She fumbled with her mobile phone, trying to get its torch to work.

Clarissa crouched down and shone the torch directly at it, and remembered what she had read in the book.

Putto is the demon of lust and fornication. He has been described as a dark cherub who floats around the universe, causing people to succumb to their basest desires. But his evil is not a thing in itself, it thrives only where there is an absence of good in someone's soul.

She turned to Lucas then back at the amphora. 'Love not only creates good, Lu, but it can encourage evil, did you know that?'

Ben glanced over and nudged Lucas. 'I feel we should be getting out the Ouija board –'

'Ben!' said Paula in a teacher's tone of voice, still gripping his arm. 'That's not funny.'

'What does it say on the plaque? Has anyone noticed the weird smell in here, too?' asked Ben.

Clarissa shone the light again. 'It says '"*The book that claims to tell my story is a book of lies*".'

Clarissa stood up straight and shone the torch at the wall, leaning in to look at the framed photograph that was fixed there, of the orphans around the piano. 'When I was a child and visited Old Gorton Manor on my birthday, all kinds of strange people were saying weird things to me. Not horrible, but just as if they knew I had a reason for being there. The boy I saw, looked just like the boys in this photograph.'

'It almost sounds as if there were angels there that day, doesn't it?' said Paula. 'Like they were watching you, and showing you what you were going to be when you grew up.'

'Yep. Like angels, or guides. At first I thought the boy was haunting the book, but now I know that he *needs* the book because it explains how he can grow and how somebody can keep him a prisoner and how he can get himself free. And I'm sure that *this* amphora – this is his home,' she said, turning back to the pots. 'Well, his home and his prison, both, depending on who has the book.'

'But if it says that the book is all lies …'

'I think it's a riddle. I don't know who put it here, or why. Maybe the holy man who gave it to Lord Elgin. Maybe he did it to confuse the boy himself, or maybe he meant it to confuse anybody who came looking for him. But this is the biggest amphora here, and the only one with a plaque.'

'He must be a very, very old soul,' said Lucas. 'Cupids like him have been in paintings since forever. Clarissa – he must be all over the gallery!'

'Maybe fate made you get the job there!' said Paula.

'Yes – but if it *was* fate, that means that you're at serious risk – or at least the people close to you are. No light without dark, remember,' Lucas frowned.

'Yes which means no me without the boy,' Clarissa finished with a groan.

'If this boy's always trying to get hold of the book and return to this amphora, that means he's never far away. You must be the Diviner he's after next. And *you* know the truth about him because you know how to translate it. That makes it ten times worse.'

'That's one angry little angel,' Ben said.

'You're right, Ben, he *is* angry,' said Clarissa.

'And that's why we need to smash this amphora.' Nodded Paula.

'Blimey,' said Ben. 'Won't we get into trouble for it?'

'Nobody needs to know it was us. And far worse things could happen if we don't. If we smash it, he can't return to it and that will give me the chance to destroy *him* before he destroys anyone else.' Finished Clarissa.

Paula reached across to Ben. 'I don't feel so well.'

'Stop worrying. It's going to be fine. Nobody will find us here. Just chill.'

'I don't know what you are so sure about! You were scared to come here in the first place.' She snapped. 'I'm the pregnant one!'

Clarissa scowled at Ben. 'Shh. Look. Look at this.'

Ben patted Paula on the back as if to say: *it's okay.* Paula shrugged him off and rubbed at her stomach. They leaned in to what Clarissa had to show them.

'What is *that?*'

'Jeeez, it smells like somebody's thrown up in there!'

As they peered into the amphora, the smell of putrid apples and mould was so strong that Paula heaved. Clarissa placed her hands on the top of the coarse clay neck of the amphora and began to push at it. 'Help me tip it over. Come on.'

The four of them grasped the amphora and half-lifted it out of its black metal tripod. Then they rocked it, again and again, then from side to side until it toppled completely and smashed into eight large pieces on the concrete floor. A heap of fine reddish ash sifted out of it, as well as twenty or thirty small silver medallions, corroded black.

'That was easier than I thought.' Lucas picked one up and peered at it under the torch light. 'Look at the scary face on this. Looks like some god, or some monster. Maybe we could check it out on Google. Who's got their phone?'

'No, Lu. Just drop it,' said Clarissa.

'The boy hasn't got anywhere to come back to now, even if he does get hold of the book – which I'm not going to let him. It seemed a little too easy to destroy it, didn't it, but it was the right thing. So I really don't think we ought to take anything else that belongs to him. We don't want to make him even angrier than he is already. We've just smashed up his home as it is! Think about it. How would you feel?' Clarissa held Lu's hand, and squeezed it. Lucas looked at her as if to say: *fair point.* For the first time in a long time she felt that she had used her Divining talents to protect the people she cared about. Ben gave one of the broken pieces of pottery a desultory kick, and then the four of them began to make their way back out of the room, but after a few paces, they stopped dead.

'Wait.'

'What?'

'Can you hear that? Listen. It's coming from over there.'

'What is?'

'Just sounds like a dripping tap,' whispered Paula. 'Keep moving.'

Clarissa urged them to hurry. 'We need to get out of here, now.'

Just then, as she turned to check on Lucas, she saw that he had stopped. 'Come on!'

'I can't move,' said Lucas. 'I – I – my feet won't move. I'm – I'm *stuck.*' Within seconds Lucas realised that his shirt had become saturated with blood, which had started to drip from the cuffs. Lucas looked at Clarissa, terrified. 'It wasn't a tap dripping Clarry … it was blood,' he said.

'Lu – stay still – everything will be okay, he's haunting me, with Craig's death. It's not your blood – it's not real – it'll stop.' Just then, she felt a tugging at her back, and Ben was suddenly gasping for air as though all the oxygen in the corridor had been sucked away from him. He pulled at her and gripped his throat.

'Ben stay calm – it's not rea–' Clarissa took a sharp intake of breath herself and was shoved violently to the wall and seemingly pinned there by her neck, also gasping for air and kicking her feet. The torch clattered to the floor, its light flickering.

'Clarry!' Paula screamed. 'Get off of her! What's happening? *Leave her alone!*'

Just then, Paula started choking, too. Clarissa fell to the floor, wheezing while catching her breath at suddenly being released. Then, at the doorway behind them, the boy appeared.

He glared at them as he raised one arm, pointing.

Ben scrambled to his feet and picked up a chunk of the amphora, throwing it toward him. 'Leave her alone! Leave her alone!'

The boy stood there, unphased, with a dark, menacing look on his face.

Paula managed to take in a shallow, panicky breath and began to cry.

'Clarry you need to get out of here! Leave us! Just go!' shouted Lucas. 'Get yourself to safety!'

Clarissa scrabbled around for the torch, coughing. The boy stared at her, his arm pointing back towards her. The uneven floor beneath her started trembling, and gushing something from between the cracks in the flagstones. It was freezing cold water with a strong smell of the sea , and within seconds it was sloshing over her hands and feet and soaking into her clothing. Stumbling and splashing to get to her feet, she ran to Lucas and pulled at him. 'Come on, come on, think *Afiste Mas* – you must get free! He's going to drown us!'

Clarissa heard an ear-shattering screech as the boy jumped in front of her, his head tilted. Through the noise she shouted at him: 'You're the boy with the scratched out face from that picture at the orphanage! It's you, isn't it!'

The boy didn't change his menacing expression, but instead his mouth stretched wide open, and twisted, as the building began to grind and creak, as though they were surrounded by timbers on an old ship in a violent storm.

'It must be the ship he was on – The *Mentor* – he's making us re-live it before he kills us.'

'Wait! I'm going to be sick!' Paula cried.

Clarissa looked at Paula, shining the torch at her instead of Lucas and gasped. 'Holy shit what's wrong with your eye? It's bleeding!'

Paula jolted forwards and gripped tightly at her stomach, to her unborn baby. As she did so a howling wind swept through the chapel and a huge flash of electric blue light lit the chapel windows.

'Paula!' Clarissa shoved Ben out the way and leaned across to her friend. 'Paula!'

Paula grabbed Clarissa's arm. 'We need to go, I don't want to die!'

'Be strong! You must be strong!'

Lucas managed to move himself and grabbed Clarissa's arm. 'I said, go, Clarry, hurry!'

'I want to kill him – before he hurts all of us!' shouted Ben.

'You can't! It's too late! It's started!'

Clarissa fumbled for the antidote tooth vial in her pocket but she could no longer find it.

Ben grabbed for his mobile phone, and reached out pulling at Paula, passing it to her. 'Go – get out! Get help!' But as he did so, the boy wiggled his fingers and he felt a sharp scratch. Ben tried the door handle behind him that lead to the library, but it seemed to be locked. 'We're trapped.'

Clarissa and Paula struggled as they waded and splashed along the corridor through the rising, icy water, towards the door as the remaining lights above them swung and flickered and timber continued to creak. The chapel felt as though it was moving and small parts of brickwork splashed into the water and the howling wind sent debris and leaves into a violent whirl around them.

'This is the only way out!' Clarissa shouted.

Paula turned to look back along the corridor at Ben, who was now next to Lucas, shouting and throwing bits of brickwork at the boy to distract him away from Paula and Clarissa, who, in desperation, tugged at the door against the weight of the rising water.

Trembling, Paula's expression was terrified. 'Guys we can't do it, help us, it's too hard!' she screamed, looking to Ben. He got closer to them, only to realise he was bleeding. 'Ben?' He raised his arm and squeezed hard on it.

'I'll be okay, come on, don't stop trying!'

'Let us out you bastard!' yelled Paula. 'These are my people! Have you never cared once in your miserable, evil existence? *Let us go!*'

'Pull!'

'The water's freezing!'

'Come on, we have to survive this!' Clarissa lost grip on the torch and watched in despair as its fading beam sunk into the dark, churning water.

Lucas and Ben tugged harder and harder at the chapel door as the building continued to be at the mercy and anger of rolling waves and cracking lightning. Eerily, the boy was rising with the level of the water, raising both his arms, and something slithered around their legs as the water continued to rise, splashing fiercely onto their faces.

Clarissa remembered the photograph. *Maybe if I destroyed it his power would fade or he would disappear.* She turned and waded back through the water along the corridor to the room with the amphora.

'Clarry no – where are you going! It's getting deeper!'

Clarissa fought against the movement of the waves and managed to get a grip on the picture fastened to the wall. She thumped at the glass until it broke, the salted sea water stinging her cuts. Scratching at the photograph, she heard the boy whine. She carried on, until she managed to rip as much out as possible and tore at it with such aggression that she found herself shouting with hatred: *'There's no way you're getting back, or free – no way!'* She ripped it over and over and threw the pieces into the water around her.

The boy moaned and screamed but there was nothing he could do. To Clarissa, his face seemed to flicker as if it were being torn up, like the photograph.

The door that Lucas, Paula and Ben had been wrestling with burst open, and they were pushed out with the pressure of the water and tumbled in a heap to the ground, the water eagerly rushing out beyond them onto the grass.

They helped Paula to her feet, and staggered away from the chapel and the mournful screeching of the boy. Clarissa edged and paddled her way around the room far away from the boy as fast as she could and followed them out, as the photograph's sodden pieces settled in the lowering water.

Outside, Clarissa coughed trying to catch her breath in the cold night air, running from the chapel door.

It was so dark that they could barely see, and the shrill, unearthly screeches of the boy echoed through the night air so hauntingly that Paula began to sob with fear.

'Keep going, get far away from the building!'

'My stomach, it hurts, it hurts so much! My baby! He's done something to me, I'm sure!'

'Keep trying for an ambulance, or give me the phone, hold on babe!' said Ben.

In the darkness Clarissa stumbled on tufts of grass and the stone edging of a path between the graves, as she ran ahead with Lucas, toward the gate, with a deep sense of unease inside her as the dark shapes of trees swayed in the wind all around them, not knowing if the boy would appear in front them, angry at their escape.

Lucas tugged hard at the bars of the iron gate until it moved in with him, and in return there was a slow rusted creak as it opened wide, and they pushed through. The trees were silhouetted against the moonlight and crows sat scattered in the trees above them, watching them, as though awaiting their fate.

Once they'd made their way out, they stopped, trying to catch their breath. Clarissa looked back toward the chapel as Ben and Paula caught up, and Clarissa pulled them through onto the pavement. Enormous flames lept up, bright white and orange patches flickering all around the chapel, in an angry display of the boy's revenge as his distressing shrills continued to pierce the night air. Then, the flames began to fade, as though the boy was losing his power, or giving up, and suddenly, they sucked back into nothing and disappeared.

'Ben, Ben you're hurt, he cut you, you're losing so much blood, you need a medic,' sobbed Paula, trying to put pressure on the wound.

'Help is on its way. Won't be long now babe,' he said soothingly, as he put his good arm around her and held her tight. Paula hugged him back.

'I love you babe, everything will be okay.'

Paula didn't say anything but instantly, she stiffened, then buckled in pain, gripping her stomach and collapsed to the pavement, letting out a high pitched mewl.

'Paula?' said Ben.

'Paula!' Clarissa dropped to her knees in desperation to help her.

Ben knelt down beside her. 'Paula? Paula! No, *Paula*!'

With blood trickling from the corners of both eyes and bubbling from her mouth, she winced in pain, crumpling up on the cold pavement, her eyes strained and skin turning whiter by the second.

Clarissa brushed the hair from her friend's forehead, and cried out with such anger for the boy, and so loudly in distress that the crows flapped away and there was a sudden deathly stillness in the air.

Clarissa lifted Paula slightly, cradling her, and wiping her face. 'No!'

Ben let go of her hand and slowly stood up, stepping backwards.

Clarissa held her friend's body as she felt her precious life leave it. Paula went limp, and Clarissa knew she was gone.

Ben covered his mouth in horror as Lucas tightly hugged him.

There was the faint warble of a siren, and Lucas hurried into the road. At the brow of the hill, in the distance, a blurry flicker of blue light became visible through the night's misty, fine rain.

'Stop!' he yelled, waving his arms as it got closer. 'Over here! Help us!'

The ambulance slowed, and stopped, as two male paramedics jumped out, grabbing a bag each and rushed over to Clarissa, who was still holding Paula.

'What's happened? What's her name?

'Thank God you're here,' Clarissa said. '*Thank God*. Her name is Paula. She's ... she was ... is ... pregnant.'

The paramedics lifted the trolley carrying Paula's body and clicked its wheels into place in the back of the ambulance, and shut the doors.

Ben sat inside the ambulance staring numbly as the paramedics treated his arm, knowing there was nothing he could have done to save her.

Outside, Lucas paced beside the ambulance on the phone, talking to Paula's parents.

Wrapped in a heavy blanket, Clarissa sat, trying to accept the death of her friend, *another death, because of me*. Her eyes suddenly crowded with tears.

'*Is it over now?*' she whispered to the paramedic tending to the cuts on her hands. '*Is it?*'

He didn't answer, but he smiled at her; a smile that understood what it was like to have felt great loss, time and time over. She looked in his eyes, and even though he had said nothing, she could instantly divine his goodness and heartbreak, and saw her own kindness reflected back at her.

We're safe, at last. She thought. *We're all safe now.*

AFTER

Impression

Hugo Walker welcomed Clarissa at the top of the mezzanine floor. 'Bon Voyage, Clarissa!'

Inside the gallery people gathered around them, clapping and grinning.

'We wanted to give you this gift for your new home to wish you all the very best in your move, and your next chapter in life.' Hugo leaned in and kissed her on the cheek, whispering: 'We're sorry for what you've been through lately and hope this brings you a little comfort or joy.'

She bowed her head, with a smile, 'Thanks.''We'll be sad to see you go!' he announced.

Clarissa felt dreadful in herself after recent events and was aware she looked drawn and tired but didn't want to let Hugo down; after all he had gone to a lot of trouble to arrange the leaving drinks at the gallery. Because it had been a crucial part of her life she felt she had to be here, if only for a couple of hours.

Lucas smiled at her and kissed her. She wished every day that she could tell Paula how much in love they had become. At the same time she couldn't help but wonder if Craig was here, watching.

Some of her colleagues dabbed at their eyes and Lisa called out: 'You'll be missed!' as she waved at her, blowing a kiss.

Just then, Hugo nodded at one of the gallery staff and a few moments later, two of them came shuffling through the crowd with a large painting, with a bow fastened to the corner. She clapped along with the others, blushing, and thanked Hugo.

Smiling at Clarisa, the gallery staff wished her good luck, gave her a quick hug and left the painting with him, who steadied it and tapped it, smiling at Clarissa. 'We chose this for you.'

Clarissa's hands covered her mouth, as she felt a mild surge of delight. A feeling that had been dormant for a little while. *A painting, for me?* 'Thank you!'

'You *do* like it, don't you?' I've heard you talk about it so often.' Hugo crossed his arms and looked at her expectantly.

Clarissa nodded, but she couldn't quite get her words out, and couldn't help feeling happy yet alarmed at the same time because the painting was *The Woodman's Daughter*.

The little girl figure and the little boy figure had happy expressions on their faces, and they both appeared to be smiling at her directly. The feeling of the painting was different, warming and full of rich colours as it should be. *They're smiling, and everything looks okay ... something must have changed, maybe the boy has gone*, she thought.

'Yes,' she said hesitantly. 'Yes, I do like. It's a very influential painting for me, thank you,' she smiled. 'I love it!'

'Great! She loves it!' said Hugo, raising his arms, smiling to the crowd of staff and clients as they cheered and clapped.

'We'll have it sent to your new address.'

Light of Day

As they put the last of the cases into the removal van, Clarissa asked Maggie: 'Any man in tow?'

'Who needs a man when I've got Harold the dog,' she oozed. '*You'll* never break my heart, will you boy!' Harold the stocky French bulldog made an affectionate whine as he sat, wriggling into a comfortable position.

Ma leaned into Lucas, squeezing his arm. 'This is it, a new start. But you will come and visit me, won't you? I'm more than happy to help with any decorating too darlings.'

Clarissa looked at Lucas, knowingly. 'Of course! I'll tie in the trips with the gallery, as I'm helping on their seasonal launches. We're only a few hours away.'

'And besides,' said Lucas, 'you're both welcome any time. The ferries run regularly. Afternoon tea, beach walks – you'll love it. That invite extends to Harold, too, Mags.' Harold snorted as he looked up at Lucas, while blinking in the afternoon sunlight.

Maggie looked at Ma, who was holding back her tears. She nudged Clarissa as if to say: *look at mum.*

'Remember to send me the address, and the Carragh-Hughs … they always ask after you,' said Ma.

'I remember our trips to Blackgang Chine as kids, is it still there?' asked Maggie.

'Hardly,' Clarissa said, 'so much erosion. We can go over there for a tour when you visit, it's very eerie now, apparently.' Maggie smiled and nodded, a tear welling up in her eyes.

Lucas hugged Ma, then Maggie, and said: 'Okay, right, we're all set, we should get going, we need to get to the ferry by six. Clarry, shall we?'

Nursery Rhymes

It took only a few weeks for Clarissa to feel that moving to live by the sea was one of the best decisions they could have made. Every evening, as the birds sang, and the ships' horns sounded in the distant night as they sailed across the Solent, she was reminded just how far she was from the pressures of her old life and the horrors that had trapped her.

Most of all, she didn't feel the presence of the boy here. As each day dawned, she felt more and more confident that they had left him behind, that his attack at the Chapel had been the last desperate attempt: with no book to guide him, no amphora to hide in, and no idea where she and Lucas had actually gone, she was safe.

Most evenings she slept so soundly after a walk along the clifftops or the water's edge, that she felt there was nowhere else she'd rather be. They'd wrap up warm, and head out at sunset, down the cliff steps and onto the beach. From there, they would turn and look up to see the lantern lights on the veranda, looking at their home nestled high on the cliff-top. The house seemed so grand. They'd cuddle with the breeze against their faces, as they looked out to sea: the vast, breathtaking image of solace and simplicity. Her memories of Craig and Paula were peaceful ones now, and she knew that they would be happy, at peace, and that she herself was once more feeling calm and settled. She had felt so calm, in fact, that she had even taken to painting at her easel in the garden, with the vast sea view in front of her, listening to the seagulls squawking as they circled the nearby lighthouse, and the waves as they crashed against themselves, at the turning of a high tide.

After they had taken their early-morning weekend walks, she would always be filled with inspiration. She missed the village shops, the smell of Gretta's Bakery and going to Ma's house for

Sunday lunch, but her visits to Ma had now become sentimental treats to look forward to.

They had finished decorating and furnishing most of the rooms now, except for the nursery, and so yesterday the remainder of their belongings had been delivered from storage. Clarissa stood by the window admiring the sea view, finishing off her morning mug of tea while Lucas was at the DIY store. She waved at a neighbour walking by, and then she turned to the last pile of boxes and books in the corner of the room.

She crouched down next to the boxes and pulled out one marked NURSERY. Smiling, she peeled off the brown tape and opened the box.

'Your daddy and I are going to paint your room, soon, Little One! How is buttercup yellow and duck egg blue for you? Hmm?' Her baby bump slowly turned over, which she felt was acceptance. 'Thought so. You're going to have the loveliest cosiest little room. Let's see what's in your box, shall we?'

Bartholomew mewed and jumped onto Clarissa's lap, she sunk her fingers into the fur on the top of his head and rubbed all around his ears. 'Hey boy.'

Clarissa reached in and pulled out a small white box. Inside was a snow-globe picture frame, with a photograph of her and Lucas outside Bembridge Windmill. 'This is for your bedside table. It's mummy and daddy.'

Next she pulled out a very soft, ribbed giraffe toy that had a button to turn on a soft purple glow from its belly while it played a lullaby. 'This is Roddy the giraffe. He is from your auntie Maggie. Aah, and this is a framed nursery rhyme of *Hickory Dickory Dock* from Nanny.'

Once she had opened all the nursery boxes, and admired the cot that Lucas had built, she went into the next room, where she still had bedroom mirrors and pictures to unwrap.

'Oh, look at all these! Shall we try and get some of these unwrapped and see if we can hang them up ready for when daddy gets home?'

Rubbing her baby bump, she selected a wrapped frame. 'This one first, although it looks a bit heavy for mummy to lift up alone! I think this could be the one from Hugo as it's so big. Maybe I'll get it ready where I want it and then daddy can help me hang it. Now, let's get all this wrapping off.' She crouched down, and carefully peeled off the envelope with her address written on it first, that was sellotaped to the packaging. Opening it, she pulled out a card which read:

Dear Clarissa, with fondness and sincere sadness at you leaving us. We hope the picture brings you happiness. We look forward to seeing you again soon. Do come along to the seasonal events! All the best in your new home. With very best wishes, Hugo and team, Milltower Gallery.

With a smile, she placed it down beside her and started to tear off the padded brown-paper packaging.

As she had seen in the gallery, the little girl figure and boy figure had smiles on their faces. '*The Woodman's Daughter,*' she whispered. '*Just as you should look.*' The feeling of the painting was still warming. The green tones were strong, too, rather than looking drained with evil, or as though the colours were fading with tiredness. The little girl was still holding a fabric-bound book, and there was a positive feel to it. *They're still smiling,* she thought. *Everything looks normal, and nice – I think everything really is going to be ok now.* She let out a sigh of relief and smiled at Bartholomew. 'Everything is just fine!'

She pushed all the wrapping aside and admired the picture for another moment. Just then, she heard a wet, dripping noise. She assumed it was Bartholomew nuzzling his fur for fleas. 'Oh Barthy, not in here boy, please!' She decided to prop the painting up safely against something, and so supported herself on it as she stood up. All of a sudden, Bartholomew jumped away with a hiss, arched his back and ran out of the room. But the wet noise continued. As Clarissa looked back to the painting to lean it against the wall, she too recoiled in panic. She hurriedly stepped back, letting go of the painting, and it fell to the floor with a loud crash, landing flat on its back on the parquet floor. '*Oh my God!*'

Clarissa stared at it, her hand clamped over her mouth, feeling as if she couldn't breathe. It wasn't *The Woodman's Daughter* as she had just seen it. The little girl in the painting had vanished, and the woodman himself had turned his head away and the rich colours had drained. Right at the front of the painting stood the boy, staring up at Clarissa. He was baring his tiny irregular teeth in a menacing grin, and his hands were smothered in blood.

The baby inside her contracted, as if yearning to help, or escape, making her double up and squeeze her eyes shut in pain. When she opened her eyes again, she looked back at the picture, hoping that she had imagined the boy, but he was still there, and still grinning. And she knew *why* he was grinning. He had found her. He had tricked her. He had been in the painting all along, following her, giving her false hope. She had tried to get away from him, but now he had found her.

'*You!*' she said, backing towards the door, her heart thumping and her stomach throbbing. 'Please, God, not you – no, *please*!' She threw the wrapping at the picture so it landed on top of the painting, and then she left the room and slammed the door behind her, frantically turning the old key in the lock.

Lucas came home late that evening, because he had tried to get every last thing they needed for the nursery in Newport town centre.

Clarissa sat watching him while he ate his reheated supper, but he hardly spoke at all, except to say how tired he was, and he didn't even ask her what she had been doing all day.

Clarissa had intended to tell him about *The Woodman's Daughter*, and ask him what they could do with it. She felt like giving it away, or throwing it away, over the cliff edge, or burning it, but she wasn't sure if that would only anger the boy even more – and now, of course, he knew where she lived.

Lucas was so aloof, however, that she decided to say nothing for the time being. Perhaps he was simply exhausted after a long day, but Clarissa was also worried that he might have been influenced by the boy as soon as he walked in the door –

especially since he was so tired rather than excited about his purchases that they'd been saving for.

Before they went upstairs to bed, she shut the dining-room door and pressed her ear to it. She thought she could hear whispering, but it could be nothing more than the draught from the fireplace, and memory of the whining of freshly burning wood.

'What are you doing?' asked Lucas. 'Come to bed, for God's sake.'

The Return of Evil

Clarissa was woken from a nightmare by the sound of glass smashing. The bed was showered in glittering splinters and a freezing chill blustered around her.

'Lucas? Lucas wake up. What was that? There's glass everywhere!'

Lucas didn't answer, and the bed beside her felt flat. Clarissa pushed the covers aside carefully and clambered out of bed slowly, breathing heavily, cradling and stroking her baby bump. Her hair flapped in the gusting wind coming in through the broken window and as she tucked her hair behind her ears, she felt the wetness of blood from a cut on her cheek. She switched on the bedside lamp and looked around the room.

'Lucas?' she called, panicking. 'Where *are you*?' Lucas' side of the bed was empty and glass was scattered over the bed and floor. She looked up at the window. 'What the hell *was* that?'

She grabbed her dressing gown from off the bed and hurriedly put it on. She picked up the telephone handset to dial 999, but there was no dial tone.

'Lucas? Lucas!' she called again, as she slammed the handset down and grabbed her mobile phone from the bedside table, avoiding fragments of glass. Frantically, she tapped on the keypad but her battery was dead.

'*Shit.*'

Moving toward the door, she trod gingerly across the wooden floor in order to avoid cutting her feet. She turned on the main light and pulled the bedroom door open.

No one was there. She couldn't hear a sound, apart from Ma's old long case clock ticking downstairs. There was a strong dull smell in the air, too, engulfing her senses.

'Lucas?' she whispered into the dark landing. '*Where are you?*'

Had he smashed the window or was it someone from

outside? The boy perhaps?

She followed the sound of something vibrating, and could see a glow of light on the floor by the wardrobe. It was Lucas' mobile phone. *OLVENS* said the display. She picked it up and answered.

'Hello?'

'Clarissa?' It was Sally Olven. 'We've been trying to call you. We called Lucas earlier but we were cut off. Love may have silenced him. We are on our way to see you, something is going to happen and you must be ready.'

'The battery's dead on my mobile – and I think someone has cut the landline – listen – it's Lucas, I can't find him – his phone was on the floor. He must have dropped it – and my window's smashed. Something has already begun but I don't know what. I'm scared, Sally. It's nearly three in the morning, how did you – and what do you mean *love* may have …?'

'We're on our way,' Sally interrupted. 'But Clarissa, be ready.'

Clarissa dropped Lucas' mobile phone on to the bed. Stepping across to the chest of drawers, she grabbed the knobbly wooden handles of the top drawer and tugged it open. Reaching inside, she frantically scrambled for a phone charger. She knew it was in here somewhere, amongst the photographs, old receipts and a bottle of near-empty cologne.

Just then, as though she were standing right beside her, Mrs Ball's voice whispered softly in her ear: *Love is strong but you, Clarissa, are stronger.*

Clarissa found the charger and threw it onto the bed. Then opened the second drawer down and reached to the back of it, carefully pulling out the book from its hiding place. Inside it was a letter that Ma had given her and underneath it a small bundle of birthday cards from Mrs Ball. They were wrapped in cloth together and she placed them on the surface of the chest of drawers, next to Mrs Ball's framed photograph.

'Lucas, where are you?' she called out. She placed her hands on her baby bump and said: 'Be strong, little one. I think, it's *time.*'

In spite of the rotating beam of the nearby lighthouse, it was still dark enough outside for anybody to be standing there watching the house, watching her, without her being able to see *them*. Her instincts were telling her that the boy was back for his revenge. She could sense jealousy and anger stronger than ever, as though the boy himself may be stronger, and closer, and she was more aware than ever before of his presence. Was he watching her and her unborn baby but unable to harm her while she slept? So had *he* broken the window in anger? Why didn't she feel or hear Lucas get out of bed?

She tugged open the third drawer down and took the tooth vial out of the drawer and looped its chain over her neck, and then she tucked the book and letters into her dressing gown pockets 'Oh Lucas where are you I need you!' she screamed. Suddenly she didn't feel alone anymore. She sensed something in the room with her.

She slowly pushed the drawer shut, and turned around.

No-one was there. Just the bed and the flapping curtains in the cold gusty wind.

'*Afiste mas!*' she blurted, just in case.

She stood there, listening, but she heard nothing at all. Only her own breath. The boy could be right next to her, almost touching her, and she wouldn't even know until he decided to show himself. Something seemed very different, this cold, cold night.

She kept the painting that had hung in her childhood bedroom covered in cloth down the side of the wardrobe, and she wondered if the characters from her painting were warning her, the way they had when she was younger.

The lights flickered and went out, plunging the room into darkness.

Clarissa slowly edged her way to the opposite side of the room, holding out her right hand until she could feel the wardrobe. The lamp flickered as though it had a loose wire, and the rotating beam of lighthouse flooded the room with light – in, then out, rhythmically. She could see no-one, but could *sense* someone was there.

She opened the wardrobe and from the top shelf removed a small box containing her bottle of holy water. Gripping it tightly, she could feel the embossed image of Mary in the palm of her hand, and she found that strangely reassuring, as if it was confirmation that this water really *was* blessed, and that goodness was on her side. She placed it on the bed next to Lucas' phone.

She could feel her heart thumping, racing against the faint ticking of the clock downstairs.

'Where are you, you horror?' muttered Clarissa. 'Show yourself. I know you're here and I know exactly who you are. Real love never scared me and neither will you!'

The wintry coastal air came gusting in now, bringing a spattering of rain with it, and the clock downstairs struck three.

She knew that nobody would hear her even if she screamed – the wind was south-westerly and her neighbours were at least three hundred yards away.

She looked around the room once more, and her breath froze in her lungs.

There he was.

The boy, the Cupid, was standing to her right, in between the edge of the bed and the wardrobe, with one arm raised. Clarissa took a few steps back until she reached the bed and couldn't go any further.

Before the light flashed round and faded again, Clarissa had time to recognise so many of the boy's various faces – every face of love and lust and every face of evil: endearing, harmful, enchanting and persistent. Somehow this creature was all of them – showing her who he was and who he had been, and how he could manifest himself as anyone he pleased.

'*Go away!*' she shouted. '*I meant it, love never scares me!*' Although she was exhausted, her voice was angrier and stronger, high-pitched with pain and terror both at once. Her baby kicked inside her, as though trying to help her. She pulled the book from her pocket and tried desperately to read from it, although the bad light made it almost impossible.

'*Afiste mas!*' she screamed at him. Then cried: '*Just get out, get the hell away from me! Get out of my life you evil son of a bitch! I was warned about you!* Afiste mas!'

She crouched down against the edge of her bed, rubbing her

stomach. *'Please! I'm pregnant you bastard!'* She was screaming at
the boy, but she knew her anger was also at Mark, and the way
he treated her, and for Craig for not fighting back at the boy, and
for letting Paula come to the chapel, pregnant, and at the smeary
man who had leered at her daily when she was a child.

The beam of the lighthouse turned again. In the momentary
bursts of floodlight she grabbed Lucas' phone again and tried to
guess his numerical password while the tears rolled from her
cheeks. Just then, however, the boy stalked towards her with both
hands stiffly extended and pushed her backwards. She dropped
the phone and it skittered across the floor to the edge of the bed.
Stumbling, she grabbed the edge of the duvet as she fell. The
room became filled with a screeching noise so high-pitched that
the other window smashed and a water glass beside the bed
exploded. Clarissa covered her face and cowered down.

It was then that she saw a foot protruding from under the bed
– and it was glistening red with blood. On another turn of the
light, she could see that it was Lucas'.

She screamed, straining her eyes to see under the bed, but at
the same time trying to keep watch on the boy, who hadn't
moved. The room fell quiet.

She scrambled over to Lucas' body and looked back at the
boy. Her eyes filled with tears and she screamed at him: *'No!'*

The boy looked back at her with all of its many faces of love
and gave her the slightest of smiles, as if he had been waiting for
this moment for so long; waiting for her strength to be exhausted
and her will to be worn down. *You may be a Diviner, Clarissa, but
our patience is endless. Love will always win.*

She froze as she stared back at him. She felt beaten with
exhaustion but reached beneath the bed and began pulling at
Lucas' feet.

'Lu! Darling what has he done to you? Lucas!' In the light she
could see the boy's lips drawing back to expose his array of small
crowded teeth. 'Get away from us you bastard! Get away you
murderer!' Her hatred for him was so intense that she was
quaking.

'Afiste mas!' she shrieked. She continued to rub her stomach,

soothing the deep pain inside her. 'It's okay baby,' she whispered. 'It'll be okay!'

She stood up slowly, her face wet with tears, and held the book in front of her.

She faced the boy.

Keeping her eyes on him, she took in a deep breath. Her determination was stronger than ever, because the thought of losing another man she loved was unbearable, as much as the distressed, discomfort of her unborn baby. She flicked through the pages until she sensed that she had reached the right one. Lowering her eyes, she stared hard at the words in front of her. The lighthouse beam revolved again in the moonlight and the wind and rain continued to bluster into the bedroom. She stared at the book and willed it to help her.

The boy began to cry, wheedling her to feel sorry for him.

She paused, and remembered Mrs Ball's words: *Love is strong, but you, Clarissa, are stronger.*

Through squinted eyes, she saw that the words on the pages began to glow brightly, and reform themselves, as though translating into English for her to read not only clearly, but in this awkward, alternating light.

The boy groaned when he saw the pages light up, illuminating Clarissa's face. He was clearly angry and frightened because he couldn't harm her, even though he was able to destroy everyone she loved, and would ever love.

The pages flicked over, then suddenly stopped again, and the glow became more intense.

'I know who you are,' she said, softly at first. But then she took a deep breath, feeling the kick of her unborn child, as if it were urging her to sound stronger. With all her might, she screamed '*I know who you are!*'

The boy raised both his hands stiffly, his face completely drained of colour and emotion but she could see tears sliding down his sallow cheeks and his skin appeared to be rotting.

'*You are all of those people who have ever hurt me, frighten me or unsettle me! You are all of those people who have hurt my friends and family! You have killed people I loved because they loved me!*'

The book's pages began to flick backwards and forwards at speed, and now the letters were so radiant that her face shone, like a stern and righteous angel in a painting. When the pages stopped, she looked at the boy. Her strength was certain.

As if giving her instruction to read, the book glowed then faded, and the words shone.

"'Love will not survive when misused,'" she read from the pages. 'You are the perverted man that would wait for me along the lane when I was seven years old!' she said – and as she said it, the boy appeared to grow in size, and his clothes formed into a dusty brown coat, and his face stretched into a solemn smear of bruising and blood reds.

The pages flapped forward and again stopped, in a pulsating glow.

"'You are love's evil; jealous and cruel.'" Clarissa declared. 'You are Mark. You were inside him, hating me, and when he was making love to me. You forced yourself on me.'

Again, the boy changed, and jolted, and became taller, and there was Mark standing in front of her, in a grey suit, his eyes hollow, his teeth tiny – the way his face had looked when she had seen him on top of the staircase, but this time his hair was thinned and broken.

Again, the pages flurried and flapped over, backwards and forwards. Clarissa began to feel even more powerful, a confirmation that she was doing the right thing, and it was working.

Right in front of her eyes, at rapid speed, the boy changed in appearance from one person to another: into the school's headmistress, into the girls that she had thought were her friends, and the man from the courthouse steps.

She stated who she saw: 'You're Mark's gardener, looking up at me from your lawn-mowing! You're the vicar who married my parents! You're Laura, who used to share my flat!' she screamed. '*It's been you all along! Watching me, hunting me! But I have what you need – you will never take it from me to be able to return!*'

He became figures from her childhood paintings, and faces from portraits that she had seen in the gallery. He had always been there, all of her life, always following her, always trying to get her to lead him to the book that she was now using to expose him, for what he really was. She recognised so many of his faces, all those who had lied to her and tried to trick her with false promises, intimidate her and make her feel like an outcast.

'"A false love is no love,"' Clarissa read out loudly. '"Be gone with the hours of the day from existence. Your days on this world are done for all eternity. You have been exposed to end your existence here."'

Again, the pages flurried over at intense speed, as if a storm force gale had increased, peaked and suddenly dropped. She read out: '"Your heart is darkened and plagued by tricks. You reflect the cruelty and confusion of your own soul. You are the darkest form of love."'

Now she looked over the book, and stared straight at the boy. He had shrunk back into his usual scruffy, curly-headed guise, the way he had appeared when an orphan, with all of the figures and faces exhausted, or freed.

'It doesn't matter who you look like and who you possess,' she said, trying to keep her voice steady.

She held the book with one hand under its spine, and lifted one arm to point at Cupid, as though channelling all of her divining powers though to her finger tips. She pointed at him, the words on the pages now beaming, and said: '"You are Cupid – the child of love. The child of trickery. *Amorino!*"'

The boy's mouth stretched open so wide that his jaw looked dislocated. He then jolted and clenched his bloodied fingers, and there was a dazzling flash of light as the lamp's dull bulb exploded, and the door swung shut. The trinkets on the chest of drawers rattled and fell over, books on the shelf flew off and crashed beside her. The wind picked up and whirled round the room, swirling with hurricane force, blowing items of clothing and objects across the floor and the shards of broken glass from the windows. She stood as strong and still as she could, determined not to give up.

'*Relinquere!*' she said loudly and sternly as the pages of the book flicked over again, before the boy had fully changed.

Clarissa read: '"Love has many faces! Truth will always win and love can only survive if it is true! You are malleable and therefore untrue!"'

The boy buckled and jolted. As he became weaker it looked as though he were trying to take on the shape of someone bigger and stronger, and as he did so a shrill whining noise began. For a split second Clarissa thought she could see Mark's face again, and his steel grey eyes staring out at her from Cupid's face, but then the boy doubled up in pain, and as he became even weaker, he began to shrink again. He continued to whimper like a wounded animal.

Then there was silence.

She repeated, shouting loudly, '"*Love can only survive if it is true! It will not survive in the hands of ill-intent. Love doesn't always win.*"'

Just then, as the wind suddenly dropped, Clarissa watched and guarded her face as objects fell back to the floor and the pages of the book flapped gently over, and faded, as though it had done its work, as if the same words had protected other Diviners in the past, perhaps hundreds of times, over hundreds of years.

It was then, at the other side of the bed, an image of Craig appeared. He faded like a clearing of winter fog and smiled, and watched as the boy buckled and flickered and whined. Next to Craig, Paula and Mrs Ball appeared and then Clarissa's father. They all watched, as though bringing her even more strength and spiritual confirmation that she had conquered him. *Cupid. Love.* For a moment though, she wondered if she had died, or was about to, and was going to join this company of ghosts.

Right in front of her eyes, however, the boy began to jerk backwards. He jolted and convulsed and as he did so, his whining became louder and louder, until it was an ear-shattering screech.

Clarissa closed her eyes and gripped tightly onto the book.

Then, as the wind calmed entirely, the unearthly noise stopped.

It took a few moments before Clarissa opened her eyes again

and looked around her, panicking as she couldn't see the boy. Where was he?

Then she stopped, and almost instantly her anger and fear dissolved with the sinking of her heart, as she turned back and looked to the floor to see Lucas' blood-covered body, glistening and naked, half showing from under the bed.

She crouched down to him and tried desperately to move his legs and pull him out. His legs were sticky with blood and cold.

'Lucas,' she sobbed. 'I love you. *I'm sorry. I'm so sorry!*'

There was a gentle glow within the room from where Craig and Mrs Ball and her father had stood, and it was then that she felt a warmth drift over her as she cried.

'Lucas please wake up, don't leave us, the baby and me – we need you.'

She brushed aside some broken glass and was about to reach underneath the bed to pull at him again, harder, when once again she realised they weren't alone. From the corner of her eye she could see two figures standing by the doorway, now open, and in a glowing light.

'Tw – twins,' murmured Lucas from under the bed.

Clarissa gasped. *'Lucas! Lucas! You're alive!'* she sobbed and scrambled as low underneath the edge of the bed as she could physically manage, to try and pull him out farther, but he was too heavy to move. *'Oh Lucas!'*

Clarissa felt violently sick and retched at the sight of him and the smell of his blood, which was now soaking her pyjamas and dressing gown too. Removing the antidote tooth vial from the chain around her neck, she unscrewed the lid frantically and reached under the bed to tilt Lucas' head. She put the vial to his lips. 'Drink this,' she said, her hands trembling. *'Drink it!'*

She stroked his hair, crying, as his lips moved and he swallowed the contents.

With a great effort, she then crawled over to the foot of the bed, with tiny shards of glass cutting the palms of her hands and knees. Sarah and Sally Olven hurried over to her to help her up. As she looked at them, she noticed that their eyes were glowing, and that their hands were extremely warm. They had been the figures in the doorway.

'*Cupid – where has he gone? Has he gone? Have I done it?*'

'He had gone before we arrived,' said Sally. 'You dismissed him, Clarissa. It was always your destiny to dismiss him.'

Clarissa knew she had to find the will to leave Lucas and get help from her neighbours.

'Stay with Lu, please, I have to get help. My neighbour is a doctor.'

'He could die, he's lost a lot of blood,' said Sally.

Clarissa grabbed Lucas' mobile but the battery was dead. 'It's no good. I'll have to go. I'll take his phone.'

Although she couldn't see clearly in the darkness, Clarissa shoved at the wooden gate to force it open. She could make out shadowy shapes of the trees and she knew this was the only way. The wind had picked up and she was so terrified and heartbroken for Lucas that she could hardly walk straight. There was a small path where she could walk toward her neighbour's cottage, away from the danger of the cliff edge.

She could feel her heart beating, in a slow, swollen thump. She was exhausted, and her stomach was aching. The blood on her pyjamas had cooled in the air and made them stick to her skin. Rain had thinned and washed away some of the blood on her face, leaving a metallic taste as it trickled past the corners of her mouth. Her dressing gown kept her warm enough to keep a little energy, but the sky rumbled with thunder and a fine cold rain was blowing with the wind.

Beneath her feet it was muddy and squelchy, but she didn't care, because she had to get help for Lucas and her unborn child.

She passed the coastal footpath and stopped. In front of her at the end of the path stood a figure, though the moonlight played tricks with her eyes, and she tried very hard to focus, *was it a man?* She peeled some her hair away from her face, strands stuck together with the blood and tears and rainwater. She narrowed her eyes but still couldn't quite make out who, or what it was. The rain became heavier as she continued to stumble forwards.

She then decided it didn't matter who it was, she needed help. She screamed with all her might. *'Help me! Please help me!'*

She stopped at a bench, and leaned against it, exhausted. 'Please,' she sobbed. 'Somebody *help* me.'

The figure in front of her grew closer. *'Help me – it's my husband!'* she cried.

The figure stopped and stood motionless, and there was rustling from a nearby wooded area.

Clarissa took in a deep, jittery breath and sobbed. She straightened, staring at the figure. It was definitely a man.

Something ran from the trees, catching her attention.

'Hello?'

The man seemed to get closer with an outstretched arm toward her as a dipping and wavering glow of torch light shone before her.

Out of the shadows from the trees and in the lighthouse beam, she caught a glimpse of his face.

Clarissa sat down, with increasing pain in her stomach. *'Hold on baby, nearly there,'* she cried half to herself. *'Mummy is okay.'*

What if this man is the boy? What if he's lured me with a false image of my neighbour and his dog?

She wiped her eyes of tears and looked up at the figure of a man, who could now be only ten feet in front of her. A cold, stiff coastal breeze gusted over her.

'Father? Father, is that you?' she sobbed. She had begun to feel disorientated.

'Clarissa? Is that *you?*' said the figure as it hurried the last steps toward her. *'Clarissa!'*

It looked like her neighbour. But slightly resembled Mark. Could she be sure it was him? *Surely, love's poison comes in one form at a time and the boy wasn't strong enough now to manifest himself again. And besides, he's gone, for good, hasn't he? That's what Sally Olven said.*

'Clarissa? Clarissa don't be frightened it's me, Doctor Jones. From the cottage. What's happened?'

Clarissa could see now that it really was Doctor Jones. He was wearing an oilskin raincoat and had dark, kind eyes.

She felt breathy and fell to her knees onto the cold, wet and muddy ground, but cried out 'It's Lucas – he's – he's been badly hurt. He's bleeding. I couldn't call for an ambulance the phone is dead. *Please*, you must call an ambulance!'

'I'll do that we need to get to the cottage – I don't have a mobile on me. Come on, Clarissa you poor thing, you're covered in mud and freezing cold, let's get you indoors quickly – what *on Earth* has happened? Look at you! Let's get you looked at right away.'

She cried in relief: '*Thank you. Thank you so much.*'

Just then, a further rustling sound came from the trees, and Doctor Jones' lurcher dog came bounding over and made a fuss of her as the doctor helped her to her feet.

She continued to sob and as she looked at the dog, she knew that dogs sensed malevolence, just as Diviners could. It was inquisitive and affectionate, not timid, which confirmed there was no need for her to worry. Not for now, anyway. For now, the boy was gone and she was in good hands.

As Doctor Jones walked her along the muddy path, Clarissa began to remember all the moments that the boy had caused her suffering. She understood now, with a powerful and intimidating clarity that she had the ability to see further in people than they do themselves, and that love comes at a higher price than ever imagined. Love was not only endearing and playful, but entrapping, and can be cruel and dangerous and overbearing, and that love has many, many different faces. Her ability to see the *real* faces of love and expose the ugly truths of it could make it impossible for her ever to find love for herself – or at least not without mortally endangering anybody who came close to her.

Maybe she had dismissed Cupid for all time. But how could she tell if he might one day reappear in yet another guise?

'Clarissa?' said Doctor Jones, as they reached the lobby door. 'We're at the cottage now. Everything will be okay. Are you all right?'

'Please, we have to get help for Lucas.'

'Of course, I'll call for an ambulance any minute now, I'm just unlocking the door. I'm worried about you. You're pregnant.'

Clarissa grimaced as she wiped her hands on her soaked and bloodied night clothes, and managed to stand up straight.

'I am myself, doctor, I am. In fact, none of this would have happened if I weren't who I am, if you must know,' she said.

Doctor Jones frowned at her for a moment, but she knew that he would never understand what she meant, even if she had the time or energy to explain it to him.

Without saying anything else, she stepped into the cottage, and he followed her.

About The Author

Dawn G Harris is a writer and artist from the South East of England.

From a young age she has put pen to paper and been keenly interested in psychology, nature and science, which is reflected in her writing today. She has varied experience in many business fields and management, giving her added insight into human nature and the complications we face. Alongside her devotion to writing, she has been acknowledged for her successes and dedication as a manager of charity work and her compelling support for others.

Dawn has written a series of children's books, short stories and mottoes.

Diviner is her first full-length novel.

Other Telos Horror Titles

TANITH LEE
BLOOD 20
20 Vampire Stories through the ages

TANITH LEE A-Z (forthcoming)
An A-Z collection of Short Fiction by renowned writer Tanith Lee

SIMON CLARK
HUMPTY'S BONES
THE FALL

FREDA WARRINGTON
NIGHTS OF BLOOD WINE
Vampire Horror Short Story Collection

DAVID J HOWE
TALESPINNING
Horror Collection of Stories, Novels and more

RAVEN DANE
THE MISADVENTURES OF CYRUS DARIAN
1: CYRUS DARIAN AND THE TECHNOMICRON
2: CYRUS DARIAN AND THE GHASTLY HORDE
3: CYRUS DARIAN AND THE FIERY FOE (forthcoming)

PAUL FINCH
CAPE WRATH AND THE HELLION (Horror Novella)
TERROR TALES OF CORNWALL (Ed. Paul Finch)

PAUL LEWIS
SMALL GHOSTS
Horror Novella

ZOMBIES IN NEW YORK AND OTHER BLOODY JOTTINGS
Horror Story Collection

THE DARKNESS WITHIN: FINAL CUT
Science Fiction Horror Novel

CTHULHU AND OTHER MONSTERS
Lovecraftian Style Stories and more

STEPHEN LAWS
SPECTRE

RHYS HUGHES
CAPTAINS STUPENDOUS

TELOS PUBLISHING
www.telos.co.uk

Printed in Great Britain
by Amazon

33442154R00194